ALSO BY S.E. Lynes

Valentina
Mother

THE
PACT

S. E. LYNES

bookouture

Published by Bookouture in 2018

An imprint of StoryFire Ltd.
Carmelite House
50 Victoria Embankment
London EC4Y 0DZ

www.bookouture.com

ISBN: 978-1-78681-353-4
eBook ISBN: 978-1-78681-352-7

This book is a work of fiction. Names, characters, businesses,
organizations, places and events other than those clearly in the
public domain, are either the product of the author's imagination
or are used fictitiously. Any resemblance to actual persons, living or
dead, events or locales is entirely coincidental.

The wolf thought to himself, "That tender young thing would be a delicious morsel, and would taste better than the old one; I must manage somehow to get both of them." Then he walked by Little Red Riding Hood a little while, and said, "Little Red Riding Hood, just look at the pretty flowers that are growing all round you; and I don't think you are listening to the song of the birds; you are posting along just as if you were going to school, and it is so delightful out here in the wood."

Little Red Riding Hood glanced round her, and when she saw the sunbeams darting here and there through the trees, and lovely flowers everywhere, she thought to herself, "If I were to take a fresh nosegay to my grandmother she would be very pleased, and it is so early in the day that I shall reach her in plenty of time"; and so she ran about in the wood, looking for flowers. And as she picked one she saw a still prettier one a little farther off, and so she went farther and farther into the wood.

—*Grimm's Fairy Tales*

PROLOGUE

It's tough work, out on the Ham Lands in the thick, dead night. It's dark. It's cold too, and their hands freeze against the handles of their brand-new spades. They bought these spades this morning, from the vast DIY warehouse on the outskirts of town. But none of this was their plan. It was never their plan.

Despite the cover of the trees, rain sticks the thin shirts to their backs, runs into their eyes and off the rounded points of their noses. Neither of them could have done this alone. Nor could they have trusted anyone else to do it. And so they are bound together. It could not be otherwise. This is the dark business of siblings, the wrestling of skeletons into the closet, the locking of the door. This is a blood bond severable only by death.

Through the rush of wind in the leaves she calls out, 'Are you all right?'

No answer, only the thump of blade on sod, a grunt as the turf is sliced and lifted away.

Anxious, she switches on the torch to check. Catches a wide eye, a grimace.

'Switch it off!'

'Sorry.'

The darkness returns, blacker still. Lips pressed tight, she digs on. The rain has softened the ground, but still the work is hard – harder than she could possibly have imagined. Everything hurts: her arms, her back, her neck, her legs. But dawn will catch them red-handed if they don't hurry. And so she must work, keeping her mind on the rush of the wind in the leaves, the blunt cut of blade on soil. They have been here for hours.

A while later, though how much later she cannot tell, the rain abates. The wind drops and a vanilla moon filters through the treetops. Not a single car on the road. It is calm, silent – almost beautiful. The hole they have made is deeper now.

'Grab the feet.'

'OK.' She takes the stiff, bare ankles in her filthy hands. Her cold, muddy fingers slide against the marbled flesh. The touch, the way the skin feels against her hands, makes her shiver.

'On three.'

Her arms pull at their sockets. A burning pain in her back when she straightens up; she leans forward to ease it.

'One.'

The body swings like a hammock towards the grave, since that is what it is, this hole they have made.

'Two.'

She focuses on her hands. She must stop them from slipping. Pain sears her neck and shoulders; hot needles prick the base of her spine.

'Three.'

The larger weight hits the ground before the other, smaller weights: the torso followed by the collapsed jumble of limbs. Eyes closed, one arm flung across the belly, a snapshot, frozen in grotesque and helpless laughter. Not a dead body, not a person at all – a photograph, a memory, a bad memory best forgotten.

She closes her eyes. The scent of the soil is fresh and damp. She can smell her own sweat too, drying now to an icy film on the raised bumps of her skin.

'Keep going.'

She startles, opens her eyes. Those are her shoes, wet and muddy at the edge; this is her then, staring down into the shallow abyss. This is her. This, now, is part of who she is. She grabs the spade and shovels the broken earth.

CHAPTER 1

ROSIE

Mum? Mummy? Are you… are you…

Rosie, love… Rosie?

Someone calling me… but I can't ans— can't open my… I feel… I feel… I'm at the bottom of… you're… you're… you're somewhere. Mummy? Mum?

You're up above.

I'm below. I can't see anything. Water. Is it? Thick. Soup. I want to swim. I want to swim to you, but I can't get… can't get up off… I can't get up off the seabed.

Sea. Bed. A bed with covers and a soft white pillow. There's a chemical smell. A seabed… a bed for the sea… Abed is a boy from drama. C is for caution. A cautionary tale. A mermaid's tail. Flick, swish. The water is thick and dark. It's full of weeds. Why was the sand wet? Because the sea weed. Smoke weed. We'd better not… we'd better not… we'd better not do that…

Hold on, Mummy. I'm coming up.

Wait for me, Mummy. Wait for me.

CHAPTER 2

TONI

I remember the day you were born. You were perfect. A miracle. Knotted hands clasped together, face old and angry, skin deep red and purple, scrunch-eyed fury.

'And you?' you seemed to say. 'What the hell are you doing here?'

Your daddy and I were lost, like that, in an instant. We bent over you like lovesick idiots, brushed your tiny cheeks with our knuckles, cried without knowing why.

'It's such an everyday thing,' your daddy said, his voice high and choked. 'But it feels like we're the first people ever to do it, you know? I know lots of people do it. I know that in my head, so I do. But it feels like we're the first.'

'She's so beautiful.' I couldn't think of anything more original to say. I didn't have a more original thought in my head. In all your bloodied, fist-clenched rage, you were beautiful. You *are* beautiful.

You are my beautiful little girl.

'Congratulations, Mrs Flint,' the midwife said. 'And does this little bundle have a name?'

I looked at your lovely daddy, my Stan, and we shared a secret smile. There was one name we'd agreed upon. And there you were, soft russet flames rising from your furious little head, waiting for us to give this name to you. Still smiling, I turned back to the midwife.

'She's called Róisín,' I said, bursting with a pride that was fierce, new, unstoppable. 'It means rose in Irish.'

And that's what we called you, on your birth certificate. In life, we call you Rosie. Our sweet little Irish rose.

The midwife laid you on my chest. You were still hot, hot with our shared blood. We were still attached, you and me. Me, overcome with love beneath your sweet, warm weight, and you, still furious, spitting with indignation, hacking like a cat. I knew we would have to cut the cord soon, I knew they would have to separate us.

I didn't want them to.

CHAPTER 3

ROSIE

Smell… it's… don't think it's coming from outside. I think… I think it's up my nose… like… like a Vicks inhaler. Or is it the sea? Scratch on my arm. Ouch. Can't feel tape on my mouth. But I can't move it. I…

Ó Maidrín rua, rua, rua, rua…

Someone is singing. Daddy?

Ó Maidrín rua, rua, rua, rua, rua…

Oh red, red, red, red, red fox… Daddy? Is that you? You call me red fox, don't you, Daddy? I'm your little red fox.

An maidrín rua tá dána.

An maidrín rua 'na luí sa luachair,

Is barr a dhá chluas in airde.

'Little Red Fox'! My song!

The little red fox,

The little red fox so bold.

The little red fox lying among the rushes,

And the tops of his two ears sticking up!

Dad? Daddy? Keep singing, Daddy, don't go… don't go, Daddy…

D-dum, d-dum. My heart. My pulse. D-dum, d-dum. Mum? Mummy? Auntie Bridge? Emily? Can anyone… can anyone hear?

A piece of paper in my hands…

You are invited to Stella Prince's 16th Birthday Party.

Neon letters. Old-school font. Where am I? When is this? You're there. You're on the sofa watching the news. I'm standing up. I can see the top of your head, your parting white and straight. This is in our flat. I recognise our floorboards, our patterned rug. In my hands, the invitation to Stella Prince's party. Stella Prince has got 2,000 followers on Instagram and she lives in a massive house in Strawberry Hill.

Mum, oh my God, look at this…

That's my voice! I'm speaking. I'm saying, *Stella's having a marquee and waiters and a DJ and everything. Can I go? Please, Mum, can I?*

I'm stoked because no way would I be friends with Stella Prince normally, because I'm in the year below. But I know her from theatre group. Not gonna lie, I'm well gassed to get the invite, because this is a whole year before I get the main part in *Little Red and the Wolf.*

I give the invitation to you. You read it fast, muttering the words, and then you say, *For her sixteenth? What's she going to do for her eighteenth, hire a yacht? When I was a kid it was a meal at Pizzaland if you were lucky. Round here's Crazyland more like.*

Yeah, Mum, good one.

So can I go? I chew my cheek. I like the feeling of my teeth cutting through the soft, knobbly bits of flesh. I suppose I must swallow them down. I guess I'm eating myself, if I think about it like that. Gross. *Mum? Can I? Can I go? Please, Mum?*

You're looking up at me with *that* face now. Like I'm driving you nuts but you're trying to keep it together. When you speak, you do your soft voice, your let's-be-reasonable voice. That's enough to drive *me* batshit, Mummy. It makes me want to scream, because I know you've already decided I can't go, and no matter what I say, you've already won.

Sure enough, you say, *You're too young, Rosie. There'll be drugs, and don't tell me there won't be – these posh kids always have drugs because they have the money, don't they? And next thing we'll be calling an ambulance.*

But, Mum, I'm nearly fifteen!

You're nearly fifteen – exactly. Which means you're currently fourteen. You're not a grown-up, you're still a child, and while you're under my roof you'll live by my rules—

But even Ellie Atkins is going! And her mum literally doesn't let her do anything!

You didn't let me go, obvs. Everyone else went. I had to see all the photos on Facebook, see them all laughing with their arms round each other, the banter in the comments. I'm never allowed to go to parties. I had to wait till, like, a week after my fifteenth birthday before you even let *Auntie Bridge* take me to a gig. Not even a gig with my friends, no. I had to go with my auntie, for God's sake. I mean I know Auntie Bridge is a legend and everything, but she's still my auntie.

Come on, Toni.

That's Auntie Bridge's voice.

What about Frozen? she is saying. *We can have a singalong?* Pitch Perfect?

Where am I now? When is this? I'm… I'm in the living room in our flat again. Except I'm sitting next to you and I'm in my panda onesie and you've got wet hair and you're in your dressing gown. We're all cosy. We're about to watch a movie. We have a good TV because you don't go out at night. Auntie Bridge is kneeling on the floor in front of the telly, scrolling through the choices.

What about Bridesmaids? I say. *Naomi said it's hilarious.*

It's a 15, you say – so this must be before my birthday. Knowing you, it's probably the *week* before. You didn't let me watch a 15 until the actual *day* of my birth, probably after 10.13 a.m. because that's the exact time I was born. I practically needed a birth certificate. So savage.

Auntie Bridge is looking at the TV screen, but I know what she's thinking; she's thinking: *Who waits till their kids are the actual exact age of the film certificate?* But she doesn't say anything and neither do I because hello? Pointless.

So can I take her to see Honey Lips next month, then, Tones? Auntie Bridge's scrolling through the films, acting casual. She calls you Tones, which is even more of a cringe than Toni *barfs into sleeve*. *Shepherd's Bush Empire has seating,* she is saying. *And I'll only give her a little bit of coke, just a line or two.*

You laugh a bit, but then you say, *I don't know, Bridge. These things get so crowded. What if she needs to go to the loo?*

Auntie Bridge nods slowly, like someone trying to get a gun off a crazy person. *They are crowded, yes. But it's you that's scared of crowds, yeah? And I'll hold her hand if I have to take her to the loo.* She winks at me. *I'm not wiping your arse though, all right?*

I laugh; you sort of laugh, maybe because Auntie Bridge said *arse*.

You hate crowds. And you hate gigs. You always complain that you can never see anything, or it's too hot, or it's all just tuneless noise. Naomi's mum is the same age as you and she goes to gigs, like, all the time. And clubs, although that's a bit dodgy to be honest.

OK, so you let me go to the Honey Lips gig, but you hardly ever let me do anything. Can't you see? Can't you see, Mummy, you were so worried about drugs and boys and dark nights, it's like those things made all this noise in your head and it was so loud you couldn't hear what I was actually saying? It's like that time you found tobacco in my room. Oh my God, I haven't even tried weed or anything and everyone else has tried it and some of the guys at theatre have taken MDMA and one of them has tried ket, but you went as mental as if you'd found skunk or something. I can see you, pulling it out of the drawer of my desk and holding it up like evidence.

What the hell is this? You're shaking the yellow pouch, your eyes so round I can see the whites. You look like a bush baby on speed or something. *What the hell do you think you're playing at?*

I'm minding it for a friend. I'm trying not to laugh; you look so stupid with your nose in the Golden Virginia. I didn't even buy it; Naomi's brother got it for us from Waitrose near Twickenham station when he bought us some Kopparberg Summer Fruits for a party. Oops, I didn't tell you I was going to that party. I told you I was staying at Naomi's.

Soz.

If I smell pot in this, young lady, you say, *you'll be grounded for a year.*

You can ground me forever if you want. And I won't even care because I'm practically a prisoner in this flat anyway.

You come over to me and put your face so close to mine your eyes go all blurry. You almost slap me! I hate you when you're like that, Mum, you're soooo savage.

We made up; we always do. I sat on your lap and kissed your cheek.

I'm sorry, no, I'm sorry, I love you, love you more, wrong, I love you more…

But I kept my roll-up stuff hidden after that.

Like other things.

Like my Instagram account.

Like Ollie.

CHAPTER 4

TONI

So here we are, my love. West Middlesex University Hospital. West Mid, as it's known locally, the place you were born, where I have worked for most of my life. It's my hospital – that's how I think of it. Only today I'm not organising patient data, I'm not giving birth in a delivery room and no one is saying *Congratulations, Mrs Flint.* This time – oh my love, my darling girl – this time, fifteen years on, your dad is long gone, and you're lying in a bed. Saline drips into your arm through a tube. And I… I'm right here by your side with nothing better, nothing more productive to do than bury my own stupid head in my own useless hands.

This is my fault. How did I let things get this far?

Come back, darling girl. I can make everything right if you just come back. I don't know what to do, where to put myself without you.

Without you, I make no sense. I am alone. I am pointless.

Come back…

We were all right before all this, weren't we? We thought we weren't but, looking back, we were. We were so much more all right than we realised, as all right as anyone, our good days as happy as anyone else's, our bad days no worse: the car not starting, or getting soaked in a sudden downpour, or a bank card getting eaten by the machine. Normal bad stuff – black-sock-in-the-white-wash stuff.

Maybe it had taken us so long to get to that level of all right that we didn't realise we had got there, that we had made it.

Did we forget to start living *afterwards*, Rosie? Yes, at first. Of course we did. We were taken up with the business of surviving. But I like to think that, these last couple of years, we had started to live, you know, in the sense of taking joy in everyday things, like laughter, food cooked for deliciousness and company rather than for the sole purpose of nutrition. Each other. Your auntie Bridge, you and me, we were getting on with it, weren't we? We felt joy; we *achieved* joy, didn't we? Not all the time, but sometimes, and that's enough, isn't it? For anyone.

And now here I am by your side, alone with my thoughts, but I can't tell you what I'm thinking, or that I'm sorry, because you can't hear me. I hope we're going to be all right again. Sometimes I call your name, but you don't respond. I hold your hand, but it is limp in mine. They said you will wake up, not to worry. But worrying is what I do, Rosie – you know that. Your auntie Bridge says I'd win gold in the Worry Olympics, doesn't she? When you wake up, then we'll talk. We'll really talk this time. We'll move on from all of this, if you allow us to, but first I must tell you I am sorry. I am so very sorry.

The floor squeaks.

'How's you?' A nurse appears at my side. She lays a hand on my shoulder a moment, unhooks your chart from the end of your bed. *Overdose*, that's what she's reading there. That's the word on the sheet. I fight shame, the urge to explain. The less I say, the better. She puts the chart back on its hook and looks at me with a compassionate expression. 'Can I bring you a cup of tea, Mrs Flint?'

Tea. The British cure-all. Makes me think of World War II, of the poster that was all the rage the other year: Keep Calm and Carry On.

'Call me Toni,' I say. 'Everyone does. I work here, actually, in Records.'

'Do you?' She smiles and folds her arms over her chest. She doesn't have a large bosom, a bosom you could lay your head on and cry, but she should have, do you know what I mean? She has that comforting manner about her. 'So you know your way about then.' It's a statement, not a question, but I answer anyway:

'Yes.'

'So.' Eyes on mine, she raises her eyebrows for a new question. 'Milk and sugar?'

'That's very kind.' I check her name badge. 'Thank you, Linda. Milk and half a sugar.'

She touches my shoulder again, lightly, before walking away. Her white rubber clogs squeak, squeak, squeak as she disappears into the corridor.

I turn back to you in hope, but nothing, no change. I can only talk to you here in my head. I'm thinking about you, and I'm thinking about me and about how I thought I was looking after you. I thought I was protecting you, but I think now you were protecting me, weren't you?

Me, you, Auntie Bridge. Auntie Bridge looking after me and you, me looking after you and Auntie Bridge, you looking after your auntie Bridge and me. You could put us on a diagram, couldn't you? We would be a triangle. But would you, would anyone really be able to look at that triangle and know which was the base and which was the point?

Tell me, Rosie: who was looking after whom?

CHAPTER 5

BRIDGET

Heart pounding, Bridget searches through her box of memorabilia: old programmes, her scrapbook of reviews and photographs from her TV work, from theatre work, from some of her early gigs. She should be packing some clothes to take to the hospital, making sandwiches, filling a flask; she should be...

Where *is* that programme? *A Midsummer Night's Dream*... Where the hell is it?

'I'm your only niece,' Rosie says, loud in Bridget's mind, as if she were right here in this room, as if she hadn't just been driven away, unconscious, in an ambulance.

'You're my favourite niece,' Bridget will have replied. Yes, she can remember saying it; it's their script, as old and worn as her leather jacket. 'You're going to nail it tonight,' she remembers telling her. 'It's in the genes, yeah?'

Rosie. *Squirt*, Bridget calls her when she's teasing. Her goofy wide smile, her eyes almost shut. Rosie, for the love of God. That cheeky face alongside Bridget in the cab of the van, the gangly teenage legs shrink-wrapped in ripped black skinny jeans, blue Doc Martens crossed on the dashboard. That was the first night of *Little Red and the Wolf*. April – not quite three months ago. That's right. Bridget was running her up to the theatre while Toni got herself together after work. Funny, the things you remember.

'You're so mad.' Rosie, giggling.

Bridget pushing her on her skinny shoulder. 'I think you'll find madness is the only reasonable response to the world.' Pulling onto the roundabout.

Rosie moves her feet down from the dash, wriggles in her seat. She's pale suddenly, and her smile has gone. 'I feel sick,' she says. 'What if people think I'm crap?'

'Come on, Squirt. Don't panic. One, feeling sick won't kill you. The more you think about it, the more sick you'll feel, so try and forget about it. Two, you won't mess up, and three, as far as other people and what they think goes, I've told you – you have no control over that shit.'

'You said shit.' The smile is back, but it doesn't reach her eyes.

'Stuff, then, smart-arse…' Bridget grins at her niece, changes back into fourth gear. 'I tell you what – if I thought about that *stuff*, I'd never do anything. No acting, no band, no nothing. You can't worry about what other people think, yeah? Do you get what I'm saying? You've just got to do what you do, in the way that you do it, and whatever anyone else thinks is up to them. You have zero control over it. None whatsoever, yeah? I'm not saying go round beating people up or anything, but if people want to laugh or take the mick or criticise, let them. Honestly, it says more about them than it can ever say about you, all right? So do yourself a favour and let that shi— *stuff* go right now.'

'Thought you told me to put it in a box and shut the lid.'

'Don't be pedantic.' Bridget glances at Rosie; the two of them exchange a smirk. 'You'll be great. Do your exercises and your breathing, you'll be fine.'

Rosie pulls a silly face and salutes – this Bridget catches out of the corner of her eye. 'Do re mi fa so la ti do,' she sings, then makes an exaggerated show of a deep, yoga-style breath. 'Yes, boss.'

She was fifteen by then. She's still fifteen, not sixteen until August. Bridget's jaw clenches at the thought. She empties the box onto her bed. The paper trail of her life scatters, slides onto the bedroom floor.

Where is that bloody programme?

The opening night of *Little Red and the Wolf* – that was the night Emily introduced herself. Came bowling into their lives pink-cheeked and waddling like a jolly character from a Christmas card. Except it was Easter, not Christmas, and she wasn't waddling – she was limping, on account of her hip, but they only found that out later. Bridget can see herself and Toni in the theatre bar. Rosie has just that minute come up from the dressing rooms to join them, flushed with adrenalin and beaming from ear to ear.

'Bloody brilliant, kid.' Bridget recalls her niece's bony little body in her arms. 'You beat the nerves and you nailed it. Told you you would. Got your auntie's designer genes, innit.'

Rosie is laughing. Blushing crimson with delight. People come over and congratulate her on her performance – *wow; amazing; you were awesome; well done, Rosie!* – friends from the cast, parents of those friends. Everyone's so nice, so generous, and it's so bloody brilliant to see Rosie get the fuss she deserves, see her squirm with pleasure. She's worked so hard, rehearsing like a demon since January. Toni's a basket case by this point, of course: can't speak for tears, bless her, which is understandable after all she's been through. She just looks so happy. She looks like the old Toni, when Stan was alive. Bridget's struggling to keep it together herself, but it's all over when Toni take Rosie's hands in hers and whispers:

'Your daddy would have been so proud of you.'

Too much. Bridget has to grab one of the little black paper napkins they put under the drinks and use it to blow her nose.

'Hay fever,' she says, to no one in particular. 'Must be the lilies on the bar.'

And that's when she notices the middle-aged woman limping towards them, smiling away and sticking out her podgy little hand.

As Bridget watches her, a smile forms, even though she has no idea that things are about to go from brilliant to full-on amazing.

All of this she remembers as if it were yesterday. That feeling, that life was finally getting better for all of them, that this was the break they needed to put tragedy behind them once and for all.

But like theatre itself, there was already so much going on behind the scenes. And neither she nor Toni would realise until it was too late.

CHAPTER 6

ROSIE

I am alone. Alone in the soupy dark. Thick, heavy eyelids. Dead, lead limbs. Still can't get up off the... my neck is fixed to the pillow... my head... my head so heavy. I... Ollie... Ollie?

You're too pretty to play rugby... cool auntie... so tell me, how was school today?

I like your eyes.

I like your hair.

You are so crap at techy things, Mum. Soz, but you are. We had that on our side, Ollie and me. You made me be Facebook friends with you so you could see what I was up to. I couldn't get Snapchat because hello? Too risky. So I got Instagram. But not as an app. I turned off notifications. I deleted recent history...

Delete recent history...

I wish I could. I would delete everything: bleach it out, scrub this sicky shame feeling away...

Mummy? I want to... please, I...

But literally all my friends have tattoos. Stella Prince has, like, three, and Naomi's mum said she could get one.

This is a different memory. Where am I? When am I? You're there. This is you and me. We're in the kitchen at home. This is quite recent, I think – a few months ago. Auntie Bridge isn't there. I don't tell you that Naomi's mum said she can only get a tattoo when she's eighteen. She's going to get a Thai letter N, which I think is a mistake because in, like, two years she'll think that's lame.

You're like, *That's ridiculous. It's not even legal.*

I'm like, *You can get fake ID. Stella's got fake ID.*

That's legit, she actually has.

I don't care what bloody Princess Stella's got! You'll have to wait till you're eighteen, by which time, hopefully, you'll have come to your senses and gone off the idea.

You turn your back on me then. You always do that when you want the conversation to be finished. I'm not gonna lie, you can be pretty savage sometimes.

So harsh, I say and you tell me off for banging the cup on the worktop, which I didn't – I just put it there. *Auntie Bridge has got tats and you don't say anything to her.*

You reach for the chopping board. *I can't tell her what to do, can I? She's my sister!* You pull the sharp knife from the drawer. You go over to the fridge and rummage around in the salad-tray bit, but roughly, as if you're angry with the vegetables. Eventually you straighten up, a big brown onion in your hand, holding it up like, *One more word from you, lady, and the onion gets it.*

You don't really say that. That's just me messing about. But you never ask me to pass you stuff when you're cross; it's like you're trying to make some sort of point or something.

She's my sister is what you actually say. *And she's a grown-up.*

So?

Don't so me. You go all huffy and puffy, as if I'm so impossible. I'm thinking: *do re mi fa so la ti do,* which is one of my exercises for stress. You put the onion on the board and slice off the top, your mouth closed tight. I feel sorry for the onion. *If you want to be an actress, you can't go covering yourself in tattoos, can you?*

Auntie Bridge is an actress and she's—

You hold up the knife – psycho alert. *Your auntie Bridget is a grown woman. This discussion is over.* Chop chop chop.

I walk off. You shout after me not to slam the door. But I didn't – it just closed loudly behind me. In my room, I lie on my bed, pick up my phone. Swipe, Safari, hello, Instagram… a red circle, a message. It's from him, from him, from him… a message for me… from Ollie, my Ollie… my…

I only wanted to have a space. Everyone else has Snapchat, Instagram, Facebook, everything. Just FB and Insta, that's all I have. I'm being completely straight now. I'm not going to lie to you. I'm not going to lie to you ever, ever again.

CHAPTER 7

He would come into my room at night. He would wait until the house was asleep then creep along the landing. A soft knock at the door, a knock I'd been waiting for – and dreading. Why knock, I used to wonder, because he always came in anyway. He wasn't asking my permission, but he liked to pretend he was.

I would lie under my covers with my back to the door, pretending to be asleep, my whole body tense. I would wait for the change in the air, the slow creak of the floorboards.

'Hey,' he would whisper, his breath hot, his mouth right there by my ear, and I would stare at the gap in the curtains, the lamp post outside with the broken bulb, listen for the hoot of an owl, or the violent mating of the foxes. The foxes were the worst. They sounded like babies screaming, and I could not stop myself thinking of babies, hundreds of them, being murdered in their cribs. I would lie still, rigid, and stare at the gap in the curtains. And I would think of those babies.

'Are you awake? Wake up now. I just want a cuddle. You can give me a cuddle, can't you? No harm in that, is there? A little cuddle?'

CHAPTER 8

TONI

I wonder if your auntie Bridget is on her way. I wonder if she's called the police yet.

No. No, she wouldn't do that. Not without talking to me.

She should be here soon. There was no room for her in the ambulance so she said she'd grab a change of clothes, some food and a flask of coffee, and come up in the van. But surely she'd be here by now? Oh my God, what if she's driven off? Really, what if she's run away, before it all comes out? I wouldn't blame her. But please God, I hope she hasn't. I need her. I can't do this without her.

I can't get hold of Emily either. I've sent a text, but nothing yet. When she gets it, she'll be here as soon as she can, I'm sure.

I know I shouldn't, but I can't stop wondering if anyone's been to the house. If they have, they will have discovered the body by now. It's too soon for anything to be on the news, so I suppose there's no way of knowing. I suppose it might be days before it's discovered. Weeks, even.

I can't think about it. I can't.

Do you know what? I'm going to think about when you called me to tell me you'd got the part of Little Red instead. It's a nice memory, a battery charger for my soul. It was last December, wasn't it? We were coming up for the Christmas holidays. You'd turned fifteen in the summer and it was a Saturday afternoon; you'd remember it as clearly as me, I'm sure, if you were awake. You'd auditioned in November and you had to go up to the Cherry Orchard to hear the results.

'No matter which role you get,' I said when I dropped you off, 'your auntie Bridge and I will be super proud of you just for trying. It's being a part of something that counts, isn't it, love? And don't run, by the way, it's icy.'

You kissed my cheek and, as if I hadn't even spoken, ran into the theatre. I watched you open the door and disappear inside, your red hair flashing behind you like a fox's tail.

A couple of hours later, my mobile rang. You were supposed to be doing a workshop – you weren't due to finish until six, so when I saw it was an unknown number, my heart leapt into my mouth.

'Mummy?'

'Rosie?' I said, trying but failing to keep the panic out of my voice. 'Are you OK, baby girl? Is everything OK?'

'Mum, I'm fine. I just forgot my phone.'

'Again? What have I said about going out without your phone?'

'Oh my God, stop stressing.' Your teenage irritation was palpable. 'I'm just borrowing Abed's, it's *fine*. They let us out early, that's all.'

'Oh, thank God.' I pressed the phone to my chest a moment and sighed before I put it back to my ear. 'Sorry, baby. As long as you're OK. I'm on my way, all right? I'll be there in ten minutes. Well, twenty.'

'It's not that, Mum. Just listen a sec, will you? I had to call because… well, because guess who got the lead?' You giggled, and I knew instantly, of course.

'Erm, let's see,' I said, stalling. 'Toby Marsh?'

You giggled again. 'No-o.'

'Sarah Peters? Maggie whatsherface? No, I'm joking.' I paused. 'It was Stella Prince, wasn't it?'

You knew I was teasing but you had to say it anyway – you were like a shaken-up bottle of lemonade. 'I did!' Cap off, out it fizzed. 'Me! I got it! I'm going to be Little Red Riding Hood!'

'You're joking?'

'I'm not!'

'Does that mean I have to make you a cape now? Couldn't you have got something easier, like a tree or something?'

You laughed then, a big loud hahaha! – pure, delicious, unguarded. 'You won't! They have proper wardrobe and everything. There's a lady at the theatre that does it; it's, like, her job. They said to not have a haircut between now and Easter, but that's about it.'

Your lovely russet hair. Hair to make people turn in the street. Your father's colouring. My God, how ecstatic he would have been, I thought. How filled up, how proud. 'My little red fox,' he would have said, and fifteen or not, he would have picked you up and spun you around for joy.

'I still think Toby Marsh should have got it,' I said.

We were both helpless with laughter now, caught up in the wonder of the moment and all it meant, all that lay behind it: the accident and its terrible aftermath. We both knew, I think, that we were at the top of some kind of hill, looking down on what had been the most arduous of climbs. We couldn't believe that we were there, at the summit. We had only to raise our eyes to see the view clear and blue before us. We had only to step into it and it would be ours.

I found myself blinking back tears.

'Mum?' you said. 'Are you still there?'

'It's amazing, baby girl,' I managed to say. 'Seriously. Wait till I tell your auntie Bridget. She'll be over the moon. I'm so very proud of you.' I bit my lip, wiped my wet cheek with my free hand. 'What I mean is, I'm proud of you for fighting those nerves. That took guts.'

'Thanks. I did the exercises like Auntie Bridge said and I... I just went for it.'

'That's brilliant. And you're still at the Cherry Orchard?'

'I'm just at the entrance. The others are going for the bus. There's, like, five of us. The 33 goes right to the end of our road.'

'No, no. I've literally already got my bum in the car. Wait there, OK?'

'But, Mum, I can get the bus!'

'No, baby girl. Stay there, I'm coming for you.'

You sighed. 'OK.'

'Don't go off anywhere, will you?'

'I won't.'

I rang off, unable to wipe the smile from my face. You, who had been so quiet for so long, you were blossoming once again like... like cherry blossom – why not? Beautiful and white and bold on the tree. I felt your confidence, my love. I'd felt it grow those last few years since you'd joined that theatre. I had allowed myself to believe, or start to believe at least, that the feisty six-year-old you had been, with her dressing-up clothes and her little picnic-tabletop stage, the little Rosie who had been ours before the accident, was back.

And then, months later, when we came to watch you perform, all dressed up and lost in the part and giving it your all, and Emily approached us in the theatre bar afterwards, I was so proud of you that I felt if someone tapped me on the shoulder or whispered something too kind or cruel, I would shatter into pieces on the floor. Your auntie Bridget was proud of you too, of course, but not like me. I'm your mother. There is no one, no one who loves you more than I do. No one ever will. No one could.

Blossoms fall, though, don't they? I didn't think about that.

CHAPTER 9

BRIDGET

'May I be allowed to congratulate the marvellous Little Red?'

That's what she says, the woman, as she limps towards them across the theatre bar. Her huge eyes blink behind strong lenses, a slightly manic smile on her face, the programme rolled up in her hand. Bridget half expects her to start bopping them all on the head with it.

To Bridget's surprise, Rosie doesn't clam up as she usually does in front of strangers.

'Thank you,' she says, all smiles, offering her hand to shake. 'That's really kind.'

'Emily,' the woman says. 'Emily Wood.'

'I'm Rosie Flint, and this is my mum, Antonia, and my auntie Bridget.'

'Lovely, how lovely.'

As they say their hellos, the lenses in Emily Wood's glasses flash under the downlights.

'Now,' she says, hands on hips, 'I won't beat around the proverbial; I'll come right out and say it. I'm wondering if Little Red here would be interested in a conversation about possible representation.' The woman is as rambunctious as Toad of Toad Hall, as hearty as Father Christmas.

'Wow,' Toni says, glancing at Bridget. 'I was *not* expecting you to say that.'

Rosie meanwhile has gone pink. When Bridget catches her eye, her smile reaches her ears.

'I'm in the business, as they say,' Emily goes on, 'but I'm moving from acting to agency, as it were. Scouting for talent, I suppose you'd call it.' She leans back and chuckles – a real old-lady chuckle. 'Scouting for talent, what on earth do I sound like? A silly moo, that's what.'

Bridget can't look at her niece or her sister. Knowing she has to be serious always makes her lose it, and if she gets the giggles now, she knows she won't be able to stop. At Central, she had a reputation for corpsing, especially during scenes involving love or death.

'Scouting,' Emily continues. 'Sounds like something to do with tents and knots and dyb dyb dyb, doesn't it?' She chuckles again, rounds it off with a kind of hoot and a sigh.

Bridget focuses on her boots, bites her bottom lip against growing hilarity, the increasing and horrific possibility of a full-on snort. The woman is crazy. *Batshit*, Rosie would say – will say, Bridget is sure, once they hit the privacy of the van. As for the woman, she's borderline hysterical. She pushes up her glasses and draws her finger under her eyes to wipe away her stray tears.

'Antonia,' she says, letting the glasses fall back onto her nose. 'Your daughter really is the full package.'

'You make her sound like cheese,' Toni says, laughing. 'Or drugs!'

Bridget and Rosie exchange a smirk. Toni can be heroically tactless sometimes.

'Sorry, yes, quite,' Emily says, apparently not fazed in the slightest. 'Cheese, indeed. What I mean is, she has the lot. She's as beautiful as a peach – look at her skin! And she really can act. Her singing voice is… well it's nothing a voice coach can't fix. Does she have any other talents?'

'She has a brown belt in taekwondo.' Toni nods at Bridget. 'Her auntie takes her every week.'

'Oh for God's sake, Mum,' Rosie mutters, rolling her eyes.

Bridget keeps her mouth shut, as she always tries to when things have nothing to do with her. She's been careful to stay an aunt, especially since she had to move in. This conversation is about Rosie, and Toni is Rosie's mother, no one else.

'No, that's good, that's good.' Emily closes one hand into a fist and swipes the air. 'It shows athleticism. Fitness is so important in this game. And the martial arts are marvellous for discipline of mind and body.'

'And self-defence,' Bridget adds – can't help herself.

'Self-defence indeed.' Emily blinks at Bridget a moment. In those glasses, the effect is of a fish stunned by a flashlight. Blink! She turns back to Rosie and smiles. 'Yes. Really. The whole package.'

The crowd is dispersing, the hubbub quieting. Emily tells them that she trained at the Central School of Speech and Drama. Bridget almost chips in to say that so did she, and ask Emily which year, but again, it's Rosie's moment, so she keeps shtum.

'I spent most of my career in the theatre,' Emily says. 'Character roles mainly, once the old beauty faded. Some television – *Casualty* and twice on *The Bill* – but that was when I was younger and prettier. The television work has dried up over the last ten years or so. Plus my dicky hip. Theatre work is so demanding physically, so I said to myself, Emily, I said, it is time for a change.'

'Do you have a business card or anything?' Toni says. 'It's just that I really need to get this little girl home and to bed.'

'Of course. Silly moo, wittering on. Yes, yes.' She digs around in her handbag. 'I don't expect you've thought about anything like this, and that's fine. You'll want to take a moment, I'm sure, but I think I could get Rosie a lot of work. Commercials at first, mostly, I'll be perfectly honest. They're not art, but they pay well. Obviously it won't be Steven Spielberg straight away, but it won't take long for this one to get noticed, mark my words. She would need a headshot of course, but I can arrange that.' She throws up her hands. 'Listen to me, getting ahead of myself. Shut up, Emily, don't frighten the horses!' She hands a card not to Toni but to Rosie.

'Rosie,' she says. 'Such a pretty name. So feminine, and perfect for a famous actress, wouldn't you say? And Flint. Flint is good too – shows strength, a cutting edge, a romantic heroine!'

Rosie giggles. Bridget can tell her niece thinks Emily's a bit bonkers too. She will definitely imitate the woman once they get home: the frequent blinking, the jolly-hockey-sticks turns of phrase, her constant chuckling. But Bridget has begun to wonder if this last is a sign of shyness, no more than Emily's way of being in the world, and the thought softens her. Everyone has to find their way of being in the world, don't they? No one knows that more than Bridget.

'We should go,' Toni says, throwing out her hand to shake. 'Nice to meet you, Emily.'

Seeming not to have heard, Emily traces her forefinger across the card. 'Into the Light Agency,' she says. 'That's the website address. Some small miracle there, I can tell you. Emily Wood is not exactly known for her technical savvy, to put it mildly. But do have a perusal. If you think you'd like to work with Madame Belle, aka *moi*, there's an email on the old calling card there.' For the second time she throws up her hands. 'Stop talking, Emily! Rosie, my dear, you must be tired after your magnificent performance. Antonia, Bridget, lovely to meet you both. Goodnight, all. *Bonne nuit. Buenos... nottes, noches*, or whatever they say in Timbuktu.' She raises her hand in a wave, blinking all the while. 'Enjoy the rest of your evening.'

Off she goes, a lopsided heel-toe, heel-toe, her white-grey hair fading out of the theatre and into the night.

CHAPTER 10

ROSIE

I can't get up off… I have to get up off the seabed. I'm… Shame. I'm ashamed. I've done something very bad, something shameful that's making my stomach tie itself up in knots. Mummy? I'm sorry. I'm sorry, Mum. Am I awake? Emily? Auntie Bridge?

Hey, Squirt. Did you remember your ankle support?

Auntie Bridge! That's my auntie! That's her voice!

Where am I? When is this?

Course. I put it on in the flat. That's me! That's my voice!

I can see my legs: crossed, white baggy trousers. My blue Doc Martens on the dashboard – the left on the right, the right on the left. We are in Auntie Bridget's van. We so are because I can hear the rattle of the engine, can smell her vanilla air freshener. Fags, a bit, underneath.

You… you're not with us, Mummy. You're probably at home because it's the evening and you don't go out, so you'll be lying on the sofa watching some Netflix series.

Ankle support… white baggy trousers…

Auntie Bridge must be taking me to taekwondo. She always takes me. She stays and watches and shouts *Yes!* or *Get in, girl!* when I do a good kick or something, which is so embarrassing. I tell her to shush, but I don't mind really 'cos the others say she's a legend. All my friends say she's a legend. *Your auntie's so cool,* they say and I'm like, *So?*

I have my kit on, my brown belt tied round my waist. I know taekwondo is good for strength and self-defence and everything, but secretly I like it because it's given me abs. Naomi is jealous of my abs. She always pokes me in the stomach and says, *That's just freaky.* I have Instagram abs #nofilter.

Reckon you could still kick someone in the neck? I ask Auntie Bridge. We're on Twickenham High Street, near Poundland. *You know, like, if they were mugging you or something?*

She laughs. The van lurches as she changes gear. *I could kick you up the arse.*

We both laugh. Auntie Bridge is a black belt, second dan, but she doesn't do it any more. Auntie Bridge has six piercings and seven tattoos. You said if I get a tattoo you'll *bloody kill me.* Bloody is your worst swear word. You're weird about swearing. *We've got enough stacked against us as it is*, is what you say, *without a foul mouth on top.*

I'm sorry, but that's just weird.

Auntie Bridge is a grown woman… grown woman… groan, woman… I am a girl who thought she was a grown-up. But I wasn't. I'm not. And now I can't see you, Mummy. I don't know where you are…

Everything slots into place; everything comes around. Auntie Bridge has this tattoo on the inside of her wrist. Everyone thinks it's a Celtic sign, but it's not. It's an A and a B joined together so that the right leg of the A and the spine of the B are one line.

It stands for Antonia and Bridget, Auntie Bridget says.

Where are we now? When are we?

The Italian café, that's where. Café Bellissimo. I recognise the chairs. I can see Waitrose out of the front window, further up, towards the station. Auntie Bridge wouldn't be seen dead in Starbucks because she's an anarchist. She says that all the big chains are fascists. I go to Starbucks with Naomi sometimes, but I don't tell Auntie Bridge.

Antonia and Bridget. Antonia – that's you, Mum, obvs. But everyone calls you Toni. The name Toni is so lame, but the only reason you're called Antonia is because your dad wanted a boy and he was going to call you Anthony, LOL. But he left Granny Casement literally just after you were born, which is proper savage even though you say you were better off without him because he used to hit Granny and stuff. You say Antonia sounds too posh, but Toni is plain cheesy. *Cheesy peas*, you say when you're messing about, or when someone takes a photo. It's from some old comedy show you used to watch. You hate having your photo taken. Cheesy chips, like we get in Dorset. Remember when we were watching the TV that time and they asked that footballer what his favourite cheese was and he said, *Er, melted*. We laughed our heads off at that, didn't we?

I could have a tattoo somewhere you wouldn't see – on my bum!

Bottom, Rosie. The word is bottom.

Bottom, Puck, Titania. Auntie Bridge was Bottom in *A Midsummer Night's Dream*, she told me. It was when she was young. Bottom of the ocean… a seabed… Auntie Bridge got that tattoo done when she was twenty. It was her first.

What does it mean, Auntie Bridge? We're back in Café Bellissimo. Auntie Bridge has her Led Zep T-shirt on; her arm is on the table, wrist face up. The A and the B.

What do you mean, what does it mean? she says. *I told you, it's your mum and me.*

I mean, like, why did you have it done?

Because… Auntie Bridge stops, like she can't say it. She looks me in the eye, as if she's deciding whether she should say it or not. *I had it done because… well, when I found out about Uncle Eric.*

Do you mean with Mummy?

She nods.

You told me about what happened with your uncle, but you never talk about him. Literally never. I didn't know it was why

Auntie Bridge got that tattoo – as in, the exact reason. The way I'm remembering this, that's how it feels, like I didn't know that before.

Auntie Bridge looks more serious than I have ever seen her. She looks like she's going to cry, and she never cries. *Interfered*, you said, but I don't think you've said that word to me yet. In this memory, I mean. I think you told me later. I know what *interfere* means. You think I'm a kid, but I'm not. I could get married next year, legally. I could have a child. I could go to the GP and get the pill and they wouldn't have to tell you because it would be patient confidentiality. There are different types of abuse: verbal, emotional, physical. Sexual. We had a talk about it in PSHE last year. Personal, social, health and economic education. So many abbreviations! GCSE… General Certificate of Secondary Education. PE… physical education. YOLO… you only live once. ROFL… roll on the floor laughing. You like FFS. I read that on a text you sent to Auntie Bridge.

I'm locked out, FFS.

Her reply: *Spare key under geranium, you muppet.*

You say FFS means for flip's sake, as if I don't know. You're so weird. I'm fifteen not ten, you know.

The water is thick and dark. It's full of weeds. I'm all alone in the moonlight. There is music. The wind is in my hair.

I'm in Emily's car. I'm in the passenger seat and she has the roof down. We're singing along to her tape. *Cats the Musical.*

Midnight…

I'm being sick into a bucket. Your hand is cool on my forehead. *That's it*, you say. *That's it – good girl. You'll feel better now.*

I'm in the kitchen. There are Rice Krispie cakes, my favourite, on that three-tier cardboard cake stand we've got.

Can I have one, Mummy?

Not now, baby girl. You'll spoil your appetite. You can have one after dinner.

The tabletop comes up to my chest... how old am I? Eight? Nine?

I'm in the Italian café. I'm with Auntie Bridge. She is wearing her black leather trousers. I have hot chocolate with little pink and white marshmallows. It is after school. I'm maybe eleven? It's *afterwards*...

Auntie Bridge always picked me up from school *afterwards*. Auntie Bridge drinks black coffee: an Americano. She goes to the gym and she's quite dench. But your arms are even more dench than Auntie Bridge's. You always twist the lids off jars when we can't. Auntie Bridge has a patch on her bicep. Trying to give up smoking. Again. Auntie Bridge is six years older than you. Six piercings. I was six when Daddy died in the accident. I was six *before*.

We shared a room when we were little, me and your mum, Auntie Bridge says.

Was that in Hounslow?

Yes. At Granny and Grandad Jackson's in Benson Close. That's your great-grandparents, Squirt. Your grandad Casement, that's our dad, ran off with another woman, back to Scotland, we think, and your granny had no job and no money so she moved in with Great-Granny and Grandad Jackson. And Uncle Eric lived there too. Our uncle, I mean. He was your great-granny Jackson's son from her first marriage, to a guy called Patrick. She had your auntie Patricia with him as well. I'm sorry, I'm not explaining this to you very well.

I get it. I try and keep it in my mind, but it's complicated, and even as I'm holding on, it floats away. I know Eric is my half-great-uncle, but I've never met him. I think he's in a mental hospital, but I can't remember. You told me he was ill. *Ill-in-the-head ill,* you said. You never tell me the whole truth. Auntie Bridge told me what happened. Not in detail or anything.

Uncle Eric started on her when I left for drama school.

Started interfering, you mean?

We are talking about you. I am trying to be mature; I am using the correct terms. This isn't in the Italian café now – this is at the flat. It's another time. I am older. I already know about your uncle Eric. I have Doc Marten boots that Auntie Bridge bought me, and she didn't buy me those until Year 9, so I'm thirteen or fourteen. You are out. You are probably at your charity meeting or at work, because you never go out anywhere else, like to the pub or anywhere, except to see one of Auntie Bridge's gigs, but even that's only, as you would say, *once in a blue moon*, because you are always tired.

Auntie Bridge nods, but it's a grim nod, like when they identify bodies on the television.

He only got to her because I wasn't there to protect her, sick bastard.

Auntie Bridge swears in front of me sometimes when you're not there. She says the F-word, but she told me not to tell you, because when you guys were growing up, she always told you never to swear. *People like us have enough holding us back without a foul mouth*, she used to say to you when you were growing up. Hmm, where have I heard that before? LOL. That's why you're strict about table manners as well. *Hold your knife and fork properly, don't hunch over the table, put your cutlery together to show you've finished…* blah. Auntie Bridge smokes on the back patio, too, when she's supposed to have stopped.

Why didn't you call the police? I ask, even though I know our family don't trust the police.

She shakes her head. *The pi— the police are useless. Were, anyway. We called them once, when Dad… when your grandad gave our mum a black— when he hit Granny Casement. They stood outside and did nothing. There's Mum with a shiner like a big bloody plum and Dad fobbing them off with some bullsh— some rubbish about the cupboard door…*

Why didn't you tell them what happened?

We did. They did nothing, Squirt. Sweet FA. Said they couldn't intervene unless it was physically happening in front of them. And they would have done nothing to that sick, feckless bastard Eric either. Sorry. Anyway, I did it. I beat him up myself.

My mouth drops open. *Your uncle Eric? What, like, with taekwondo?*

She smiles. *Something like that.*

My mouth is still open with shock. I've never heard either of these stories before. At that moment I think Auntie Bridge is more than a legend; she is a double-hard kickass legend! But at the same time, I can't imagine it because she is so peaceful and chill. I don't know when any of what she's telling me was, except that it was in the past.

So that's when I got my first tattoo. She sips her Americano. We are back in the Italian café, so I suppose I'm at primary school again. She must have told me different versions of this story at different times. Grown-ups do that. You have to get those versions and slide them on top of one another like coloured filters until you build a picture that looks real.

I stroke the inside of Auntie Bridge's wrist with my fingertips. I trace the Celtic sign that isn't. Her wrist is soft, and I think about how she has the same blood as me and you. *What does it mean, Auntie Bridge?*

It's a pact. Like a promise.

Like your band, The Promise?

A bit, yeah. Except a pact is maybe more serious.

Like a contract?

Yeah. Except there's no paper. And you can end a contract; you can pay your way out or give notice or whatever. This is forever.

But what does it actually, actually mean? As in this pact, yours and Mum's one?

It means… She looks out of the window. Her eyes dart like fish as the traffic goes by outside. *It means I'll never let your mum down again.*

CHAPTER 11

TONI

On the way home from your *first night*, the three of us were screeching with excitement, laughing at nothing, ecstatic. You had done so well, overcome so much. You had the whole theatre in the palm of your hand and I was so proud. In the van, you imitated Emily to perfection. Your auntie and I were helpless. We weren't cruel about it – well, maybe we were, a bit – but Emily really is a funny one, isn't she? And besides, I didn't know her then. And I had no intention of getting to know her – nor of letting you sign up with a total stranger. But I didn't tell you that there in the van, because, well, because I didn't want to burst your bubble.

'Oh my God, Mum,' you said when we got home. You could barely get your arms into your PJs for excitement. 'I can't believe, like, a proper agent wants to sign me! I could end up being on telly or in the West End or something!' Your eyes twinkled.

'Let's talk about it in the morning, eh?' I said, pulling back your duvet. I hoped that if we waited until you'd had a full night's sleep, you would have calmed down. I hoped you'd be able to see sense.

'Can't we just have a peek at her website?'

'Absolutely not.' I stroked your hair, kissed your forehead, gave you a last congratulatory cuddle. 'Now lights out and get your rest. You've got to do the whole thing again tomorrow.'

'Night.'

'Night.'

'Mum?'

'What?'

'This has been the best night of my life.'

Your auntie Bridget was in the kitchen. I thought she might be out on the patio, having a cheeky cigarette, but she wasn't. Your auntie has the odd roll-up, you know. Don't tell her I told you.

'What a night,' I said.

'She was something, wasn't she?'

'She absolutely smashed it.'

Bridget had brought out her best whisky. 'A small nightcap to celebrate, methinks. I was just sitting here trying to figure out if I recognised Emily from Central.' She eyed me in the way she does, then poured out two small measures into the Edinburgh-crystal glasses that someone, I can't remember who now, gave me and your dad for a wedding present. 'Good confidence boost for Rosie though.'

'"The whole package",' I said. Scoffed, actually. 'Honestly. She's a person, not a designer sandwich. And who talks like that? She sounded like one of those people from Radio 4.'

'That's drama school. Projection, darling.'

I did understand that Emily had been talking commercially, honestly I did. It's just that, well, a) I didn't trust her, and b) I hate all the pressure on kids these days: to be half supermodel, half athlete; to be perfect; to be a beautiful person living a beautiful life – it's why I limit your phone time, why you're not allowed Instagram, and why I've never pressured you into any after-school clubs or anything. It was your auntie Bridget who suggested the theatre group. And the taekwondo for that matter.

'An actor is a product just like any kind of talent,' your auntie Bridge said. She was scrolling through her phone.

'I know that,' I said. 'But some of your auditions have been brutal, haven't they? And what about that director that came on to you that time?'

She shrugged, still looking at her phone. 'She did that to everyone. You get used to it when you're as hot as me. Ah, here she is. Emily Wood. Yes, Central. Two years before me. Yep. *The Bill, Casualty, An Inspector Calls* at the Almeida, *View from the Bridge* at the Old Vic, *Taming of the Shrew*... bloody hell, she's done a shitload of theatre.'

Your auntie Bridget's a clever one, Rosie. She was pretending to check for herself, but she was checking for my benefit. She was trying to reassure me that Emily was genuine. *Legit*, as you would say. Your auntie knew that if I felt reassured, there was perhaps a tiny chance of me letting Emily represent you. Crafty, you see? Except that Bridget and I know each other better than we know ourselves. She can't fool me, and she knows she can't. She will have known that I could see right through her. It's a dance we do.

And she will have known that there was no way I was letting you get an agent. Not at fifteen.

'If she's only just starting up,' your auntie was saying, 'she won't have much of a name yet, so it could take her ages to get Rosie anything. Might be nothing more than something on the old CV.'

'CV?' I took a sip of the whisky, felt the burn in my throat. 'She's a child.'

'Yeah, but kids start young now, don't they?'

'I suppose they do, but that doesn't mean Rosie has to.'

Bridget drained her glass and placed it on the table. 'Did she say anything just now when you said goodnight? Was she excited?'

I sighed. 'Yes. She was in heaven.'

Stay calm. That's what your daddy would say if he were here. There's nothing else to do but wait, so I suppose I'll just have to carry on chatting to myself. I remember I did this when I was in hospital after the accident. I had my own little radio station here in my head, broadcasting my life to me like a world-record-breaking episode of *The Archers*. I can't face reading. The newspapers are grim, and the magazines in the waiting room are years old; I didn't realise half of them were still in circulation. So I'll just rattle on as if we were in the kitchen together, you setting the table, choosing tunes off your laptop, telling me about your day. It's the only way I can sit here without going out of my mind. It's the only way to feel less alone.

I suppose your auntie Bridge may even have crashed out after everything she's been through in the last few hours. She'll need trauma counselling, absolutely no doubt about that. I did tell her to grab some sleep, but I doubt she will. I wonder if she's told Emily – she might even have gone to pick her up in the van. If anyone can cheer you up, it's those two.

Talking like this, even here in my head, is helping me. It helps me to run through how we got to this point. One day, I'll make sense of it. When you come round, I hope you'll be able to tell me your side of things. I hope to God you've not been… that he didn't… I hope you're still… I can't say it. Bridget reckons he didn't touch you, and you tell her everything, don't you? But then you've not spoken since… Anyway, your auntie Bridget will be here soon. She will know what to do.

Wake up, Rosie. Wake up and just… be you. That's all I need. You.

CHAPTER 12

ROSIE

Ollie is mine… my secret. I'm so stoked to have one secret. I'm gassed to have one space without you in it.

I met him on Instagram. He plays in a band. Like Auntie Bridge…

… *Mum? Is Auntie Bridge, like, the lead singer?*

That's my voice. When is this? Where am I? This is *afterwards*. I am probably eleven… ish. We are in your car. I am in the back seat. I'm not allowed in the front.

Not lead, no, love, you say. *She plays lead guitar and does backing vocals.*

It's the first time I've been allowed to come and see Auntie Bridge play. You are taking me, but I'm not allowed to stay until the end.

Only backing? I'm disappointed. Auntie Bridge is a good singer. She harmonises with songs on the radio, but she also does the descant over random things in the flat: the washing machine, the kettle, the hum of the fridge. Once, when the smoke alarm went off, she did the bass harmony and we all cracked up. There was no fire, obvs.

Do you think they'll play the O2? I am defo quite young, because that question is so lame.

You laugh. *Not the O2, baby, no. Not quite. They play in pubs round here mostly… Richmond, Twickenham, Barnes, Chiswick. But they do OK.*

Secret: Auntie Bridge's band is so not cool.

I feel bad thinking that. I would never say it to Auntie Bridge or anything. She wouldn't care if I did – well, she might – but I still wouldn't say it. She doesn't care what anyone thinks of her, does she, Mum? The Promise is, like, a rock band and I prefer bands like Jungle and Hot Chip. It's not her main job. She does websites and fixes computers for people, or teaches them how to set up a blog, that kind of thing, and acting-wise sometimes she gets work in plays, but not very often. She's done a bit of television, and she does voice-overs and what she calls *corporate work* – which I think is when she teaches straight people to have better, more fun personalities.

Auntie Bridge owns five guitars and she keeps them on these special hooks on the wall in her room. She lives in our flat with us. She moved in… *afterwards.*

Why am I telling you this? Am I even telling you this?

I am telling *me* this.

I am keeping me company here under the soup water. Mum? Mummy? If I talk to you, here in my mind, will you hear me?

If you hear me, will I exist?

If I hear you, can I come back?

I want to come back. I'm trying to find my way to you. I'm sorry for what I've done. If I wake up, you can tell me what it is. It's big – I know that. I feel it in my guts, like I've eaten something dodgy. Something. I have done… something.

All Auntie Bridge's tattoos mean something. There is an H on her other wrist, for Helen. She left Helen and moved in with us… *afterwards.* That's why she's serious when she talks about Helen.

Putting two and two together, I suppose Auntie Bridge came to live with us because of the pact – the pact she made with you,

Mummy. She came to live with us after the accident, which I don't remember. I don't even remember much about moving here, just light coming in through the back door, and boxes in my room, and thinking it was cool having everything on the same floor but weird too at the same time not having to go upstairs to my bedroom. I remember before, when we had Dad, and we lived in the house on the river, and afterwards, now, with Auntie Bridge.

Everything comes around… everything slots into place…

Hel and me were splitting up anyway, Squirt. Don't think about it.

Auntie Bridge said that, but I think now that she said it so I didn't feel, like, bad or anything. They are still friends, her and Helen. Why am I telling you this? I'm telling me this. I'm pouring words into myself. I'm making myself exist with words. I'm looking for the something very bad. I'm calling out to you, Mummy.

I'll keep calling.

Sorry. Sorry. Sorry.

… Alone at the bottom of the sea. A loan at the bottom of the C. C word. C u next Tuesday. *#washyourmouthoutwithsoapand-wateryounglady…*

A funny smell. Like something from chemistry lessons – a reaction in a conical flask held over a Bunsen burner. A dark tin space. It's noisy when I bang on it with the side of my head. Ow. My hands are tied… it's dark. It feels like the back of Auntie Bridge's van. Why am I tied up in Auntie Bridge's van? That's impossible. Why would Auntie Bridge tie me up and put me in a van? It's… it's… I'm… hello? Hello? Who is that?

Van doors opening. Blinding light… I close my eyes… can't speak… tape on my mouth… someone rips it off. Ouch. It… it kills…

I can't tell if I'm crying. I feel like I am. My throat stings like I am. Mum? Mummy?

I know we've had our disagreements. I know I've pushed you too hard. I can see that now like I couldn't before. I have grown up, I think. Whatever I've done, I hope you know that.

Funny… no, not funny, *ironic*… ironic how, here in the dark, I can see more clearly.

I can see e.g.:

That I was stupid.

That I was secretive.

That I lied.

But all my friends were allowed to do more stuff than me. It wasn't fair. I just wanted…

You said you never checked my phone. You said you had a friend at school whose mum read her diary and you didn't like that – you didn't think it was right. You lied. You did check my phone. And my computer. Not just on our weekly check-throughs when I am there with you…

We're close, Mummy. Sometimes you say what I'm thinking before I even know myself. When I was sick, you knew it was nerves before I did. But that's not from checking. That's because we're close. I pushed us apart.

Hear my mind now, Mum. Hear this: if I make it from the bottom, if I find my way back to you, I'll always let you know where I am and who I'm with and what I'm doing. What I'm saying is: *I get it.* I proper get it. I promise.

I'm sorry.

CHAPTER 13

It started in his room, not mine. I didn't mean to go in, and he wasn't even in there at first. I only went in because I couldn't find my pencil case and I thought he might have borrowed it, because sometimes he stomps around the house shouting, 'Has anyone got a pen?' But my pencil case wasn't in there. I looked under the bed in case it had fallen on the floor and been kicked or something. But it wasn't there either. And that's when I found the magazines.

I only looked at one. It was disgusting. I thought it was disgusting. I was only a child. I couldn't understand why he would want to look at these things. I wanted to close it up and put it back, but I couldn't stop turning the pages, shocking myself with each new photograph.

I didn't hear him come in. I only saw the light dim, but it wasn't the light, it was him, standing in front of the window, standing over me.

'Like those, do you?' he said.

'I… I was looking for my pencil case.'

'Well you're not going to find it in there, are you?' He sat down next to me on the floor.

I was burning. I couldn't move.

'Don't let me stop you,' he said.

'I don't want to…'

'Don't want to what? Come on, it's only pictures.' He took the magazine from me and turned the page slowly. 'What about that one? Do you like that one?'

I shook my head. 'I have to go.'

'No you don't. Dinner's not for ages yet.' He turned another page. 'What about this one? She's pretty, isn't she? She has nice breasts.'

I got up. 'I have to go.'

I ran out of the room.

But that was the start of it. Thinking about it, that was the start.

CHAPTER 14

TONI

I'm going to hold your hand. There. I hold it to my cheek, and at its warmth, at the thought of it ever being cold, the tears come. I rub a little lip salve on your pale mouth. Your shoulders look so small under the white cover. Saline drip drip drips into your arm. My God, the tissues here are like tracing paper. Tell you what – if you got the corner of one in your eye, you'd blind yourself.

Will you be the same when you wake up? Will you still be shy, yes, outside the house, but inside it so funny, so clever? You were always clever, Rosie. At two you could dress yourself. You could make me a cup of tea by the age of five – five! – when other kids were barely able to hold a piece of toast, blow their nose, write their own name. When you ate ice cream, you hardly got any around your mouth. I've known adults eat more messily than you. Packets of baby wipes lasted months, nappies no longer necessary by the time you were thirteen months old. And when that day, no more than six years old, you came downstairs wearing my gold top as a dress, when you went into the shed and brought out the hard plastic picnic-tabletop and laid it on the living-room carpet and stood on it and announced you were going to be an actress, I knew in my bones that you could do it.

I know, I know. I know what you would say now if you could speak.

'All mothers think their children are talented,' you would say. You'd probably throw in an eye roll for good measure. 'All mothers think their children are special. Oh, Mum, you're so embarrassing.'

*

The nurse came a moment ago, to check on you.

'Can I get you some more tea?'

'No thanks.'

I can't drink any more. I don't want to go to the loo until Bridge or Emily gets here. I don't want to leave you. If Richard were here— You remember Richard? From records? I'd text him and ask him to pop up to Jupiter Ward while I take a break. But he won't be in until tomorrow. I hope Bridge remembers my phone charger. I texted Emily, did I say that? She texted back to say she's on her way. Emily or Bridget – I'll calm down at the sight of one or the other of them. But I won't get this knot out of my stomach until you open your blue eyes and talk to me. And then… and then we'll have to find a way to go forward.

Anyway, where was I? Your acting, that's right. It was Auntie Bridget who suggested that we get you into a theatre group.

'It'll be great for her confidence,' she said. This will have been one Sunday, her and Helen over for lunch when we lived in the house on the river. You will have done one of your tabletop plays, your Bratz and Barbie dolls your co-stars. 'She'll love it,' Auntie Bridge said. 'She'll make friends outside school – it'll widen her horizons.'

I never minded Auntie Bridge giving me advice when it came to you – still don't – and to be honest, I agreed, not because of talent or anything like that, but because it hit me in that moment with particular force that the little plays you used to make up were always about sisters. And you would never have one. Your daddy and I tried. But it wasn't to be, even before. *Before. Afterwards.* We both know what we mean when we say those words on their own.

It's our shorthand, the door to the abyss, a way of acknowledging the door without having to go through it. *Before. Afterwards.*

Before, when my biggest worry was the fact that you were an only child, I thought that a social group that had nothing to do with winning or achieving and everything to do with camaraderie would do you good.

'If you really think so,' I said to Bridget, 'I'll look into it.'

Someone is being sick in another ward. It started a few minutes ago and I can still hear them retching. I almost went to help – old habits and all that – but then a porter scurried past the entrance to the ward with a bucket and a mop. It could be worse. There's an old lady in one of the wards moaning constantly. You can hear it all the way down the corridor. It's hard to tell if she's in pain or delirious or horribly aware. It strikes me that being oblivious would be better. Oblivious, that's what I'd like to be, at the end.

Not very cheery, am I? I'm worried I'll fall asleep and miss you waking up. If you wake and I have fallen asleep, for God's sake say something. Make a noise. Fart, even. Go for it! I guarantee you won't hear a word of complaint from me.

You never joined a drama group, not when you were six, because soon after, everything changed. Soon after was *afterwards.* Just as well you can't hear this bit actually, but who knows, it might do me good to talk about it, even to myself. I haven't been there for a very long time. After all the therapy, and to put it in therapy speak, I put it in a box and closed the lid. There was no other way to move on.

But now I need to go there. Because I need to get to the place where I can tell you I'm sorry and ask for your forgiveness, and to get there I need to travel through this – our life, the story of me and you. And Bridget, of course; your beloved auntie Bridge.

I know the accident wasn't long after Bridget said about the theatre group, because I'd already booked you in for drama club after school, starting in the September. You were going to be seven in August. You were the youngest in your school year. It was the summer – July. We were going camping to our favourite place: the Isle of Purbeck. Your dad and I couldn't wait to get there, throw the tent up, then walk over the fields to the Square and Compass, our usual pub, and sit in the garden and look out over those sheep-dotted fields, the stone walls sloping down, defining the green, the old-fashioned telegraph poles, the mottled cottage roofs, and the sea, the sea! Oh, Rosie, if I close my eyes… that sky, so wide, a liquid blue you could drink and feel it sustain you.

'What's that thing supposed to be?' I remember saying to your dad one of those times, gesturing towards the weather-wrecked wooden sculpture in the middle of the pub garden. You were clambering all over it while chickens clucked about on the scrappy grass.

I remember him looking at me, amused, quizzical. 'Are you kidding me?'

'No. Why, do you know what it is? Looks like a star or something.'

'It's a square and a compass, you bloody eejit.'

'Oh God, as in the Square and Compass pub? Duh.'

We got the giggles so badly I had to run to the loo.

But I remember that sense of peace, Rosie, which tells me I once felt it. I remember your dad sitting on the bench, his raincoat collar sticking up around his neck, his hair thickened by the salt air, his face freckled by the sun. I can see him so clearly, more clearly than I have for a long while. Your daddy – your lovely, kind, funny dad.

It is scant comfort to know that it wasn't his fault, nor that the bloody imbecile checking his phone while driving was also killed in the collision, crushed by the wheel of his stupid pimped-up

Escort. When I try to remember it, I find it vaguer each time, as if I'm losing the before, losing you as you were then, losing your daddy. Stanley Flint. My Stan. I see him turn to me. I know he's smiling, but his face is fading. I feel his hand on my leg, a squeeze.

'All right, Bun?' Him looking at me, his hand on my leg. That's all I remember.

Bun. Bunny. He called me that after Rabbit in *Winnie-the-Pooh* – the overthinker, the worrier to the point of confusion. I called him Stan, or my love, or darling, or honey. If you could hear me, you'd be kicking your feet in horror or grimacing or something. You can't stand soppy talk, let alone the thought of my romantic life, even if it's long passed into history, left in the *before* like an artefact. What is it you would say? *Urgh, Mum, gross. Barfs into sleeve.*

Your dad said things like:

'Hey, Bun, why don't we go to the Witterings at the weekend?'

He'd say:

'Hey, let's get chips and eat them on the beach.'

And:

'Bunny. Wake up. Look at the sky.'

His lips on my pregnant belly, kissing me, kissing you, through my skin.

I was never a great looker, never anything special. But your dad made me beautiful. Your dad made life beautiful.

'All right, Bun?' Him looking at me, his hand on my leg, a squeeze.

Then nothing.

I woke up in the place I work. But this time I was strapped to a bed.

I met your dad here. Well, not in this ward, in A&E. You know that. He'd broken his left femur playing football.

'Truth be told,' he said a little later, grinning while I cleaned the blood off the cut on his forehead, 'I tripped over a sports bag on the way, so I did. Never made it to the pitch.'

I was still a nurse then. He asked me to write my number on his plaster cast. Which I did. Can't imagine doing anything so reckless now. But I did then. He was the first man who, when I told him I'd always wanted to be a nurse, didn't say: *So why not a doctor?*

I have often wondered why it was your dad, particularly, who finally settled me. There were so many men before him. Too many. But it was as if we knew each other instantly. That's the only way I can describe it. Like we knew everything important and fundamental about each other in those first moments. The rest, the stuff that came later, as we peeled off one another's layers, was, if not irrelevant, then peripheral. Detail. Decoration. Nice enough, but not relevant or necessary.

Me and your dad were so different. Me a fusspot; him so laid-back – *chill*, as you would say. Me with dark hair, brown eyes, skin that tans; him with freckles, blue eyes, skin that blistered after five minutes in the sun. So maybe there was an element of opposites attracting. But do you know what I loved most about him? It was that he never needed me to be anything other than exactly who and what I was. I never felt that I had to explain myself to him, and maybe because of that I wanted to explain everything.

I told him about the missed school years, the social workers. I told him all the things I swore I'd never tell you: the alcohol-soaked chaos and drug-fuelled promiscuity, the police warnings and petty crime. I told him about my uncle Eric.

And he took it, my love. He carried it as if it were no more than a bag of apples.

'Of course you did,' he'd say, or, 'Stands to reason,' or, 'You were just a kid,' or, 'Well, yes, you were in pain, weren't you?'

I would never tell you this if you were awake. Or maybe I would now. Maybe this is the next *afterwards*. The post-after. The beyond. What good can come of what's happened if not that we, you and I, get to know each other? As people this time. I have not let you know me, I think. You needed a mum, and I was the best mum I could be.

But perhaps I forgot to be a person.

CHAPTER 15

BRIDGET

Bridget remembers the call. How could she forget it? Toni hadn't rung from Dorset to say she'd got there safely like she always did – one of their silly habits from the old days, one that had stuck. So Bridget was calling her, getting no reply, and then finally Toni called back. But it wasn't Toni, it was a doctor calling from Toni's phone: she was at West Middlesex A&E, was this Antonia Flint's next of kin?

'I'm her sister,' Bridget said. 'I'm Bridget, Bridget Casement.'

It was only later that she realised she should have said, 'No, that's Stan. Stan Flint's her next of kin.'

Later still that she was hit with the knowledge that what the doctor had said was, after all, the truth.

'OK, Bridget, I need you to listen. Your sister's been involved in a serious accident. I need you to come in as fast as you can.'

'Is she… is she alive?'

'She is. But she's been seriously injured. If you could come as soon as you can.'

Too much to think about, even now. They'd only made it as far as the M3, less than twenty miles away. Rosie had not one bruise, not one scratch, had stayed safe in the back seat of Toni and Stan's rusty old VW Golf.

Memories come in flashes. Sometimes Bridget can't place them accurately in time. Toni saving up painkillers in a jar is one. Toni asking Bridget to smother her with a pillow.

'Please, Bridge.'

'I can't. You can't ask me to do that.'

Those dark nights in the house on the river, before they moved to the flat. Bridget would go to her in the dark. She would stroke her hair.

'Go to sleep, Tones.'

'I want to die.'

'I get that. But Rosie needs you, and the sun will come up, and by then it'll be tomorrow.'

'You won't leave, will you?'

'Of course I won't leave. Go to sleep.'

Little Rosie slept at the foot of Toni's bed on her camping lilo. Bridget wonders how she never woke up, especially when the nightmares came. God knows, Bridget could hear Toni shouting from the next room. But Rosie refused to sleep anywhere else.

'I want to sleep with Mummy.'

Bridget wasn't about to argue with that. The poor kid had lost her dad. This was in the days and weeks after Toni came back from hospital, when they were gathering up the pieces, seeing what they had.

Bridget took Rosie's room until they moved into the flat. Bridget took her to school, picked her up, took her to Café Bellissimo for hot chocolate, to Helen's sometimes. In the early months, Rosie would come in and lie on Toni's bed, do her homework at her dressing table while Bridget made the dinner.

'I don't want Daddy put in the ground.'

How long afterwards did Rosie say this? Actually, it was further back. Tones was still in hospital.

'It's too cold in the ground,' Rosie said. 'Daddy hates the cold.'

Her little face at Toni's bedside. A small girl playing guardian angel to her own mother. Sitting on a hospital chair, her scuffed shoes dangling on the ends of her little legs. She still had her uniform on and she smelled like kids smell after a day at school: of dust and dirt and the detergent they use to polish the floors.

'All right,' Toni said, glancing at Bridget, her smile so full of doubt, Bridget had to look away.

'It's dirty as well.' Rosie spoke with the gravity of a lawyer, counted the points on her fingers. 'And it's got worms.'

But my God, the denial was worse.

'Auntie Bridge? When's Daddy coming home?'

Bridget stopping, squatting down on the pavement on the way home from school, meeting Rosie's blue eyes. 'Remember, Squirt. Daddy's gone up to heaven, hasn't he?' And her, Bridget, an atheist, but you do what you can.

'But you said he's in the hospital.'

'He is, poppet. But he's in the morgue, isn't he, yeah? And that's just his body, isn't it? His soul is in heaven, which means he can see you but he can't come back in his body, and if you need to talk to him you have to pray.'

She nods, so solemn there on the pavement as life ploughs forward around them, people so oblivious that some days Bridget wants to shout: *What are you all doing? How can you carry on when this has happened? Have you no shame?*

Rosie's face, the penny seeming to drop. But then: 'So when will Daddy come home?'

Bridget standing up, holding out her hand. 'Shall we go to the café? How about a hot chocolate?'

Rosie's tiny hand, a hand you could crush just by holding it too tight. Yes, Daddy's coming home next week, Bridget wanted to tell her. But she couldn't, could she? And then one day in the hospital, like that, Rosie said about the ground being cold. It was maybe a week, maybe two, after.

'Remember I said about making special ashes,' Bridget said gently. 'So that we can keep him at home with us?'

Rosie nodded. 'Are we going to do that then?'

'I think so.' Bridget looked to her sister for help, but Toni couldn't even nod. She still had the chin support, was still being fed mush on account of losing most of her top teeth, breaking her soft palate. All she could do was whisper *yes* and blink, which sent two fresh tears coursing down her cheeks. Bridget thought of Stan's clothes, still hanging in the wardrobe, of his book still on his bedside table, his glasses folded on top – he had forgotten to take them on holiday. She wondered if she should move these things, clear them out, if she should ask whether or not Toni wanted her to. What would be worse to come back to – evidence or absence?

'We can buy a special jar,' Bridget ploughed on. 'We'll maybe buy a nice vase from one of those posh shops in Richmond. I could take you there tomorrow, Squirt, how does that sound? Or we could even get my mate Cath to make something.'

And that's what they did. Cath, Bridget's potter friend in Teddington, made an urn, and that's where Stan is now, on the top right-hand side of the bookshelf that the fireplace divides into two.

And all their lives divide that way, into two: before and after.

CHAPTER 16

ROSIE

Mum, the thing is, I would never have had a chance with a boy like Ollie, no way would I have even followed him because he's so out of my league, but there was this group photo from *The Wizard of Oz* from Easter last year. I wasn't in that because I was too nervous to audition, wasn't I? But I helped with props and I did some ushering too, do you remember? You let me do some of the matinees, but you wouldn't let me do the evening performances unless you came to pick me up, and I didn't want you to have to come out at night because, well, *because*.

You see, I do think about you sometimes, Mum. I'm not completely selfish.

Anyway, Stella Prince, you know, cool Stella whose party you didn't let me go to? She was Dorothy, obvs, and she'd posted about it loads on Instagram, and on one of the photos she'd tagged us all, the cast and crew and everyone. This was before she went away to uni. Stella has more followers than anyone I know, and she posts such cool pics, and I was stoked to be tagged on her feed even though it was only because she'd tagged everyone.

But that's how Ollie found me. This was before I got Little Red – ages before actually. Before we met Emily and things started to go well for us again. It was May last year or maybe June. I feel bad now. That's a long time to keep a secret.

I don't let, like, *anyone* follow me. I'm not one of those girls who just want loads of followers so they can say, hey, I've got 4,000 followers. I'm not like that. Mine's a private account so people have to ask to follow me. You see? I do listen to you. For some things, I do. I'm so much better behaved than anyone I know, Mum, you just don't realise it because you only know me and Naomi and Cat and about five of my other friends, and they're all really nice but even they do way more naughty stuff than me. Naomi smokes, like, ten roll-ups a day and Cat's had weed, but don't tell her mum or she'll kill me. Seriously, Mum, don't.

So when Ollie requested to follow me, I was like, what? I clicked on him to check him out – I'm not completely stupid – and saw, well, first of all that he was dank. Sorry, but he was *so* hot. And second, I saw that he followed Stella and a load of others from drama, and Stella and some of the girls followed him back. I even looked him up on Facebook and saw that we had twelve mutual friends, so I was careful, Mum, I *so* was. I accepted his follow request and followed him back. That's just what you do. His account was an open one. I stalked him a bit and liked his most recent picture: a flat white at Butter Beans in Richmond next to a copy of *Impro* by Keith Johnstone. I wanted to comment, *I've got that book!* and to ask if he was an actor too, but that would have been so embarrassing, and I didn't like any of his other pictures or he would know I'd looked through all of them and that would… well, no. Just no.

Ollie was following loads of beautiful girls, not normal ones like me, and I wondered why he'd bothered following me. He had this picture of him on holiday in Spain or somewhere, with his top off, and he was so dench; he had abs and he had, like, this really intense gaze. He's got beautiful brown eyes. I took a screenshot, but I deleted it later in case you checked through my photos and asked me who he was. I even deleted the deleted album, to be sure. But I kept it in my phone for a bit first so I could look at it. It's a bit like when you want, say, new trainers or a top or something but you can't afford it so you take a photo of it in the shop and sort of carry it around for a bit and imagine what it would be like to just, like, go out and buy it. Have it.

Anyway, then I posted a picture on Instagram of me and Auntie Bridge at her last gig, at the Orange Tree pub in Richmond. Auntie Bridge had her guitar round her neck and she looked quite cool for an old person, and it wasn't too bad of me obvs because I'd put it up there. I had put:

Me and Auntie Bridge #thepromise

Underneath, he had put:

Cool auntie ☺

I screamed. *He* had commented on *my* picture. Oh my actual God. If my friends saw it, they might click on him and they'd see that a total babe had commented on my feed. Loads of my friends get comments and likes from hot guys all the time, but they post selfies in bikinis, in their underwear, where they're wearing red lipstick, photos of them out drunk or on MD. I don't post selfies like that, like the others girls do, because, well, because 1) you would kill me; 2) I've never gone out and got drunk apart from one time when I went to that party when I told you I was staying at Naomi's, but I've never taken anything; and 3) those pictures are so embarrassing and I can't even do them. I tried once but it was such a fail so I just choose ones where I don't look too bad, for me.

I never get likes from hot guys, not normally. But this was *more* than a like – this was an actual legit comment. This was a move.

I liked his comment, but I didn't comment back because hello? Internet safety.

CHAPTER 17

TONI

After the accident, I told myself for years you were not harmed. But in your new quietness lay the truth. Whatever had made you stand on that picnic-tabletop and perform for us had died with your dad. Stanley Flint. Stan. The picnic-tabletop was… before. Now we were… afterwards. After the accident, you put it back in the shed. Soil from the trowel fell on it. Snails made a home on it – like barnacles on the bottom of an abandoned ship.

You had become shy. Overnight. You're still shy, in a way that you never used to be, and that makes me sadder than I know how to say. Sometimes, even now, when you make me laugh or tell me your stories, I long so badly for you to be able to share this wonderful side of yourself with the world. That was why I was so thrilled when you got the part of Little Red. It was Bridget – again – who suggested I sign you up for the local youth theatre, not to explore any potential you might have but to give you back your confidence. You were around ten or eleven by then… so, three or four years after the accident. It was the summer before you went to secondary school. The hospital had moved me to Medical Records, which was good of them. No longer able to cope with dealing directly with the needs of patients, I could have been out of a job completely.

We didn't talk about talent any more. We didn't talk about being special or gifted or anything like that. We had passed the prolonged and breathless shock of the first years and we were surviving, holding hands in the dark cave of grief. Bridget was right, as she so often is. You excelled in the art of becoming someone else, maybe because you wanted to be.

The girl in the bed opposite keeps trying to chat. Her tone hovers uncomfortably close to belligerence.

'That your daughter?' she said when we first came in. *A' ya doh'a?* That's what she sounds like. Thank goodness I nagged you to pronounce your words properly, although how I can get you to stop saying 'like' every second word is anyone's guess.

I wanted to say, 'No, it's my mother, who do you think it is?'

Except that wouldn't have felt right, with your granny being dead, and it's a bit rude.

'What did you say she was in for?' she asked, about ten minutes ago.

I didn't. I didn't say.

What you're in for is your own business, no one else's, not even the police's. If they trace the body to us, well, then we'll have to take a view, but until then I'm saying nothing. And nothing is exactly what I said to her. I looked at her coldly, mouth tight shut. That worked. She muttered something about only asking (*arxin*) and looked out of the window. If I leave your side, I'm sure she'll be over here straight away, reading your chart before you can say *nosy bitch*.

Anyway, let's talk about something nice, something life-affirming that will do just that: affirm your life, now that we've retrieved it. I was talking about your first night as Little Red, wasn't I? About how excited you were when I put you to bed, how full of the famous actress you were going to become. I hoped it would pass, this euphoria, but of course it didn't, and the morning after, you were still full of Emily this, Emily that.

'Listen, Rosie,' I said. 'We don't even know her. She could be anyone.'

'Anyone could be anyone,' you said as you set the table. 'We can still look at her website though, can't we? Just a look?'

'All right, all right. Just a look.'

You fetched your laptop and we looked up the Into the Light Agency. With hindsight, I suspect you'd already looked it up in bed the night before on your iPhone. Your auntie Bridge had gone to the gym, I think, because it was just us two that morning. I'd made waffles, and we ate them with maple syrup, do you remember?

The agency was exactly as Emily had said: there weren't many actors on it, maybe eight or ten or so, and they all looked to be in their late teens, maybe early twenties. I tell you what, Rosie, and I don't expect you to understand this, but as you get older, the sight of young people can bring a tear to the eye. Youth: so beautiful, so full of innocence, curiosity and hope. Maybe it's because I know I'm looking at the blemish-free faces of people who have yet to experience real pain, have yet to have their lives irrevocably compromised. Why would they not be curious? Why would they not hope? Life hasn't yet taught them not to.

Sorry, I'm being morbid, not to mention making assumptions about people I don't even know. I mustn't let the old bitterness overtake me. That's in the past, where it needs to stay. Where were we? Oh yes, those photographs. Professional shots like you see in theatre programmes, and my thoughts turned immediately to the worry of how much a photograph like that would cost. There was one shot in particular: a girl with sleek black hair, flawless skin and the biggest brown eyes you've ever seen. Sunita Philips, I think her name was.

'Oh my God,' you said. 'She is so amazing.'

I could tell you were thinking about what it would be like to have a photograph like that taken, to have yourself presented in that way and how wonderful it would be. And I wonder if that's the moment I thawed. I could see that the website was very professional; your auntie had checked Emily's credentials online. I didn't trust her, no way, but then I didn't trust anyone.

'You really want to do this, don't you?' I said.

You nodded once, twice, three times. You were tucking into your muesli and you grinned at me, your cheeks pinking with delight. Another drip fell from the melting iceberg that was me.

'You'd have to keep on top of your school work,' I said, pouring coffee into my flask for work. I said nothing about the money, another worry that was running through my mind. I knew I'd find the cash somehow.

You nodded again – three, four, five times – your brow furrowed in a show of commitment. It reminded me of when you were four and I said I would only buy you tap shoes if you promised to stick at the lessons. You stuck to the lessons, all right. I found some tap shoes second-hand. You wore them out. In fact, you wore them until your big toenails went black, and when I asked why, you said you didn't want to ask me for another pair because they were expensive. Bless your heart, darling. My darling girl.

You probably couldn't believe I was even considering it, could you, because of how I am – my limitations, my paranoia. I smiled to myself, put my flask into my bag with my packed lunch, made sure your sandwiches were ready in your rucksack with your water bottle and one of the chocolate Rice Krispie cakes I still made for you safe in its Tupperware. I was busy, as usual, scooting about, but as I came past you, I reached over and laid my hand on your soft cheek.

'This doesn't mean I'm saying yes to drama school or anything like that,' I said. 'That's a whole other conversation, all right?'

'I understand,' you said, washing down your multivit with a slug of orange juice. 'She said it'd only be for adverts anyway at first, for experience and coaching and all that stuff. Even if I don't get anything, it'll be good to put on my CV, and I won't fall behind on my GCSEs or anything.'

'And how will you get to these auditions?'

I saw you stop yourself from rolling your eyes.

'Mum, I take a bus when I go into Kingston or Richmond, don't I? I've been on the train to Waterloo. I'm fifteen.'

'You've only been on the train once, with Naomi. And that's with no changes and no Tube. What if it's at night?'

'They don't do auditions at night! She's not going to send me to anything dodgy, is she? She's not going to send me across London at, like, midnight. Her agency wouldn't last long if she did that, would it?'

I chewed my lip. 'I'll give her a call once the play's finished its run,' I said after a moment. 'No harm in seeing what she's got to say.'

CHAPTER 18

ROSIE

The next time I posted a picture, Ollie liked it even though it was only my dinner, but he didn't comment. It was Auntie Bridget's pasta that she makes, with anchovies and tomatoes and stuff, which is well tasty, and it looked amazing because she'd put chopped parsley on it, and Auntie Bridge says chopped parsley makes everything look good, even your lentils, which otherwise look like diarrhoea. No offence, LOL.

Ollie posted a picture of a racing bike. Lime green. Single-speed. Because we were doing more than likes now, I commented:
Cool bike ☺
He liked my comment and commented back! He put:
Thanks ☺
We started liking each other's pictures and commenting. Our comments weren't serious or anything, they were just banter. My iPhone 5C is a bit crap, but it takes quite good photos and I tried to start taking more arty shots to post. I was posting for him, no one else. That's so embarrassing, but it's true. Every picture I put up, I hoped he'd see it. I hoped he'd see it and think it was cool – that I was cool.

I hoped he'd like it enough to click on my heart.

I suppose we must have done that for ages, all through last summer. It was just likes and bants. He wished me happy birthday on my fifteenth birthday, good luck when I started Year 11, happy Halloween, happy Bonfire Night, whatever. Then at Christmas, he liked the picture of our Christmas tree and put:

I wanna send you a card. What's your address? He had added a Christmas-tree emoji – sweet!

I didn't know if he was joking or not, even though we'd been friends for, like, nearly eight months. If he was, and I DM'd my address, I'd look like a total nerd. And then I thought you'd see the card and ask me about it, so I put:

Next year! LOL. I thought for a second then added a winking-face emoji.

In January, when I got the part of Little Red, I started taking more pictures – rehearsals and things – and he liked all of those. I so wanted to ask him to meet me, but I was way too scared. Loads of girls followed him. He was one of those guys who has a million girls hanging on, like Sam Hanson, this lad in Year 12, who is a total flirt but never commits. Naomi says guys like him have all their little chicks in the nest and they give the worm to whoever has the widest beak just so they don't give up and drop out of the nest, dead. Ollie was probably going out with some hot girl like Stella Prince, but Naomi said he'd still be keeping loads of other girls interested, waving a worm over their heads, like, *Heyee, chickee, open your beak, it might be you next.* I love Naomi. She's so jokes.

I didn't comment on too many of his pictures or ask if he was going out with anyone. That would have been a bit needy. But I kept on taking photos, kept on getting a thrill when he liked my posts. I would say he liked, say, nine out of every ten. I always felt so gutted when he didn't like one, proper stoked when he did – I'd be, like, *Yay!*

Then I started messing about with the filters, taking pictures of anything I found funny or weird or lovely. I even started to take pictures of food, like on the arty food accounts. Remember when you made Rice Krispie cakes when I got my first audition and you put them on that cardboard cake stand that Richard from work gave you for your birthday, and I took a photo of that?

What are you taking a photograph for? you said.

Nothing. No reason. They just look so yummy.

I started to notice the world more, if that makes sense? And I felt like I could make a world just for me. I could cut out all the bad stuff and just pick the good. I didn't have to tell anyone about the accident. I didn't have to tell anyone about you, or about Dad dying. I could like other people's lives too. I could even like older kids from drama's posts, even kids who had gone away to uni. And that was cool.

It was all for Ollie. *He* had made me appreciate things, little moments that usually I'd be, like, yeah, whatevs. And no offence, Mum, but the other reason I put pictures there instead of on Facebook was because you weren't on it. Sorry, it's not against you or anything, I just wanted to put my stuff somewhere my mum wouldn't see it. Or comment! Sometimes when you comment on my feed it's such a cringe. I'll put a funny picture of me messing around with my friends and you'll put some moist comment like *You all look so beautiful.*

It's sooooo embarrassing…

A glow from above… white… whiteness… beep beep… That's a good sound, I think. I'm going to run towards that sound… Help… Help me…

Je suis, I am.

Tu es, you are.

Il/elle/on est… Honest, guvnor, we weren't doin' nothin'.

Got a French test tomorrow morning. *J'ai un examen de français demain matin.* Squeak. Trainers on lino, or an animal… a mouse? A cough… dry cough… a walkie-talkie?

Nous sommes, we are.

Vous êtes, you (posh) or you (lot) are.

Ils/elles sont, they (men)/they (women) are. Unless they're mixed and then they're men again. Begin again, Michael Finnegan. He grew whiskers on his chinnegan…

Lying on the seabed, a bed for the C… C word is rude… C u next Tuesday… The water is thick with plants. They wave at me like Dementors in Harry Potter… Mum? Mummy? Emily? Auntie Bridge?

Cough, cough. Throat-clearing or walkie-talkie? No radios at the bottom of the sea. Can't get a dry cough under water, can you? Walk the walk, talk the talk. *When I was one, I'd just begun, the day I went to sea… Ó Maidrín rua, rua, rua, rua…* Daddy used to sing. Daddy made me try tea for the first time, put some sugar in, stir it up. *There you go, my little red fox, get that down your neck, put the hairs on your chest…*

I make you cups of tea, you make me cups of tea, tea says I'm sorry, I love you, you look tired, let me do something nice to make you smile, the kettle crackles with calcium, the water here is hard… *This kettle's buggered, Rosie. Hey, Rosie, what do you fancy for dinner? Poached or scrambled? I've got oven chips… Pass me a carrot, lovey, there's a doll…*

I love you.

I love you more.

Wrong. I love you more.

It's complicated, Mum. *We* are complicated. I didn't mean to be secretive. I love you more than anyone else in this world. I'm sorry for what I've done. I know it's bad, whatever it is. I can feel it. It is very, very bad.

CHAPTER 19

TONI

A week later, once the show had finished its run, I emailed Emily and invited her over to the flat to chat to us in more detail. It was a Saturday afternoon in early May; Bridget was at rehearsals for that evening's gig at the White Cross pub. When Emily pulled up outside in her bright red Mini convertible, you ran out and jumped into the car and directed her round to the car park at the back. I could hear the two of you laughing as you approached the back door together and that reassured me a little. I know, I know, you would have told me I was mad or embarrassing or mental – your favourite phrase when it comes to me – but one day you'll be a mother and you'll realise it's not easy letting your children out into the world, especially now with the internet and all that it has brought to our lives.

Once in the kitchen, you invited Emily to sit at the table and made us a pot of tea.

'What a helpful daughter you have, Mrs Flint,' Emily said.

'Yes,' I said. 'She is. Thank you for saying so.'

You are helpful, Rosie. I don't tell you that enough.

Once you'd come to the table and poured the tea, Emily chatted to us some more about the agency. A lot of what she said she'd already told us in the theatre, and of course we'd looked online, but it was good to hear it all again in the calm environment of home.

'So far I only have nine actors on the books,' she said. 'But I have a house in Suffolk, and I plan to run residential workshops in the school holidays with my business partner. I'm doing the rounds of the youth theatres currently. My idea is that I would be a kind of stepping stone to a larger agent. I'm offering a contract that is non-binding so that, should they find someone bigger, they can fly off like birds. Hopefully by then they'll have had some experience and coaching in a safe and nurturing environment.' She smiled, her eyes almost closing at the edges.

'It sounds great,' you said.

'*Little Red* got such rave reviews,' Emily chatted on, 'as I'm sure you know. It's been featured in the *Richmond and Twickenham Times*, and the *Richmond Magazine*. Heady heights!' She chuckled.

'It's been on Facebook too,' you said.

'I saw that,' I said. I suppose I was keen to join in.

'And Twitter,' Emily chipped in.

'I don't do Twitter,' I said. 'I'm not really one for all that stuff.'

'Me neither, Mrs Flint, but it's the world we live in now, isn't it? One has to move with the times.'

I bristled. The implication was that I hadn't, I suppose. But I do have Facebook, don't I, though I haven't got a profile picture, nor do I ever post anything, and I only went on so I could be Facebook friends with you and keep an eye out. I know your friends have every social-media gadget or website or app or whatever they're called under the sun, but I still think it was reasonable to limit you to one. Facebook is more than enough to keep up with your friends, make arrangements and so forth. I know your friends got Facebook when they were twelve and I know you had to wait until you were fourteen. But that's just it – you were only fourteen, your life open wide to anyone who wanted to look. You're still only fifteen now, and I've read so much about teenagers and the internet and mental health. I can believe it! I can't imagine what it's like having to look at all the pictures of a party you weren't invited to. We never had to cope with that when I was young. If you didn't make the cut, it was tough but that was it, although I hope to God you never go to the kind of parties I went to. Nothing that went on there would be worthy of Instagram. Unless you want to show people pictures of smashed windows, police hammering on the door, some skank shooting up in the corner. Worse.

Something else occurs to me now, talking to you like this. I wonder if another reason for me not letting you have these things was that I couldn't see the point. I can't think of a single thing in my life that I would want to put up there and say, here, look at this. Apart from pictures of you – which you wouldn't let me post up or stick up, however you say it – what would I have to share? Updates from West Middlesex Hospital records department? Not exactly a thrill a minute, is it? For all that I personally find people's medical issues fascinating, I understand that so-and-so's liver failure or whojamaflip's skin condition would leave most people cold. Maybe if I posted the bottle-inserted-in-the-rectum shots I'd get a following – but I'd soon be Instasnapping my P45 if I did that, so let's not go there.

'You've gone off on one, Mum,' you would say to me now if you were awake, if I were talking to you for real.

But I hate social media, and that's why, when Emily stood up to go and held up her cheap black plastic phone, I thought we'd get along just fine.

'This thing can't do your Twittergrams and your Snapfaces and what have you,' she said, 'but it's good enough for phone calls and the old texting, and that's all I need when I'm out and about.'

I held up what your auntie calls my *vintage* Samsung. 'I've not quite joined the Apple revolution either, Emily, as you can see.'

She chuckled. 'Technology is the apple of temptation,' she said. 'Question is, who took the first bite, eh? Was it Adam or was it Steve?'

I laughed – what was she on? Did that even make sense? 'Buggered if I know.'

She limped over to the back door, wincing a little as she went, and paused there a moment.

'More of a person-to-person person myself,' she said as she grasped the door handle. 'Sorry, too many persons in one sentence there. Don't take it personally.' She chuckled again, and this time you chuckled too – I think for the same reasons as me. She just comes out with the funniest things without meaning to.

'Thank you for your time, Emily,' I said. 'We'll be in touch.'

'Oh, Mum, she is so nice,' you said when you came back into the kitchen after waving her off. You had your arms around me, your nose against my neck. 'I know she's only the same age as Auntie Bridge, but she seems more like a granny, don't you think? Person-to-person person.' You laughed. 'Classic. And she knows someone who does headshots for, like, two hundred pounds. That's really cheap, she said, and she said she can take me. I can pay. I've got, like, two hundred pounds in my post-office account.'

'I haven't said yes yet,' I protested, but you didn't need to know about acting to hear that my conviction was failing.

'I don't mind paying for a headshot, Mummy. Honest.'

'I said we'll see.'

I didn't want to take your cash, my darling. But at the same time I think there's something to be said for putting your money where your mouth is, and that's exactly what you'd done, offering up your savings like that. Determined, that's what you were. I'm hoping your determination will pull both of us through now, my love; that it will help us face what we must face.

I hope you'll appreciate how difficult it was for me, letting Emily into our lives that day. I hope you can acknowledge that I never said how worried I was. And I was, my love. I was terrified. I just want to say that for the record. Even if Emily was the real deal, I knew you were throwing yourself into a world fraught with danger and disappointment. I wondered if it was because you idolised your auntie Bridge so much or whether it was just in the genes. Your dad was a real extrovert too, you know, never needed asking twice to pick up his guitar.

Whatever it was, the thing that made me thaw, that made me change my mind and bite my lip against all that frightened me was this: when you'd joined that theatre group, I'd seen the confidence you'd had when you were little start to come back. I'd seen you grow. And so I fought against myself. I swallowed down my own feelings on the matter as best I could. Like when I've arranged flowers in a vase or straightened a picture on a wall or lit the last candle on a birthday cake and I stand back and catch my breath, not daring to move for a moment in case the flowers droop, the picture slips, the candle goes out. So it was with you, my darling. You were blossoming before my very eyes, and at that fragile sight of you, my lungs filled with fresh air.

So when you kissed my cheek and said, 'Please, Mummy? Please can I sign with Emily?' I thought: this is our turning point. This is us moving from *afterwards* to *beyond*.

'Yes,' I said. 'All right. Yes.'

CHAPTER 20

BRIDGET

Bridget gets home to find Toni waiting for her in the kitchen. She looks up, as if startled, her eyes wide. There is a mug of tea beside her, the top filmed with grey.

'Emily has a photographer,' she says without saying hello. 'For this headshot thing, you know? She said she'd take Rosie.' She bites at her ring finger, which is already red, the nail chewed to the quick. 'What do you think?'

'OK.' Bridget fills the kettle, biding her time while she figures out what her sister is asking her for. Not that she would ever ask. 'Has she said how much it'll be?' is what comes to her. Perhaps this is about money.

'She said it would be cheap. Two hundred there or thereabouts.'

Bridget pulls a mug from the cupboard and drops a teabag into it. 'Stop biting your nail,' she says over her shoulder. 'You'll make it sore.'

'Doesn't your friend Saph take photos?'

Ah.

'Sure,' Bridget says, turning to face her sister. 'I can ask her. If you prefer that.'

Tones withdraws her hand from her mouth and frowns. 'I think I'd be more comfortable with someone we know. Am I being weird?'

'No weirder than usual.' Bridget points to Toni's mug and then to Toni: *tea?* Toni shakes her head: *no thanks.* 'In fact,' Bridget continues, 'Saph owes me anyway for installing her antivirus the other week. I'll give her a ring, maybe take Rosie next Saturday morning.'

'I can take her.'

She has that look in her eye, that I-don't-need-your-help-even-though-I've-just-asked-for-it look, so Bridget leaves it there. Experience has taught her that this is by far the best option.

'Sure,' she says. 'Do you want her number?'

'Oh… would you mind calling her, as she's your friend?'

'Course not.'

The following Saturday, Bridget walks her sister and niece out to the car. She leans in at the passenger window while Toni gets into the driver's seat.

'So Pope's Lane's just off Twickenham Green, yeah?'

'I know where Pope's Lane is,' says Toni. 'Stop fussing. It's literally round the corner.'

'I've just thought,' Bridget says to Rosie, who has climbed into the back seat. 'You know it's Saph from the band, don't you? Sapphire?'

'I know.' For some reason, Rosie blushes beetroot – Bridget can see even from outside the car. Why would she go bright red about that? Teenagers are strange sometimes. 'We don't know any other Saphs, do we?'

Bridget rests her hand on the roof and peers in so she can see them both better. Toni has started the engine but is fussing now with the fan settings, trying to clear the windscreen.

'Her parents were mad for *Sapphire & Steel*,' Bridget says to her niece. 'That's why they called her Sapphire. Tell her I told you that.'

Rosie presses her face between the front seats. She will stay there until the last possible moment, when she has to put on her seat belt. Toni would make her wear two if she could.

'What the hell's *Sapphire & Steel*?' Rosie asks. God, these kids could make you feel like you were a hundred years old sometimes.

'Put your seat belt on and don't swear,' Toni says. 'It's a crap show from the seventies.'

'Joanna Lumley was in it,' Bridget chips in. 'You know, Patsy from *Ab Fab*?'

'From those DVDs?' Rosie says.

'The sensible daughter and her crazy mum,' Bridget says, rolling her eyes towards Toni and winking.

Rosie's face brightens. 'So was Patsy, like, famous? I mean, Joanna Lumley? I mean, like, before?'

Bridget laughs; so does Toni. They exchange a glance. Rosie sits back and clips her seat belt, looking at both of them, perplexed.

'What?' she says. 'What's funny about that?'

CHAPTER 21

ROSIE

On the way to Saph's you're like, *That was nonsense before, by the way. Auntie Bridge was only teasing.* Sapphire & Steel *was a show from the eighties, and Saph's older than your auntie Bridge so she can't possibly have been named after* that *Sapphire.*

Maybe it's Sapphire like the actual jewel?

Most probably. Actually, the daughter in Ab Fab *was called Saffy, wasn't she? But I don't know what that was supposed to be short for. Anyway, I think your auntie Bridge's Saph played drums for The Bangles once, so that's her claim to fame.*

Who are The Bangles?

You laugh and shake your head. *Never mind.*

Saph is The Promise's drummer, obvs. She's a photographer too, and she also makes this leather jewellery with silver on it for shops all over Britain. Until this day, the day of the headshot, I've only seen her on stage and said hello to her, but I've never talked to her properly. She is so cool even though she is old, and when she opens the door I feel myself go bright red.

Hey, babe, look at you. Her long grey hair is so straight and shiny the light bounces off it. She tucks a lock behind one ear. The top of her ear is pierced with a silver hoop with a tiny butterfly on it. *You ready to look beautiful?*

Me with a cherry face. I wish she would stop looking at me. I'm like, *Er, no, I… Not sure.*

Come in, come in, babe. Let's sort you out.

You're all, *Hi, Saph. So lovely to see you, it's been ages. How are you?*

I can tell you want to come in just by your body language; we do loads of work on body language in drama. You're leaning towards her and that means you like her and you'd like to stay. If you wanted to go you'd be backing away. Maybe you'd have your palms up.

I'll see you later, Mum, I say, in a nice voice. But my hands become fists and you tilt your head a bit and back off. I can tell by your smile that I've hurt your feelings. Your smile is like one I would do if I took a hockey ball to the shin and it killed but I didn't want to admit it. I'm sorry, thinking about that now. You came all the way to the door with me and then I brushed you off.

All right then. You have this weird, cheerful voice. *I'll be back in, what, an hour, Saph?*

Sure. Saph's pushing back her shiny hair. *No rush, hon. Actually, give us a couple of hours, yeah? She's safe with me, aren't you, babe?*

I giggle. My cheeks have gone hot again. So embarrassing.

I don't even wait for you to get into the car before I go inside. I don't wait and I don't wave you off. I pretend to forget. I can see myself now on Saph's front step, as if I'm someone else. The way I turn away, the way I step into Saph's house and let her close the door. The way I leave you behind.

That was mean, I think. I'm sorry.

Saph chats to me for, like, twenty-five minutes, without even taking a single picture! She makes me this cool tea. I can't remember what it's called but it's not PG Tips or even Earl Grey. I think it's called red bush but she says it another way – something like roebuck, like the pub on Richmond Hill. That's probably so she doesn't have to go around saying red bush all the time because hello? Rude!

So how long have you been acting? She's setting up this umbrella-dome-satellite-dish thing in the corner of the living room. *Bridge tells me you're really talented. Sorry I missed you in* Little Red, *Bridge said you were amazing. You're very pretty when you smile, do you know that? You have a really lovely aura and your hair is amazing. I'm so jealous of your hair.*

No way, I'm jealous of your *hair!* I so don't say because that would be lame.

Saph talking to me is like having a spotlight on me. It doesn't burn my eyes but even so I can't look at it. I can't look at Saph. She is too cool. On stage, I've seen her wear these hippyish clothes, like she's wearing today: a pink maxi skirt with silver patterns on and big black biker boots like Auntie Bridge wears and a cream-coloured peasant top with pink and peacock-green embroidery on it and plaited cotton strings at the neck, and on her fingers she wears loads of silver rings, and I wish I could be like her. That's why I can't look straight at her – because I want to *be* her so much. Well, be her but my age version? I don't want her to look at my clothes – they are so boring. Skinny jeans and a T-shirt. So *conventional.* When I'm older, I'll go to second-hand markets and buy cool second-hand stuff and put loads of plants on my windowsills like Saph has and hang loads of different pictures on the walls of all the plays and TV stuff I'll be in.

I will be way less conventional.

Are you OK, Rosie babe? The tea OK?

Oh yes. Thanks. Tea's nice.

It's not – it's rank. But I can't say that. I think I have fallen in love with Saph except I don't want to, like, kiss her or anything. That would be gross.

She makes me laugh while she takes the photos.

Think of the most annoying boy in your year.

Urgh.

Now pretend he's asked you out on a date.

Oh my God, no!

OK, think of a hot boy in your year. The hottest.

I think of Ollie. I think of all the photos of him, how his hair flops over one eye, how his teeth are all even and white. My face is probably radioactive by now. Thank God no one can see my thoughts. I laugh with Saph and feel my face go even hotter. I bet I look gross. I bet I've got a big fat cherry head. I bet the concealer on the zits on my forehead has worn off.

Snap snap. Snap snap snap.

She has a thing called a light meter, which she makes me hold under my chin. Her drum kit is in the opposite corner. After the photos are finished, she lets me have a go on it. It's awesome – so loud. Then she plays the drum opening for 'Middle of the Road' by The Pretenders and I say I know it because Auntie Bridge is a Chrissie Hynde nut, and she says, *Yes, I know, she is.* I take a photo with my phone for Instagram. Then I get back on the drums again and ask Saph to take one.

Later, I put it on Instagram: *Me on the drums at Saph's #thepromise.*

Ollie likes it. He comments: *Looking cool, rock chick.*

Which is a bit lame, but I don't care.

Saph sends the pictures through a week later. Normally, clients can only have three, she puts in the email, but she sends, like, twenty or something and says we can use whichever we want. We will have to put them on a USB stick and get them printed at Boots or somewhere, save on costs. She says she doesn't want paying for the shoot.

You're all teary. *That's so kind of her*, you say. *She's basically done that for free. And she's got to make a living just like the rest of us. We'll have to think of a gift for her. Honestly, Rosie, the less people have, the more generous they are.*

You always say that last bit: *The less people have, the more generous they are.*

You are generous, Mum. You are kind. Even though things are tight for us, you always make sure I have what I need and most of what I want. I do know that. I do appreciate it. I wish you would get yourself some new things sometimes. You never buy new clothes or shoes, and your boots went out of fashion in, like, Tudor times, LOL. I've got an iPhone and you've got an old, crap phone. You haven't even got a laptop and you know Auntie Bridge would get you one – she's always offering.

Anyway, on the pictures, Saph made me look much more beautiful than I am in real life. She made my eyes bluer, my freckles cuter, my hair richer. She made my skin glow. I thought I'd have a bright red face but no, it was kind of lit up and peachy.

Who's afraid of the big bad wolf? I say when I see those photos for real. *Not me!*

This is the next day when we pick up the actual physical pictures from Boots in Kingston, and you want to look at them properly, straight away, so we go across the courtyard to Caffè Nerd. It's Caffè Nero obvs but we call it Caffè Nerd because that's what the sign looks like and that made us laugh once and then it stuck.

Hot chocolate? you ask.

Actually could I have a cappuccino?

Your face, like I've said something confusing. *A cappuccino? Since when did you like coffee?*

Since… I don't know. Not a big deal, is it?

No, of course not. Just didn't realise, that's all.

You give me your card to go and order while you get us a table. I carry the drinks over. You are still flicking through the photos even though there are only three.

You're so like your daddy. Your eyes are wet.

I look Irish. I hope you're not going to start crying – what if someone I know comes in?

Irish, yes, you say. *He had that Celtic charm, did your dad. He was from Cork – you know that, don't you? And he was so funny. He adored you.*

I know. I know. And I know.

You press your nose to mine, and your eyes go all fuzzy because we are so close. *I know you know and you know and you know.*

I know you know I know and I know and I know.

You're silly.

You're sillier.

That night, I make one of the photos my Facebook profile pic. Later I check it to see how many likes it's got: 146, which isn't even all that many for some people, but it is for me, and loads of my friends have commented. All of them are really nice, apart from Zac, this lad in my year, who has written *Sket*, which means slag or whatever. But he's a weirdo and no one likes him.

After that, I change my Instagram profile pic to my favourite headshot. A second later, Ollie comments: *Beautiful.*

That's so quick, I think. As if he's been waiting.

CHAPTER 22

TONI

Emily emailed us to say she would get your photo onto Spotlight ASAP. I felt my guts flip at the thought of your image out there for public consumption, beyond the realm of Facebook. Things were moving so fast – too fast. I tried to remember that your picture had been in the programme for *Little Red and the Wolf*, alongside your name, and reassure myself that it was all part of the process, but I was still uneasy.

In the past I would have called my misgivings instinct, but since the accident my instincts had been well and truly cocked up. It's one of the things that came out in the post-trauma counselling. I got, still get, nervous about things that turn out to be fine. More often than not, it's just my own fears about life and death manifesting themselves in these smaller worries. That's what the counsellor said anyway, and what that means in practical terms is that my instinct has joined the long line of things I can't rely on any more. *Don't sweat the small stuff*, they say, don't they? You'd think, having gone through the big stuff, I would know that. But I do sweat the small stuff, now more than ever. I've tried so hard not to let the way I am affect you, my darling girl, but I know that it has. It did. Perhaps that was inevitable. But I'm still sorry.

Anyway, according to Emily, before we could upload the photo to Spotlight and to her website, there were forms to fill in. In the meantime, she said, she would send your headshot through to a couple of casting agents she knew on a friendly basis. She'd copied me in, so I replied:

Thank you so much, Emily. All very exciting. Let us know if we should be doing anything.

When you got home, I showed you the email and my reply on your laptop, and honestly, your outrage was such you'd have thought I'd rolled naked down the high street on a carnival wagon, singing *aye aye yippee yippee aye.*

'I can't believe you replied for me,' you shouted at the top of your lungs, as if I'd burned all your clothes or sold your childhood toys without asking. 'I'm capable of replying to an email, you know. And Emily's contract is with me. She's my agent. Mine.'

'All right, all right, keep your voice down. You're fifteen, not twenty. And you haven't signed anything, there's no contract yet, so strictly speaking she's not your agent. She's not anything.'

'I'm fifteen years old!' You threw your rucksack on the table so hard your Tupperware bounced out and onto the floor. I didn't remark on the irony of you getting cross with me for treating you like a child while still allowing me to make your packed lunches for you.

You sighed and gripped the chair back. I could see you were making a great effort not to lose it with me.

'Look,' I said. 'I wasn't being overprotective; I was trying to help. You've been a child since you were born; you were a child a year ago. Six months ago, you liked hot chocolate, now you like coffee. I can't suddenly switch into treating you like an adult' – I snapped my fingers – 'like that. It's a gradual thing. And you're not an adult yet. You're an adult when you're paying your own rent, buying your own food and doing your own washing, and until you're doing that, you're a kid. A child. My child.'

You threw your eyes to the ceiling. 'Do you realise, Mum, that in less than a year, I could go by myself to the GP and it would be, like, confidential?'

I struck back. 'Why, what's the matter, are you not well?'

'That's not the point.' You were shouting again – you didn't pick up on my flippancy. 'That's not what I'm saying. I'm saying that I'm old enough to email my own agent!'

'All right. All right. I get it, I get it.'

You sighed again, softer this time, your frustration ebbing. 'I know you're trying to help,' you said. 'But don't, OK? Just don't.'

'All right.'

From that point on, you must have emailed Emily directly and asked her not to copy me in, because that was the last email I saw live, or however you say it. I had to wait for our weekly checks to see any further correspondence, and even then, you wouldn't leave me alone to read anything. Looking back, you could have deleted whatever you wanted. The next thing, you were telling me that your first audition had come around. It must have been a week, maybe two weeks later.

'It's for a soap advert,' you said. You were jumping up and down with joy. 'I have to go into London. I have to be there by 11 a.m. the day after tomorrow.'

'London? But what about school?'

'It's only double PE, which is, like, a waste of time, and Naomi said she'd photocopy the biology notes and I can catch up on maths in, like, ten minutes.'

'Hold on a second. You can't miss school.'

'It's just PE, Mum! I want to be an actor, not an athlete.'

I met your eye and saw ice. You were so passionate. And I thought about how I had missed not the odd day but *years* of school for much less edifying reasons. What was one day if it was for something that meant so much to you, something worthwhile?

'You're sure it's OK to miss lessons like that?' I said.

'Of course it is! Everyone does it and that's not even for anything important. I'm doing something towards my, like, professional career.'

'How are you going to get there? I can't take the day off just like that. I won't be able to drive you.'

'I know how to get on a train, Mum.' You laughed sarcastically. 'It'll be fine. Anyway, Emily said she'd come with me. She might even drive.'

'But we don't know Emily that well.'

Another laugh, dripping with disdain, as if you, not me, were the one who knew about the world and all its terrors. 'Oh, Mum. Don't be mental.'

'Don't say that, it's offensive.'

'Soz. Don't be silly then. Emily wouldn't be much of an agent if she… I mean, what do you think she's going to do?'

I felt my chest sink. You were right – I was being paranoid. And the thought of you, in the centre of the capital, on your own…

'As long as Emily goes with you,' I said, 'that's fine.'

You sat on my knee and kissed my cheek. Were you manipulating me? I think you probably were. I can't believe now I agreed to any of it, frankly.

'This is *so* what I want to do with my life, Mum,' you said. 'The rest of the time, it's like I'm living in black and white, but when I act, I, like, go into colour. Do you know what I mean?'

'I do. It's just—'

'So will you call the school and tell them I'm sick?'

I know you think I'm too strict, but it's you who's in charge, my love. Always has been. I told you it was OK, but that you'd have to keep in touch. I would need Emily's mobile number as well as yours.

'Yes, Mum, yes, Mum, three bags full, Mum.'

The next night, I made lasagne for dinner, to celebrate. It's been your favourite since you were a little girl. I even made Rice Krispie cakes and put them on the cake stand. You took a picture of them, do you remember? You stood on a kitchen chair like a real live food photographer.

But that night, in the early hours, you crept into my room.

'Mummy,' you whispered, 'my stomach's killing me.' You climbed into my bed and seemed to sleep all right, but in the morning you were as white as a sheet.

'I haven't slept at all,' you moaned. 'I feel so sick.'

The involuntary gesture of mothers everywhere: I laid my hand across your head. 'You're not hot or anything. And your auntie Bridge is all right and I'm all right. You feel sick, did you say? Is it nerves, do you think?' It occurred to me as the words came out of my mouth that it could conceivably be anxiety.

'I was on the loo all night,' you said, your mouth set in misery.

'Do you think you're well enough to go?'

You closed your eyes and shook your head. I felt so very sorry for you. I know I'd had my misgivings, but now that you were sick, I felt awful. But it was more than just sympathy. It was the old, old fear: that you'd never be the same little girl you were before the accident – fearless, tap-dancing on her picnic-tabletop, needing nothing more than the little things to keep her happy: a glass of lemonade in a pub garden, her favourite dinner, a Rice Krispie cake made by her mummy. I had thought after your success in *Little Red* that your nerves would go away or at least become something you could control.

But why would you be able to go back to your old self any more than I could?

We think we've got over things, don't we? We think we've made our peace with trauma, that we're strong again. We keep going, we smile, we manage day to day. Then something comes along, something so very small compared to things we've faced before, something we think we can more than handle, and it floors us once more. And we realise we're not strong after all. The fault lines have not healed over. We're not living, not really. We're still surviving.

You were strong, my love, getting stronger all the time. But in that moment, I knew you were still afraid. The fearful, quiet thing you became in those terrible years after we lost your dad had returned.

No, it had not returned.

It had never gone away.

I left you sleeping and promised to take the afternoon off. I called the school to let them know, then texted Emily:

Hi, Emily. Toni here. Rosie's been very poorly in the night so won't be able to make the audition today. So sorry. T x

A few seconds later, she replied.

Oh heavens, what a shame! Tell her not to worry. Always lots of young girls at these things, they won't even notice. I'll let them know. Tell her to get well soon. Regards, Madame Belle x

You'd woken up. You were calling me. I went in to see you and you said you wanted me to help you into the living room so you could lie on the sofa.

'Of course, darling,' I said. 'Lean on my shoulder and we'll take it slow.'

I helped you into your panda onesie and together we made our way to the living room. You lay on the sofa, and I tucked you under your duvet and left the remote control and a glass of water within reach.

'I don't know how you can wear that onesie,' I joked. 'If I had that on, I'd boil.'

'If you had this on, you'd look insane.' You gave a weak laugh, then smiled.

'Best not to eat anything until this evening, eh?'

You nodded and gave me another wan smile. 'You're the nurse.'

'Listen, I've got to go to work, but I'll be back later. You going to be OK?'

'I'm fine.'

'I'll keep my phone with me, all right?' I kissed you on the cheek and made a dash for it.

I was fifteen minutes late to work – not too bad considering.

'Afternoon, Mrs Flint,' said Richard as I babbled my apologies. He tapped his watch and winked. 'Don't you worry, babe. I covered for you.'

'Sorry, Richard.

'I gave him the usual kiss on both cheeks. 'Rosie was sick in the night. I've had to leave her on the sofa.'

He pursed his lips with concern. 'Babe! Do you need to go home?'

'I'll probably go after lunch if you think you can manage without me.'

'Of course. If anyone comes, I'll tell them you've gone to the loo. Don't let those bastards take any more off our shitty pay, eh?'

You've never met Richard, have you? I bet you feel like you know him though, with all I've told you about him. Oh, the laughs we've shared in that place. Richard is a real tonic. I would never have thought working in hospital records could be so much fun. A lot of it is gallows humour obviously. We see a lot of sadness. It was the same when I was a nurse. You have to cope with it somehow, and humour is as good a mechanism as any. We like to diagnose too, Richard and I. We love to see if we were right.

The morning you were off sick, I remember Richard calling me over to look at something on his computer screen.

'Look at that,' he said. 'Bet you that's a cyst.'

'I think you're right. It's huge, isn't it? Must be the size of a football.'

He pressed the ends of his fingers to his chest and looked at me over the top of his glasses. 'I wouldn't know, babe. Football's not really my thing.'

'Do you think she'll be in the waiting room later?'

'She might be. But that thing's going to need its own gurney.'

We giggled. Which we should not have done, but that made it funnier obviously.

Later, on the pretext of needing the loo, I did actually pootle up to the waiting room to see if I could spot someone who looked like they'd swallowed a Space Hopper, but I couldn't, obviously, and a little after lunchtime, I drove home.

You were up and about but still in your onesie and still very pale. I poured you a can of Sprite and stirred it to get the gas out. You sipped that and ate some salt and vinegar crisps, and together we watched a film on Netflix, snuggled under the duvet on the sofa. And like mothers everywhere whose children are safe at home, I can honestly say that in that moment, I felt a deep peace I had not known for a long time.

CHAPTER 23

ROSIE

Ollie has sent me a friend request on Facebook. When is this? This is last year… is it? I think it is, but I can't remember how long after we start commenting on Instagram this happens. Anyway, I'm like, *OMG, I can't believe it.* His Instagram name is @makeurOllie, but his Facebook name is just his normal name: Ollie Thomas, like two first names together. I press accept and scream into my pillow so you won't hear. That's it. We are now Facebook friends as well as Instagram buddies. Later, when I'm cleaning my teeth, he DMs me. The phone is propped up on the sink; I nearly knock it off, LOL!

Gr8 to c u over here on FB. Do you have Snapchat yet?

I spit the toothpaste foam and rinse my mouth. I go out into the hall to check on you. You're on the sofa lying down. There's half a bottle of red wine on the coffee table and you're watching *House of Cards* on Netflix. Your eyes are closing; you won't be getting up any time soon. You always say I have to leave my phone in the kitchen overnight, but you're always so knackered you forget. I kiss you on the top of your head.

Night, Mum.

Night, love. Sleep tight. Love you.

Love you more.

Wrong. Love you *more.*

I run back into my room and jump into bed. My phone lights up the space under the covers like a magic underwater cave or something – you know, like when a diver shines a torch into it? I can see my bare legs, my toes. I swipe the screen and read Ollie's message again

Gr8 to c u...

My stomach is full of butterflies, like before an exam. We've only liked and commented over on Instagram but that was in front of everyone. It was public. This is more. This is private. This is just us. I want to tell him everything! I want to tell him my fears because I have this deep, deep feeling he'll understand. I want to tell him I've never had a boyfriend before. I want to tell him I've never even kissed a boy apart from Paul Briggs, but that was in Year 3. He won't laugh. He won't take the piss out of me, I just know he won't, because he's cool but, like, kind cool not cruel cool. He's the cool where you're nice to people even if they're not hot or trendy or whatever. Anyway, you don't know about Instagram, and let's not even go there with Snapchat. You won't let me have it, obvs, and I can't get it in secret without you finding out. It's not as easy to hide as Instagram, but I can't tell him I have to keep things secret from my mum because it's so lame. My friends all have Snapchat, obvs. They've all had a boyfriend or at least kissed someone, like, say, at a party or something. Two girls in my year, OK, they're not my friends but I know them, they've gone all the way. Loads of girls have done other stuff, like blow jobs. This one girl, Louisa Simms, she gave Josh McCann one behind Sally Franklin's cabin when she had a party… that I wasn't allowed to go to, obvs.

I just want to kiss someone to see what it's like.

I want to kiss Ollie.

Gr8 to c u...

I reply: *Cool. No Snapchat cos CBA. Also, my mum's a FB friend so...* I add a gritted-teeth emoji.

CBA… can't be arsed. Do you know that one? We shorten it to ceebs when we talk. That's my favourite abbreviation. Ollie replies on FB literally seconds later.

DW… I've come off Snapchat anyway. Too busy. Better 2 PM you on Insta instead if u worried about ur mum? He's put a gritted-teeth emoji and a monkey-covering-eyes emoji – hilarious!

DW. Don't worry. Phew.

I reply: *Cool. Thumbs-up emoji. Monkey-covering-eyes emoji.*

Oh my God, this is basically a conversation!

Over on Instagram we have a full-on private-message conversation. Our messages are just banter, chit-chatting about what we've seen on Netflix, about college, drama stuff, whatever, but they're ours, just his and mine, and I'm proper gassed. I flick over to his Facebook while I'm PMing him and scroll through. There are the same pictures on his Facebook as on his Insta: him on holiday in Spain; one where he's put: *In Mauritius.* The sea is green, he has these sky-blue shorts on and his hair is wet and pushed back, and oh my God, the abs! Like a chest of drawers or a tortoise's shell. Literally. He is ripped. There are two pictures I haven't seen where he's cropped off his head, but it looks arty, and he's holding a bottle of San Miguel, which looks cool. He is so tanned in a way I could never be because you make me wear, like, factor three thousand million when it's not even that hot, and a hat and a shirt when it's boiling – so embarrassing.

I take a screenshot from his Instagram. When we finish messaging, I look at it for a bit there in my duvet cave of light. I look at his tanned skin. How would it feel to put my hand on his stomach, or have his hand on mine?

Rosie?

Shit, you're right outside my door.

Rosie, baby, have you got a light on?

Oh yeah, soz, was just reading something.

Lights off now, OK? School in the morning, baby girl.

OK. Night.

Night.

I delete his picture. Delete it from my deleted album.

GTG, I message him. That means got to go BTW.

Sweet dreams.

I turn off my phone, listen for you out in the hallway. I hear you cleaning your teeth, switch the phone back on and check I defo deleted the picture. I did, phew. But I didn't delete it from my head.

CHAPTER 24

BRIDGET

Bridget touches the teaspoon to the red sauce, blows on it to cool it a little before putting it to her tongue. Bloody hell, that is good, though she says so herself. The trouble is the old bittersweet Proustian thing. Puttanesca sauce always takes her to Sicily, to that place she and Helen found in San Vito Lo Capo. Hardly a discovery though, was it, right on the seafront, overlooking the vast white sands, sands pinked by that astonishing mass of coral running across where the sea reached onto the beach. Their second night in the town. After that, they ate at that restaurant every night for two weeks.

'Bridge, you have to learn how they do this.' Helen, enraptured as ever by good food, a little tanned, a little flushed and bright-eyed too from a crisp bottle of Bianco d'Alcamo.

In execrable Italian, heavy on the hand gestures, Bridget had asked the waiter for the recipe. But Sicilians being as they are, she ended up being invited into the restaurant kitchen the following afternoon, where she was introduced to the chef, Gianluca, who promptly gave her a starched white apron and stood at her shoulder while he supervised her first foray into Italian cuisine.

'*Si, ecco. Poi, metti gli alici. Brava.*'

She stirs the thickening tomato sauce. She knows how to make this for no better reason than wanting to make it for Helen. She knows how to cook because of wanting to cook for Helen. For no better reason, then, than love.

Does Helen return to Sicily sometimes, Bridget wonders, to that restaurant on the seafront? Has she been there with anyone else? Bridget takes another mouthful and closes her eyes, searches for the moment one more time. The rush of traffic outside momentarily transforms into the crash of the waves... No. No it doesn't. Fuck. She opens her eyes. Get a grip, woman. It doesn't work like that. You can't force memory; you can't make it happen. It has to take you by surprise.

The kitchen door flies open, clatters against the side of the fridge.

'Mum! I've got another audition!'

Rosie. This flat, this life. This is Bridget's life now.

'Oh soz, Auntie Bridge. Thought you were Mum.' She sits quickly, the way young people sit, digs in her bomber-jacket pocket and throws her phone on the table. 'Oh my God, guess what?'

'Erm, you've got another audition?'

'LOL! Yeah.'

'Brilliant. You'll be buying us a mock-Tudor mansion next. And just so you know, if you're choosing a motorbike, I'd like the Ducati Monster.'

'It's only an ad.'

'All good experience though. Pass me a beer, will you?'

Rosie jumps up – young people jump everywhere – grabs a bottle from the fridge, opens it and passes it over. 'I'm so stoked.' She is grinning. She is grinning her head off.

'Sure you're on top of your mocks?'

An eye roll. 'You sound like Mum.'

'Haven't you got your French oral tomorrow?'

'*Oui.*'

'Smart-arse. Make yourself useful and set *la table.*'

Rosie lays out the cutlery and the plates, chatters away. Emily is coming over the following night to discuss the casting apparently. It's all arranged.

Bridget wonders what Toni will say. She seems to be taking it well so far. Maybe she's beginning to come to terms with the fact that sometimes there are things that Rosie has to do by herself.

And that has to be a good thing, doesn't it? Moving forward, moving on?

CHAPTER 25

TONI

I'd just finished assembling dinner when the buzzer went. You were in your room. I couldn't hear any music and you didn't dash out, so I assumed you were busy studying. It was about six o'clock, and Emily wasn't due until seven, so when I went to the door I was expecting one of those guys who sell the terrible cleaning products for extortionate amounts. You always laugh at me when I come back to the kitchen with some lurid neon cloth or a packet of anti-static wipes for the computer screen, or some other piece of crap that has cost me the best part of a tenner.

'You may as well put those straight in the bin, Mum,' you say, or, 'You know that'll fall apart after you've used it three times, don't you?'

'I know, but he's just trying to get back on his feet, you know?' I'm always a bit teary after I've spoken to these men. It's their furrowed brows. Like someone's etched their lives there with a chisel.

You roll your eyes at me and say something like: 'He should sell better stuff then, shouldn't he?'

Typical teenager, you, with your black-and-white opinions, your moral outrage, your judgement. Too young to know that life doesn't always give us clear colours like that, that everything and everyone has been chipped at and damaged and complicated beyond imagining. No matter how happy a person's face, you never know what battles they're fighting behind the scenes... I'm sure I've seen that on your Facebook somewhere, one of your bumper-sticker philosophies. But I suppose I should have been pleased you were just a normal teenager, as black-and-white and morally outraged as all the rest.

You won't be like that any more, will you, baby girl? You've experienced first-hand how life can unravel, haven't you, my love? How it can change us, irreversibly, forever.

Anyway, it wasn't one of those men at the door – it was Emily. I couldn't help but smile when I saw her. She was so *herself*, if you know what I mean. She was wearing walking shoes, jeans that came up over her belly like Humpty Dumpty's trousers and, even though it was warm out, a woollen sweater with a Fair Isle design running across the breast and shoulders, and over that, a navy-blue raincoat. She blinked at me through those lenses that make her eyes look as big as a bush baby's.

'Toni!' she said. 'How the devil are you?'

As she stepped into the hall, I was already fighting the urge to giggle. 'I'm well, Emily, thank you.'

'I'm sorry I'm so early. I was banking on traffic on the A316, but it was completely clear.' She raised her eyebrows at me. 'Obviously, if I'd been running late, there would have been a traffic jam from here to Timbuktu, but... anyway, I just thought... I can go away and come back if you'd prefer?' She gestured towards the street. 'I've parked out at the front there, but I won't get a fine, will I? Not at this time? I can easily go to a café and wait, Antonia, it's no trouble.'

So funny. So herself. Although not quite. I remember thinking that she was less sure, somehow, although I couldn't put my finger on why I would think that. She had the big voice, yet she was small; she was full of bravado, yet full of doubt.

'Don't be daft, Emily,' I said. 'And call me Toni, please. Everyone else does. Rosie's here. She'll be delighted to see you.'

I shouted down the hall to you. No answer. I knocked on your door and opened it a crack.

You weren't at your desk at all; you were on your bed, staring at your phone. I know now why that was, of course.

As soon as you saw me, you pulled the headphones out of your ears and pushed the phone against your chest. 'What?'

'Have you been listening to music when you should be working?' I said.

You rolled your eyes and shrugged at Emily over my shoulder as if to say: *See what I have to put up with*? 'Music helps me concentrate.'

'Concentrate on what?' I asked. 'YouTube? Facebook?'

'No-o.' Ah, the two-syllable *no*, beloved of all parents of teenagers. 'I had to research something for history. I was doing *that*.'

'Come on through to the kitchen, Emily,' I said, just to get away from you and your lip-curling, your dripping disdain, your constantly rotating eyeballs.

'Mu-um.' The two-syllable *mum*, up there with the two-syllable *no* in the irritation top ten. 'Emily and me can talk in my room.' You met me with your clear, intransigent eyes, but I was having none of it. I know our flat isn't large, but to chat to a fully grown woman in your bedroom? I'm sorry, but that's just inappropriate.

'Don't be silly,' I said.

'But it's my room,' you said. 'It's my only space.'

'Oh, I'm sure the kitchen will be fine,' said Emily. Her usual bluster had vanished. She was bouncing the tips of her fingers together and looking from left to right as if to try and figure out where to put herself. I suspected she was embarrassed, and quite right. No one wants to get caught up in other people's bickering, do they? I know every daytime show has people airing their grievances for all the world to see, but I'm still very much of the old school. The way I was brought up, what happens in the family stays in the family.

We had just sat down in the kitchen when I heard the front door open and close. Your auntie Bridge. She had no acting work that week, so she'd picked up a couple of shifts in the Italian café as well as her website jobs.

'Hey up, Squirt,' she said, ruffling your hair as she came into the kitchen.

'You remember Emily, Bridge?' I said.

'Agent to the stars,' your auntie Bridget said. 'What's she got, the lead in the new Scorsese?'

Emily chuckled. 'Almost.'

'I'm starving,' Bridget continued, wandering over to the stove and peeking into the pan where I'd prepared the broccoli. Before I had a chance to speak, she dropped the lid back onto the pan and said, 'Emily, are you staying for dinner? Not sure what it is, but it smells good.'

Emily looked from Bridget to me to you. And back to Bridget. 'I…' she began. 'I'm sorry, forgive me, but do you live here too?'

'I do, yes.' Bridget smiled. 'Unless Toni's moved my stuff out again. She's always doing that, but I just move it back in.'

I laughed. She's such a nut, isn't she, your auntie?

'Well I never,' Emily said, eyebrows almost hitting her hairline. 'I didn't realise that. How funny, I mean. I met you at the theatre, of course, and Rosie's shown me pictures of you and her at your concerts. The Promise, isn't it, your group? Concerts? Or do you call them gigs? It's gigs, isn't it, for pop?'

'Rock,' Bridget said, but she was smiling, as amused as we always were by Emily's way of putting things. 'You should come along sometime.'

'I'm sure Emily has better things to do than hang out here with us,' I said. 'Don't you, Emily?'

'No, stay,' you said. 'Mum always makes enough for about ten people anyway.'

Honestly, you and your auntie do gang up on me sometimes. I was hoping to save half for the next night so I didn't have to cook again. As for poor Emily, her eyes were as round as a rabbit's. And the headlights were flashing off her spectacles.

'I…'

'Emily, don't let these two bully you,' I said. 'But if you'd like to stay for dinner, you're very welcome. It's nothing fancy – just cottage pie.'

She stayed, as you know, and I realised immediately that we'd done the right thing, asking her to eat with us like that. That's typical of your auntie Bridge, isn't it? Whatever the circumstances, she always does the most open, the most generous thing. It never occurred to me to ask Emily to stay, just as it had never occurred to me to think about what her home life might be like, whether she was married, or had kids. Whether she had ever wanted those things. But I thought about it then, and when I asked her about it over dinner, she said that no, she wasn't married, and no, she didn't have children.

'But I'm a busy bee,' she added with hasty joviality, and I had an inkling that, despite all her bluster, she might be a little lonely.

'Good to stay busy,' I said. 'Stops you from thinking too much. It does me anyway.'

You glared at me, but I didn't think I'd said anything wrong.

'Oh, I'm like the proverbial whirling dervish,' Emily went on, 'zipping round all the youth theatres in the borough and beyond. And I have a keen interest in film, too, so if I'm not watching a play locally, you'll find me in the cinema with my popcorn.'

That chuckle. You take her off so well, Rosie love. You make me laugh. I love it when you make me laugh.

'Whereabouts are you based, Emily?' I asked.

'Richmond way,' she said, placing her hand to her chest. 'With my brother, for my sins.'

For my sins. Hadn't heard that phrase in years.

'Little two-bed terrace,' she went on. 'Nothing fancy. Keep the old overheads low.'

While we chatted, you set the table and Bridget pulled a bottle of lager from the fridge for herself and poured a glass of Cab Sauv for me.

'Heavens, no,' Emily said when Bridge offered her a glass. 'One sniff of that and I'll drive the car straight into the hedge! But thank you.'

As we ate, we exchanged stories, got to know each other on a personal level. Bonding, you'd call it. Emily didn't ask about your dad or the accident and I wondered if you'd already told her, if you even bothered telling anyone about it any more. I guess I'm used to people avoiding the subject, and as for you, you've spent most of your life without your dad, so for you the way we live is normal.

Anyway, Emily told all those funny stories about her days on *The Bill*, do you remember? The pranks they pulled! I couldn't believe my ears.

'Ah yes, I remember one day we…' Emily could hardly get it out for chuckling. 'We stretched cling film over the loo seat, under the seat, I should say, on the porcelain bowl itself. We stretched and stretched it tight, tight, tight, so you couldn't see it. We were laughing so much we were crying. And then we put the seat down and you couldn't tell there was anything there.' She gave a hoot, pushed up her glasses and wiped her eyes with a piece of kitchen roll. 'Anyway, so me and my friend, we waited, her in the other cubicle, me at the sinks, pretending to, I don't know what, fix my hair or my lipstick or something.'

'And then?' You were perched on the edge of your seat, desperate to know.

'And then the superintendent, as it were, came in. I said hello, but casual, nothing-naughty-happening-here sort of thing, and she went into the cubicle. Next thing, we hear this shriek! Poor woman had peed all over her knickers, her tights, her you name it—' She broke off, helpless.

Well, that really tickled you, didn't it, Rosie? Your forehead was on the table; your shoulders were shaking. I hadn't seen you laugh so much in a long while. And when she told us the one about smearing strawberry jam on the actual loo seat and that famous actor – what was her name? Oh, it's gone. Anyway, she sat on the jam, and your face when Emily told us that was an absolute picture.

'Sticky Bum we called her after that,' she added, just as you hit your peak of hilarity, pushing up her glasses and wiping her eyes again. Honestly, I thought you were going to spit your cottage pie across the table. 'Sticky Bum!'

We laughed so much that evening. The surprise of it was moving for reasons I can't really explain. I guess, when I remember times with your dad, I remember having people over for dinner, meeting up with friends in the pub. I remember laughing a lot more. Emily is one of those people who's funny by accident, isn't she? Except I suspect she knows exactly what she's doing. Disingenuous, I'd say, but in a lovely way. She kind of bumbles through what she's saying, but actually, her comic timing is perfect. And when she showed us that picture of herself when she was twenty, well.

'Emily,' I said. 'You were absolutely stunning.' Her face was smooth, her long blonde hair fell straight over her shoulders and she didn't have her glasses on. Really, she was quite beautiful.

'Ah yes,' she said, a little sadly. 'I was never tall, but I did have a nice face. You'd never think it to look at me now, would you?'

'Oh no, that's not what I meant. I just meant…'

She patted my hand. 'It's quite all right. I know what you meant. I'm a great deal older now, and after the fall, I put on weight and never lost it. Plus the old limp isn't exactly desirable, is it? So the television parts dried up, and I found I wasn't as physically strong as I had been.' She smiled and looked at you.

None of us asked her about her fall, perhaps for the same reason she didn't ask about our set-up: out of politeness.

'You'd be surprised how physically demanding theatre is,' she said after a moment. 'That's why I was pleased that you do your karate and what not.'

'Taekwondo,' said Bridget, who, I realised, had barely spoken. But then, knowing her, she probably wanted to stay in the background and let you and Emily get to know each other.

'Bridget's a black belt second dan,' I said. I suppose I was keen to lighten the mood. I didn't want to go from her misfortunes to ours and end up with us all crying over our cottage pie.

Emily's eyebrows shot up. 'Black belt, eh? Do you teach it?'

Bridget shook her head and stood, her face deadpan.

'Too dangerous,' she said. 'For the others, I mean. I'm a deadly weapon, Emily.'

You and I started laughing, and seeing us, Emily caught on and laughed too.

'I'll clear these plates,' your auntie said, grinning. 'Would you like some coffee, Emily?'

After you'd helped your auntie Bridge clear away the plates and make coffee, Emily got down to business and told us about your audition.

'Now, this one is in Islington,' she said. 'I'll send details. It's at a casting agency, so it's all above board. You'll see when you get there. Quite an elegant suite of offices, I would say. There's a main reception where you give your name and they'll buzz you up. The offices are on the third floor, and the lady you're seeing is called Kate Paxton.'

'When is it?' you asked.

'This Friday at 5 p.m.' Emily checked her watch. 'What are we now, Wednesday? I suppose that's tight for you, Toni, with your work, but I can take Rosie if you'd like. I don't have any appointments that day, so it's not a bother.'

'Thanks,' I said. 'I'm sure we'll manage.'

'Well let me know if you change your mind. I'll send the script through with the details. It's all pretty straightforward. You speak into the camera and the casting agent will read the other part. Toni, perhaps you can rehearse it with her?'

'Sure,' I said. 'Happy to.'

I was thinking your auntie Bridge could take you, but once Emily had gone, she said she had a client that Friday and couldn't turn down the cash. As Emily had said, there was no way I could get you there for five, and after all the time off I've had, I couldn't really ask for more. There was no way I would have let you go all that way by yourself, so there was no choice.

We would have to rely on Emily after all.

CHAPTER 26

ROSIE

I'm in my bedroom. I'm under my covers, in my cave of light. I know when this is! I can tell by the feeling in my tummy that it's December. Not the Christmas feeling; I'm tingling because I've just got the main part in Little Red and I know *that* because I'm texting Ollie to tell him. I'm so stoked. I haven't told anyone else about it yet except you. And Auntie Bridge, obvs. Not even Naomi.

So. *Me and Ollie, sittin' in a tree, t-e-x-t-i-n-g. ROFL!*

Texting! Not even on social media, literally just directly on our private numbers. Afterwards, I always delete, even if it's not phone-check night.

That's amazing, he's written. *Congratulations.* He has added a party-popper emoji.

My stomach flips. *Thanks. Where do you live BTW? House emoji. London.*

Duh. I want him to know I'm joking so I put a crying-with-laughter-face emoji.

Near Kingston. He's put a winking face with a tongue!

Cool. He lives near Kingston! That makes sense, if we have loads of mutuals. I want to ask where exactly, but I don't want to be weird and stalkerish. I want to ask if he has a girlfriend, but hello? Psycho alert. Another message:

Guessing you live near Richmond if you're in the Cherry Orchard. This time he's really gone for it on the emojis – there are two cherries and two theatre masks.

Twickenham. Near the rugby ground. I find a rugby-ball emoji! I had no clue that was there, literally.

Do you play rugby? Rugby-ball emoji.

No. LOL. Three crying-with-laughter faces.

You don't look like a rugby player. Winking face.

Don't I? Shit! No emoji fits. I just press send.

No way. You're too pretty. Smiley blushing face.

I feel myself go bright red even though there is no one in my room and no one can see me. I'm so gassed that he said I'm pretty, even though that's, like, anti-feminist and wrong and I know it's not about looks, it's about what a person is like underneath. He sends another text without me even replying!

You're supposed to say I look nice too. Winking-with-tongue-out face.

Oh no. How embarrassing.

Soz. You do. I like your hair. (And your eyes and your chest, I so don't say, LOL.)

I like your eyes. Are they green or blue??? Mad-eyes emoji.

Blue. Bright-red-face emoji.

Have you gone red for real? Send me a picture. Grinning face.

My heart feels like it's beating in my throat. I push the phone to my chest and take two deep breaths. Auntie Bridge always says that's the best way to cope with stress, because it gives you oxygen and oxygen makes you feel energised, so I always do that and my *do re mi fa so la ti do*, except I'm in that moment again now, here in my soup, and I'm looking at myself as if from the outside, except with the feeling from the inside, and I'm not stressed. Stressed is not what I am. Not exactly.

Send me a picture…

I push back the covers and sit up. I still have the phone against my chest. This is mad. It isn't like he can see me through the phone or anything, but I'm literally hiding myself all the same. I run to the bathroom and splash my face with cold water. My eyelashes go darker and clump together a bit. They look longer, as if I have, like, mascara on or something. That makes my eyes look bigger, so I dry my face without drying my eyelashes and lean into the mirror and say *what big eyes you have* and laugh. I am still laughing as I leave the bathroom. That's when you shout through – our flat is so small we hear everything.

You OK, love?

Ye-es. Just needed the loo.

OK. Night then, baby.

I jump back into the bathroom. Make the landing silent by bending my knees loads. I flush the chain and call out:

Night, Mummy. Love you.

Back in my room, I put on some of that strawberry lip salve you got me for Christmas and scratch my lips with my teeth to make them look bigger and redder. I smile and take a selfie. It's horrible, so I take another. I look gross. My nose looks big and white and… urgh – blackhead alert. I feel so ridiculous. How do my friends even do those selfies? The ones that if I did, you would kill me. How do they know how to do that face… like they've been caught by surprise in their underwear or they've been embarrassed but they're actually pretty confident all at the same time? And most of them have loads of make-up on even though they're just chilling at home, even when they're in their PJs and sometimes their pants. Do they, like, sleep in their make-up or do they put it on just to take the picture? Do they spend hours alone at home doing make-up just to take one selfie? I would ask but Naomi doesn't do those pictures either – she's like, *no way* – and I'm too embarrassed to ask the ones who do. I can't do a pretty filter or puppy ears or anything because I haven't got Snapchat either, or an iPhone6.

I can't change my face so it looks right.

I try taking another picture. It's still crap, but I'm so stressed now I actually have gone a bit red for real. I PM the picture to Ollie and dive back into bed. I pull the covers over my head and do a little scream into the pillow and then I stare into the phone.

Nothing.

The screen fades.

I tap it back into life.

It fades again.

I tap back, scroll through Instagram, but there's no new posts. Then the message icon goes red. OMG. It's Ollie.

Beautiful. Blowing-kiss emoji.

Beautiful.

CHAPTER 27

TONI

Emily sent you the script for the audition. It was an advert for toothpaste; I forget now which one. I thought you had a really great chance of getting it because you do have lovely teeth. They are like mine, actually, well, like mine were before they got smashed out of my— sorry… before I lost them in the accident, I should say. The top front row of my teeth are all false, as you know, or maybe you've forgotten. I never take them out. It's too upsetting seeing my mouth collapse inwards like a crone's, not to mention the thought of you or your auntie Bridge having to see them in a glass on the bathroom shelf.

No. I'm too young for that.

Anyway, you came into my bedroom and sat on the bed to chat to me while I was putting away some clothes. Once I'd finished, you asked me to test you on your lines and handed me the script.

Nothing in life is perfect…

That was the first line, I think. On it went, the usual nonsense.

So I can't buy designer clothes? So what? I'm happiest in my comfy old jeans. So I can't afford cosmetics like the fashion magazines? So what? I prefer the natural look…

That kind of thing. Bullshit, basically, sorry to swear.

And then you had to flash your pearly whites and say:

But if there's one thing I never compromise on, it's my smile...

We laughed about how cheesy that was, didn't we? Once you'd got it off pat, you sent it right up, doing an American accent and swishing your hair like the L'Oreal ad. I love it when we laugh together like that. We have the same sense of humour, you and me. And in that moment, I loved the fact that, even though your auntie Bridge was the actor, you'd come to me for help.

You'd come to me.

I began to get concerned when late on Thursday night, you complained of stomach pains.

We were sitting in the living room watching a movie on Netflix together when it started. Your auntie Bridge had a gig at the Fox in Twickenham. I was supposed to be going with her, but I wanted to stay with you the night before your big day. I'd treated us to a microwave dinner for two and we'd eaten it on trays on our knees.

'It's probably nerves,' I said. 'You got sick last time, so you maybe have association on top of everything.'

'What?'

'Last time you had an audition, you were too sick to go, weren't you? You've got an audition tomorrow, so I'm just saying maybe your subconscious is worrying you'll be sick again and is making you have those symptoms. They're not real.'

'But I feel really sick,' you said, 'like I'm going to throw up. It's that microwave meal. I shouldn't have had Indian food. My stomach's all swollen, look. It's rock hard.'

'It won't be the dinner. It's too soon for it to be that, and besides, I had the same thing and I'm fine.'

'I can feel it, Mummy. My stomach's like a stone.'

'When did you last go to the loo?'

You bit your lip in thought. 'Wednesday? No, Tuesday. Maybe Monday?'

'And it's Thursday night. There you go, you see, you're probably constipated. Classic stress. You could try a laxative, I suppose, but it might send you the other way.'

'No, it's OK.' You stood up but immediately doubled over.

'Rosie, honey.'

'I'm OK.' You grimaced. 'It's cramping. It really hurts, Mum.' You met my eye. 'What if it's not better tomorrow? What if *I'm* not better? I keep doing do re mi fa so la ti do, but it's not working, it's not working, Mum.'

'Oh, come on, baby girl. Think of all the hurdles you've jumped over. You can't let a silly audition affect you like this. You were Little Red, for goodness' sake, star of the show!'

I know. I know that was the wrong thing to say. I should have said that it didn't matter, that none of it mattered. But I said what I said in the moment, what I thought was best, and I see now that I got that wrong. But it's so hard to get it right all the time, and I'm not perfect, love. I'm just a mum. Any parent will tell you how difficult it is when their child is standing in front of them looking for answers and they're thinking, *But I don't know the answers.* No guidebook can ever prepare you for the million different ways in which a child can test you. You were staring at me with your big bewildered eyes, my darling, and you looked so afraid. I wanted to take that fear away, of course I did. I wanted to make it right.

'What if it's not better?' you were asking me.

I didn't know. I wanted to tell you to stop fussing, to ignore it, but I also really wanted to say, *Don't worry about it, you can stay in bed. I will look after you.* In other words, half of me wanted you to go, half of me wanted you to stay. I guess that's every parent in the world for you.

'It doesn't matter.' I did say that in the end. 'There'll be other auditions. You go on into your room and get into bed. I'll bring you a hot-water bottle.'

You slumped away. I made a hot-water bottle and wrapped it in your white towel with the little piggies on it that you've had since you were a baby. It used to cover your whole body, that towel, when you were tiny and chubby and warm in my arms. Your daddy used to blow raspberries on your belly, used to hold you up high, his arms strong and straight: *Whee! Look at her fly!*

Ah, happy times...

Anyway, I sat by your bed and I massaged your tummy. It *was* as hard as a rock, up as far as your ribcage. I suspected your bowel was impacted, but rubbing it seemed to ease the pain. 'If you're no better in the morning,' I said, 'I'll call Emily. There's nothing at all to worry about. I'll take care of it.'

'Oh, Mummy,' you said.

'It's OK, my darling. It's all right. It's all going to be all right.'

I sang to you then, do you remember? I sang some Adele, some Birdy, and that old spiritual your dad used to sing to us both.

Nobody knows the trouble I've seen, oh yes, Lord...

I can't sing like he could, but I can hold a tune. It was enough. You closed your eyes; your breathing slowed. I left the hot-water bottle on your belly. I pulled your hand to my lips and kissed it and tucked it away under the covers. As I left the room, I heard you whisper, 'Night, Mum.'

'Night, baby girl,' I said. 'Sleep now.'

In the kitchen, I poured myself a large glass of red wine. It was about 10 p.m. Bridget wouldn't be back until midnight earliest, probably nearer 1 a.m. I wished she was there so I could talk to her. I thought of your dad and how calm he would have been and how I could have talked to him. How he would have known what to say.

'If she's sick, she's sick, Bun,' he would have said. Something like that. 'Feeling worried won't help. Feeling worried never helped anyone.'

Even thinking about what he might have said eased my anxiety, even though the soft sound of his voice remembered was wrapped up as all my memories of him are in the pain of missing him. He was… effortless. I don't know any better way to put it. He had it no easier than anyone else, had his baggage just like the rest of us, but he bore it, bore everything, with lightness, with humour, with a kind of grace. I make it sound like we never fought, but honestly, we hardly did. Even when we did argue it was always me that caused it. Sometimes I'd pick a fight just to have one.

'Bun,' he would say in those moments. 'Come on, Bunny, don't be crazy.' He would stroke my hair.

Once I hit him. Well I hit his hand. 'Get off me,' I said, and at the sight of his face, I burned with shame. He looked hurt, yes, but worse, he looked confused, as if he had no idea why I'd done that or who I was or what it meant. Oh God, even the memory of that hurts. I burst into tears and threw out my arms to him.

'I'm sorry.'

'It's OK, Bunny,' he said, holding me.

'I don't know why I did that,' I sobbed. 'I can't believe I did it. You'll leave me. You should.'

'Don't be an eejit. If I didn't have you to keep me on my toes, I'd relax so much I'd drop dead, so I would.'

I laughed. 'You're the eejit for loving me.'

'You have a point there.' He kissed my head. 'We don't have to know why we do what we do. It's OK not to know why.'

Just the thought of him: that tuft of hair at the back of his head that never lay flat; his scruffy T-shirts and jeans; the terrible trainers that I threw in the bin when I'd bought him some new ones; the way he looked at me with a mixture of amusement and disbelief when I was being nuts, with mischief when he'd bought tickets for something or wanted to take me to bed… oh, and the way he danced. Like a flickering flame, he was, a beautiful flickering flame.

My throat stung. I swallowed some more wine. I wondered if your auntie Bridge had left any tobacco in the house. Ah yes, baby girl, it's all coming out now.

'Oh, Stan,' I said to no one, imagining him right there at the kitchen table, bottle of beer lolling lazy in his hand.

Your phone was on charge next to the toaster.

'Should I check it, Stan? Should I?'

'I don't know, Bun. Your call. I love you.'

'I love you more.'

'Wrong. I love you more.'

'Should I check…'

He disappeared. From outside somewhere came the violent screech of mating foxes.

I told myself I was worried you were suffering from nerves and that I should scroll through your social media to make sure you weren't being cyber-bullied. I told myself that I wouldn't be a good mother if I didn't check. Thinking back, I reckon I checked it for no more reason than to keep you near, to have someone with me there in the howling emptiness.

Photos: you'd taken a screenshot of the street map where the audition was in case you couldn't get 3G, and I'd given you the A–Z too, which you'd already packed in your rucksack. You were looking forward to being Emily's co-pilot.

I went through your other photos. There was nothing untoward, and even though I hadn't expected to find anything alarming, I felt my breathing settle. I checked the deleted album, but there was nothing in there either, just couple of snaps I remembered you taking: the strawberry sundae you made at the weekend, the Rice Krispie cakes I made the other night. You built a tower with them and sprinkled them with that new food glitter we bought. A picture of your new Converse boots.

There was nothing worrying on your Facebook page either, or in your messages, so I didn't need to worry about anything there. I trawled through some of your friends – 273: how can you possibly know all these people? You tell me that's not even a lot. I have to say, Rosie, some of your girlfriends post some seriously worrying pictures. Another thing we've fought about.

'Look at that girl,' I remember saying once when we were going through your Facebook page together. She had her arms crossed, knowingly, to give herself a cleavage, and she was pouting like an advert for a sexy phone line. Underneath she had written: *Cheeky little selfie, how do I look?* There was another one of her in her underwear. She had taken the photo in the mirror; there was a star where the flash had bounced on the glass.

'Look at this one!' I said. 'She looks about twenty-five!' She did, love. She looked as wise, as knowing and as cynical as a fresh divorcee. At fifteen!

'Oh, Mum you're so stuck in the Ice Age,' you said. 'They're celebrating their bodies and that's their right. You're just body shaming.'

'But – but…' I stuttered. Body shaming? I had no idea what you meant. 'They're not celebrating anything, baby girl, they're asking for approval. These are advertising posters, they're shop windows displaying their wares, like, well, like prostitutes, frankly, like you see in the knocking-shop fronts in Amsterdam. Honestly, Rosie, some of them may as well put a price tag on and have done with it. I might be stuck in the Ice Age, my love, but at least we didn't confuse being attractive with being a commodity.'

'It's not like that any more.' Your voice was thick with exasperation. 'Women should be allowed to do what they want with their bodies. They're proud of them. They see it as, like, a powerful feminist statement.'

'Powerful, my backside.'

'Don't say that! You're putting it all on the girls. We should be allowed to wear what we want and do what we want. It's not our fault if some perv can't control himself, is it?'

'You're all so flaming naïve. You've no idea how dangerous it is to post pictures of yourself like that. You don't know who could be looking at those pictures, and I tell you what, lady, if I catch *you* doing it, you can say goodbye to Face—'

'Oh, don't worry, you won't.' You had raised your voice – you were almost shouting. 'Because I won't be doing anything normal, like, ever, because you just want me to be a weirdo. I'll carry on being the only girl in the entire world who doesn't have Snapchat or Instagram or go to parties or clubs or drink or smoke, and then I'll just go and live in a convent or something or, like, like, like a Buddhist retreat, and I'll never have a boyfriend or do anything normal, ever, in my whole, entire life.'

And with that, of course, you stomped out and slammed the kitchen door, leaving me with nothing to do but sigh and turn to my shaky reflection in the window.

'That went well, Toni,' I said to my own fractured image in the glass. 'Fabulous bit of parenting. Congratu-fucking-lations.'

At least you weren't posting sexy selfies. That's what I told myself, to make myself feel better. But of course, just because I couldn't see any sexy shots on your page didn't mean you weren't taking them, did it?

CHAPTER 28

ROSIE

You're pretty… you have nice eyes… these shop windows… these knocking-shop fronts…

Ó Maidrín rua, rua, rua, rua, rua…

An maidrín rua tá dána.

Silly moo, ignore me… Emily?

Your mum and I have a pact… It means I'll never let her down again… Helen and me, we… Auntie Bridge?… *Sexy shots…* Mum? Mummy?

I'm sorry… I'm sorry… I'm sorry… I'm sor—

Emily… I'm with Emily. We're in Hampton Hill… no we're not; we're in Twickenham, in a café. We're sitting at a table for two. She's bought me a mochachino. It's halfway between hot chocolate and coffee. It's a teenager in a cup, I think: halfway between being a kid and a grown-up. I smile at this idea. It's quite clever, you know, for me.

Your mother's very careful with you, isn't she? Emily's head is on one side, like an animal hearing a sudden noise.

She gets worried, I say. Foam tickles my top lip. I lick it off.

I can see that. But you're a big girl, my dear. You are a young woman, and a very talented, very beautiful one at that.

My face goes hot. *Er, no, I'm not.*

Emily laughs and shakes her head, and she gets this, like, look on her face, sort of smiling and looking at the ceiling and then shaking her head again.

Ah, how youth is wasted on the young, she says. *It is our great shame and tragedy that we don't see how beautiful we are until later, when it's gone, and we look back and wonder why we didn't see, why we didn't know. Why we didn't seize it and use it to conquer the world.* She leans across the table. Her bosom squashes against the tabletop. Her eyes are shiny, as if she's about to cry or something, but she looks pretty stoked too. *I was beautiful once*, she says. *I was lovely, like you.*

Yeah, I saw your photo, I say. She's being weird, but I don't want to be rude. *You're still pretty though, just in a different way.* She's so not, but she seems a bit down about it and I'm trying to be nice.

She smiles again but she looks sad, and she's like, *I was. But I didn't fight my corner. I let things get out of my control. Sometimes you have to fight, Rosie. People try and cage you up, but you can't let them. You can't be a prisoner of other people's madness, do you know what I mean? You have to leave the nest if you wish to fly. You have to get out!*

I think Emily's been smoking weed. Her eyes are a bit red and she sounds proper batshit.

Yes, I say. I don't know what else to say. She's not scaring me, she's just, like, gone a bit weird. The menopause drove Auntie Bridge crazy. Maybe Emily's got that. She is fifty-three.

When is this? When did we go to this café?

Emily melts, her face runs like thick sauce… like thick…

Auntie Bridge… there's noise… new noise… the bubbling sound of people talking… we are in a pub. It's the Cricketers on Richmond Green, I recognise it – hurray! We are outside at the tables at the front. It's still light. There are people on the green, the air is warm and mellow – it has absorbed the sun. The air smells of heat from the pavement, of bodies, and of Auntie Bridge's patchouli. The people on the green drink beer from plastic cups, sit around on picnic rugs with bottles of wine, bags of crisps, ice creams. Two men kick a football and hold their pints at the same time. We are drinking lager too, from glasses, and Auntie Bridge is smoking a roll-up. It smells sweet, and I think she's put some dope in it, but I don't ask her because that's not cool. She has a pint. I have a half because I'm *an underage squirt*. I think this is just after my fifteenth birthday, like a week or something before I went into Year 11. I don't even like lager. I only drink lager with fruits of the forest in it, which Auntie Bridge says is *an abomination*. She has chewing gum for both of us for afterwards, to disguise the smell of alcohol for me and cigarettes for her.

So that you don't find out.

We are waiting for Helen.

Do you think you and Helen will get back together? I ask.

She shrugs and pulls on her fag/joint. *Depends.*

On what?

On Helen. On me. On your mum.

Mum's fine. She's fine now.

But you'll be off to uni in a year or two, won't you, Squirt?

Yes, but that doesn't mean…

I don't know what I was going to say. I don't know if I ever knew.

Neither of us has found anyone else, I suppose, and… Bridget takes a drag of her cigarette, and her eyes narrow like they do when she's going to say something difficult. She's about to say it, but then Helen arrives.

Hello, you two. Pissed again? She kisses Auntie Bridge on the back of her neck, which is weird considering they're supposed to be ex-partners, and nods to me. *I told you to stay away from her, Bridge. That Rosie Flint is a bad influence.*

Helen is smaller than me. Auntie Bridge calls her Titch. Grown-ups have more nicknames than teenagers, I think, or maybe it's just Auntie Bridge. Helen has long brown hair, which she always ties back because she says it's like rats' tails, which it so isn't. She has cool glasses, like 1950s ones, and a wicked sense of humour, which if I tried to do it would just come out wrong or cruel or sarcastic but when she does it, it's funny. She's an actor like Auntie Bridge but she doesn't do any acting any more, she writes screenplays for television. She writes for *EastEnders* and earns a lot of money. She is the love of Auntie Bridge's life, but Auntie Bridge told me that when she'd had *a few too many*, and in the morning she told me never to tell anyone what she'd said.

Not even your mum, OK, Squirt? Especially not your mum.

Grown-ups are weird… grown-ups are…

I'm just home from rehearsal for Little Red. You've made leek and potato soup. It's delicious. You watch me as I eat it, smiling like I'm doing a good thing, but I know you like it when I enjoy eating what you make. You're a good cook, Mummy. Sorry, I don't really say that. No one's cottage pie is as good as yours.

Auntie Bridge makes better chilli con carne though, LOL.

Peng munch, Mum, I say, dipping my toast in.

What? What does that even mean?

Peng munch? It means nice food, duh.

You shake your head, but you're still smiling. *Honestly, you speak a whole other language.*

I say goodnight early. I tell you I'm tired, but I'm so not. In my room, I check my phone. Ollie has messaged! I get into bed with my clothes on and pull the covers over my head. I make my cave of light.

Hey, beautiful.

Beautiful! Like it's my name! I start to reply, but I think, wait, leave it a few minutes. I look on his Facebook page instead. He's posted a cute photo of himself as a little boy. His hair is practically blonde in it, and he looks so cute in dungarees and a little stripy T-shirt. His cheeks are bright red and he has put the caption: *Human cherry.* I like the picture, then back over on Instagram:

Hey, ugly mug. Jokes. Saw your pic on FB. Winking-with-tongue-out-face emoji.

You're in the living room watching the news, but I'm still scared you'll see or hear or… just *know*, by telepathy or something.

OMG, he is typing…

What've you been up to today?

We message for a bit. You knock at my bedroom door and open it.

Rosie? You're not still up, are you?

Shit shit shit. If you pull back my covers you'll see I'm completely dressed.

Just reading.

OK. Lights off now, babe.

OK. Night. I can feel you're still there. I turn off my phone and my secret cave goes dark.

Night, love. Love you.

Love you more.

Wrong. Love you more.

Night.

Night.

I listen, still as a rock, for the shush of the door on my bedroom carpet. I hear the water run in the bathroom and switch on my phone again. Ollie and I message for, like, forty-five minutes. That's a record for us. He's so interested in everything about me, and he knows about acting because he asks if I've read any Ute Hagen and I'm, like, *Oh my God, yes!* We talk about Stanislavski and our favourite actors. His is Jake Gyllenhaal. I think Jake Gyllenhaal is too 'big', but I don't say that. He likes Claire Danes too, and I agree with that. She's not my total fave – that would be Carey Mulligan or Jessica Chastain – but Claire Danes is up there. She is awesome. Messaging him, I feel all warm and relaxed, as if I'm in a hot bath, but at the same time I have butterflies kind of everywhere. It's midnight. You are asleep in bed and I'm still awake, and I know I'm going to be wrecked in the morning, so I make a *mature decision.*

GTG.

What is GTG?

Got to go, silly! Crying-with-laughter face.

OK. Kiss emoji. Crying-face emoji.

I am in love. I am in actual love. But I can't tell you or Auntie Bridge. And I can't tell my friends, not even Naomi – not yet. It's too embarrassing, because if I tell her, she'll ask questions and then she'll find out it's actually nothing because we haven't met or spoken or anything so she'll think that we aren't legit friends. She won't understand the connection. Because that's what this is: a deep love connection.

I clean my teeth and quickly pull off my clothes and put on my nightie. When I get back, I check my phone again, just in case. Red circle! He's sent a picture. OMG! A picture – a private picture just for me. I can't figure out what I'm looking out at first, and then I realise: it's a close-up of a big toe.

His. Big. Toe.

Normally that would creep me out, but that's just Ollie – he's really good-looking but actually he's really interesting and funny when you get to know him. And even his toe is hot. The nail is a soft brown, like that golden caster sugar we get. There's a thin white strip at the top and a creamy white crescent moon at the bottom. I drop the phone. I know boys' toes aren't rude or anything, but my heart pounds and I have to breathe in and out through my mouth. A memory… toes… toes… toes wiggling in the sand. Little toes, and big toes.

Wiggle your toes, Rosie. It's my dad's voice. It's my daddy's toes! I'm giggling. It's my toes! My toes are next to his!

My dad bends all his toes except his big toe, which sticks up from his foot. *Look at my toe, Rosie. Look at it. What does it look like to you?*

A toe, silly. My tiny little voice is so cute. Happiness warms my guts like spices.

No, not a toe. That's no toe, young lady. That, my little fox, is a spaceman.

Silly Daddy!

The memory dissolves. I pick up the phone again and read the caption:

Show me yours?

My heart kind of blows up. I think it will jump into my throat and right out of my mouth. I sit on the edge of the bed and try and figure out which foot is the best. Neither – they're both bluey-white and gross. I run and grab the nail scissors from the bathroom and trim my toenails. I run back into the bathroom and grab your bag of nail varnishes from the cabinet. I tell myself it's OK to take them because I always paint your toenails for you so you kind of owe me. I choose bright red, like Lego bricks. Oh my God, you will so kill me if you see I've painted my toenails. With *your* nail varnish.

I paint my right foot, thinking I can do the other one later, once I've taken the photo. The varnish smudges, so I run my fingernail along the nail's edge to neaten it. There is nail varnish all over my thumb now, bright as fresh blood. It looks like I've cut myself, but it doesn't matter because my toe looks proper dank and that's all that matters. I wish I had a toe ring or something cool like that, but I don't. It's twenty past midnight. I'm gonna be so wrecked. The toe will have to do.

It takes less than a second to take the photo. I play around with the filters, decide on no filter, up the brightness. Attach.

Here is my toe, LOL. Blushing-grinning emoji.

Send.

Waiting for him to reply is torture. I paint the other foot. Hopefully he'll think I have my toes painted all the time, just for,

like, hanging at home. I'll have to hide my feet from you for defs.
After ten minutes – ten years, more like – he replies.

Your toe is very sexy. I'm going to call u Sexy Lady from now on.
Goodnight, Sexy Lady.

Sexy Lady? Me? O to the M to the G.

CHAPTER 29

TONI

The girl in the opposite bed keeps trying to chat, Rosie. She's friendly but with an edge, do you know what I mean? I just get the sense she could flare up at any moment, that she's someone you keep at arm's length. But she's had no visitors this evening, poor thing. I wish someone would come for her. Where is her mum? Her dad? She is terribly thin, and she has bandages on her arms. I didn't ask what she was in for. I can guess, obviously, but I don't want to know.

Not for me to make diagnoses anyway, is it? The doctor diagnosed you. You were intubated, and they gave you flumazenil. I would have done the same. I could have told him what to do, but I didn't. It's not my place to diagnose or to prescribe. I'm only a nurse.

Was a nurse, should say.

I wish Richard was here. He'd cheer me up. I could do with some gallows humour right now, like the other day, when he called me over to his desk.

'Toni, come and look at this.' He was already giggling by the time I got there. 'What do you reckon the scenario was here? Think he slipped at a wine tasting?'

On the screen was an X-ray of a pelvis. Male. And clearly lodged in the back passage, neck end up, was what looked like a wine bottle. 'Whoops,' I said. 'No more Pinot Grigio for you, sir.'

We were both giggling, which we absolutely should not have been.

'Now if you ask me,' said Richard, eyes glittering, 'that's gonna create one hell of a vacuum on the way out. I mean, he could lose his lungs.'

'I just hope his teeth are his own.'

We see strange X-rays all the time, but ones like this never get less funny. They make up for the bad news: the nightmare bloods, the harrowing CT scans, the obvious domestic abuse, the kids' medical notes that would make a grown man weep. It's part of the job. And of course having a window on all of that is fascinating. The human body and its weaknesses: the diseases, the conditions, the injuries, the breaks, the malformations and, as in this particular case, the foreign bodies. I never get bored of all the things that can go wrong with a human being and all the ways we as a species have found to put them right. When we can. We can't always put everything right, as you and I know.

Richard knew I was worried that day too. This was the morning after you'd got sick for your second audition, so I suppose he was trying to cheer me up. But the moment the laughter died down, I was back to thinking about you, at home, under your duvet. I'd put your Jellycat rabbit in with you for company. Funny, no one would have done that for me, growing up. My mum was at work or out with her latest skanky boyfriend, my grandparents were too old and my dad was nowhere. Kids thrive on neglect, sure. But there's a limit.

Richard was looking at me with concern. 'You worried about your Rosie?'

'I'm fine,' I said. 'Actually, I was thinking I need to stop worrying all the time. At her age, I was up to all sorts.'

I've never told Richard about Uncle Eric. I've never told anyone apart from your auntie Bridge and you – bits and pieces for you, of course, what I thought you could cope with. I've never told

Richard about my teenage years. Or my early twenties for that matter. At your age, I was what I'd call wild. If you'd known me at school – not that I was there much – perhaps you'd have called me a slut, a slag or whatever the term is now. Auntie Bridge blew Eric's cover when I was fourteen. He left soon after. I've never told you this, and I don't know if I will when you wake up, but I was thirteen when he took my virginity. A child. If he was alive, he'd be on the sex offenders register. Or in jail. Possibly. I told you he'd gone to a psychiatric hospital. Your auntie Bridget and I decided we had to say something in case his name came up. You see, our mum never told us Dad had left her, can you believe that? She said he was working away. Then when we moved in with Granny Casement, into the house in Hounslow, she didn't tell us it was because she was so broke we'd have been on the street otherwise. But we knew all the same, your auntie Bridge and me.

Kids know. They know when adults are lying to them or not telling them things. It's a form of gaslighting, however kindly meant. Kids know when their parents don't get on, if their father or mother is having an affair, if their dad has buggered off and left them to fend for themselves, if a close relative is dying or sick. Hard as these things are to say, you have to give kids something that makes sense of their feelings, otherwise they exist in a state of fear and confusion.

So I told you that your great-uncle Eric was a bad man and that he'd interfered with me when I was young. There was no need for any more details, and when I told you I was not OK for a long time but that I was OK now, I meant it. I am. In that sense. And any traces of emotional scarring were removed by your lovely dad. But I put myself in a lot of danger growing up, Rosie. I've had three terminations. I sometimes wonder if that's why I had difficulty conceiving again after you. I don't know if I'll ever tell you any of this, but I like to think that I will, some day. I'd like you to get to know me, for us to get to know one another, in all our flawed completeness, if not as friends then at least as grown-ups – as women. But yes, I was chaos, a void that could not be filled. Sometimes I envy your auntie Bridge, who has never slept with a man, even though she tells me life is no simpler for her.

I've kept too tight a rein on you, my love. I know that's why we're here. I accept that. I can't rewrite my history. I can't wash away the stains, and I realise I can't use your life to do it either. Your life is yours. I need to try and love you exactly as you are. That's what love is. Stan, your dad, understood that. He knew everything about me, saw my limitations and loved me anyway, and every day it occurs to me as if for the first time that there is no greater gift one person can give to another. Love is everything. It is all there is.

But I ran riot, Rosie. For years.

And there was no one, no one to stop me.

'I got up to all kinds,' Richard was saying. 'Used to hang out down by the railway tracks, high as a kite, or pissed on cheap vodka. Never had to be home, never had a phone, and all the phone boxes were smashed up back then, weren't they?'

'So you were a tearaway like me then?'

'Oh God, yeah, babe. My mum never had a clue where I was. Never had a clue where my dad was either, come to that. I remember once I shacked up with some guy and didn't go home for a week. No one said a bloody word.'

I love Richard's honesty. We need more honesty in this life, don't we, my love? It makes everyone feel so much better. Less alone.

'But do you think kids are any safer now?' I said. 'With all these checks, all this technology and helicopter parenting?'

He shook his head. 'I don't think so, babe.'

I remember I ate lunch at my desk that day so I could knock off early and get back to you. I was all right, I think. I was working calmly, until Richard came back from the coffee machine having nicked the *Richmond and Twickenham Times* from the waiting room.

'Oh God,' he sighed. 'Have you seen this?'

And I don't know why, but my heart started pounding the moment the words left his mouth. Something had happened to you. You'd been in an accident, you'd been harmed, someone had broken into the flat… Like I say, we think we're OK, we think: I've survived, I've got stronger, I'm all right. But the truth is, the smallest thing can send us into panic, and in those moments we know, deep down, that we're not all right – we're not all right at all.

'Girl gone missing in Putney,' Richard was saying, his pale blue eyes flicking left to right across the page. 'Not been seen since the day before yesterday.' He handed the paper over to me.

'Oh no,' I said. I already felt weird, even as I took the newspaper from him. Ethereal, like I was no longer tethered to the earth. I knew it wasn't you, of course I did, but the twists and turns in my guts, the metallic taste in my mouth, the accelerating beat of my heart… those things came to me as if it was.

I read the article. A fifteen-year-old girl. Cosima Wright. She was meant to be meeting her mother in a café after school prior to going to tennis club. Witnesses saw her in the café but no one saw her leave. She was gone by the time her mother arrived. Never seen again. Just like that. There was a picture of her in her tennis kit: brown hair, pale skin, pretty but nothing special. She was shy apparently. A studious girl who kept herself to herself. The police were asking for anyone who had any information or who might know where she was to come forward.

'Richard,' I said. 'I've got to go home.'

I texted you from the car:

U OK, baby girl?

No reply. Bloody kids, I thought. All this technology, and making contact's like trying to get an audience with the bloody Pope.

I drove home too fast, jumped an amber-to-red on Twickenham Road. I parked out front, but I was so flustered it took me ages to get out of the car. No one answered the door, and I spent another few minutes trying to find my key. It was where it always is, in the side pocket of my bag, but I hadn't been able to see it for stress. I unlocked the door and raced through the flat, pushing open your bedroom door as I passed.

'Rosie? Rosie love?'

You weren't in your room. I dashed through to the kitchen, heart banging in my chest. The back door was locked. Grateful to have the keys still in my hand, I unlocked it and went as fast as I could up the garden path to the gate.

'Rosie! Rosie!' My heart was in my throat. I opened the gate and headed for the car park. 'Rosie!'

A red Mini. Emily's red Mini. You were just getting in.

'Rosie!' I called out. 'Thank God.'

'Mum?'

Emily got out of the driver's side and waved to me over the bonnet. 'Toni! I was just taking Rosie for a cuppa. Would you like to come?'

'I…' My hand was flat to my chest. I couldn't talk. I was still panting like I'd run a mile.

'Mum? What's the matter?' You ran over to me. 'I was only going for a cup of tea. I feel better.'

'I didn't know where you were.' My voice shook. I hated that I couldn't stop it, knew it would irritate you.

Sure enough, a change in the air.

'Mum, I'm fifteen. I was feeling better and Emily texted to see if I fancied meeting up. We were going to talk strategy. It's three o'clock in the afternoon. It's broad daylight.'

'I know. It's just… Did you see the paper?' A silly question. You never read the paper. You never watch the news. We could be in the middle of World War III and you'd still be laughing at those photos with the captions or watching kittens chase after balls of wool.

'What paper? What are you going on about?'

'There's a girl gone missing in Putney. Yesterday.'

'Oh, for fuck's sake,' you whispered. But I heard you.

'Don't swear at me! In fact, don't swear at all!'

'I'm not. But really? Really, Mum?'

'And don't take that tone. You didn't answer my text. Can't you see I'm upset?' I made myself look at you and met your gaze. There was something in your eyes, a hardness, that was new.

'Mum.' You slid your phone from the back pocket of your skinny jeans. 'I've just got your text now, OK? Just chill, will you?'

My God, is there anything more annoying than being told to chill by a child? I'll answer that for you, Rosie. There is not. Not even being talked down to by shop assistants and baristas, patronised by patients. *Just chill.* As if I've *forgotten* to relax.

But I said nothing. I'd gone from panic to embarrassment… to wanting to slap you in the face.

'Mum, we'll be at Harris and Hoole on the high street and I've got my mobile, OK?'

'OK,' I said through gritted teeth. 'All right.'

In the kitchen, I listened as Emily's car pulled away. The silence had barely returned when I burst into tears.

CHAPTER 30

It always happened on bath night. Sunday night. The night when parents got their kids clean and ready for the week. Money was tight. There wasn't the budget for gallons of hot water every day, and of course we had to share the water. It got so I would dread the sound of the taps running thunderously into the tub. Even now the smell of lavender has the power to make me sick. I wanted to tell my mummy. But I was scared of him, of the hissing sound he made when he was angry, the pulling of his fingers, crack crack crack. It was easier to let him.

He started to bring the magazines into my room with him. He would put on my night light and make me look at the pictures. I could not turn away from them. When I did, he would grip my chin in his hand and pull my head back around.

'What about that one? Shall we try it? Would you like to?'

I would nod. I had to pretend like it was something I wanted to do too. For him, it was a game. I could not speak. I watched the gap in the curtains, the moon and the stars. When I could. It was not always possible – I could not always see. In my head, I spoke. In my head, I survived. In my head, I became other people; I lived other lives.

CHAPTER 31

ROSIE

Mum? Mummy? Are you there? Emily? I'm not underwater. Not really. I am dry… soft… softness below me… cleanness… crispness. Beep beep…

Smell of coffee… clank of the coffee machine, roar of milk on the steam jet. A man's voice shouts, *One large skinny latte, one regular cappuccino for Emily.*

Emily. Light flashes like cream on the lenses of her glasses. *So what's this getting-sick business all about?*

Emily. She's opposite me. We're in the coffee bar. Her cheeks are like Pink Lady apples.

I know when this is!

Mummy? Mum?

Hold on, Mum! I am… OK, this is in the café with Emily. This is after you went mental at me in the car park. That is when this is. That was so embarrassing, Mum. Oh my God, you were being proper mental.

But I was mean to you in front of Emily. You were stressed, and I made you look stupid. I'm sorry. But that's not what I'm really sorry about. There's something else, something bigger, like a fist in my gut, but every time I think I remember, it disappears… What is it?

Do you think you can tell me? Emily's voice is soft and near. Her face. Light flashing on her glasses. She is not chuckling. We are in the café. She is not saying silly moo or any of her batshit stuff. She is like Auntie Bridge – when she's serious, she's very serious. I am drinking cappuccino, which is coffee. OK, so it has cocoa on the top, but it is not a halfway house; it is a proper grown-up drink. I have put three sachets of sugar in it.

Tell you what? That's my voice. I hear it inside my head; see myself say it there in my memory.

Emily lays her soft, dry hand over mine and pats it once, twice, before taking it away. *Whatever you want, my darling. But I'm wondering about this nervous-tummy thing. That's twice now, isn't it? I'm wondering how I can help or if we can stop it before it becomes a real problem.* She smiles. She blows on her coffee, but she doesn't drink any. She's on a diet, that's why she's having a skinny latte. *I suppose I wondered if perhaps you'd like to talk about it. God forbid, I would never want you to say anything you didn't want to. Of course it goes without saying that this would be in the strictest confidence. Do you think you can talk about it?*

She blinks. Her face is kind.

I… I say. *Sometimes I get nervous.*

She gives a slow nod. On her neck, the skin crinkles. Her hair is kind of white at the front, dark grey at the back, and her cheeks droop at either side of her chin. I don't want to look like her when I'm older. I want to look like Auntie Bridge. Auntie Bridge's hair is spiky. My tattoo will be theatre masks on my wrist. I stare down at my hands, flat and pale on the table, the nails bitten, patches of black nail varnish. I need to clean that off – it looks rank. You need nice hands to be an actress. You need to look after yourself.

You know, Rosie darling, nerves are all part of it. She lays her hand on mine again: her right, my left. Her palm is dry and warm. This time she leaves her hand there. *We all get nervous, my dear. It's the business we're in. Nerves, emotions, feelings, they're what we trade in, aren't they? We emote. We give. So those emotions, those nerves, what have you, they're important. They give us access to the things we need to convey. They allow us to move people through our art, do you see?*

I nod my head, yes.

And I know you suffer, because I too suffer. We artists, we suffer. We suffer more than most – it is the cross we must bear, my dear. But nerves, or super-sensitivity, or whatever you wish to call it, give us the energy we need to shine. And I know you can shine, Rosie. I have seen you. We should maybe think about finding ways of coping, how do you feel about that?

Do you mean like CBT? Auntie Bridge did CBT. She's taught me some things to help with anxiety.

As soon as the words leave my mouth, I feel miserable. You're not supposed to tell others what the people closest to you tell you not to tell, especially if they're family. You taught me that, Mum. And I've just told Emily something Auntie Bridge told me to keep to myself.

We had CBT classes after the accident. I only say this to try and make up for what I said before, but I think I've made it worse even though I know she knows about the accident and everything. *Mum saw a counsellor for ages.* That's definitely worse. That's private. I shouldn't have said that either. *I think I saw one too, but I can't remember. Auntie Bridge gives me exercises, like I have to say the notes: do re mi fa so la ti do, and I do breathing and it calms me down. That's how I got the part of Little Red. It's how I go on stage.*

Emily gives me a big smile, as if I've done something brave. She sips her coffee and puts the cup back into the saucer so slowly and gently it doesn't make a sound.

Good, she says. *Good girl. That's a start. It's good that you've all had help. Sometimes we need help. It's natural, under the circumstances.*

I stare at my black, scabby nails. I am heavy with guilt. You tell me guilt is a wasted emotion, but I think it is telling us to look at what we've done and ask ourselves if we should have done it, and if the answer is no, then it's a way of thinking, well I won't do that again. I can't go back and not say those things, can I? I can't not tell Emily our family business because I've told her now. It's too late to put the words back in, and I have a pain of shame in my gut.

But I can promise not to say those things again, can't I?

It's not too late, is it? Is it, Mummy?

CHAPTER 32

TONI

They never found that girl who went missing from that café in Putney. There was a follow-up article asking whether her disappearance was linked to that of another girl who had gone missing ages ago and had never been found either. She had the same profile: shy, pretty, but not an overwhelming beauty – a nice girl. I wonder, do we bring our girls up to be too nice? Are their manners putting them in danger?

It's the photographs that break my heart.

I wonder if they'll find those girls now, once they discover the body. It's possible he's behind them too. They'll be dead, of course. They might even be buried in the garden. My God, just the thought makes me feel sick. One day you'll understand how that feels. Once you're a mother, you'll watch the news and there'll be *that kid,* the kid who's gone missing or who has been found dead, and you'll feel it. You'll feel it, Rosie, and you'll feel the fragility of this life like a blown eggshell in your hands. Because *that* child is yours and mine, that child belongs to all mothers everywhere, and when you put your baby to bed that night, you'll take her in your arms and you will not want to let go. You will never want to let go.

When you went for your cosy coffee with Emily, shall I tell you what I felt most of all? Jealous. I'm ashamed to admit it now,

but I could see how well you and she got on. You came to life
around her. You were lighter, your smile readier, your very bones
looser. She knew how to tease you, how to take you seriously,
how to be your friend without smothering you. I wanted to be
your friend too, but that's not what I am, my love. I'm your
mum, and there's no dad on the scene so I'm the A, the B, the
C and the D. It's down to me to do all the jobs, the shitty ones
as well as the lovely stuff like seeing you up there on stage. By
shitty, I don't mean laundry and shopping and all that, although
yes, there's that too. I mean like nagging you about homework,
tidying your room, filling the dishwasher; worrying to death
when you're out later than you said you would be; freaking
when I realise you've forgotten to take your phone with you yet
again and I have no way of getting hold of you. I mean having
to endure a love for you so strong, so utterly consuming, that
some days it feels like terror.

You were still out with Emily when Bridget got home. Unusu-
ally for her, your auntie looked strained. Her eyes were rimmed
in red, as if she'd been crying. But Auntie Bridget never cries,
does she?

'Are you OK?' I said.

'Hay fever,' she replied. 'Where's Rosie?'

She had put the kettle on and was rooting around in the biscuit
jar. She took out a digestive and ate half in one bite, then opened
the fridge and pulled out an onion, a carrot and some bendy celery.

'She's gone for a cup of tea with Emily. Sit down, Bridge. I'll
make dinner.'

'It's OK, I'll do it,' she said. 'So she's meeting her agent, eh?
Meryl Streep watch out.'

I told her about how I'd freaked out, how you'd sassed me.
Bridget made us both tea and listened without interrupting. She
left her mug on the countertop, where she began peeling the onion.

'Do you think I'm mad?' I asked.

'No madder than anyone else.' She turned from her task, her eyes even redder now, on account of the onion, and reached for her third digestive biscuit.

'You'll spoil your dinner.'

'Thanks, Mum.' She grinned, crumbs on her teeth, before ramming the rest of it in with a rebellious flourish.

'Your eyes look sore,' I said. 'Is it definitely hay fever?'

She sniffed and turned back to her task. 'Probably. Something to add to the post-menopausal cornucopia of delights alongside stiff joints and back fat, I suppose.'

We both laughed.

'Don't worry about it,' she said after a moment. 'Teenagers. They're twats, aren't they? Sure I read that in *Good Parenting*.'

I don't need to tell you she was only joking. I smiled and sipped my tea. I don't take sugar, but Bridge always puts half a teaspoon in because she knows I prefer it that way. It was like nectar, as they say, and I wondered why I bothered trying to drink it without – why any of us bother with these sticks we use to beat ourselves.

'What've you been up to?' I asked her.

'Website job up in East Sheen, then a mate of his in Strawberry Hill with a blocked iPhone. Called in on Helen on the way home.' Somehow she'd already got the frying pan on the gas, and the smell of fresh garlic in olive oil filled the kitchen.

'How's lovely Helen?'

'Good. She's off to LA, remember? Tonight, in fact.' Her back straightened a moment before she bent again to her task. I heard the chop-chop of the knife on the board. 'That big script I told you about, jammy bugger.'

'The romantic comedy?'

'The very one. Musical, would you believe? Did I tell you that? She said she wouldn't have got it, but one of the commissioning bods had seen that indie she did last year.'

'How long will she be there?'

'Six months. She'll be even more loaded when she gets back.'

'Wow.'

'Like you say.' Bridget slid the onions hissing into the oil and turned down the gas. She reached for a piece of kitchen roll, pressed it to her eyes.

'Bridge?' I said. 'Are you all right?'

'Course,' she said and gave a loud sniff. 'Bloody onions.'

CHAPTER 33

ROSIE

So, Rosie my love, next time you have an audition, do you think you can try some of those marvellous exercises your auntie Bridget gave you? Maybe start the day before you go, even a few days before, and sort of build up?

I stir my cappuccino and nod, but I don't meet Emily's eyes because I feel too awkward, and I still wish I hadn't told her about your counselling.

I did do them this time, I say, *but I'd got sick the time before so I think I was, like, worried about getting sick again. You know, like, on top of being worried about the audition? And that was, like, too much worry.*

All right. Right you are. You must try not to worry all the time. Your mum… and I don't mean this in any way critically… your mum is a super, super mum…

I understand. I look her in the eye and smile.

She smiles back as if she's passing an apple pip through her teeth to spit it out, and cocks her head to one side. *She's very protective of you, isn't she? Do you think that's… because of the accident?*

I shrug. I don't want to talk about this stuff. This stuff is in a box with the lid closed. I'm defo not going to tell her about Uncle Eric, no way. But something bubbles up in me, now, remembering… Emily… this… it's… this is… this is not the first time we have had this conversation. Or it is the first time but we had it a few times, maybe after. Whatever, it's déjà vu. This is what they call déjà vu! I've never had that before. I've always wanted to see what it was like. I'm defo having it now. Cool. Or was I having it then, in the café with Emily? Or later, another time, not that one, not this?

I don't know.

Emily presses her hand onto my cheek just for a moment and her warm palm feels so nice I want to lean my head into it and close my eyes.

That's OK, Rosie darling, she says. *You don't have to tell me. It's just that sometimes, when someone we love worries that we can't do something or we can't cope with something, we lose faith in our ability to do that very thing, indeed to do the things we want to do, do you see?*

I nod but say nothing. I feel like I'm going to cry.

And sometimes that feeling of not being up to the job can make us nervous, do you see? And if we get a case of the old jitterbugs, we can feel sick or even be sick or suffer a migraine or what have you. The mind can make us very poorly. It is a very powerful organ indeed.

I have tears in my eyes now. I'm trying not to let them spill out. I sniff.

Oh my darling. She squeezes my hand. *Sometimes the people we love most, lovely as they are, are in fact harming us. Do you see?*

She is being kind – I know it. But I don't like what she's saying, though I don't know why I don't like it.

Mum would never hurt me.

Of course not, darling! Not intentionally, no. I would never suggest that – don't be silly. She stops, pushes the handle of her coffee cup around so it faces the other way, then back again. She takes a breath, like a gasp, and closes her mouth for a few seconds before she speaks again. *But if your mother is nervous about you going out into the world, then it could be that you're picking up on that. Do you think that's a possibility?*

I nod. She is only trying to help.

It could be that you've internalised the feeling that you can't cope with the world and its slings and arrows, as it were. And that might be what's causing the old collywobbles, and hence the sickness, hmm?

I nod.

But I'm here to tell you… She says this a bit louder. *I, the great Madame Belle, mentor and agent, I am here to tell you that you* can *cope, Rosie. You are capable and bright, and you can do anything at all you set your mind to, do you see? You can do it.*

I nod. I am properly crying now. How embarrassing.

She takes her hand away and digs in her handbag. *And somewhere inside your mum, she knows that too, all right?* She pulls out a tissue and gives it to me.

Thank you. I dab my eyes.

We just have to show her that you can do these things, all right? So I need you to work on these naughty nerves of yours and really fight them. Can you do that for me? And that might mean that sometimes, just sometimes, you might need to protect your mummy in return.

Protect her? I blow my nose. It makes a honking sound. OMG, now I'm going red. *What do you mean?*

From what you're doing. Do you see? As in, you could try not telling her every single thing you're up to, to protect her from worry. It's normal not to tell your mum everything. That's what it means to grow up. I don't mean go to Timbuktu for a week without telling her, or join the foreign legion. She chuckles. *But explore – take a risk or two. When I was your age, I was such a scamp! I used to tell my mummy I was staying at my friend Trisha's when I was actually staying over at my boyfriend's.*

I laugh. I can't imagine her having a boyfriend. *Where did you live?*

In Hampshire then. On a farm. Now I'm just over the river from you. Emily is blinking at me from behind her silver glasses. *So what do you think, Rosie? Little Red? Do you think you can protect Mummy?*

I nod. The tears are stinging my eyes and my throat is hollow. To agree with her about you feels wrong. Mum? Mummy? I don't like remembering this. I don't like remembering these feelings and what I said. I know you only worry because you love me. I know you don't let me do stuff because you love me. I know all you wanted was to keep me safe. But when Emily said those things, I saw what she meant – you thought I couldn't cope and that made me think I couldn't cope…

And that made me want to get away from you.

CHAPTER 34

BRIDGET

Bridget parks the van and turns off the engine. From the car park she can see the light on in the kitchen, the silhouette of her sister bent forward over the kitchen table. Is she crying? It's possible. It's always possible. But Bridget needs a minute, just today, just this once. In her leather-jacket pocket she finds her pouch of Golden Virginia, her tips and her papers. It only takes her a minute to roll a cigarette and, digging her Zippo from her other pocket, she pushes her back into the driver's seat and opens the van window. The sun is sinking. It's turned chilly, but her jacket is warm. She hunches her shoulders a little against the cold that blows on her neck. In the momentary peace, she lights her cigarette. The lighter has her initials engraved on the side: BC. A gift from Helen.

Helen will be at the airport by now, bound for LA. Bridget wonders how she'll get on, whether she'll be happy there in the City of Angels. Who she'll meet. Less than an hour ago, Bridget called in on her way home, to the house they used to share, rooms full of stuff, full of memories, full of so much that still belongs to both of them. She called in, as she often does, but this time to say goodbye. Helen has always stopped writing by late afternoon, so even in the early days after the accident, when Bridget used to pick Rosie up from school, she would take her for a hot chocolate and then on to see Helen. Now there is no need, no reason, no excuse to call in, but it is a habit neither of them seems able to break. And besides, who would feed the cat when Helen is away, if not Bridget?

'I want you to be happy,' Bridget made herself say in the moments before she left. She's become superstitious about journeys, and especially about goodbyes.

'I'm not totally unhappy,' Helen replied, smiling the way a person smiles when they've burnt their finger or stubbed their toe in front of people they don't know well.

'Me neither,' Bridget said. 'Not, you know, totally.'

Helen took Bridget's hand, rubbed her thumb across the knuckles, down to the silver skull pinky ring. 'I worry about you, Bridge.'

'You need someone to worry about, Titch.'

'Do you ever call anyone by their actual name?'

'Only my probation officer.'

'Very funny. Stop diverting. You could find someone.'

'So could you.'

'I know, but you could find someone nice.'

'Nice-looking girl like me, you mean?'

The living-room door was ajar. Through the crack, through the front window of the house, she could see the light already falling. There in the hallway, it was all but dark. Helen's eyes are green. Bridget thinks of them now as she stares across the backyard at the flat she now shares with her sister, that hunched silhouette crying in the kitchen.

She tips back her head, sucks, feels the rush of nicotine.

I'm not totally unhappy. It's enough, isn't it? It has to be. The pact with her little sister was made not years but decades ago now. God, she's old. She feels it then with the force of a punch. She's always looked out for Toni, ever since they were kids. Too far apart for sibling rivalry, she used to take Toni out in her pushchair, show her off on the streets of Hounslow. She took her into Richmond for her first legal drink (albeit years after her first actual drink), took Rosie to the same pub for hers, illegally, just the other month, when she was fifteen. Not that Toni knows that – Christ, no, she would kill her – but some things belong to her and Rosie. Auntie's privileges, small comforts. So much has been lost; so much has been broken. The kid has been her consolation. When Rosie was born, Bridget was the first person at the hospital after Stan, and he'd been there for the birth.

You make a promise like that, a pact, it doesn't go away because you've grown up. It is inked into the skin, branded into the heart. Toni is her sister. She and Rosie are her family. And that is all.

She pulls on her cigarette. There is a little grass in the tobacco, which she mixed in, anticipating this moment when she would unpick the tangle of herself after saying goodbye to Titch. And here she sits, teasing and laying out the tattered threads one by one.

I'm going to fucking kill you, you fucking sick bastard.

She had thrown Eric against his bedroom wall so hard his head made a dent in the cheap wallpapered plasterboard. She won't forget the whites of his eyes, the flash of black, panicked iris. His sweat, his stale tobacco breath, his stale, spunky room.

'And after that, I'm going to call the police myself.'

'Aw, Bridge. Bridge, mate. Don't. Don't be like that. I don't know what you're talking about.'

He was shaking like the coward he was. Not admitting it even now that his grimy secret was out. And then, when she had her hands around his revolting little throat, when, gasping for breath, he confessed to what he'd done, he had the audacity to blame it on Toni. She'd led him on. She'd given him the eye. She was a slut, a prick-tease.

'She's fucking fourteen, you fucking piece of shit.'

She never called the police. No one did. Her family don't do police, and family affairs are no one else's business. If she went back to that moment, she'd do the same: the threat, the pact, everything. But sometimes, on dark and lonely nights like this, she realises she never anticipated the practicalities. Does anyone, about any kind of choice? Marriage, children, anti-establishment, corporate, free spirit, committed partner, raise your voice in protest, stay silent… everything, everything has a practical side.

Everything has a price.

CHAPTER 35

ROSIE

Sometimes everything is clear. I know where I am and when I am and who is there. It is coherent. I like that word. Opalescent. I like that word too; I used it in a poem, but it's not relevant at the mo. Sometimes an image flickers but then it's gone. Sometimes it's cloudy, like when you dissolve painkillers in water. Or Alka-Seltzer, like you take, Mummy, sometimes, in the mornings. In those cloudy bits, I don't know when it is, or where I am, or even *if* I am.

Like the tin space. The back of Auntie Bridge's van. Is that what the tin space is? And if it *is* Auntie Bridge's van, then why am I so scared when I'm in it? The funny chemical smell in my nostrils. The tape being ripped from my mouth. White light stinging my eyes. A silhouette at the door of the van… who are you?

Now I'm in my room, I know that. My Hello Kitty duvet cover, my lava lamp that Auntie Bridge got me for Christmas glows pink… blue… green. On my desk is an empty glass where I've had some milk. On a plate, there are chocolate crumbs from a Rice Krispie cake. You make them every week. It's your thing – you've made them since I was little. But this glass, this plate, are not from today – they're from yesterday, and I haven't brought the empties back into the kitchen yet. You will tell me off about that. It's hot in my room. The milk will start to smell like sick. I am revising for, like, the billionth test. It's near to GCSEs. The teachers are so stressy they test us all the time; it's so annoying. In my exercise book, there's a crap drawing of a Bunsen burner and a conical flask. Underneath, the teacher has written *1* in red biro. That means top effort, but my drawing is so lame I wonder what I'd have to do to get a 2 or a 3. Chemical reactions are so boring. I can't wait to finish my GCSEs and study only interesting subjects like French and drama and English literature.

You've forgotten to take my mobile, as you always do. You are always totally done in when you get in from work. After, like, two glasses of wine you practically pass out in front of the telly, and right now you're making dinner so there's no way you'll check on me. I promise myself I'll only go on Instagram for a bit. For, like, a few minutes. I tell myself I'm literally just going to scroll through, see who's posted, do my likes, check my notifications, but really there's only one notification I'm interested in.

There's a red circle! A message! Let it be him let it be him let it be him.

Hey, Sexy Lady. Was thinking shall we swap mobile numbers? Only if you want. Then we can text. Easier? And maybe soon we could even chat. Like chat chat. Chat chat chatty chat, LOL. This is my number anyway…

I'm flapping my hands in front of my face, which has gone all hot. Oh my God. He's given me his number. I think about calling Naomi, because I've waited so long for this and now there's really something to tell her. It's legit. But I don't, because Ollie is my secret, and I'm not ready to take him out of the box. I'll tell her at school tomorrow. But she'll have to, like, swear not to tell anyone else. Oh, what do I do? I know I don't *know* know him, but we've been friends for ages and I know him soooo well. It's like those quizzes in magazines where they ask you a question and you have to pick an answer, like multiple choice but for fun, e.g. A hot guy asks for your number. You've never met him but you have friends in common. Do you:

a) Tell him he has to write a letter to your parents requesting permission
b) Say yes, but maybe we should get to know each other better first
c) Say hell no, back off, what kind of girl do you take me for?
d) Give him your number immediately – what are you waiting for, girlfriend?

I don't think it's right to send him my number if he has an actual girlfriend. I've had loads of chats with you about this kind of stuff and you always say that if you're talking about a friend behind their back, make sure you're not saying anything you're not prepared to say to her face. I do say things I wouldn't say to my friend Sasha's face. But she's such a bitch, and I would only slag her off to Naomi because I trust Naomi with my *absolute life*, and anyway Naomi says that's not bitching, it's just venting. Also, we don't criticise Sasha's clothes or her legs or anything; we just, you know, offload, like the time we were at a party and she knew that Naomi was really into this lad and she went over and started flirting with him, and then when Naomi asked her what she was doing she was like *What?* as if she didn't know *exactly* what she was doing, so I think it was OK to talk about that because otherwise we would have exploded or something because she is SO ANNOYING.

Whoops. I've just told you we were at a party. I mean, I know you can't hear me but I've told you in my mind. I've been to three parties, Mum. I said I'd been to one, but I've been to three. You may as well know that now. I told you I was staying over at Naomi's and that was the truth, but we went to parties those nights and one of them was in Barnes at a friend of Naomi's I didn't even know. We got back at one in the morning.

Soz.

Anyway, I don't want to ask Ollie if he's got a girlfriend 'cos then he'll know I like him in *that* way, so I check his Facebook page and go back through his pictures. There are a couple of him with girls, but there's more than one girl and the pictures look like they were taken at parties. The girls are hot and that makes me feel like *why am I even bothering?* but I carry on. In another photo, he has his arm around a girl, but it's not just her and him, there's another boy and he's got his arm around the girl too. She is very pretty and she is laughing in a confident way and again I feel rubbish because I know I couldn't laugh like that, like when you throw back your head and push your shoulders forward. I have tried this in the mirror and I look like I've got problems with my bones or something.

Rosie! Rosie love!

You're calling me for my dinner.

Coming!

I copy his number into my contacts under OT, because, well, why not? If you check and ask me I can say it's Ophelia Thomas or Olga or Olivia and she's just a mate. I text him quickly:

Hi. It's me. You have my number now.

I put a heart emoji but then panic and delete it and send the message like that. I'm about to come to the kitchen when my phone beeps.

What, no kisses? Crying emoji. Heart-broken-in-two emoji.

Heart broken in two! OMG! My hands clench into fists. I want to squeal but I can't. I don't want you to hear.

I text kisses. One big, one little. And a heart.

Coming now, I call down the hall. I race to the bathroom, pretending I need to wash my hands, which I do, but really I want to splash my face with cold, cold water. Scream – that's actually what I feel like doing. So I press the towel to my face and say *aaaah*.

It sounds like someone who has been kidnapped and gagged and is trying to shout for help.

That sound.

That sound.

That sound is me.

That sound is me.

Help. Help me. Is that what has happened to me? Is that the bad thing? Is that why I'm here in the soup?

Here she is, says Auntie Bridge when I come into the kitchen. *We were about to send out a search party.*

Funny. I shake my non-existent belly with my hands and sit down.

Auntie Bridge's made pasta, you say. You look at me all weird, like you're wondering what's wrong with my face.

What?

Nothing. Have you washed your face or something?

So? I say. *It's not illegal, is it?*

It's tuna bol, says Auntie Bridge. *We're going veggie this week.*

Pescatarian, I say. *Because fish.*

Which you'll be wearing in a minute, you cheeky monkey. Auntie Bridge winks at me and I laugh.

Now when I think about that meal, I remember you laughing too. It was like we both realised at the exact same moment that we were being grumpy cows. I love our family. Our funny triangle family. We are jokes, but we look after each other.

Whichever way up we are, you say, *there's always two of us at the base, supporting the other.*

This triangle is how we are, how we have become, how we have had to be.

At dinner, you ask me if I had a nice time with Emily, and I know we're friends again, but I get a stomach ache because I know we talked about you, and now that you're there in front of me, I feel bad.

Yes, I say.

That all? What did you talk about?

Nothing really. Acting stuff.

OK. You raise your eyebrows at Auntie Bridge even though you know I can see you.

She's a secret agent apparently, says Auntie Bridge, smirking.

I don't laugh. For once, Auntie Bridge is being a bit annoying. Keeping anything to yourself in this house is a big crime. Apparently.

What've you been up to today? you say.

I shrug and I'm just like, *Stuff.*

Fascinating.

After dinner, Auntie Bridge goes to get ready for her gig. I rinse the plates and pass them to you to put in the dishwasher. I wipe down the kitchen table. You hold out your hand for the dishcloth so you can wipe the hob. Your expression is sad.

I'm sorry, you say. *About before. With Emily. I was just worried. I get worried.*

I know. I'm sorry too.

You throw the cloth in the sink. I sit on your knee and press my face into your neck. I'm not sad or happy or especially anything, but the fruit smell of your skin makes me cry.

Hey there, baby girl, you say. *It's all right; it's all right.*

I love you, Mum.

I love you more.

Wrong, I love you more. Idiot brain.

Don't be cheeky.

I want to tell you about Ollie. So much. I want to show you our messages and his pictures and giggle with you about how hot he is, even though he's not my boyfriend and I know deep down that he never will be.

But I don't tell you.
I can't.
I'm sorry.

*

My phone is vibrating. It's Ollie. He's calling me. He's CALL-ING ME. I never thought this would happen. I can't believe it. When is this? Is this the same day or, like, way after? Oh my actual God, this is more than a worm in the beak, this is a total move! I close my eyes, open them. I slide the screen.

Hello, beautiful. It is a man's voice. Oh my God. A man, all deep and posh. I'd expected a different voice, more like the lads in my year. But he's eighteen, nearly nineteen, so obvs he's more mature.

Hello? Is that Ollie?

Finally I get to talk to you. He sounds so, like, *Downton* or something. My stomach flips right over.

Finally. I laugh, like a nerd.

You sound nice. I like your voice.

I like yours. You sound older.

I'm very old. I'm actually seventy-three.

I laugh. I can't think of a comeback – way too gassed.

So did you finish your studies?

Just had dinner actually.

What did you have?

Just pasta. What about you?

Steak and chips. Ice cream. Not together obviously.

I laugh.

So what've you been up to?

I tell him about my trip to the café with Emily.

You have an agent? That's exciting.

Yeah. Well, sort of. She's, like, mentoring me? She's a bit old, but she's funny and kind and she has a lot of contacts and stuff.

She sounds… cool.

She's so not! I laugh again, tell myself to stop laughing all the time or he's going to think I'm a dork. *But she's only my first agent. I'll try for a bigger agent next year or the year after, once I've done more shows or maybe some adverts and stuff like that.*

Have you thought about modelling?

I think that's mad but I like him saying it. *Er, no!*

You should. You're easily beautiful enough and it pays really well.

Beautiful! He said I was beautiful. And he is so posh!

I do a little modelling here and there, he says. *It's not what I want to do though – it's just to fund me through university. Ultimately I want to be a doctor and do voluntary work overseas. I'm hoping to finish my studies without too big a loan and then I'm going to go to Kenya or join Médecins Sans Frontières.*

Wow. Oh. My. God. That is so cool. And his French accent is *très chaud.*

A text comes in – holy frickin' crap, it's you!

Come and say goodnight, you have put, which is Mum-speak for go to bed. I realise it's 10 p.m. and I still haven't done any homework. Like, none. My chemistry test is tomorrow.

I've got to go, I say.

That's OK. I'll miss you though.

There is this pause, but it's more than a pause, it's like *a moment,* like we are talking without words. I can hear him breathing. I wonder where he is – lying down, I think, in his room, on his bed. In his boxers, his hair kind of flopping over one eye, one hand on his stomach. OMG.

Chat tomorrow? he says.

I can barely speak. I don't know what else to say so I say, *Bye then.*

Bye, Sexy Lady.

Bye, er… Bye what, Rosie? Say something, say anything, you total loser idiot brain.

Darling? he says, and I can tell by his voice that he's sort of smiling down the phone. *My prince? My knight?*

I laugh. *Er, yeah. Bye.*

I hang up and cover my face with my hands. Oh my God, that was the biggest cringe EVER. I am such an idiot; he will think I am a total nerd. If I was him I would never call me again. Literally, I would unfriend me, delete me, block me for crimes against… crimes against banter.

You're on the sofa drinking red wine in front of the news. I don't want you to see my face in case you can tell I've been talking to a boy, so I kiss the top of your head from behind the sofa.

Night, Mum.

Homework go OK? You've got your chemistry test tomorrow, haven't you?

Yeah. It's fine.

All right. Night, baby girl.

Night.

After I've cleaned my teeth, I get into bed. I pick up my phone to switch it off but there's a text from Ollie. Now that we can text, I will have to remember to delete them.

Great talking to you, Sexy Lady. Check your Instagram messages. Winking-face emoji.

I bring up Instagram and see the red circle. My stomach flips over. There is a photo from him, like a mouth in an O. But it's not a mouth. It's his belly button.

Underneath it says:

Send me yours.

CHAPTER 36

TONI

'Rosie? Rosie love?'

I thought I saw your eyes flicker just then, but no. Nothing. Under the white cotton sheet, the landscape of you rolls out: your feet the highest peak, your knees, sharp hips, your breasts that don't budge an inch even when you lie down, and you're too young to even know how incredible that is, how much you'll miss it one day.

'Everything all right here?' It's our nurse, the nice one.

'Thank you, yes,' I say. 'Actually, I was just thinking, will that water in the jug there be stale? Maybe I should freshen it up in case she wakes. The doctor said it could be any time.'

She lays a hand on my shoulder. 'You stay where you are, Toni. I'll change it right this second.' She smiles, takes the plastic jug from your bedside table and off she goes. I watch her leave; let my eyes drift across the ward. Those two beds won't be empty for long, I'm sure. The young girl is asleep.

In my text, I told Emily you'd had a funny turn, that's all. It didn't feel right not letting her know you were here, but I didn't think she had to know the whole story. She's stuck with you when others might have given up. She's been very patient. When you got sick for the third audition, I thought she'd fire you. Very gently and nicely, of course, but you're no use to her if you can't make auditions, are you? No use at all. And the third audition was a film, a terrific opportunity that would have had you filming in France!

You were so elated I thought you'd got on top of your emotions, found a way to turn your nerves into excitement. *She's going to do it this time*, I thought. But you followed the same pattern as the two previous times: all right the day before, didn't seem too het up about it, but by that evening you complained of stomach pains and I thought, *Uh-oh, here we go again.*

'Try not to worry,' I said as I tucked you in with your hot-water bottle. You'd already had a fair few trips to the loo. I'd put a bucket next to your bed just in case you couldn't make it to the bathroom. 'Try and breathe and don't fret. Fretting won't help – it won't help at all.'

You were crying so much you became short of breath. Your auntie Bridge came to your room and sat on the end of your bed. She glanced at me and we shared a look.

'Oi, Squirt,' she said, 'what's all this, you big skiver?'

But even she couldn't cheer you up.

'Should I take her down to A&E?' she said quietly.

'I don't think so,' I said. 'It's just an upset stomach at the end of the day. She'll need nil by mouth and just sips of water for another twenty-four hours.'

'You're the nurse.'

'I'm beginning to think we need to leave this audition business for a year or two,' I said. 'It's all too much too soon, isn't it?'

'Stop talking about me in front of me,' you wailed. 'Don't say that. I just need to do my do re mi and I'll be fine. Just stop talking about me as if I'm not here!'

I stroked your forehead and shushed you as best I could. I didn't shout or get cross. I knew you were taking your anger out on me because I'm the closest one to you. I took your empty milk glass and your plate into the kitchen. I could hear your auntie Bridge trying to cajole you, you whining back at her, miserable. After a minute or so, even Bridge gave up and joined me in the kitchen.

'Poor kid,' she said, sitting down.

'We'll see how she is in the morning,' I said. 'I'll text Emily now and give her the heads-up, but frankly, it'll be a miracle if she rallies in time.'

'I think you're right,' she said.

'About tomorrow?'

'About too much too soon. She's been through a lot. She's only fifteen, Tones. I didn't do anything serious until after drama school.'

'Do you think she'll ever be able to face it?' I said. 'Out there, I mean?'

'Out there in the world? Of course she will! Just maybe not now. Not yet. She's still so young.' Bridget got up and opened the wall cupboard nearest the stove.

'There's no wine in,' I said.

'I'm not after wine.' She moved aside a bottle of cooking brandy and pulled out the Glenmorangie that Helen had given her for Christmas. She grinned. 'Medicinal.'

'How old were you when you did that play at the Wimbledon theatre?' I said.

Your auntie Bridge screwed up her eyes a moment. 'I'd forgotten about that one.' She pulled down the two crystal glasses, put them on the table and poured two small measures. 'Eighteen? It wasn't serious – I didn't get paid or anything. When was that then? Was that before I went to Central?'

'The summer before. You were in the local paper. The toast of Hounslow! We went to Pizzaland with Mum and Terry, that disgusting boyfriend with the gold tooth she had for a bit. It was a big deal.'

Your auntie Bridge shrugged. 'Your memory's better than mine, but yeah, maybe she should stick to the youth theatre for now, you know, where she feels safe. There's no rush, is there?'

'Exactly. I want her to have a childhood, Bridge.'

We exchanged a glance, the smallest nod. Neither of us said anything, but I knew she was thinking about me, about what happened to me. My childhood was finished at thirteen.

You slept all that night and all the next day. I rang in sick, checked on you every hour. At least asleep, you looked as if all your fears had dissolved and as if, wherever you were, you were at peace. I didn't check your phone. I didn't think to. I was too caught up in my mother's vigilance, eyes fixed with terrible concentration in one direction, little realising that, like the victim of a dodgy street magician, following the marble in the cup, the ace in the pack, the rabbit in the hat, I was oblivious to the sleight of hand, ignorant that what I was training my sights on had been taken long before.

CHAPTER 37

ROSIE

I'm on the swings. My daddy is there. His face. Near, far, near, far… we're in the park. He's gone behind me now. His hands on my shoulders, then not, then on again. Where are you? You are on the bench. You look up from your magazine and wave. I can't take my hands off the T-bar because I'm concentrating on keeping the swing going, so I shout:

Look at me! Look at me, Mummy. Daddy, I'm doing it!

You are. Keep going; keep going.

You stand up and half walk, half run over to me. You are smiling a big smile, your eyebrows up near your hair.

Brilliant, Rosie!

I can do the swing!

Concentrate; concentrate… Daddy's voice behind me. *Legs straight and lean… That's it. That's it, Rosie. Keep going. Bend… and legs… that's it… Look at her, Bun, she's got it. You're doing grand, Rosie – you're flying to the moon. You're a star in the sky…*

I'm a star in the sky, Daddy. I'm a red star in the sky… I am a red jewel in a gold crown… look at me… look at me… look at me look at me looooooook at meeeeee…

I'm in bed. You are beside me. You are holding my hand… Is this now soup or long ago soup? I think it's now… I think it's now,

Mummy! I'm coming up… wait for me… I'm coming up… I'm coming up… I'm…

Listen. I was thinking, would you like to meet up? I mean, only if you wish to.

Wish to? I laugh. Ollie is soooo posh. *Who says wish to?*

He laughs too. *Want to, wish to, whatever. So, would you like to meet?*

Er, yeah. I can't believe this is happening. My legs are literally shaking.

I hear him smile. Don't ask me how smiling sounds, but I do, I hear him. I hear him because I know him so well.

All right, he says. *I'm going to say… do you know Hampton Hill? Is that near you?*

Mm hm. Yeah. I know where it is but I haven't been there by myself, just gone through it in the car with you or in Auntie Bridge's van.

There's a coffee shop opposite the park gate. It's Hampton Gate, I think. The café's called Thyme for Coffee – thyme as in the herb – do you know it? It's by the zebra crossing.

My stomach does a somersault. I know where he means but I think, *I've never been there before and what if I get the wrong bus?* But then I remember Emily telling me I can do things, that maybe you have made me feel like I can't because you're always so nervous. I can do this. But I'm not going to tell you I'm doing it. I'm going to protect you from YOU, Mum, from your worrying.

Yeah, sure, I reply. *I can get the bus.*

Will you come alone?

Of course! I'll tell my mum I'm meeting Naomi in Twick or something. Genius plan. Even you can't say no to that.

Good. Good. Shall we say Saturday, eleven thirty?

Cool.

He rings off. I scream into my sleeve and throw myself on my bed. Oh my God. It's, like, an actual date. That's it. I'm actually going to see him – for real.

I text Naomi. She's cool. She's excited. She says I have to take a selfie with him. I don't tell you, obvs. I think of you though when we check my computer. I think of the way you make me say the rules out loud, as if I'm an idiot:

Do not make friends with someone you don't know.

Never agree to meet someone you've only got to know online.

If a teacher or an adult tries to befriend you, tell your main carer… blah blah…

But this is going to be broad daylight! There will be loads of people around! And I know girls in Year 11 that use Tinder and they're, like, fine. This girl Tash, she's been with her boyfriend for, like, six months and they met on Tinder, and she said he's really sweet. Ollie has over twenty Facebook friends in common with me and one of his friends is Stella Prince, and she's the coolest, most savvy, most dank girl ever. So I know I'll be fine.

I wait until Saturday morning to tell you. After breakfast, I pretend to check my phone and then, all casual, I'm like:

Oh, Mum, Naomi's saying she wants to meet. Can I?

You're in a good mood. You're going to hang out with Auntie Bridge. She is going to take you out for coffee too! She is going to buy you a bun the size of your head. Apparently.

That's fine, you say. *Where, what time?*

I am so ready for you.

Caffè Nerd. I say it fast because you don't hesitate when you tell the truth. We did that in drama.

Good, we know where to avoid, says Auntie Bridge, and winks at me. *Don't want these squirts ruining our image, do we, Tones? Embarrassing us in public when we're trying to dance. Not that I'd be seen dead in that fascist joint.*

Your face is weird, like you're giving Auntie Bridge some sort
of look.

All right, you say to me. *What time are you meeting her? And
what time will you be back?*

Half eleven. I'll be back by, like, three?

Nice try. You can be back at one, for lunch.

*I don't need lunch. I'm stuffed. I'll get, like, a muffin or something.
What about two o'clock?*

Now Auntie Bridge is giving you a look.

OK, two, you say. *But no later. If you're a minute late, it'll be a no
next time, all right? And don't forget your phone and your Zip card.*

Mu-um. For God's sake. I'm not stupid.

On the way there, I'm nervous because I haven't caught this exact
bus before and I can't remember how far down the high street the
café is and what if I miss the stop? In the end, I get off too early,
but it doesn't matter because I have Google Maps on my phone
and it's just a bit further down in a straight line. Actually it's easy.
Piece of piss, Auntie Bridge would say.

I cross at the crossing. I know it's the right crossing because
there's a gate to Bushy Park about a metre further on, which is what
Ollie said. I pass a church and a shop on the corner but by now
I'm, like, check me out, because I can see the café right there and
it's 11.29 a.m. See? I can do stuff on my own. I get to the café at
11.30 a.m. on the dot! What's genius about this plan is that you and
Auntie Bridge will never find out I'm not in Caffè Nerd, because
no way will Auntie Bridge let you go in there and spy on me.

Gene. Ee. Yus.

Inside the café, I look all around but I can't see Ollie or anyone
who looks like him. But he's got to come all the way from Kingston,
which is much further, and Saturday mornings are pretty busy
on the roads and there's always, like, roadworks and stuff. In the

corner of the café at the back there's a group of two families with four little kids between them, and a golden Labrador; in one window there's an old man with a bald head with, like, strands of hair going over the top and thick glasses reading a newspaper; in the other window, two women about your kind of age are having coffees and sharing a raisin Danish.

At the till, I order a hot chocolate.

'Sit,' the waitress says. 'I bring.'

She has a foreign accent; I think she is Polish or Romanian. I wish I was confident enough to talk to her so I could listen to her accent. The accents I can do so far are Scottish, French and Spanish, but Welsh is impossible, and when I try Polish, Auntie Bridge says I sound like the Count, which is some lame vampire puppet or something from the olden days, so that needs practice. Anyway I keep looking round in case Ollie arrives. I begin to worry he'll stand me up. Then I think he defo will.

What am I even doing here?

He's probs just stringing me along.

I've been an idiot.

I am an idiot.

I basically loop through those four thoughts, round and round. There's another waitress, with blue hair, thick black eyeliner and about ten piercings in her ears. She wears black jeans, black Docs and an old White Stripes T-shirt. She looks so cool in a way I could never be.

I sit down at the table next to the old man's. He has a pot of tea, not coffee. If Ollie checks through the window he'll be able to see me from there. The man smiles at me and I say hello, to be polite. He goes back to his paper: *The Times*. I'm hot in what I'm wearing so I take my jumper off and flap my T-shirt to cool myself down. Still Ollie isn't here. I check my phone. There are no messages.

The waitress comes over with my hot chocolate. I get the Wi-Fi code and go on Instagram. There are no messages on there either, nothing on Facebook, no texts. I like everyone's posts on Facebook.

After that, I go on Instagram and like everyone's posts on there as well. There are pictures of a gathering from last night. I didn't even ask you if I could go. What would be the point?

'I hope he's not stood you up,' says a man's voice. It's the old man. He's put down his paper and he's drinking his tea. He looks at me over the rim of his cup and his eyes crease up as if he's smiling.

'No.' I shouldn't answer, but it's rude not to and we're in a public place.

'I wouldn't wait too long,' he says. 'You don't want him to think he can walk all over you, do you?' He puts down his cup. 'Or is it a girlfriend?'

The way he says 'girlfriend' gives me the creeps. I know old people say girlfriend when they mean a friend that's a girl, but it sounds weird coming from him. His hair is greasy and the lenses of his glasses have dry spots of what looks like milk on them. I don't say anything. I sort of smile but go on my phone and pretend to scroll. I almost message Ollie but stop myself. I don't want to seem needy. It is 11.38 a.m. I've been stood up for defs. How embarrassing. I should've known. No way would someone as dank as him go for someone like me. He's probably got, like, a thousand girlfriends. He's probably one of those boys who like to have irons in the fire. That's what you call it when a boy or a girl keeps lots of people dangling by flirting with them just enough to make them think they have a chance but never actually committing. Sasha does that with boys so it makes sense that boys do it to girls. Sasha's a bit of a bitch, to be honest. What's the boy word for bitch? There isn't one because sexism.

I drink my hot chocolate. I check the window again.

Mistake. The old man is staring at me, and when I accidentally meet his eye he doesn't look away. It is 11.41 a.m. I'm just gonna leave. If that man follows me, I'll call Auntie Bridge. She will rescue me without telling you, is what I'm thinking. But then I remember that you and Auntie Bridge have gone for coffee together. You don't know where I am. You don't know where I am 'cos I didn't want you to know. Because I lied. I feel sick. I feel sick like when I had the auditions. My stomach cramps and for a minute I think I might actually *be* sick.

I stand up.

'Off so soon?' says the man. His eyes are red at the rims. He looks posh even though his hair strands are greasy. He is well spoken. But still.

'I've… I've got to go.' I'm still smiling, for God's sake. Still being polite. 'I just remembered, my mum is meeting me outside.' That sounds lame. It sounds like a lie. Which it is, obvs.

'Quite so. You'd better skedaddle.' He stands up. He puts on his coat and pats his pockets as if he's checking for his keys. Shit. Shit, man.

I throw my money on the table, walk quickly to the door. I get to the door before the man. I step out onto the street.

'Excuse me,' the waitress calls.

'I've left the money on the table,' I call back, but the door has already shut and I'm on the street. I look left and right but the traffic is heavy and I can't cross. I don't know which way to go.

The door opens again and the man steps out. Now we are both on the street. Whichever direction he goes, I will go the opposite way. I will not go into Bushy Park. No way. That would be suicide.

The door opens again. 'Hey.' It is the waitress.

'I left the money on the table,' I tell her. I want to tell her that the man is bothering me, but he hasn't actually done anything and I can't form the words. I can't, it feels too rude, and he's probably harmless – harmless and lonely.

'You forgot change.' She smiles, puts fifty pence in my hand. 'Thanks.'

She goes back inside. The door shuts. Inside the café one of the nice women throws back her head and laughs. The man hasn't moved. He is just kind of standing there looking all dithery.

'Rosie!' It's your voice. 'Rosie, love!' Your voice is calling me.

I turn away from the man. You and Auntie Bridge are coming up the street.

'Lovely day to you, dear.'

I turn back. The old man is walking away and I feel bad for thinking he was a pervert when he was probably just trying to talk to someone. He probably lives on his own, that's why he wants a bit of conversation, why he's got no one to tell him his glasses are dirty. He is already level with the zebra crossing. My heart is beating. The sun is in my eyes.

What are you doing here? you say. *I thought you were in Twickenham.*

I... I... Naomi changed her mind at the last minute.

You laugh. I can't believe you're being so relaxed. *How funny. We came here because we didn't want to cramp your style, didn't we, Bridge?*

I wanted to go to Caffè Nerd, says Auntie Bridge. *I wanted to come over and sing some popular show tunes to you both, but your mum said no. Boo, hiss.*

I put my hand to my forehead to block out the sun. The man is going through the gate to Bushy Park. He looks like he is talking on a phone. He doesn't look back. My legs feel like jelly even though nothing's happened. Nothing's actually happened.

So where's Naomi? you ask.

Oh, she cancelled.

What? You look like I've just told you she shat on my shoe or something. *Oh, that's not on. That's not on, is it, Bridge?*

It's OK, she texted. She went to meet her boyfriend. I feel a bit bad because I'm making Naomi out to be a flake, but she's not, she's really nice.

Oh, that's shoddy. Auntie Bridge is shaking her head. *You don't throw your mates over for a lad, no way. Come on, Squirt – let me buy you a hot chocolate.*

I just kind of nod and go into the café again, even though I don't want another hot chocolate. I want to go to Naomi's now and tell her about my epic fail, but I can't because I've just said she's seeing a boy. So it's a Saturday morning and the sun is shining and I'm having coffee with my mum and my auntie because I've been stood up by a hot guy who I thought actually gave a shit. But he didn't. I am so stupid. I am an idiot. When I get home I will delete him, unfriend, unfollow.

In the café, my phone reconnects to the Wi-Fi automatically, and two seconds later, a message flashes at the top of my screen. I have just enough time to read it before it disappears. It says, *You missed a call from OT.*

Ollie.

A red number 1 comes up on my voicemail. It's him; I know it is. I feel myself go bright red.

Hot chocolate, Squirt?

Er, yes. Yes please.

Are you all right, baby girl? That's you, saying that. You've got that face on, like I'm ill or something. *You look a bit hot and bothered. Are you upset about Naomi?*

What? No. No, I'm fine. I just… I need the loo actually. Won't be a sec.

I try not to run. Inside the cubicle, I lock the door and sit on the loo. My breath is coming fast. There is Wi-Fi in here too. I bring up voicemail. It's him it's him it's him. My whole body is hot and filled with butterflies except they feel more like bees TBH. I clamp the phone to my ear:

I just tried to call you. I can hear dogs woofing in the background. *I've gone to the wrong café. I've been waiting here for twenty minutes. I just this second checked with the waitress and she said I'm not in Thyme for Coffee; I'm in the High Street Café up the road. It's barely ten doors down. Christ, it's like a pound in here. I'm just waiting to pay then I'll come down. The waitress is taking ages. I hope you're still there.*

My insides feel like they're melting and fizzing all at once. Ollie didn't stand me up. He didn't stand me up at all. He was in the wrong café. Aw, he sounds so sweet, like he's really worried. He's sounds, like, proper upset. About me! And now… now… Oh my God, he's coming here. But you're here and Auntie Bridge is here and then you'll know that I was never meeting Naomi and I may as well lock myself in my room and throw away the key and get my meals delivered and pee in a bucket in the corner because *that's* how much of a prison I'll be in.

This is a disaster.

No time to text! I call him. He picks up after one ring.

Hello, Sexy Lady, he says, like he's talking and smiling at the same time. *Look, I'm on my way. I'm just paying. So, so sorry.*

I'm so relieved, I'm laughing. *It's OK, but you can't come—*

I'm paying right this moment, he interrupts me. *Are you still there?*

Yes. But no. I mean, yes I am, but no you can't come. Literally. My mum's here. And my auntie. I told them I was meeting my friend Naomi. They don't know about you, like, at all. My mum will go mad if she knows I've got a… if she knows I'm meeting a boy. I don't want to be, like, you know, savage and everything, but if she sees you she'll never let me meet you again.

There is silence.

Ollie?

You're right; I can't come, can I? This is all my fault. I should have known when you didn't appear…

I can practically feel him running his hands through his lovely quiffy hair. He sounds so disappointed. He sounds gutted.

I am happier than I can ever remember being in my whole. Entire. Life.

Don't worry about it, I say. *I could meet you next week instead?*

All right! Oh, he sounds so pleased! *Thank you for the second chance. I knew you were special. Next week, same time?*

Yes. Same time. But here, in this café, OK? And then I can go to the High Street Café and we'll do the whole thing in reverse.

He laughs. At my lame joke!

Till next week then?

Yeah, see you next Saturday.

OMG. I love him I love him I love him.

CHAPTER 38

BRIDGET

Bridget slides her key as quietly as she can into the back-door lock. It's late. Friday night, almost 1.30 a.m. Saturday morning then. A last glance across the backyard to the car park, to the black hulk of her van above the hedge. It's always silent when she gets home from a gig, and she's always done in. But she can never go to bed straight away. Too wired.

She eases the door open and lifts her guitar and amp inside. The kitchen is dark but for the night light her sister always leaves on for her. Bridget creeps across to the cupboard and pulls out the Glenmorangie – half a bottle left. She pours a small measure and steals back out onto the patio. She sits at the little metal garden table and rolls a special ciggie, lights it and gives a sigh like a smoke signal in the still of the night. She takes a swig of whisky, another drag, and feels the rush, the draining down of all that adrenalin.

The last plane has long gone over. No foxes screeching, no sirens, none of the muggy background noise that hums through the suburb's daylight hours. This is as near to silence as they ever get around here, and that's OK. By now, Rosie and Toni will have been asleep for hours. Early to bed, early to rise, that's her former scallywag little sister these days. So much easier to keep an eye on – a piece of piss, frankly, compared to the nightmare she was in her late teens, early twenties. God, she was tough! Never kept up with the social worker, never went to school, and then the drugs, Christ, the drugs, the alcohol, the boys who should have known better down at Yates's Wine Lodge, and later at Destiny's nightclub slash knocking shop. The times Bridget had to drive her clapped-out rust-bucket Renault 5 all the way to Watford to carry a plastered Toni out of the club, throw her into the back seat and take her home – hold her forehead while she puked, put her into the recovery position. Plastic bowl, glass of water, paracetamol. Even now, when she's had too much red, Toni still apologises for those times.

'You could have finished uni if it weren't for me,' she says. 'I ruined your life.'

What can Bridget say to that? Over the years she's given every reply she can think of.

It wasn't your fault. None of it was.

None of us really knew what we were doing, sis.

I could've finished uni if Uncle Eric had kept his cock in his trousers, you mean.

My life's fine. Don't worry about it.

It had to be me. Who else was it going to be?

Perhaps she should have said, 'Yes, you did. You were a fucking nightmare.'

But that's no truer than any of the others. And her sister is so strict with Rosie, sometimes Bridget throws it back at her. She can't help herself.

'Because of course you were tucked up in bed at nine every night at her age, weren't you, Tones?'

Toni tells her to shut up. 'It's different, Bridge. She has me and you. She doesn't have a mum who's off with her new boyfriend. She has a family who actually keep an eye on her, who actually give a shit. I want something better for her than I had, that's all. She won't be giving blow jobs for drug money, not on my watch.'

'I was only teasing.' Bridget is quick to know when she's gone too far. 'I want something better for her too.'

And they've done it. They've made something better for the kid despite everything. They've done brilliantly under the circs. They're not rich, they're not setting any career highs or living an Instagram life, but they are safe – they love each other. They're not totally unhappy.

'Bridge?' Toni. At the back door.

'Christ, you gave me a shock! I thought you were asleep.'

'Are you smoking weed?'

'It's flavoured tobacco. Herbal.'

Toni huffs and puffs in mock disapproval and comes out onto the patio. She has her nightie on, and her towelling robe, the sheepskin slippers that Bridget bought her for Christmas because she always has cold feet.

'Herbal, my arse.' Toni takes the joint from Bridget's fingers.

'Don't let your daughter see you doing that.'

'Have you got whisky too?'

'Yep. There's all sorts I get up to in the dead of night when you're in bed.' Bridget gets up, goes inside and brings another glass and the Glenmorangie from the kitchen.

Tones eyes the bottle with suspicion. 'Just a nip.'

'That's all you're getting, you cheeky sod. This is good stuff.'

Toni smiles and passes back the joint. 'You OK? Looked like you were miles away.'

'Yeah. Good gig actually. Good crowd.' Bridget tops up her own glass, glad of her sister's company. She'd have been falling into melancholy by now out here on her own. *Fallin' into maudlin*, as Helen says. Ah, Helen.

'Where was it?'

'The Crown. You know, Marble Hill, near the park, that little roundabout? Do you need a blanket? I can run and get you one.'

'No, it's OK. I'm warm. Do you mean where we took Rosie for her birthday lunch that time?'

'The very one. How far we've come from a bag of cheese and onion and a can of crap cola down the Hounslow Sports and Social, eh? Bag of dry roasted if you're lucky, sit quietly and we might let you chalk the cue. How's you anyway? Any curtain rings round willies to report?'

Toni sighs. 'Rosie's meeting Naomi for coffee again tomorrow.'

'That's OK, isn't it?'

'Yes. No. Yes. Just can't understand why she would go when Naomi blew her out only last week.'

'She's fifteen, Tones. I think kids are just flakier these days, that's all. If you can text someone, you can blow them out whenever you like, can't you? Nothing personal, it's just not like when we were kids, is it? Carrier pigeon would never have made it in time. And you can't stop her going for coffee with a mate.'

'I know.' Toni sips her whisky and gasps. 'Jeez, that's strong! How do you drink it?'

'Practice.'

Toni cradles the glass in her hands. The two of them stay a moment in silence, listening to nothing, looking at nothing.

'It's just…' Toni says then.

'What? Go on, you know you're going to say it, so you may as well.'

'You know last week she said she was going into Twickenham and then we bumped into her in Hampton Hill? Well, it's just she could have texted to say she was changing cafés, couldn't she? I don't know. There's something funny about it, don't you think?'

'No, I don't. She's a teenager. They're shit-for-brains. It's in the book.'

'But why wouldn't she text?' Tones ploughs on. It's better to let her. 'Why, when they have these expensive phones, can't they send a simple text? It's almost as if she wanted to go somewhere in secret. Do you think she's keeping secrets?'

'I should hope so. She's fifteen. Look at you, smoking joints like you're Chrissie Hynde or someone in your own back garden. You're not going to tell her that, are you?'

Toni tips back her head and exhales heavily, a plume of smoke rising into the dark blue night. She is amused – Bridget can tell by the set of her mouth, but she's not letting on. 'That's completely different. I'm a grown-up.'

They drink in silence. One more toke each and the joint is dead. Bridget throws it onto the patio and crushes it under her boot.

'I'll pick that up, don't worry,' she says, and then, 'Listen, it's only a coffee. And it's in broad daylight. So what if she is meeting a boy? So what if she's not telling you? Is that really the end of the world? Don't you remember all that, how exciting it was?'

'It wasn't really, not for me.'

'No, I get that. But later, when you met Stan? You were like a kid then.'

Toni smiles, at last. 'I was.'

'You didn't even tell *me*.'

'Only for a week. And I was busy.'

'Busy. That's what you're calling it, is it?'

On cue, in the darkness, the foxes are off, screeching their sex life like insensitive, rampant neighbours. Those poor females, Bridget thinks. But at least the sound is rural, somehow. And now the planes have stopped, they could be in the countryside. If the stars weren't hidden by the orange glow of street lighting, if the 33 bus hadn't just shuddered on by, if they couldn't see the looming mass of suburban houses blacker than the black sky, yes, they could be in the countryside. Almost.

'Do you think foxes have orgasms?' she asks.

Toni laughs. 'More than us, I bet.'

'Everyone has more than us, Tones. If I don't count the ones I have on my own.'

Toni laughs. 'Thanks for that.'

'You're welcome.'

The screeching stops. Another bus out on the main road. Feeling her muscles stiffen, Bridget shifts in her seat. 'We've come a long way, the three of us.'

'We have. Rosie with her two mums.'

'You're her mum, Tones.'

'You're ours. You look after us both.'

'Don't think it's as clear-cut as that.' Bridget stands and stretches. When she rolls her arms, her back gives a crack. 'We look after each other,' she says. 'And you, my love, need to go to bed.'

CHAPTER 39

TONI

I can't get hold of Bridget or Emily and now my phone's on red. I should save any scrap of battery for incoming calls, I suppose. Brilliant – just brilliant. I don't think I've ever felt so lonely, and God knows I've felt so much loneliness there was a time when I wondered if I'd feel anything else. Where is Bridge? I suppose she might well have crashed out – it's been an exhausting – not to mention traumatic – twelve hours. But what if something has happened? What if someone has come after *her*? No. I mustn't think like that. I've no idea where Emily is either. What has happened to them both?

That's a point. What if something bad has happened to Emily *and* Bridget?

Oh, Rosie. Sometimes I wonder whether once you start with trouble, it is so very difficult to stop. Sometimes I think it started with our dad leaving us. If Dad hadn't left Mum – let's face it, if he hadn't laid into her every time he'd had a skinful – we wouldn't have had to move in with Grandad and Granny. If Uncle Eric hadn't lived there… My mum, your granny Casement, didn't believe in luck. *You make your own luck*, she used to say, and I agree, to a point. But sometimes life can throw you into a hole, and no matter how many times you try to crawl out, the ground slips, you lose your footing, you're dragged back in. Your dad, my Stan, he was the one who pulled me out of that hole for good,

Rosie. He pulled me out and held me until the hole filled and the ground was safe again.

But of course, through no fault of yours or mine or his, we lost him. Another hole blown beneath us, the two of us tumbling down. I became overprotective – I see that, of course I do. I saw it even before this, but I couldn't help it. Perhaps when something really bad happens, the reason you can't stay out of the hole is because you keep throwing yourself back in without knowing it.

Thinking about it, I'm guessing that the Saturday before last, when your auntie Bridge and I bumped into you on Hampton high street, you were supposed to be meeting him, weren't you? And I'm thinking that you wouldn't have done that in secret if I hadn't been so protective, do you see where I'm going? I threw us back in the hole, Rosie. Me. If I'd been normal, you could have been normal too. If your dad had been here, he would have helped me to be normal, but he couldn't help, could he, because… because he *isn't* here. He *isn't* here any more.

Oh God, I'm tying myself up. I can't stop thinking about how shocked you were to see us; how shocked I was to see you there, not where you'd said you'd be. What did you do – text him to warn him away? Or did you spot us through the café window and he sneaked out through the back? I remember you looked very hot and bothered and you went to the loo. Did you text him from there? Did you talk to him? Was he in there with you?

No, of course he wasn't, what am I saying?

If only I'd seen him that day. I would have known. I would have realised. I wouldn't have recognised him from your hundreds of Facebook friends, would I? Of course not. But if I'd seen him, I would have known immediately. I could have saved you. As it was, we saved you that time but only enough to put you in danger once again. Your auntie Bridge said there's no way we could have known. She said there's no way any parent can keep tabs on everything their kids are up to. All we can do is tell you to stick to the path and trust that you won't stray into the wood. And at the end of the day, it's about trust, isn't it? I thought you trusted me, but I suppose now I realise that trust is like respect: if you want someone to trust you, you have to trust them in return. I didn't trust you to stick to the path. You saw that. And to shake me off, you strayed into the wood.

Thank God I trusted my instincts that following Saturday though. My God, can it really only be this morning? That's enough to make my head explode. I think I got suspicious because I couldn't understand why you would agree to meet Naomi again after she'd stood you up only the previous week.

'Oh, Mum, you don't get teenagers,' you said. 'We're not like adults. We don't get all stressy about things like that. Stop putting your old-person stuff onto my social life.'

I stood corrected but something didn't square up. I can't put my finger on what it was, but I got the feeling you were lying to me.

'When did you say you were meeting her?'

You shrugged and looked at your trainers. 'Same.'

'Same what? Place? Do you mean Caffè Nero or that Thyme place?

'Time? Eleven thirty.'

'Don't be smart with me, young lady.'

'I'm not.'

'So what time?'

'Thyme for Coffee.'

I almost slapped you. I almost wrapped my hands around your neck. 'Don't be so bloody cheeky. You know what I mean! What time are you meeting her?'

'Eleven thirty. I just said, didn't I? God, Mum, you are *so* controlling. You're suffocating me. I literally can't breathe.'

'And this is you asking if you can go? This is your attitude, is it?'

'You already said I could go! Oh my God, you can't change your mind, it's not fair.'

I grabbed you by the zip of your hoody. Oh my love, I actually grabbed hold of you. What was I thinking? I wasn't – that's the point. I'd, as you would say, *lost it.*

'I can change my mind any time I like, young lady,' I said. 'I can change my mind and do you know why? Because you're fifteen, you are a child, you are *my* child, and I'm a grown-up and I'm your mother and if I say you can't go then you can't, do you understand?'

You met my gaze, your eyes like coals.

'Why won't you just fuck off?' You shouted this into my face. 'I hate you.'

And before I'd even had time to process the words that had come out of your mouth, you turned and ran down the hall. You grabbed your rucksack and jacket from the coat hook. You left.

I hate you.

That's the last thing you said to me.

CHAPTER 40

BRIDGET

Bridget is still in bed when she hears them arguing, hears the slam of the front door. It's 10.30 a.m. Probably should be getting up anyway; got to feed Helen's cat for one.

She finds Toni in the kitchen, her face flushed, her eyes red. 'Went well then?'

'She's impossible. Bloody impossible.' Two tears trickle down her sister's cheeks, but they're tears of frustration and they're running out of steam. 'And I made a mess of it as usual. I just… My senses are tingling, Bridge. I can *feel* that something is wrong. She wouldn't look me in the eye. And then she just flew off the handle about absolutely nothing.'

'Oh dear.' Bridget touches the flat of her hand against the kettle. It's hot – there's enough water for coffee.

'She said she hated me.' Toni's voice is high and frail. 'She told me to F off, Bridge.'

'Parents fall out with teenagers all the time, Tones. It's in the manual.'

'But you don't fall out with her. She doesn't tell you she hates you, does she?'

'That's a different dynamic, isn't it?'

'You always say that.' The pain shows on Toni's face; her cheeks sag and she looks so tired. Poor thing. If Bridget had a magic wand, she would wave it, she really would. She'd have waved it a long time ago. She tweaks her sister's nose like she used to when they still lived in Benson Close.

'Thing is,' she says, 'I am much, much cooler.'

This works, to a degree. Toni manages a smile at least. And at least she talks things through instead of walking round with a sword through her neck saying she's fine, like that meme Rosie showed her. And she's talking now, nodding when Bridget holds up the coffee jar. She tells Bridget that she's shaken – by the coals in her daughter's eyes, by the way she ran from the house.

'Biscuit?' Bridget asks.

Toni shakes her head. 'I know you think I'm being neurotic, but I know something is not right.'

'You're fretting about nothing. Honestly, she'll be back here in two hours like the cat that got the cream. If you act casual, she'll probably tell you everything. Maybe you should try telling her something about yourself, you know, from when you were young.'

'You think so?'

'Yeah.' Bridget has no idea, but what else is there to say? 'Edited, obviously. Maybe leave the crystal bongs out for now.'

After coffee, while Toni's in the shower, Bridget texts Saph, who she was meant to be meeting later this morning.

Tones not in a good way. Gonna hang out here this morn. Soz, mate.

No prob. Love to u both. Drink later?

Maybe. I'll text, but if u get a better offer, go for it.

No such thing as a better offer than u, babe.

Bridget smiles. Saph is straight as an arrow, but she's the world's biggest flirt.

The water is still running. Bridget decides to clean the top row of cupboards while she waits. It's at least a year since she last did them. There are some jobs that have stayed hers, and this is one. After the accident, she did everything, pretty much. It was the only thing that made sense. There was no way she could have seen Rosie go to a childminder, not under those circumstances. It was easy enough to build freelance work around the 3.20 p.m. pick-up, and there were one or two mums in the playground who weren't too bad. Some of them were fucking torture though, with their wooden heads swivelling on their wooden necks, their blonde hair, their smiles thick, as if they had something unsavoury stuck in their teeth.

'I'm sorry, are you Rosie's mummy?'

Mummy? What are we, ten? 'No, I'm her aunt. I'm Toni's sister.'

The slow nod, the step back. The mouth fighting to stay in shape. They all knew about the accident. But tragedy is in poor taste when there's a summer fayre to organise, organic carrot batons to hand to their children. No, that's not fair. Bridget was in a bad place then, she knows that. They were just people, people as fucked up and insecure as anyone else. They meant well. Maybe they didn't. Who cares? That whole time was chaos. She meant to leave Helen cleanly, set her free, but she's not even managed that, and now here they are, years later, and not a week has passed without them seeing one another. Bridget knows that if she ever met anyone else, she could never tell Helen, and if there was even one thing she couldn't tell her, then everything between them would be lost.

And so, abstinence.

Abstinence makes the heart grow fonder.

CHAPTER 41

ROSIE

I hate you. That's the last thing I said to you.

I can't move my mouth. But I'm telling you I don't hate you. I love you, Mummy. Mum? Are you still there? I need to tell you…

I'm in my bedroom. I know when this is! It's today, this morning. I'm going to meet Ollie in, like, an hour. I'm trying on outfits. My phone is ringing. Emily's rosy apple face is on the screen.

Hi, Emily.

Hello there, dear. Lovely out, isn't it? A real corker.

Dunno. I've not been out yet.

Quite right. What kind of teenager worth their salt is even out of bed at this ungodly hour, n'est-ce pas? She chuckles, and I laugh too because she is such a wally. I love her but she's pretty batshit, to be honest, and I really want to look nice for Ollie so I'm like:

I'm going out in a minute, Emily.

Right you are! I hope he's handsome! More chuckles. Batshit on speed, no word of a lie. Why do old people always assume you're going to meet your boyfriend… *sweetheart* in old language. *Well now, I'll be brief. The reason I'm phoning is that I was wondering if you feel ready for another audition? I don't want to rush you, but remember we talked about trying to get on top of this nasty nervous sicky business.*

I'm not sure, I say. *My mum's been saying we should think about leaving it for a while, until I'm older.*

Yes, yes, dear. Of course, it's up to you. I'll drop the notes over anyway and you can see how you feel. Are you in today?

I'll be in this afternoon. I know you'll make me be back by then. Because psycho Mum.

Jolly good. Now, off you go and I'll catch up with you later, all right? Just have a think about it and let me know what you decide. Toodle-oo for now.

OK, I say. *Bye, Emily.*

You're in the kitchen. Yeah, this is defo today. I'm wearing my black skinny jeans with rips and my Docs and my white crop top with a kiwi fruit on it. I'm coming to tell you that Emily's going to bring some notes over later, even though I know you'll tell me off for the top. I bought it online and you won't like it 'cos it shows my belly, but all of my friends wear tops like this, literally all of them, and they haven't even got sick abs like mine. I'm about to tell you but then you freak out on me. I'm trying to tell you something, I'm trying to talk to you – you know, communicate? And you start going on about Naomi even though we've already arranged all that and you're not listening. As usual.

I hate you. I only say it because that's how I feel in that moment. I love you even when I hate you. You're my mum, for flip's sake. But you're doing my head in, and I've had enough. I just want to meet my boyfriend. I don't care about you and your fussing and who's a flake and who's not.

I'm sorry for saying that now.

I'm so sorry, Mum.

And I'm sorry for telling you to F off, obvs – that was way harsh.

But… even that's not the big thing. There's something bigger and the shame of it is making me feel sick. What have I done, Mummy? Why can't I remember? What have I done?

On the bus, I start to feel bad that I haven't told you about Ollie. I've wanted to. But I want to meet him so badly, Mummy. I want to meet him more than I want to tell you. I want a bit of life that's mine – do you get that? If I'd told you I was meeting an older boy, you so would have stopped me. I haven't even told Auntie Bridge because I was worried she'd tell you. And Mum? If you'd seen him, you'd have seen that he's so fun and so hot. I'm in love with him, Mummy. I'm in total, deep love with him.

But there's something bad in my gut and it has to do with him, I can feel it. I've done something worse than all the lying. Something worse than telling you I hate you or even telling you to F off. But I can't figure it out. It's here on the edge of the soup; it's down in the dark water, floating in the weeds. It's got something to do with the back of the van. The smell in my nose and the tape on my mouth. And the smell of baking. And the van door opening and the light. And the figure… Auntie Bridge? But that doesn't make sense with this fear that fills up my insides every time I remember it. It's something, it's someone, but it's not Ollie. It can't be Ollie. I can see Ollie, I can, but it's not… it's not… it's only a photograph.

I'm getting near the bad thing. I'm coming up, Mummy. I can see light above the soup water. The weeds are clearing. My mouth opens but my heart blocks my throat. I can't scream. There is no sound. I am covered in sweat. Sweat in my hair. It runs down the sides of my head, my body. I am in the café. I am at the counter. The girl is putting cups on the shelf behind the till. It is 11.25 a.m. There is a smell of coffee and bacon. It's coming. The bad thing is coming towards me. My body fills with heat.

'Decided to give him another chance, eh?'

I swing round. The bald man from last week is in the window seat. His newspaper is on the table and he is pouring his tea. He looks up as if it wasn't him who spoke just now, but I know it was. I recognised his voice. The light bounces off his dirty glasses. Outside a red bus thunders past.

I glance away, willing the girl on the till to stop putting cups on the shelf and look at me. Look at me look at me look at me… The heat in my body gets hotter. A line of sweat runs down the side of my forehead.

The girl stops doing the cups and turns to me.

Hello, she says in her accent. *Hot chocolate?* She smiles; this means she remembers me from last week. I wish I knew her better. I wish she was my friend. If she was my friend I would say, *Help me.*

Yes, I say. *Thank you.*

Take seat. I bring.

OK.

It is OK. It is OK because it's broad daylight. There are lots of people around and this time Ollie knows which café I'm in. Ollie knows where I am. He will save me. He knows me. He loves me.

I go and sit at the back of the café on the other side of the bar. It is as far away as possible from the baldy man. I know he's just, like, some lonely old man who thinks he's being friendly, but I don't want him to talk to me. There are nice leather sofa seats here and a low coffee table. I can't see the man from where I'm sitting. Even if he's a total perv, it's not like he can, like, pull me into a van and drive off with me from here, is it? But my heart is beating fast.

Hot chocolate. The Polish girl smiles at me as she puts my drink on the table.

Thank you, I say.

She walks away before I can say any more – before I can say, *Help me.*

The sweat dries on my face. I rub at the sides of my eyes and it flakes off, soft and salty. I lick it from my fingers. I go to check my phone. It's not in my bomber-jacket pocket. I open my rucksack and root around. My purse, my iPod Shuffle, a packet of tissues, half a packet of cherry menthol chewing gum, my lip salve. Where is my iPhone? Where is it?

I was going to put it in my bag but then I saw it needed to go on charge, and after Emily called I left it there because it was only, like, sixty per cent. After our fight, I ran out of the house. I grabbed my bag from the hook and I ran because I knew you'd never catch me. I thought my phone was in my bag. But it wasn't – it was still on charge.

Shit.

My phone is in my room.

It's in my room on my desk. I left it there when I went to talk to you in the kitchen. I was going to go back. I wasn't planning to run out. But you didn't listen to me. You were going on about Naomi. And then I ran out. I grabbed my bag and I ran out. It's your fault I don't have my phone.

Where do you think he's got to, eh?

The baldy man is standing at my table. His newspaper is folded under his arm. He is wearing pale jeans and his shoes are black leather and they look like those special comfortable shoes that old people wear. He still has little whitish dots of what looks like dried milk on his glasses.

He's on his way, I reply. I don't know what else to say. I don't look at him. I just want him to go away.

You look hot, he says. *It is awfully hot in here, isn't it? We should go outside and wait for this fellow of yours. We could wait in the park.*

We. Park. What?

It's OK. I'm OK, thanks. My hot chocolate is a weird shade of brown, almost purple. I blow on it and it ripples like old skin.

Are you sure you don't want to take the air? I could wait with you until lover boy gets here.

Lover boy. Gross. Where is the girl? I can hear the steamer heating up the milk. Where is the other girl? The one with the blue hair? I can't speak.

I'll join you here if you don't mind. No fun being lonely, is it? He sits next to me on the sofa. I can feel the heat from his body. I can smell the grease on the thin strands of his hair, the oil on his skin. His leg is almost touching my leg. He pats my thigh and says, *Ollie won't be long.*

My heart is in my throat. There is a buzz in my ears. How does he…

Hello, Sexy Lady. His voice is lighter, higher, younger. It is a voice I recognise.

Who are you?

He laughs, leans in close to me. *Don't you know? I'm Ollie.*

CHAPTER 42

BRIDGET

It's 11.30 a.m. when Toni comes out of the shower. Bridget hopes the warm water has relaxed her, returned her to herself. Standing there on the chair, soapy cloth in hand, she stops cleaning and listens. Hears her sister in the hallway – hears that she doesn't go into her own room, which is next to the bathroom, but further on, to Rosie's room. Bridget can hear this because the door hinges squeak. She has been meaning to fix this for weeks and makes a mental note to fetch the WD40 from the shed later and get it sorted today. There's no reason for Toni to go into Rosie's room, no laundry to deliver; the washing machine's still churning the week's dirt out of Rosie's school uniform, and, at fifteen, she is expected to hoover her own room and keep it tidy. In theory.

But Bridget doesn't wonder even for a moment why her sister has gone into Rosie's room. She knows why.

Resisting the urge to call out, to save Toni from herself, Bridget carries on with her spring clean, singing one of The Promise's songs to block out the noise of drawers opening and shutting, the sound of her niece's privacy being invaded.

> *You and me, you and me, in deep water, baby*
> *You and me, you and me, two in the pack*
> *You and me, you and me, to the slaughter, baby*
> *Like lambs to the wolf, there's no going—*

'Bridge.' Toni is at the kitchen door. She's dressed, but her hair is wet, combed back from her face. She hasn't put on any make-up yet and her face is still a little puffy. She looks exhausted. In her hands she holds a yellow iPhone 5C.

'Is that Squirt's phone?' Funny how, in these moments, we ask questions we already know the answer to.

Toni nods. 'She left it on charge. I know you're going to say no, but I think we should check it.'

From the cupboard top, a thick clump of grey fluff, made entirely from dust, floats down to the floor. Bridget climbs down from the chair, crosses over to where Toni is sitting and takes the phone from her. 'But I thought you checked it regularly?'

'I do, but…'

'You're going to find something you don't like,' Bridget says quietly. 'You know that, don't you?'

'What makes you say that?'

'Because that's what happens when you snoop around in other people's affairs, Tones. Come on. How would you feel if I checked through your phone? Or your diary?'

'You could check through my phone any time. There's nothing exciting on it anyway. Messages from you, mostly. I should imagine checking through my phone would be the most boring thing anyone could do, to be honest. Not like I have much of a life, is it? I haven't even been to the pub since…' She looks up, finally. Her eyes are shining, rimmed as if in red eye pencil. When she blinks, they overflow.

Bridget feels more sorry for her than she can put into words. Even if she knew how to phrase what she feels now, she would not say it. She wants to throw her arms around her sister's neck and ask, *How can I fix you?* but right now, at this moment, it would be like trying to hold a bramble.

'It's not right, Tones,' she says softly.

'But she ran out before I...' Toni sobs, looks desperately out of the kitchen window, as if by some miracle her daughter will come bounding across the patio, all smiles. 'And I can't text her because she doesn't have her phone.' She looks around the kitchen then, as if searching for something. 'I think I'll drive to the café. I won't go in. I'll just drive past slowly and see if I can spot her. Or I could go in and say, hey, you forgot your phone.'

'Don't do that.'

'Or I could text Naomi, couldn't I? Say, hey, I know you're with Rosie so can you tell her she's forgotten her phone? Her number will be in here. In fact, I've got Naomi's number in *my* phone, I could call her from mine...'

Bridget feels a tightening around her heart. 'Look, why don't you and me go into Richmond instead? We can go for coffee in that new Danish place. Saph said the cakes in there are better than sex. We could have one each and see if we can remember far enough back to compare.'

'Don't.'

'Don't what?'

'Stop trying to make me laugh.' Toni's mouth presses tight before she opens it again. She breathes sharply in, as if to make an announcement. 'You can't joke me out of this. Either you help me check this phone, or I'm getting in my car and I'm going to see if she's really where she said she'd be.' She looks into Bridget's eyes.

'Hold on, wait a second. What do you need me for anyway? If you want to check it, then check it.'

'I... Come on, Bridge. You know more about these things than me.'

Bridget turns away. She throws her cloth into the bucket of soapy water, leans her hands on the countertop, one on each side of the sink. Behind her, her sister sniffs. In the quiet flat, Bridget hears the thrum of a plane as it passes overhead. Over thirty years ago, she and her sister made a pact. And there was, there is and there will forever be no going back.

She turns from the sink to see Toni weeping determinedly, elbows on the table, face in her hands.

'All right,' she says. 'Give it here then.'

It is quarter to twelve. Bridget sits down next to her sister. There is no justification for doing what she is about to do, and part of her feels dirty even holding the damn phone. So she hands it to her sister.

'You go as far as you can. If you get stuck, I'll help, all right?'

Toni inputs Rosie's password. The neat square apps bloom in orderly rows on the screen: Weather, Messages, Calendar, Photos, Camera, Clock, Maps, Videos…

'This is wrong,' Bridget mutters.

'Please, Bridge. Just sit with me, will you?'

Safari, Mail, Phone, Facebook.

Toni presses the Facebook icon. Immediately, Rosie's feed comes up in white, the familiar blue band across the top. On the globe icon there is the red notification flag: 15. Fifteen, like her age, like a ranking on this silly little world.

'I've checked through her friends,' she says. 'I mean, I don't know all of them, there's hundreds, but there's no one dodgy-looking, none of her teachers or school staff or anything; I checked against the staff list, including the caretakers.'

Bridget wishes Toni would shut up – leave her out of it. She no longer wants to put her arms around her. She would prefer, frankly, to wring her neck.

'So you're going to access her private messages? She'll know you've checked her phone if you do that – you know that, don't you?'

Her sister is biting her thumbnail and blinking over and over like she has sand in her eyes.

'I have to,' she says. 'That's the whole point.'

In an attempt to slow things down, in the hope that her sister will see sense, Bridget leans back in her chair. 'OK. Let's just scroll forward a second. What if you find a message from a boy? What then? Have you thought about that? She's fifteen years old. She can have a boyfriend, can't she?'

'I'm not saying she can't.' Toni's voice rises. 'But she needs to know she can't do that without telling me, or there'll be consequences. She needs to tell me the truth.'

Bridget regrets having said anything. Regrets being here. She should have gone to Saph's.

'Otherwise how can I look after her?' Toni continues, her voice as high as a child's. 'How can I protect her, Bridge, if I don't know where she is or who she's with?'

Bridget thinks of herself at that age, and all that she had to hide, the consequences if any of it had come out, and even after so many years, a wave of anxiety passes through her.

'OK,' Toni says, eyes fixed on the phone. 'There's a message from Naomi. I'll just…' She presses the icon.

Despite herself, Bridget leans in to her sister and reads the screen.

Rosie Flint
Hey babes. Can u do me a fave? Can you tell your mum you're meeting me on Sat morn? In case my mum checks? Gritted-teeth emoji. Kissing-lips emoji.
Thursday 23.30
Naomi Philips
Ooh. Is it Ollie? Yes BTW. But text me after. I wanna know all the deets. Winking-face emoji.
Thursday 23.35

'Oh my God,' Toni shouts at the phone. 'That's this Thursday just gone. She's not meeting Naomi today. I was right – I was bloody right. She's… she's been deceiving me all this time. Hang on, what's this one…?'

Naomi Philips
Hey doll, wanna meet up this morning?
19 May
Rosie Flint
Hey Nomes. Nah. Because homework. Frowning-face emoji.
19 May

Unease rises in Bridget, thickens.

'The nineteenth,' Toni says, her voice loud in Bridget's ear. 'That's last Saturday. So she wasn't meeting Naomi then either. I bloody knew it.'

'Tones, wait. It's not the end of the world. She's probably—'

'There's no probably, Bridge. Stop sticking up for her. You're always sticking up for her. She's meeting a boy, and she hasn't told me.'

'All right, all right.' Bridget snatches up the phone. 'Calm down, Tones. Just calm down.'

'What's that message?' Toni grabs the phone and stares into it. 'What's this one? Who's Ollie Thomas?'

'How should I know?'

'Has she mentioned him to you? Is he from the theatre?'

'I… I can't remember. How could I possibly remember? Look, let's see what his message says and then we'll have a think, OK?'

Toni puts the phone in front of them on the table. There is an exchange of messages with this Ollie Thomas. Even from his tiny thumbnail picture Bridget can see he is good-looking. A real heart-throb, if you like that sort of thing.

> *Ollie Thomas.*
> *Gr8 to c u over here on FB. Do you have Snapchat yet?*
> *18 May 2016*

> *Rosie Flint*
> *Cool. No Snapchat cos CBA. Also, my mum's a FB friend so… Gritted-teeth emoji.*
> *18 May 2016*

> *Ollie Thomas*
> *DW… I've come off Snapchat anyway. Too busy. Better 2 PM you on Insta instead if u worried about ur mum? Gritted-teeth emoji. Monkey-covering-eyes emoji.*
> *18 May 2016*

> *Rosie Flint*
> *Cool. Thumbs-up emoji. Monkey-covering-eyes emoji.*
> *18 May 2016*

'May 2016!' Toni cries. When she speaks again, it is through her fingers. 'That's a year ago! What does he mean, over here? What does that mean?'

'I don't know yet,' Bridget replies quietly, chastened. 'I don't know.'

CHAPTER 43

ROSIE

In the café, his breath on my face. His face in my face. His dirty glasses make me feel sick, Mummy. Can you hear me? I can feel you near. I am here in the café but it's not now, it's… When is this? When am I? I am today. I am this morning. I am now. I am in two moments in time, travelling but not travelling. Being. I can feel the pillow under my head. I can see the water above me… I am lying under the dark, the weeds… the hard seat hurts my bottom… not enough padding, you say… when do you say that? Did you hear me say that to myself? My mouth is dry, Mummy, but I'm not thirsty. He is sitting too close too close too close. I want to call you, Mummy… you are near but you are foggy. I can't shout to you. I can't call you. I left my phone in the… I ran out in a rage… You are such a pain, you won't leave me alone. I was so pissed off with you, but now I need you and I can't call you. You're always nagging me to call, and I don't want to have to call all the time but now I do – I do want to call and I do have the time, but I can't call because I left my phone in the flat I can't I can't I can't. Mummy, help me, help me, help me escape from this horrible man. He's saying he's Ollie. He's not Ollie, he's someone else – he's an old man and his glasses are dirty and he's making me feel sick.

The man smiles. *I sense you're disappointed, which is a shame. I'm really rather a nice chap if you get to know me. I like your jeans,*

*by the way. Is that the fashion, to have the rips and the holes in them
like that?* He chuckles like an old man. He *is* an old man.

You're not... what have you done to Ollie?

The girl from the till comes over. The man smiles at her and
asks her how she is. She replies *OK* but her eyes are dead like she's
bored. I try to talk to her with my eyes, Mum. *Help me*, I try to
say. I really try, Mummy, but I can't speak. I can't speak. Is this
now or then? Where are you, Mummy? Are you outside the café
with Auntie Bridge? No. No, you're not because that's last week
and this is today. Today – this morning. I'm opening my mouth
but no voice comes out. The girl looks at my hot chocolate, but
when she sees that the cup is still half full, she walks away.

Come back, I shout to her with my eyes. *Come back, come back.*

What's the matter, Sexy Lady? Cat got your tongue?

I have to do someth— I have to... I have to move get out run
away. Come on, Rosie. Come on. Get your arse off the chair for
fuck's sake and run. Run, Little Red, run.

*I must say, I feel like you're cross with me about something. Are
you sending me to Coventry, young lady? After all the encouragement
I've given you?*

I... I have to go, I've got a... a thing. I have to be... sorry.

*So soon? Why not stay a while longer? We can chat. You can get to
know me better. It seems a shame not to spend a little time together
after we've got to know each other so well. You've grown up through
knowing me, don't you agree? You're more confident now. I think if we
talked you'd learn that beauty is only skin deep and that a man like
me actually has a great deal to offer. Experience, for one.* He leans
forward. *Tell me, are you wearing that wonderful red nail varnish
on your toes?*

What has he done with Ollie? He has killed him! Oh God, he
has killed Ollie and stolen his phone and hacked into his computer.
He has seen my... he has seen my... oh God.

I pick up my bag. I thread my arms through my jacket sleeves. *My mum's waiting outside*, I say.

Is she, dear? I don't think so. That was last week, wasn't it? You're getting all muddled. We're doing so much better this week, aren't we? Last week you left and before we had the chance to chat, we were interrupted by your mummy.

There is no Ollie.

It hits me like a kick in the chest.

People do this. Fake profiles. We learnt about it in PSHE. Oh, Mummy, you will be so cross with me. This is the bad thing. I think this is it. I don't get away, do I? He takes me and ties me up in his van. It's not Auntie Bridge's van. It's his. He throws me in the back and drives off with me. I remember the tin space, banging my arms, my head. It's him, standing in the light when the door opens. It's him ripping the tape from my mouth. He knows everything. He knows everything because I have told him everything. Me. I did that. I gave him that. Everything. Idiot!

Am I dead? Am I dead, Mummy? Is this heaven's waiting room? *What's the matter, cat got your tongue?*

He is leaning towards me. His breath smells. What should I do, Mummy? Keep it nice – stop it from turning nasty? Keep it safe and nice. Shout? I can't shout. I want to, but I can't.

It was nice meeting you, but I… I really have to go now.

When I get home, I will tell you everything. I am so sorry I lied. I am so, so sorry. This is what I am sorry about. Yes, this is the nasty thing.

I get up. My legs shake.

He gets up too. *Perhaps a walk in the park would be better, what do you say?*

No! I mean, sorry, I… I actually have to go home.

Then at least let me pay for your hot chocolate. I wouldn't be much of a gentleman if I didn't pay for your drink on our date, would I?

I've already paid, thanks. I back away. He stays at the table, thank God.

I turn away from his horrible big blinking eyes, his dirty glasses. I try not to run. I walk quickly towards the door. The girl on the till isn't even looking; she is serving someone, chatting, smiling. The other girl, with the blue hair, is at the back, putting cooked breakfasts on big white oval plates onto a crowded table. The café is noisy but no one is even looking at me. How can this be happening in front of everyone? In daylight? In this nice, busy place? Why can't I ask for help, Mummy? Why can't I tell him to leave me alone? Why can't I shout to her, the girl with the blue hair? To the four women who have just come in, laughing together? To the Polish girl on the till? They would help. Blue-hair girl would be cool. What is wrong with me? Why can't I tell her what's happening? It is broad daylight. Why can't I speak out?

If I get outside, I will be OK. I will get the bus.

No, I won't, because he could get on the bus too, and if no one else gets off at my stop or if there's no one out on our road, I will be toast.

I will walk home.

No, I won't. He could follow me, wait until we are alone, until there is an alley or a quiet street or a doorway, and just push me into it, quick, while no one is looking.

I will call you, and if you don't answer, I'll call Auntie Bridge. No, I can't, can I? I've left my phone in the flat.

I will walk… around. Just around. I will stay here on the high street where there are people. I will do my breathing, like before a performance. It is broad daylight. Do re mi fa so la ti do.

I will calm myself down. I will go into a shop and politely ask to use their phone. If he follows me in, I will say, *This man is not my father, I don't know him, he is following me. Help. Help me. Call the police.*

Beep beep… Is that you? Is that you, Mummy?

I step out onto the street. The light hurts my eyes. I feel the door behind me not quite close, open again. It's him. I know it without having to turn around. I can *feel* him. My mouth is dry. I am gulping. I am moving my tongue around, trying to create spit.

Heavens, you are in a hurry, young lady.

Beep beep…

I turn left, walk towards the crossing. I will not cross. I will not go into the park or near the park gate. I will walk slowly. I will do my breathing. Do re mi fa so la ti do.

There are people on the pavement. There are couples, there are families with dogs, little kids in buggies. I smile at them. A mum smiles back. A kid eating a croissant in his buggy waves at me. I wave. I smile. Can't they see the sweat on my face? Can't they see him behind me, talking to me like he knows me?

Good idea, he is saying. *A brisk stroll around the town on this fine Saturday morn. I don't often get out, you see. This is quite a treat.*

It's OK; it's OK. I will calm myself. I will do my breathing. There is a church on the left just before the crossing. There are old people outside selling plants and second-hand books. I will buy a second-hand book! Or a plant. I will buy you a plant, Mummy, to say sorry. You love plants. I will ask them, politely…

Hey, slow down, he says from behind me. *Don't you want to stroll in the park with me? It's such a lovely day and so crowded here.*

Beep beep…

Calm. Breathe. I will pretend to buy a geranium here at this nice church. You love geraniums, Mummy. I'll buy one and I'll whisper to the lady with the short grey hair: *This man is following me. Help. Help me.*

Rosie darling, you can't ignore me like this. He says it quietly but his head is near my head and I hear him. *All I want to do is talk – get to know you a little. You could come back to my place…*

Beep beep… Beep beep… Beep beep. I know that sound. That sound saves me, doesn't it? Doesn't it, Mummy?

Cooee! Rosie! Rosie darling!

Beep beep. Beep beep beeeeeep. A red Mini. The sunroof is down. It's Emily! She stops at the crossing. She is waving. I burst into tears and run to her.

Rosie my dear, fancy seeing you here! I was just on the way to your place with the notes. Your mum mentioned your printer was on the blinkeroo. Do you want a lift, or is the Pope Catholic?

Her car is half a metre away. She has her hazards on like you do, Mummy, when you need to pull in. I run, fast, open the car door, can't believe I'm getting in Emily's car, can't believe I'm safe. I am safe I am safe I am safe.

Thank you! I say. I am full-on crying now. *That man – that man was…*

Her smile fades. *Oh my dear, whatever's the matter?*

Behind us another car beeps, wanting us to get going. Emily turns around and holds up her hand. She calls out:

Just a tick. She turns to me. *Is that man bothering you, dear?*

I nod. *Please. Let's go.*

The man has reached the car. He is right there. He has stopped talking to me; he is pretending to stroll. He passes the car as if nothing has happened. I look at Emily and she reads my eyes; she hears me without me having to say. She raises her eyebrows and looks from me to the man. She gives him a stern look. I've seen this look before – she calls it her Paddington Bear stare – but he doesn't see her; he is facing ahead. Emily drives slowly, until we're level with the man. Someone beeps; she waves them past, she doesn't care. Go, Emily!

Excuse me, she says to the man. *My young friend here says she'd rather not talk to you. Do you hear? I say! You should know better than to talk to young girls who do not wish to talk to you. Now go and bother someone else. Goodbye!*

She guns the engine. The car behind beeps her again, in an angry way. The man doesn't look at us, but I can tell he's heard. His face is red. He is looking at his feet. We drive away. I don't turn around, because I never want to see him again.

I am crying but laughing at the same time. Emily is laughing. We repeat the whole conversation and laugh at ourselves.

You were brilliant, Emily, I say.

If I see him again, I will jolly well poke him in the eye! She chuckles. I love Emily's chuckle; I just love it. I am safe.

CHAPTER 44

The first time he hit me, it was because I hadn't filled out his benefit form for him. The second time it was because he found out I'd been out with a boy. I was a bit older by then, but still not old enough to get away. The third time? Oh, who can remember? I couldn't possibly keep a tally. All I remember, really, is the feeling. The fear. The way the mattress sank when he got into my bed. How I tried to keep my eyes on the gap in the curtains, tried not to hear the foxes, not to think of screaming babies being murdered in their cribs. His hand on my shoulder.

'Wake up.'

He should have gone to a hospital. He should have had medication. He wasn't well. He wasn't well at all. And I had no one to tell. I was too afraid.

So I waited. When the time came, I laid the foundations. I prepared. By then of course he relied on me for everything. Funny thing, power. It seems so solid, so immovable. But I found another power. One that shifted, viscous as oil, one that filled and moulded itself to whatever shape it had. I became fluid. I filled the space. And I used his power against him.

I wanted freedom. That's all I ever wanted. Not this. Never this.

CHAPTER 45

TONI

When I saw those messages on your phone, baby girl, my heart broke.

'The little shit!' I said and burst into tears. 'I'll kill her.'

I can't think about myself saying that now, and yet it was only today. All parents say it, all the time: I'll kill her, I'll kill him… it's just a phrase – everyone says it. We don't mean it. No one means it, my love.

'Just… keep your hair on,' your auntie Bridge said.

'Keep my hair on? Are you serious? Come on, Bridge, you can't possibly be on her side, not this time.'

'I'm not on anyone's side, Tones. Stop saying that. I'm trying to help. And you're right, she's lied to you, but that's what teenagers do.'

'Let me guess, it's in the manual, is it?' My God, I was so horrible to your auntie Bridge, Rosie. That's families, I know, but still. 'Any more flippant remarks up your sleeve,' I went on, my voice trembling, 'to calm your lunatic sister down? Any more platitudes? Why not make a few jokes while you're at it?'

'Tones, don't. I'm not… you're not…'

'Not what?'

'Nothing.'

For a moment, neither of us spoke. It was horrible, just horrible. We never fight, not like this. And I know your auntie Bridge is a tall, strong, impressive woman; I know she's tough, but she's not hard, Rosie. There's a difference. Underneath all the leather and the tats and the spiky hair, she's soft – softer than anyone I've ever known.

Bridget picked up the phone, face like thunder. 'Looks like they've been messaging on Instagram.'

'She doesn't have Instagram.'

'She doesn't have the app, you mean.'

Well, you can imagine, baby girl. I didn't know what the hell she was talking about. 'The what?'

Your auntie Bridge laid the phone on the table. 'The larger iPhones have much more storage. A phone like this has less megabytes—'

'Oh God,' I interrupted. 'Don't talk techy to me, Bridge, you know I hate that stuff.'

'I know. I'll keep it simple.'

'And besides, how is this helping to find Rosie? We need to call the police!'

She laid her hands on my shoulders. It was the closest we'd been all morning. I saw her kindness, there in her eyes, and it made me so ashamed I couldn't look at her. I didn't squirm out of her grip. I wanted her hands on my shoulders, just for a moment. It helped.

'Listen to me,' she said, and oh God, I could hear how hard she was fighting to stay calm, and it reminded me of your dad and of what a madwoman I can be, and I made myself stop, breathe, calm down. 'We do *not* need to call the police,' she went on, almost whispering. 'Rosie is not missing. You've got to stop saying that. She's gone to meet a boyfriend in a café in broad daylight. She hasn't told you because that's a secret she's keeping. She hasn't told you because, I suspect, she thinks you might stop her. So she's not missing, all right?'

I felt my eyes fill. I nodded. 'All right.'

'So,' Bridget continued, 'data is just stuff you have on your phone. It's like… it's like food in the cupboard. You have a big cupboard, you can get loads of food in it, loads of tins of beans and tomatoes and stuff. A small cupboard, you can only get so much in, yeah? Only so many tins of beans. So these smaller phones have smaller storage space, OK? Smaller memories, if you like. Apps are things like Facebook and Instagram and Snapchat, that's all. They're your tins. And the problem with these smaller-capacity phones is, if you have too many apps, they use too much storage and then your phone clogs up and doesn't work or doesn't work as well.'

'I see.' I did, Rosie. I got it, for once. You would have been proud of me.

'Good.' Bridget smiled at me. She looked relieved. 'Rosie isn't necessarily trying to deceive you by not having Instagram or Snapchat, or whatever she has, as an app. She might even be on Twitter, who knows? But whatever accounts she's got, she's accessing them through a web browser, and that could be because her phone hasn't got enough storage, do you get that?'

I nodded. 'The browser? That's like the Google?'

'Well,' Bridget began – I think she was going to correct me, but she thought better of it. 'To all intents and purposes, yes. It just means that her accounts aren't stored on her phone. They're on the internet, do you see? So we need to access her Instagram account through the browser if we want to see what she's been up to on there.' Your auntie Bridge got a strange look on her face then, like she was explaining something to herself and only understanding it in that moment, or as if the fact of snooping around on you, as she saw it, was making her feel ill. At least that's what I thought at the time. Now I think she too was starting to feel like something was wrong.

I swallowed hard. I could see her discomfort, but I knew I had to push her further. 'And will you help me find her Instagram account?'

'It should be straightforward enough. If I'm right, we'll go into her browser and whatever she's looked at recently will come up.

My guess is she'll be logged in, so we'll have no more to do than touch the icon. The question is, do you want to do that?'

I glossed over the gobbledegook of the first half and tried to think about the last bit, the bit I'd understood. 'I…'

'Do you want to have a cup of coffee and think about it?'

'No,' I said. 'Let's just do it. If it's all innocent, I'll leave it. I promise. I'll wait until she comes back and I'll tell her I checked her phone. I'll say I looked at her messages on Facebook, that's all, and see if she comes clean about this boy and the Instagram.' I looked up and met your auntie Bridget's eye. 'How does that sound?'

'OK. Let's see what we've got.'

Auntie Bridge swiped the screen and inputted your password again. She laid your phone on the table in front of her and let me press a square with a compass in it and the word Safari at the bottom. More neat squares lined up on the screen, squares hidden beneath the squares, a grid beneath a grid. A net. It occurred to me that a net is used to catch things, but I didn't say that out loud. Apple, I read there. Bing, Google, Yahoo – that was only the first row. Amazon, Glass Animals, Instagram.

'Instagram,' I said.

Bridget sighed. It was her who pushed the Instagram icon. 'Have you ever been on this?'

'No. Why would I?'

'We're on it. The band's on it, I mean. It's really just photos.' Bridget talked me through the screen display. The camera icon, the circular photo badges, the photos themselves and below, the home icon, the search… Jeez Louise, Rosie, it's a whole other world, isn't it?

She held up the phone. 'That plus sign is what you press if you want to add a photo, the heart is to like someone else's photo and this circle here is her profile pic.'

'So if I press that…' I pressed something, can't remember what now.

'That's Rosie's page, yes. And that's her Insta handle, the name she uses on there – see there, Theatrerose01 – and voilà: her photos…'

We fell silent. There were nine photos on the screen. Bridget coughed. I knew she was about as comfortable as if she was sitting on a spike, but I had to find out what you'd been up to. There was a picture of you with a puppy.

'That's Naomi's new dog, Benj,' I said. 'I saw that on her Facebook.'

Another photo of the puppy on some grass, a picture of a hot chocolate with marshmallows on top, a picture of you pulling a silly face, wearing your raincoat, an altered picture of you and Naomi with huge cartoonish eyes, cartoon twinkles.

'What the hell is that?' I said.

'That's a filter. You put them on a photo and they add silly features, like doggy ears or whatever. I don't think Rosie has them, I think they're a Snapchat thing or a newer iPhone thing, but this could be a picture that someone else, probably Naomi, sent her.'

'How do you know all this?'

Bridget shrugged. She knew *all this* because you had told her *all this*. And that hurt. You'd shown her all your silly pictures; your YouTube videos and things called memes – a whole other concept your auntie Bridge had to explain.

'Why does she show you this stuff and not me?'

I imagined the two of you crying with laughter, in your world of in-jokes and terminology. It was unbearable.

Your auntie Bridget shrugged.

'Like I said, Tones, it's a different dynamic, that's all.' She pressed something on the screen and together, in silence, we scrolled through. There was nothing sinister at all. But my instincts were not at peace. There was something else – I felt it.

'This boy, this Ollie, didn't he say they'd message on the Instagram thing?' I asked. 'How do you get to the messages there?'

'You want to look at her messages from her boyfriend? Have you lost your mind?'

I snatched the phone from her. 'It's this one, isn't it?' I pushed my thumb to the screen. 'MakeurOllie. That's his... what did you say it was? A handle?'

'Can't you just ask her about this when she gets back?'

I barely heard. I was looking at your messages to this boy. I could feel my eyes twitching, my mouth tightening, my forehead creasing. It wasn't fear or disgust, not then. It was confusion.

I handed the phone to Auntie Bridge.

May 26 2018 09.50
MakeurOllie
See you in an hour, Sexy Lady.
Theatrerose01
Can't wait to meet you.
MakeurOllie
In the flesh. Winking-with-tongue-out-face emoji.

Once again I snatched the phone from her hands. My mouth dropped open. I tried to close it but couldn't.

'The twenty-sixth,' I said. 'That's today. *Can't wait to meet you.* So she's never met him? Is that what that means? Sexy Lady, how weird is that? Don't you think that's weird, Bridge? I mean, it doesn't sound like a kid, does it? I mean, they don't say stuff like that any more, do they?'

'Toni?' Bridget said, as if through glass. 'We already know it's a first date.'

'Sexy Lady,' I whispered; couldn't bear to say it any louder. 'I mean, that's straight out of the seventies, isn't it?'

'Not necessarily.' Bridget caught the phone as it dropped. I pushed my face into my hands and swore. I was vaguely aware of your auntie Bridget getting up, the scrape of her chair, the weight of her arm around my shoulders. I collapsed forward, forehead on the tabletop, and groaned.

'Toni,' Bridget said. 'Tones. You're overreacting. They do this. Girls do this all the time. Some of them are on Tinder, you name it.'

'What the hell is Tinder?'

'It's a dating app. There's girls out there meeting up with men they don't know all the time. And as for meeting lads or… or whoever in secret, you used to do it, I used to do it. It's no more than shinning down the drainpipe in the fifties to get whisked off on the back of a Teddy boy's motorbike, no more than telling your folks you're staying at your friend's house when you're shacking up with some bloke. We sneaked around all the time, didn't we? For different reasons, with different methods, but the outcome is all the same. This Ollie guy is obviously someone she's met through drama or something. We could check with the Cherry Orchard, see if he's in the youth theatre. He might be a helper or a stagehand or anything. I'm not saying it's good that's she's deceived you – it's not – but a lot of girls keep their boyfriends secret. She doesn't know what she's doing. Toni my love, listen to me. She's not thinking about the dangers we think about, is she? She's not seeing the sharks in the water. Lots of girls do this – most girls do. Tones?'

I straightened up and faced your auntie Bridge.

'Rosie is not most girls,' I said quietly. 'She's my baby. She's mine, Bridge, and she's only fifteen and she's in a relationship with someone I don't know or even know *about*. He could be Levi fucking Bellfield for all we know!'

Bridget's eyes were the big sad eyes of a wounded bear. 'But he won't be. Look at his Facebook profile. Men like that don't have washboard stomachs, Tones. I know you're shocked because only yesterday she was dancing on the picnic table with her Barbies, but I promise you this is no more than a grounding offence. Stop her pocket money, shout at her, but don't… don't get like this. You're tearing yourself up over nothing, darling. Over nothing.'

'Nothing? You call that nothing, Bridge? Seriously? My daughter, your niece, is arranging to meet a boy we don't even know, in secret, when she's been told a million times about stranger danger, and you're saying it's nothing? She is out there right now with this… this pervert, and you're saying it's nothing?'

'But it's broad daylight, Tones, and he isn't a stranger to *her*.' She opened her mouth to say more, but I was already making for the hallway, heading for the bedrooms. I grabbed my keys, my jacket, my phone and went back to the kitchen. Your auntie Bridget was looking at me like she, not I, was the one in pain.

'Tones,' she said. 'Where are you going, sis?'

Going? I was gone, I tell you. I was out of there. I opened the back door so hard it banged against the outside wall.

'You didn't believe me when I said she was lying,' I said, nearly crying. 'So I don't expect you to believe me this time. You see nothing, but I see something. It's cry wolf, isn't it, for you? I understand that, I really do—'

'Toni, stop it. Tones. Toni!'

'No, you stop it, Bridge. You don't know. You're not her mother. You're not a mother at all.'

She closed her eyes and sighed. I could see how much I'd hurt her. I wanted to say sorry, but I didn't. When she opened her eyes again, her brow was low, her lips white. She took a step towards me – put herself between me and the backyard.

'I know you're panicking,' she said softly, 'and I know why. You know I know why. But she's not you, Tones. She's… not you.' She was shaking. We never mention Uncle Eric, Rosie. We never refer to him, not even obliquely like this; we never have, not since…

'She's not you, my love,' Bridget was saying. 'Yes, she's gone behind your back, but that's what teenagers do, it's—'

'Do not. Do not tell me it's in the manual, or I swear to God I'll…'

She raised her hands: surrender. 'OK, OK, I get it. But, Tones, they all do it! Especially when their parents are too…'

'Too what? Too what, Bridge?'

Bridget looked at the floor. 'Nothing.'

'Too what, Bridge?'

There was a splash of tomato sauce from last night's spaghetti crusted like a scab on the floor tiles. The tips of Bridget's ears were red. She looked every bit as furious as she used to when she was standing over me in some grimy flat, telling me to put my clothes back on; tipping me onto my own bed after carrying me out of some dive at three o'clock in the morning.

'Nothing,' she muttered. 'Forget it.'

'I know she's not me, Bridget.' My own voice, thick and low, simmered. 'I know that very well, thank you very much. I have dedicated *my life* to making sure she's not me. So don't patronise me. You of all people. I'm up to here with being patronised. I'm patronised every day of my life. I'm fully capable of making the distinction between me and my daughter. I know she doesn't have an uncle raping her night after night, is that what you want to hear? Is it? I know she isn't fucking guys twice her age behind the leisure centre. But she's my daughter and it's my job to look after her, and I'm going to find her, all right? I'm going to go and get her now, so get the fuck out of my way before I—'

But your poor auntie Bridget had already stepped out of my way. Without even looking at her, I raced towards the car park. I was coming to get you. And no one, not even your beautiful angel of an auntie Bridge was going to stop me.

CHAPTER 46

BRIDGET

The dying sound of Toni's Fiesta fades into the underlying rumble of the suburbs. Bridget sinks into a kitchen chair and puts her head in her hands. Her sister is off, chest full of rage, head full of shadows. In front of Bridget, on the kitchen table, Rosie's phone buzzes, then buzzes again a second later. A message from Emily, one from Cat Morris, whose name Bridge recognises as one of Rosie's school friends. She reads Emily's:

Will pop notes over in the post-meridian! See you later. E.

Then Cat's:

Hey, hun. Gathering at mine next Sat. Hope you can come.

Cat has added a thumbs-up emoji, a wine glass and a little yellow face blowing a kiss.

Thumbs-up. Glasses of wine. Little yellow faces. Bridget picks up the phone, lets it loll in her hand. Little yellow faces, frogs, dancing girls. Do words no longer convey meaning? Can they not express what we want to say? Is it a case of words are not enough? *How do I love thee? Let me count the ways…* let's see, an eye emoji, a heart, a ewe – I love you, geddit? *How embarrassed I am…* a blushing yellow face. *Goodnight, I'm going to sleep now*, sleeping yellow face, zzZZ.

In the silent kitchen, Bridget sits with her head in her hands. What does she feel now, her sister crying and desperate and gone, she herself shaking and shocked and fighting back tears? Frowning yellow face, that's what she feels. Sad yellow face crying blue teardrops, yellow face fuming, tinged with red, yellow face with gritted teeth, yellow face with brow furrowed in sorrow, three monkeys – hear no evil, speak no evil, see no evil…

A red heart, broken in two.

More than anything, she feels old. When she was young, they wrote letters – everyone did – actual letters on paper with pens. Basildon Bond stationery, a silver Parker ink pen with cartridges for Christmas, her pride and joy, the pen she used to write her first song. There were so many more words, somehow, then. Her best friends, her sister back at home, secret girlfriends… she would take pages to say what she had to say – they all did, if they wanted to – and no one batted an eyelid. Now what do the young and in love have to replace those long letters, those confidences, those risky paper flights? They are living a life beyond letters, beyond even a heartfelt email, maybe even beyond texts in the way that Bridget uses them sometimes when what she has to say is too difficult to express face to face.

You are the air I breathe, H. I will love you always. B.

Toni, we will get through this, I promise. I've got your back. B

The words of lovers, of friends who love, have become condensed, so condensed that, she supposes, meaning and intention can be, must be, abbreviated: a small yellow face blowing a kiss, or winking, or crying with apparently uncontrollable laughter. Bridget has seen Rosie put three crying-with-laughter emojis in a row to her friend Naomi, her own face motionless, not even smiling. Meaning is condensed, yes, but inflated.

Faked.

And after the customary two sparse words and four emojis, there's the photographs of private body parts. That's what kids do now. It's all the rage. Bridget knows that from talking to her niece. What is private now? What does private mean? A private account is still public. Facebook, Instagram, Snapchat, Twitter: kids' whole lives are documented from the age of, what? Eleven? Younger now? They know what everyone else is doing, all the time, with or without them; what they look like from every possible angle, wearing every possible facial expression; their thoughts and feelings have been packaged into bumper-sticker philosophies and pictures of baby animals before they've had time to work things out for themselves. Everything is recorded – their victories and fuck-ups, their ill-advised public confessions when in the moment it seemed like a good idea, their piercings gone septic, their misspelled tattoos, their drunken gropes and street vomits, their lingerie-clad reflections, their avocado on toast, their flat whites, their illnesses, their nail art, their haircuts.

And risk? Has emotional risk also been minimised? If there's an emoji to express it, then everyone must feel it, right? Has baring your soul in a letter become instead the baring of flesh? Is physical nakedness more or less exposing than the stripping away of our public persona, that confident imposter who faces the world on our behalf, revealing what lies beneath?

If risk has been minimised, why does the world feel so unsafe?

Oh fuck it. Fuck it all.

Bridget picks up Rosie's phone and almost throws it across the kitchen. But it isn't hers, not any more. She places it back on the table and stares towards the back gate. Toni is long gone; whole minutes have passed since the swing and clank of the back gate, the car door, the pissed-off roar of the engine. Bridget could have gone after her. She could have stopped her, overpowered her. But Toni would never have forgiven her, and already the violence of what has passed between them has left Bridget shaking and near to tears.

She turns Rosie's phone over in her hand. The last time Bridget and Toni fought was a couple of years ago, and it was over this phone. Toni had said it was impossible, she couldn't accept it.

'You spoil her, Bridge,' she had said finally, capitulating.

'I'm her auntie. I'm allowed to spoil her. And I've already paid it off.'

'But I can't afford an iPhone even for myself.'

'You wouldn't get one if you were loaded – you hate the buggers. And besides, if you had that kind of money, you'd buy her one first.'

'I can't afford one.'

'Exactly, because you have to buy her shoes and shit.' By this time, the crisis had passed and Bridget was already smiling, knowing that the phrase *shoes and shit* would amuse Toni, which it did. 'I can pay a piddly little contract because I don't have to buy her that stuff.'

'But you're always buying her stuff. You bought her the DMs and they cost a fortune.'

'One pair of biker boots once every five years, and maybe my annual Havaianas. I've got money spare, haven't I? I don't need to think about extra shoes. I only have one pair of feet to worry about.'

Toni didn't say anything to that. She accepted wordlessly what was hidden beneath Bridget's words, namely that by extra shoes she meant little shoes, shoes that could go on little feet, the little feet of the child that Bridget would never have – not now.

'You should buy more for yourself, Bridge,' she had said after a moment. By then, they were holding each other's hands over the kitchen table, idly, out of habit. Toni had not yet agreed to the phone, but they were at peace together, in the moment.

'I like giving her stuff, Tones,' Bridget said. 'She's my Squirt, isn't she? And her only living grandparents are in the land of the shamrock.'

All the while, she had known that spoiling wasn't the issue – that it was more to do with Toni and her relentless, unstoppable paranoia. The driver who had killed Stan had been on his phone; smartphones caused death, smartphones went with social media, social media was responsible for all the world's problems, another argument they would have periodically, though in general terms.

Toni refused to see the miracle of worldwide connection, the wonder of seeing your friends' children grow up on the other side of the world, as any kind of counterbalance for global anxiety and child porn. Bridget argued that all kids Squirt's age had smartphones, that this *was* the world now and they had to learn how to negotiate it whether they liked it or not.

And then Bridget delivered her ace:

'Thing is,' she said, 'there's this thing called Find My Friends. Me and Helen have it so that we know where each other is. You can turn it off if you don't want to be found, but I was thinking, if I get Rosie a phone, I can put that on it. And then if we want to know where she is, say if she's late or whatever, all we have to do is check.'

'All right,' Toni said. 'That'd be great.'

How different that argument had been. How awful this one. Bridget wonders how Toni will be when she gets back, dragging an angry and humiliated teenager behind her. She wonders how long it will take her and Toni to get over the words they have said to one another today.

The phone buzzes. But it is just Emily's message re-announcing itself. Idly Bridget picks up the phone. She cannot go back now to a time before she gazed voyeuristically into her niece's life, so she supposes there is no harm in looking again. Perhaps it is, as she first thought, that her sister's anxiety is catching, but a worm of unease has begun to wriggle around her insides. Perhaps it is not her sister's madness at all. Perhaps there is something, something small but real, in what they have seen, a clue of sorts as to why she now feels as she does. She has rationalised it all for Toni, for Toni's peace of mind, but has she also lied? To herself?

'Something,' she mutters aloud, accessing the messages first on Facebook, then on Instagram. 'Something.'

So.

Rosie and this Ollie boy agree to message each other on another account because the dreaded mother of doom, Toni, is watching.

OK, so far so clear. Snapchat is not used, not even in secret: too high a risk, possibly, of an incriminating photograph or a message popping up in full view of Toni, so they choose Instagram, no notifications, check in through the browser. Right. But over on Instagram, there are only the messages sent this morning. Rosie fled the house in a rage this morning and left her phone in her room without deleting these most recent messages. Which means there must have been others, the nature of which neither Bridget nor Toni knows. But those messages, whatever they were, led to the nickname *Sexy Lady.*

Toni is right – that is weird. *Hey, Sexy Eyes,* possibly, or even *Sexy Ass,* but what young boy in today's world calls his girlfriend *Sexy Lady*? It is, frankly, creepy.

'Something,' she says again, the wriggling worm burrowing inside her. Perhaps her sister is right; perhaps Toni simply reached the correct conclusion faster, sped along by the wings of acute maternal instinct. 'Something… something… what?'

Photos. They must have sent photos. She remembers a conversation she had with Rosie in the van, the last time she came to a gig.

'My friends all send, like, sex pics to their boyfriends,' she said, her voice calm, matter-of-fact. This was on the way home – the gig had been in the Red Lion in Barnes. 'Boys do it too. This girl in my year, right, she sent, like, a full-on naked selfie to her boyfriend, but then he, like, just *finished* with her the next day and then, right, he sent the photo to all his friends. Can you believe that? Savage! Anyway, he was suspended from school but the girl had to take, like, a month off. She had stress.'

'Oh my God.'

'I know, right? Then there was this boy who sent, like, a video of himself… you know…' She made the internationally recognised hand signal.

'Masturbating?'

'Yeah. And he sent it to a girl in the year above.'

'That's gross.'

'I know. But it was on Snapchat and they didn't capture it so he got away with it.'

'Snapchat. That's what they use, is it, to send their naughty bits?'

She shrugged. 'Mostly. For dick pics and stuff like that.'

'Dick pics?'

Rosie laughed, but at least she had the decency to blush. 'Don't tell Mum.'

'I won't. I was just thinking what a great name that would be. Hello, my name's Richard Pix. Dick for short.'

'You're so mad.'

'But listen, mate. You'd never send that kind of thing, would you? I mean, that would be on your digital footprint forever – you know that, don't you? Not to mention the dangers.'

'Oh my God, of course not.' Rosie had looked horrified.

'Thought not. When in doubt, ask what would Chrissie Hynde do, yeah? And she wouldn't stoop to that nonsense for anyone, would she?'

'I know. Oh my God, I'm not that stupid.'

I'm not that stupid. But has she been, potentially? Has someone coerced her into being that stupid? Bridget pushes her thumb to the photo icon. There are seventy-eight photos on there. She goes to albums. There is a deleted album. In the deleted album there is one blurry photo – a pocket shot. Something is amiss. The deleted album has been deleted. This could be completely innocent, a way of preserving storage space so the phone doesn't clog up.

Clog up. A few months ago, a client had a phone that had stopped working. Bridget's pretty sure it was a 5C, like this one. She rigged his phone up to his laptop, reset the date on the phone to two years earlier and rebooted it. And when she did that, all the photos and videos he had ever taken reappeared on his laptop. They'd been hidden in the dark, and floated in like ghosts. It was insane actually.

She goes into Settings. Sure enough, it shows much more storage usage than currently accounted for. So potentially, whatever photos Rosie has taken are still in there somewhere, in the dark cyber forest, hiding where no one can see them.

Bridget's chest tightens. She runs to her room and grabs her laptop, leads and phone. On the way back to the kitchen, she calls Toni. No answer. Toni must be at the café by now, or at least parked somewhere near. She's either still furious or in the middle of bollocking Rosie or… or worse.

While the laptop boots up, Bridget puts a pot of coffee on the stove. It is either that or run around the backyard shouting *help, help, help*.

The laptop awakes. She plugs in Rosie's phone and connects to iTunes. With her heart in her mouth, she resets the date and reboots. The screen tells her to wait. Bridget waits. She watches.

The screen fills. In the images fly, like spirits.

'Oh my God,' she says. 'Oh my holy God.'

CHAPTER 47

BRIDGET

Some of the photographs are innocuous enough: the usual failed blurry pictures of pavements and the inside of bags where the camera has been activated by mistake; extras of other saved photos; faces caught at an unflattering angle, eyes mid-blink, gawping mouths; Bridget herself; Toni; Rosie and Naomi, arms around each other. But others are not so innocent, and it is these that make her catch her breath. They spread before her on the screen of her laptop: hands, shoulders, ear lobes; thighs, breasts and buttocks. There is a toe, the nail painted red, a black-and-white photo of a belly button. With a sick feeling in her stomach, Bridget knows that what she is looking at is her beloved niece, her cheeky, funny, clever, nervous, shy, hilarious Rosie. Her naïve and stupid little fifteen-year-old flesh and blood. And that these pictures are the reason for that creepy nickname.

There are male body parts too. These pictures have messages beneath them. They look like the messages from Instagram – the format is the same. They must have accompanied the pictures. They must be screenshots, taken by Rosie.

A washboard stomach. She thinks she recognises it from a Facebook poolside picture of this Ollie boy. He must have cropped it and sent it, vain bastard.

Check this out, he has written. *Thoughts?*

Thoughts? My God, the narcissism of the young these days! No wonder they're all so fucked up. She scrolls down to a male nipple, deep brown on a tanned chest. How does anyone go for this level of conceit?

Like what you see? Send me yours.

'Jesus.'

There are eyes, an ear pierced with a diamond stud. There's a tattoo of a dragon on a tanned shoulder, the arm toned not from hard work but from a gym; it has that inflated look about it. A male toe. The sight of it, the message underneath, almost make Bridget retch.

Show me yours?

A toe. His. It is the last of the images of body parts to load. The first, then, that he sent, or at least that Rosie captured. It is beyond weird. Is that where it all started? With this innocent picture that is anything but? Is that how this creep began his insidious, pervasive campaign? He must have known her by then, must have seen how very shy she was, how vulnerable, how ripe. How well does he know her? What was she thinking?

And the fact that these images are clearly from Instagram, their captions below them in the shots… Why? So she could read and reread these words, alone at night, in her room, thrilled probably beyond measure by her own illicit fantasy. But why not look at them online? Maybe it was about owning them for a moment, halfway between the cyber and the real worlds, a digital image, downloaded, to hold in her naïve little hands. Whatever, she then deleted them before Toni could check, deleted them even from the deleted album. She has been so careful.

She has been so very careless.

Bridget slouches against the chair back. 'Oh, Rosie darling.'

It is a little under half an hour since Toni left. Bridget has no idea now where she is. She could be in the café, in the park, talking things through with Rosie; or, God forbid, driving frantically around the streets, searching for her daughter, the only person in the world deemed missing before they are due to return home.

Rosie's phone has faded to black. Bridget picks it up and swipes it, looks again at the laptop screen in front of her.

Show me yours. A toe. Who would send an image of a toe? She glances at Ollie's Facebook profile, flicks through his pictures. There's no denying that the boy is a honey, a beauty, the stuff of Renaissance art. His hair is slicked here, falling over his eye there, his gaze is sure and his teeth are even and white. A toe, a shoulder, a belly button, descending, teasing, like a stripper in a club… When does persuasion become coercion? When does coercion become manipulation? The manipulation of an expert?

Sexy Lady.

She shivers, shakes her head against the chills on her skin. She calls Toni. Toni doesn't reply. She must be out of the car by now – perhaps she's left her phone behind as she often does. Will she bother going through the rigmarole of getting out of the car and going into the café, or will she just slow down and peer in through the window as she drives past, maybe park outside and wait for a confrontation? They will be back soon and the atmosphere in the flat will be appalling. It would be better to be out.

But Bridget doesn't move. She can't move. Something is keeping her in her chair, laptop in front of her on the table, Rosie's phone in her hand.

It started with a toe. At his suggestion. And if he is a normal young guy, a teenager as innocently out for kicks as any teenager that has ever lived, then why, why does this feeling of unease fill her chest, make her hair follicles tingle?

She flips back to his Facebook profile. It is like trying to figure out a crossword clue, staring at the swirling letters of an anagram, hoping for enlightenment. She goes through his photos again: him on holiday, by the pool, showing off his physique like any cocksure lad his age; as a cute kid; in black and white, pouting, but again, there's no law against that. A poseur, a narcissist, a chancer with a taste for redheads and the risqué. There is nothing inherently wrong with any of it, but something, something, something…

Think, Bridget. Why does your scalp itch? What is it that doesn't fit, here in this profile of this beautiful boy, this Michelangelo's David, this Adonis? She casts her mind back to the boys at school. Peter Fisher, he was a blond bombshell, and Nick Fitzgerald, Fitzy, yes, it was Fitzy who all the girls in her year went for. Fit Fitzy, the name scrawled on the cubicle walls, on the back of the prefabs at the far end of the schoolyard. Left Bridget cold, though at the time she didn't dare to think about why, and why quite the opposite was true of Eleanor Green. Fitz, with his cold blue eyes and his fishtail parka, his button-collar shirts and his way of smoking Silk Cuts outside the chippy and later at the weekly disco in the grim community centre at the end of their road. The girls went to pieces around him, but he kept his smiles to himself like a miser keeps coppers, sparing one only occasionally, when there was something for him in exchange.

According to his profile, this Ollie Thomas is nineteen years old. A gorgeous-looking guy in the prime of his life, probably has girls fawning over him all day long, just as adults did when he was a little boy. That kind of beauty shapes a person. A person just like Fitz.

She holds the phone close to her face and scrutinises his brown eyes. You could drink those eyes like melted chocolate, spend years waiting for them to land on you, see you.

'Why would someone like you,' she whispers, there in the tense silence of the kitchen, 'be pestering fifteen-year-old girls for pictures of their toes?' Fourteen-year-olds. Rosie was fourteen when this started.

Something else about Fit Fitz – girls would do anything for him: smoke, steal, offer themselves. Nick Fitzgerald never had to ask. For anything.

So why, why would this boy offer his toe to a shy, nervous girl like Rosie and say, *Show me yours*, when surely there must be many girls willing to show him anything of theirs, in the flesh, for nothing more than a flash of those brown eyes, for the promise of a kiss from those plump lips, a smile from those even white teeth?

And in asking herself this final question, the niggling doubt, that troublesome piece of grit in the wound, rises to the surface, ready to be tweezed out.

If the question is: *Why would he stoop to such a thing?* the answer might well be: *He would not.*

And if *He would not* is the answer, then the new question is: *Why did he do it?*

And finding no reason, other questions form…

Who?

Who would cajole a child to show herself in this way, in secret?

Who, if not this boy?

Who is Ollie Thomas?

Bridget leans forward and opens another browser.

'Let's see who you are, mate,' she whispers.

She types in: *Google Reverse Image Search*. In another tab, she brings up Facebook, finds Ollie Thomas and copies the clearest photo she can find into the browser: he is poolside, wearing pale blue shorts, bare chest. The search, she knows, will only find him if this *exact* image exists somewhere else online.

Searching…

Bridget pours her forgotten coffee, stirs in a spoon of sugar and takes a sip. It is tepid but sweet.

Searching…

Does this photo exist elsewhere?

It does. A match. She clicks and clicks, finds a Facebook page that looks terribly familiar, pictures she has only just seen: the childhood snaps, the party pictures with girls, cigarette dangling from his lips like James Dean. But this man's name is Raoul Mendez: Spanish by birth, model, resident of Chelsea, actor.

Not Ollie Thomas.

Ollie Thomas, if that is even his name, has stolen this profile in its entirety and used it like cheese to trap a mouse. Or a maggot on a hook; yes, this is fishing, catfishing. She's heard about it.

'Jesus.' She is reaching for her phone to try Toni again when Toni calls.

'She's not here, Bridge.' Her sister's voice breaks. 'She's not here.'

'Tones,' Bridget says, every cell of her being focused on keeping her voice steady. 'You need to come home.'

CHAPTER 48

TONI

'Tones.' Your auntie Bridge's voice came down the line. 'You need to come home.'

'Come home?' I said. 'Why? What's happened? Is she there?'

'Nothing's happened.'

But I could tell. I could tell something was wrong. 'What, Bridge? Tell me.'

'I've found some stuff, I've—'

'What stuff?' I was shouting down the phone. 'She was here. She was here, Bridge. I asked the girl at the till, and she said she saw her. She did come here. She had a hot chocolate. It took me ages to find a parking space. I had to park four roads away – it took me ages, Bridge. I couldn't get here any quicker and now she's not here.'

I broke down, Rosie. Right there on the street. I couldn't help it, didn't care.

'Tones.' Your auntie was using her calm voice, the one she uses to talk me down from whichever ledge I happen to be on.

'Don't,' I said. 'There was a girl taken from a café in Putney. No one has seen her since. So don't. Don't handle me.'

'I'm not.' A sigh.

'Look,' I said. I was trying to get a hold of myself, trying to appear rational. 'I'm getting in the car. I'm on Holly Road.'

'Did the girl in the café see Rosie leave with anyone?'

'No. She didn't see her leave. Said she left her hot chocolate though. She didn't drink it. Oh God. She's been taken, Bridge. Someone's taken her.'

'Toni, try and stay calm for me, babe. Breathe. She left her hot chocolate last week too, remember? Maybe she doesn't like hot chocolate.'

'Stop it! Stop trying to calm me down! I can't calm down! I can't breathe. How can I breathe? She's missing, Bridge. Someone's taken her! I'm… I'm going to drive around, see if—'

'No, Tones,' Bridget insists. 'You'll be pissing in the wind. She could be anywhere. We're better off working together here. Come home.'

'I'm calling the police, Bridge.'

'No! No police.'

I put my key in the ignition and closed my eyes, made myself breathe. Down the line, silence.

I could picture your auntie Bridge, there in the kitchen, her hand gripped tight around the phone. She had her eyes closed too – I could feel it. Tears came. I sniffed.

'Listen to me,' she said softly. 'She's a teenager and she's not even late coming home yet. If you call the police now, they won't take any notice. They're fucking useless. You know that, I know that.'

A sob escaped me.

'Tones? Toni? Come home, babe. We'll find her. Together.'

'They've probably gone for a walk, haven't they?' I said. 'It's a nice day. They've probably gone for a walk.'

'They might have. But, Toni, listen to me. We need a proper plan. You need to drive calmly and carefully back home, yeah? Driving around hoping to spot her is no use at all. To anyone.'

'OK.' I started the car. 'I'll come home.'

I drove back to our flat as fast as I could, Rosie. I could barely see to drive I was crying so much. Everything I'd ever feared was coming to pass, and even though I'd lived with the conviction that one day something terrible would happen to you, I could not believe that it had. I felt and did not feel the gearstick in my hand; saw and did not see the blink of red to green at the lights; heard and did not hear the bleep bleep bleep of the crossing. I found myself parked behind the flat, clutching the leather sleeve of the steering wheel. I had no idea how I'd got there.

Bridget must have heard the car on the gravel because she ran out to meet me, her face grave. It was so horrible, Rosie, seeing her expression and just knowing that something bad lay behind it.

I threw open the car door. 'Have you had news?' I was grabbing my stuff from the passenger seat. Bridget didn't say anything. She helped me organise myself out of the car – I was shaking from head to toe, Rosie. I couldn't coordinate; my eyes crowded with blackening stars.

'I'm nearly there,' Bridget said.

'What do you mean "there"?' I looked up at her. 'Where? Do you know something?'

'Yes,' Bridget said. 'Let's get inside.' She tried to push me towards the house, but I stopped.

'Don't push me. Why can't you talk to me as we go, for God's sake?' I said. 'Don't make me wait.'

And so she began to talk as we made our way together across the backyard.

'This boyfriend of hers was fake, Tones,' she said.

'What? Fake? Oh my God.' I began to cry. 'For God's sake, why didn't you tell me on the phone?'

'I didn't want you to get pulled over for speeding or… worse,' she said. 'I had to get you here safely, and I couldn't come for you. Come on, Tones. Calm down. Let's work together, yeah?'

We went inside. Bridget walked over to the stove and stood with her back against it. She looked so serious, Rosie. Not a trace of her usual mischief. I barely recognised her. I slumped against the tabletop.

'How can he be fake?' I wailed.

Your auntie Bridge must have dashed towards me, because the next thing I knew she was holding me in her arms and I could feel her mouth pressed to the top of my head.

'It's OK,' she said. 'It's OK. We'll find him.'

'This can't be happening. This can't be happening. It can't. It can't, it can't. We need to call the police right now.'

'No we don't. I'm nearly there. I've nearly found the bastard.'

She sat down next to me, in front of her laptop. I pressed my cheek against her arm, peered while she showed me what she'd been doing, how she'd found out that this Ollie was not who he said he was.

'I know his fake identity,' she said. 'But I don't know who he *actually* is, not yet.'

'So she met him on Facebook?' My heart was pounding. I felt sick.

'On Instagram, I think. It's hard to tell. I've yet to check if they have mutual friends. It could be that he got to her by being friends with a girlfriend of hers. Some of these girls, and boys too, they have thousands and thousands of friends and followers. I remember Rosie saying – they don't care who friends them, it's a numbers game.'

'So I must have seen him on her Facebook page? But I've checked through her friends so many times, and there was no one dodgy-looking, no one much older or anything. Oh my God.'

'That's who she *thinks* he is.' Auntie Bridge handed me your phone. It was open at Oliver Thomas's profile. I stared into it, scrolling through the pictures.

'He's beautiful,' I said.

Oh, Rosie, you poor, poor girl. He was a honey, wasn't he, this boy you thought you were meeting? How would you say it, a babe? I get it. I bet you'd never think I would, but I do, baby girl, I do. I can remember.

'That's what I thought,' your auntie Bridge said. 'It's what made me wonder why he'd send a fourteen-year-old girl pictures of…'

The air filled with unspoken words.

'Of what?' I made myself say, my voice tentative as a hello called into a dark, empty house. 'Of what, Bridge?'

She sighed. She looked like she was going to be sick. She couldn't look at me, Rosie. She could not look at me.

'Well, of his toe, actually, at first,' she said.

'His toe?'

'Yes. And then... other parts.'

'Oh God. Oh my God.' I was pulling at my hair until it hurt. 'And why did you say fourteen? Rosie is fifteen, Bridge, she's fifteen.'

'She was fourteen when he first made contact.'

'Oh my God, what? I'll kill him. I'll kill him, Bridge.'

'But it's not him, Toni. This boy is not the man we're looking for. These pictures don't belong to that man – you see that, don't you? The boy in that photo is called Raoul. He's a Spanish model, from Toledo, living in Chelsea. You couldn't get more exotic. He's young, he's rich and he's a god. But someone stole his profile and used it to lure her. It's called catfishing, Tones. I'm so sorry.'

My face was burning, my neck, my chest. I opened my mouth to speak but nothing came.

'Oh my God, Bridge. My Rosie, my baby girl. We have to call the police. We have to.'

Your auntie Bridge reached for my hands and squeezed them.

'Listen,' she said. 'When have the police ever done anything for us? Never. When did they ever help Mum when Dad was knocking seven bells out of her? Never. When have our family ever relied on them? Eh? Never. And Eric? *I* sorted Eric out, didn't I?'

'Yes, but this is Rosie, Bridge. She's my daughter.'

'I know. I know that. But I sorted Eric and I'll sort this bastard in a way the pigs never could. I'll kill him. The police won't do that, will they?'

'No, Bridget! I have to call them. You don't even know where he is.'

'No, but I will. A few minutes and I'll have him, trust me.'

I faltered. 'Did she… did she send pictures, Bridge?'

'That's not important now. A lot of kids do this picture stuff. Rosie told me herself, but she said she'd never do it.'

'Why you? Why did she tell you?'

'I don't know. It's not important. The fact is, it's happened, kids make stupid mistakes, and what we have to do now is find this bastard and find Rosie. But we can't do that if we're hysterical and worrying about what she has and hasn't done, and if we call the police, they'll slow us down. They'll have to take a statement, there'll be some idiot plod on the phones… The thing I need to figure out now is how to find the postal address of whoever is behind this profile from the metadata, and then we can go and kill the motherfucker.'

'But how does she know him? Is he from drama? How old is he?'

Your auntie Bridge groaned. 'She doesn't know him, Tones! That's the point. That's all irrelevant now. You need to forget him. He doesn't exist, not for us!'

I felt so stupid, Rosie. But I was scared. My mind was all over the place. I know we should have called the police there and then, but the thing is, our family never have, only once, when your auntie Bridge called them to try and save Mum, your granny Casement. She was only six, she didn't know any better, and of course my dad answered the door and sent them on their way. Growing up, no one I knew ever called the police – the pigs, as we called them. They were the enemy. It's hardwired into us; it's part of our DNA. And then of course, there's the pact.

Your auntie was already at the computer, mumbling to herself. I picked out swear words mostly.

'So if we… gpsfortoday.com… hmm… fuck… but if I… ah.'

'You've found him?' I was at her side, heart still pounding, sweat trailing down my back.

'No. Not yet. Just let me concentrate, OK? Let's see… metadata… which social networks protect your EXIF…'

I was looking over her shoulder. She was skim-reading the screen, reading aloud for herself as much as for me – not that I could understand a word.

'EXIF… GPS location data from other users… blah blah… how to check a photo for EXIF location information… Here we go, right… what's this… blah blah… ah, Facebook, here we go… fuck.' She threw herself back in her chair.

'What?' I said.

'Facebook, in all cases, wipes all EXIF data from a photo.'

'Is that good?'

'No,' your auntie Bridge replied. 'Fuck, fuck, fuck.'

'Can you find him?'

'I don't know.' Bridget stared at the screen. 'I can't get his location from where he uploaded his fake profile. Facebook wipes that info. Instagram will be the same, then, I imagine. I can try. But there must be a way to find out who this bastard is and where he lives. There must be.' She studied the computer screen, eyes flicking over the documents. She picked up your phone and shouted into it: 'Who are you? Where are you?'

'This morning, when I brought the phone in, did we check if there were any straightforward texts?'

'There was one came in from Emily, but no, we didn't, I didn't.' Bridget flipped her thumb over the screen. 'Here,' she said. 'OT. That'll be him. It says, *See you in a bit*. And there's a love-heart emoji. Sent at 10.55 a.m. He must have sent it after she left the house. That's why she hasn't deleted it.'

'She was deleting things too?'

'Yes, I told you. Focus, Tones.'

'But… surely,' I said, 'if we have his mobile number, can't we just trace his phone?'

Slowly, your auntie Bridget turned to face me, her eyes wide. She grabbed my face in both hands and kissed me on the nose.

'You absolute beauty,' she said. She leaned back, pushed her hand through her hair, making the spikes even spikier. 'I've got all bogged down in the online stuff, and all the time, yes, yes, bloody obvious, all the time, if we know his number, which we do, we should be able to trace the bastard. I couldn't see the bloody wood for the trees, Tones! I was thinking we could only trace Rosie's phone through mine, but she'd left it here so I thought that was a non-starter… but she's got the Find My Friends app, hasn't she, so instead of finding her, I should be able to find him! In seconds!'

'Really?' I couldn't believe it, couldn't believe it was me – of all people – who had found the solution.

But your auntie Bridget's eyes closed a little; lost their shine. Her shoulders sagged.

'But there's no way he'd disclose his own location, would he?'

'What d'you mean?' My chest tightened once again. Hope, so alive a moment ago, died.

'I don't have you on Find My Friends because you're still chiselling epistles into a stone tablet, but I have Helen and Rosie so I can find them whenever. Or find their phones. But I can only do that because we all agree to it, unless…' She tapped her fingernail against her teeth.

'Unless what?'

'Well, unless in the grooming process…' She winced. 'Sorry. Unless he gave his location as a way of persuading her to share hers, as a way of tracking her at all times. It's all about trust, about getting them to think… If they get access to their location at all times, there's nothing anyone can do. Stopping her going for a coffee or whatever wouldn't work – you'd have to keep her prisoner, and even then you could never leave the house yourself. She would be a living target.'

Your auntie moved her thumb over your phone screen, her lips pressed tight together. 'But then he would've had to leave his location on, and surely he would've switched it off once he had hers. Unless…'

Despair rose within me. I didn't dare speak. I could only hope, focus on the fantasy of that hope and how, if it was strong enough, you would be delivered to me. And if you were safe, everything would change. I would be different. I would be better. Everything that was broken could be mended. We would never argue again.

It was a matter of seconds before Bridget jumped out of her chair, eyes glittering like a crazy person with a knife, and said, 'I've got him!'

CHAPTER 49

ROSIE

When we get to the junction, Emily says:

Oh blow me.

Which makes me want to laugh because hello? Rude! Emily calls cats pussies too, which I told Naomi and we absolutely wet ourselves.

What's the matter?

I'm such a scatterbrain, she says. *That's what's the matter, my dear. I've left your audition notes at home. I can see them – they're on the sideboard in the parlour. I was so busy with the tape measure… drat! Dash and drat and double drat.*

We could go and get them, I suggest.

Are you sure? Do you mind making a little detour? I'm just the other side of Richmond.

Not at all. Mum's not expecting me back till later. I was supposed to be meeting… I was supposed to be meeting a friend, but they flaked.

I want to come home to you, Mum. I want to say I'm sorry and have a hug. But I don't want to put Emily out of her way, and I don't want to get out and walk. I'm way too scared. I'm still trembling, even though Emily has made me laugh, calling the man silly names as we drove along.

It won't take long, she says. *I may as well pop back and get them, eh?*

What if the man follows us? I think. What if he has a car right there, or jumps in a cab and says, *Follow that red Mini?* No, that's mad. All that's happened is that some perv was hassling me. That's all Emily needs to know. That's all this is anyway. He fooled me by being friends with my friends, but it's easy to get friends; loads of people don't check, they just press accept, accept, accept. I've been a total dork. But I've got myself out of it, and I've learned my lesson. I can delete Ollie's profile, whoever he is. I will never ever accept a request from someone I haven't actually met again. What's the point in telling you what's happened? That's what I'm thinking now. There's literally no point making you worry more than ever, you're bad enough as it is. And if I call you from Emily's phone I'll end up having to explain everything, and if I do that, you'll never let me out of the house again. I need time to think. You don't know what's happened and I'm not going to be late coming home, so you won't be worried, not now, not yet. If I go with Emily, I'll have more time to calm down, get my story straight.

Emily is saying, *What's it to be, youngster? I can easily pop you back if you'd rather.*

No, let's go to yours, I reply.

CHAPTER 50

BRIDGET

Bridget pushes her arms into the sleeves of her leather jacket. 'Wait here,' she says to Toni. 'He's in Ham. I'll be there in ten, fifteen minutes tops.'

'But how do you know he's there?' Toni is crying.

'He left his Friends app on. I can only think he must have thought he'd swiped it off, but it didn't stay off. That happens sometimes on iPhones, but whatever, I've got him, I've fucking got him, and I'm going to get her right now.'

'No,' Toni wails, her face red and shining with tears. 'We're calling the police now, Bridge. Come on, it's time.'

'But I'll be there before them, Tones. I'll be halfway there by the time they've even picked up the phone. I'll have her in my van before some dick in a uniform can find a fucking pen. She's in fucking Ham, Tones – it's ten minutes away.'

Toni is shaking her head, sobbing. 'No, Bridget.'

Bridget crouches down in front of her sister and takes her hands. 'I get it. I do. But just… just… Look, give me an hour, can you do that? One hour. If you don't hear from me in an hour, we'll call, OK?'

They lock eyes. Both know what they see reflected there: themselves, the pact, and everything that has rested on it ever since. Even the fact that Bridget is here now, at her broken sister's side, where she has been since that terrible summer's day when all their lives were turned upside down.

'One hour,' she insists. 'But I'll be less.'

Toni sniffs. 'I'm coming with you.'

Oh Christ.

'No.' Bridget stands, grabs the keys for the van from the hook by the door. 'Think. You'll only slow… you can't… we need someone here in case… what if she comes back? The police would make you stay here, because you're her next of kin. Trust me. You've got your phone. Keep it close to you. I'll be in touch.'

'Fucking hell!' Her sister's face crumples. She bangs her fists on the table, bashes them against her head. 'I feel so helpless, Bridge! I feel so fucking trapped!'

Bridget kisses her sister's cheek and presses her lips to her ear. 'You're not helpless. *We* are not helpless. You're the one who saw the wood when all I could see were the trees, remember? And I drive faster. We're a team, so keep it together, yeah? I'll call you once I've got her. After I've cut that motherfucker's balls off with a rusty knife and made them into a key ring, all right?'

Before Toni can argue the toss, Bridget runs from the house. The van starts first time and she cries out with triumph. She is wired. She can't believe her luck. The bastard must have given his location in the early days to create trust, all part of the grooming, all part of the *I'll show you mine if you show me yours*. Sick, sick, sick. Did he know he'd left it on? Did he mean to cancel and forget? Or did he do like she does sometimes with her mobile data – think she's swiped it off and then a day later realise it's pinged back without her knowing and she's had it on 3G by mistake all this time and run up a nice fat extra cost? It doesn't matter. What matters is the motherfucker is now a flashing circle. It may have the cheesy too-good-looking face of Mr Raoul Mendez in it right now, but pretty soon Bridget will be planting her fist into another face entirely. It won't be the first time she's beaten up a man.

'Come on,' she shouts at the windscreen, at traffic too slow too slow. Come on; come on. She is going to find her niece and bring her home. She will leave whoever that bastard is sorry that he ever messed with her family. This whole situation is surreal. She can barely believe what she's doing. When she installed the tracer app, never did she think she'd be using it like this. She thought it'd be for one of the million times Rosie left her phone at Naomi's house or between the sofa cushions or at the bottom of her school bag. Not this – never this.

But the bastard isn't far, not far at all. It won't be long now. He'll wish he'd never been born.

She steers the great hulk of the van through the lights. The green banks of the Thames to her left, the water churned and brownish, she drives as fast as she dares: sailing through T-junctions, gritting her teeth at pedestrian crossings, taking mini roundabouts on two wheels. But by the time she reaches Hampton Wick, the traffic is at a standstill.

'Fuck!' She slams her fists into the steering wheel.

There are roadworks, temporary traffic lights. It was all going too well. Bridget chews at her thumbnail and swears prolifically at the road.

She fumbles for Rosie's phone, checks that the tracker is still showing the same location. It is. The bastard is still there then.

I'm coming to get you, she thinks. *I'm going to make you wish you'd never laid a hand on her.*

With a surge, the traffic moves forward. Bridget throws the phone into the hollow by the gearstick, makes it, last, through the lights and is filled with insane joy.

'Come on,' she shouts, to no one. 'Come on!'

Kingston town centre is torture. Saturday afternoon: can people think of nothing better to do than *buy* stuff? Lobotomised sheep, the lot of them. But if the traffic is moving slowly for her, it has moved slowly for that sick bastard too, and she will track him down like a bloodhound tracks a wild boar. She will track him down and rip his—

The traffic moves.

'Come on,' she shouts, overtakes, undercuts.

The sustained, angry blare of a horn. The cars slow and halt once again. With a cry, she bangs her back against the seat and thumps the steering wheel. Calm. Calm down. Focus. There is no way she'd be this close if they'd called the police. They'd still be waiting for some dope to process the call. Those photos are still on her laptop. At least Tones won't see them on Rosie's phone. But would they incriminate Bridget if the police saw them? Pictures of an underage girl, even if it is her own niece? Oh God, they might be sick enough to think that. You can't trust the pigs. You can't trust anyone it seems to her now in her sudden loneliness, the cold despair of her van.

Only family.

Through Kingston at last, left, along, and the common rears up on her left. She takes the corner too quickly, the van lurches, she fights with the steering wheel to right herself. Three more turns and she's there, the road lined with neat terraced cottages, flowers in their front gardens, twee as fudge tins. This is the edge of the estate; the back gardens of these little houses must give onto the main road that runs between here and the ragged terrain of the Ham Lands. Her eyes dart, searching for a space big enough. She should have brought Toni's little runaround but she can't bloody drive the thing. A space, maybe ten metres away. Heart pumping, she parks. Jumps down to the pavement. Checks her phone. Runs.

She is close. She is there. She is standing in front of a whitish terraced house in a poor state of repair, the window frames peeling, rotten wood. Wild flowers, weeds and long grass spring from the front garden; inexplicably, there is an upended office chair with a wheel missing. The sun is hot on Bridget's back, but she zips up her jacket all the same. An extra skin. Only now does she think about protecting herself, that she should have brought a knife, a baseball bat.

A gun.

CHAPTER 51

ROSIE

Emily drives, chattering like she does. *I was over in Kempton having a mosey around the market*, she says. *I saw the most marvellous Welsh dresser but it was too big for the dining room, and when I put my nail to it, the paint scratched off. They obviously hadn't sanded and primed adequately… preparation, dear, as we know, is key. Anyhoo, I was on my way back when I saw you there. Did you get my text, by the way? I sent it after we spoke.*

Sorry, no. I left my phone at home.

You did? Right you are. And is your mum in today?

Think so. I remember our argument. I feel terrible now. You knew I was lying, didn't you? You always know.

What about your aunt?

Auntie Bridge? She's gone to meet her friend Saph, I think.

We drive past the Prince Albert pub, then Twickenham Green. My tummy still has butterflies in it. I breathe in, breathe out. Do re mi fa so la ti do.

Not like you to leave your phone, dear, Emily says, and chuckles at her witty sarcasm.

I had a fight with Mum.

Oh dear, that's too bad. What about? The usual?

I nod. I don't feel like telling her any more. I don't want to feel that stomach ache I get when I talk to her about you. I already feel sick after that man. His breath, his dirty glasses. I don't feel like I'm going to cry or anything, but I feel like I could, like I'm near. I don't feel right. Do re mi fa so la ti do. Do re mi fa so la ti do. Breathe in; breathe out.

We pass by the end of the road that leads to our close. I wave to you. I wave to you, Mummy, like a kid. Maybe I am a kid sometimes. I don't know what I am really. We pass through St Margaret's, then over the bridge to Richmond, and I think how awesome it looks, like a postcard or a painting of an old-fashioned riverfront. I can imagine women in long white dresses in the olden days, holding parasols, strolling along in front of the tall buildings and sitting on the sloping grass verges. Men with straw hats and those twirly moustaches. There are little boats on the river. A swan trails a long V behind it in the water. My breathing evens out a bit. It's so cool with the sunroof down.

Emily turns right. We drive along the road that goes past the poppy factory. The river plays hide-and-seek between the restaurants and houses. Emily isn't talking any more, which is weird for her.

You live in Ham, don't you? I say.

That's right, dear. Good town for an actor, wouldn't you say?

I know she is joking because she chuckles, but I don't get it. What does Ham have to do with acting?

You know ham's a word for an actor, don't you? She has read my mind, probably because I didn't react. Actors have to be good at reading people.

Ham like ham and cheese?

She chuckles. *Like ham and pickle, ham sandwich, what have you. Haven't you heard of the expression hamming it up?*

Maybe.

You know when an actor is overacting, going too big; not so much brave choices but huge melodramatic gestures, hand-wringing and wailing and so forth, do you know what I mean? You've seen EastEnders, *haven't you?*

I nod, but I don't say about Helen writing the scripts sometimes.

So when an actor has a reputation for overacting, we call him or her a ham. Or you can say his or her acting was a bit hammy. In fact, quite often, if you're doing the cryptic crossword in the Guardian *or the* Telegraph, *they use 'ham' for an actor in the clues, so for example they'll put something like, I don't know, 'compass points around an actor feel this and blush'. And you'll have the s and the e for your compass points, that is, your south and your east, then you put those around the ham of actor which gives you shame – feels this and blushes – blushes with shame. That would be your answer, do you see? Not a very good example, but that's off the top of the old noggin.*

I nod. I don't really understand what she's going on about. At least she's back to normal, jabbering on, as you say, ten to the dozen.

She turns right at Ham Common. There are ducks on the pond and some people having a picnic in their coats. Another few turns and she parks at the kerb. I realise I didn't look to see which road this is.

Lucky with a space, dear, she says. *We're right outside.*

She leads the way through a little white gate in a little white fence. Number 31. The front garden is so neat; there are little red flowers in the beds and the soil is all crumbly, like when you first dig it over. There are no weeds. I think of you digging the flower beds in the garden of our river house when I was very little, your lilac gloves, the way your hair blew across your forehead, stuck to the sweat sometimes when you'd been working hard in the sun. Emily's little lawn has a pond in the middle with lily pads. The grass edge looks as though it has been combed and cut with scissors. There are two gnomes sitting by the pond, both exactly the same, both fishing. On the front step there is a rectangular parcel about the size of a shoebox for, like, men's size 12 shoes.

Ah. Post's arrived, Emily says, unlocking the door. *I know what that is. Come in, dear.*

I follow. The front door is light blue and there is a red-and-white gingham curtain across the window. It is so pretty.

I like your house, I say. *It looks, like, country-ish.*

Did I tell you I grew up on a farm? We moved here when Mummy and Daddy passed on.

Inside, there is a sugary smell, like someone's been baking.

Pop your coat off if you like, Emily says.

I take off my jacket and hang it on the hook. The hall carpet is patterned with flowers, thick and soft under my feet. I follow Emily into the kitchen at the back. The kitchen is kind of shiny, and under the baking smell it smells of lemon Flash, like she's just cleaned it this morning or something. There's a pretty back door the same blue colour as the front door, with the same pretty red-and-white gingham curtains on the window. On the countertop, next to the cooker, there are scones on a cooling rack. On the table on a tray are a butter dish, cups and saucers and a pot of honey with a cute little wooden spoon thing sticking out.

Emily tells me to sit down, so I sit at the table. She opens the fridge and pulls out a jug with the same pattern as the cups and puts it on the tray. I notice that one cup has blue flowers and the other one has orange. She fills the kettle. It is one of those ones that go on the gas. I wonder if it will whistle. The cooker is dark brown and old – it is one of those ones that have the stove and the oven all together. But it is clean. Everything is clean.

Emily lights the gas with a match and blows it out. Under her breath she is humming a tune I recognise… 'Who's Afraid of the Big Bad Wolf'. She picks up a sharp knife from the countertop and holds it up. It gives me a fright.

She chuckles. *No need to be afraid, dear. Let's see what in this parcel, shall we?*

She slides the knife along the packing tape and lifts out a box. It is not shoes. It is another gnome; at least that's the picture on the outside. She opens the box and pulls out a plaster gnome with a red hat and a fishing rod. It is exactly the same as the others and I think this makes Emily a bit batshit. But then I knew that.

Here you are. It is the gnome she's talking to, not me. She holds it up and wrinkles her nose like when you speak to a baby in a pram. *Welcome to your new home*, she says in a baby voice. *I think we'll call you Barnaby.* She looks at me. *What do you think, Rosie dear? Is Barnaby a good name for a gnome?*

Yes, I say. I wonder if the others are all called Barnaby too, but I don't ask in case she says yes. That would totally freak me out.

You can go and play with your brothers very soon, Barnaby, she tells the gnome. *But first Rosie and I are going to have our tea, all right?*

I look at my knees, where they poke out of my jeans. I feel my cheeks burn. I'm embarrassed for her, not me.

The kettle whistles. Emily makes the tea and puts the pot on the table. She gives me a scone on a plate, the same flowery pattern. Everything is so pretty and fresh and nice.

Now then, this jug is the most terrible pourer, she says. *Help yourself to butter and honey, my darling.* She takes the cups over to the sink and pours the milk while I cut my scone in half and spread some butter and honey on it. The honey spoon isn't a spoon – it's a wooden stick with a spiral thing on the end.

Shall I be Mum? Emily is back at the table. She picks up the teapot and pours tea into my cup. *Sugar?*

No thanks. This scone is delicious.

Why thank you!

She talks to me about scones. How she shouldn't eat them because they go to her hips. She tells me that the secret to baking good scones is not to over-handle them. I nod even though I'm like, why do I care?

Isn't that right, Barnaby? she says, to the gnome, and laughs.

I sort of laugh too, but then I proper laugh because I think of telling you and Auntie Bridge about this later – hilarious.

Drink your tea, Emily says.

I drink my tea.

There, she says, holding hers with both hands, her top lip puckering like a drawstring purse. *Can't beat a nice cuppa char! And Owen will be here any moment.*

Who's Owen? I ask.

Owen? she says, as if she's thinking of something else. *He's my brother, dear.*

I wish I didn't have to meet her brother. I wish we didn't have to have tea; I just want to pick up the audition notes and get home to you. But it would be rude to say that, so I don't.

Emily smiles – but not at me. It's as if she's smiling at someone or something I can't see in front of her. And she's stopped talking again.

I do a massive yawn. I feel soooo tired, like, proper exhausted.

There is a buzzing sound. It is coming from the window. It is a wasp, banging itself against the windowpane over and over. There is a plastic bottle on the windowsill. It has been cut in half and the top half has been put into the bottom half, upside down. At the bottom of the bottle is what looks like a load of runny honey. There are dead wasps in the honey, which look gross. The alive wasp buzzes along to the bottle top and crawls round and down the home-made funnel thing. It can smell the honey. I want to call out to it – stop! – but I don't like wasps, and anyway it is already at the bottleneck.

It buzzes, hovers, drops into the honey.

There are three cups and saucers on the tray now and I wonder if there were three before and I just didn't count properly or whether Emily put another out while I wasn't looking. I think about how this morning Emily said, *I hope he's handsome*, even though I've never told her about Ollie, and this gives me a pain in my stomach, but I am so tired, so tired, I could put my head on the table and sleep.

From the back garden there's a squeak like a gate opening.

That'll be Owen, Emily says.

The wasp buzzes. It is stuck in the honey. It will die there, like the rest.

The back door opens.

Well, well, well, young lady. I recognise the voice. When I turn, I see that it is the baldy man, the man from the café, the one with the dirty glasses. He smiles at me and says, *Fancy seeing you here.*

Hello there, Owen, says Emily. *You're just in time for tea.*

CHAPTER 52

BRIDGET

The front door is covered in black dust, cobwebs thick as angel hair. The brass letter box has greasy fingerprints on it, but apart from that it is as though no one ever uses this door – never goes in or comes out. Bridget's chest is tight; she locks her knees to stop her legs from trembling. She raises her fist to bang on the glass panel but stops herself. To the left of the door, there is a grey plastic doorbell. She pushes it and hears it chime in the hall, a ridiculous, anodyne sing-song. She is a caller, she thinks. She is delivering a parcel. She is selling organic veg, she is canvassing for the Labour Party, she is a Jehovah's—

A figure is making its way towards the door. A man, lumbering. Bridget's guts flip.

'Just a moment.' The voice is well spoken, with the slight tremor of age. The door chain rattles. Him, the predator, worried about his own security. The door opens a crack. His face is pale. He is anywhere between mid fifties and seventy. The top half of his large plastic-framed glasses is the colour of cinder toffee, the bottom half clear. The lenses are dirty. Behind them, his eyes are artificially huge, giving him a blinking, bovine expression.

Her fingers splay against her thighs. She grips her left wrist with her own right hand.

'Hi there,' she says. 'I'm... my name is Bridie and I'm... erm... I'm just...'

'I'm sorry, dear; I'm a little busy. Could you call back later?'

The man makes to close the door, but Bridget jams her foot inside just in time. The base of the door bangs against the metal toecap of her boot, making the rest of the door shudder.

She gives a strangled, apologetic laugh. 'I'm so sorry, but I really need to speak to you. May I come in?'

She shoves the door with her shoulder.

'You can't do that,' the man protests. 'I say! You can't barge into people's homes like that.'

She shoves again. Dimly she is aware of the chain fitting giving, falling, clattering on the bare floor. She is marching down the hall, her boots loud on the boards.

'Look here,' he calls after her, following her towards what must be the kitchen. 'If you're the police, I'll need to see a warrant. Young lady!'

The kitchen matches the grimy exterior. There are spider plants on the windowsill, all manner of bric-a-brac, a horrid Home Sweet Home sampler in a cheap thin frame, a black transistor radio, an old-fashioned spice rack, pale grey with dust, the likes of which Bridget has not seen since the seventies. She turns to face the man. He is hovering at the kitchen door. If anything, he looks afraid.

'I'm not a young lady,' she says. 'I'm a grown woman, and I've come for my niece.'

The man's hair is no more than a few strands. Beneath them, his scalp shines. He blinks his pale, enlarged eyes as if in confusion. But he is not confused – Bridget can feel it.

'There must be some misunderstanding,' he says. 'Who are you? You're frightening me.' He sucks air in, hisses it out, begins to hop from foot to foot – a strange, anxious dance.

Doubt crowds Bridget's senses. The kitchen is run-down but clean, actually, in the main. The draining board winks with soap bubbles. There is a plate on the draining rack, a butter knife.

'I was washing up,' the man says, as if to explain. But Bridget hasn't asked him a question.

'I've traced a fake Facebook account to this address,' she says. 'My name is Bridget, and I have strong reason to believe that you have my niece, Rosie Flint, here. I believe you lured her to a café pretending to be a young man called Oliver Thomas. Ollie.'

The man shakes his head, pulls at the zip of his cardigan. He is still blinking, twitching like a woodland creature. But he is not a woodland creature. His face, she sees now, is pink and rough with eczema, and he smells musty, as if he never leaves the house. The house too smells stale: of bodies, unwashed clothes and skin.

But the moment's silence sends up another wave of doubt. Bridget scans the kitchen. Is it possible she has made a horrible mistake? The man is hovering at the kitchen door. If she wants to check the bedrooms, she'll have to get past him. He is older than she thought he would be, but she will hit him if she has to.

'You have to leave,' the man says, his voice louder. He is still sucking air in through his teeth, expelling it, sucking; still hopping from foot to foot like a child. He pulls his index finger, making it pop, does the same to his other fingers, one by one. His eyes are wild, skittish.

Bridget takes a step towards him. Still sucking in and hissing out air, he moves behind the table, grips onto the back of a chair.

'Get out,' he says. 'Get out of my house.'

He is afraid of her. Good. Bridget runs for the kitchen door, back into the hallway. At the front door, beneath the coats, she sees the sole of a shoe lying on its side. A boot. Rosie's Doc Marten boot.

She runs back into the kitchen. 'You fucking worm.'

He scrabbles around the kitchen table, clutching at the chairs. Bridget darts one way, he runs for the door; she reverses, heads him off, lunges at him, sends him falling into the hallway. She's on top of him; she turns him over and punches him, hard, in the face. His nose bleeds on one side. Her hand explodes in pain. She feels another, sharper pain in her thigh and springs back.

He is holding a kitchen fork. Her jeans darken at the thigh. Blood. He has stabbed her.

'Get away.' He jabs at her, ineffectually. She catches his wrist and twists his arm, forcing him to roll onto his front. She pulls his arm up his back.

'Let me go,' he shouts. 'You have no right to be in my house. I'm going to call the police.'

'Go right ahead. In fact I'll call them for you, why don't I?'

She pushes his hand up towards his shoulder blades, hears the crack of his arm as it breaks.

The man yells. He starts to cry, giving off low sobs of self-pity. She plucks the fork from his fingers, spins him back and punches him again in the face. He wails, raises his hand to his cheek. She brings her boot to his chin, feels the metal toecap connect with bone, hears the dull thud of his head on the bare boards. His glasses skitter towards the kitchen door. His jaw is slack. Broken, she thinks. He is out cold.

Bridget runs for the stairs. 'Rosie!'

She is on the bed in the master bedroom, curled up, her back towards the door, apparently asleep. The room smells worse than the kitchen: dense, floral – lavender? – masking the heavier smell of old fabric, unwashed sheets. Dust motes twinkle in the weak sunlight. The windows are filthy: grey netting, brown floral sixties-style curtains. The whole place is a museum. Rosie's wrists and ankles have been bound with duct tape. Her mouth too is sealed with the same silvery tape. But she is clothed. She is wearing the same clothes as this morning, and Bridget closes her eyes a moment in the hope that this means something.

Bridget climbs onto the bed. The mattress sinks beneath her knees. She holds her finger to Rosie's nose and feels heat. One breath, two breaths, three. Alive, alive! Alive, thank God.

'Rosie! Rosie darling. Wake up. It's me – it's Auntie Bridge!'

Nothing.

Bridget scoops her niece from the bed and throws her over her shoulder. She is so light and thin. She is no more than a child.

In the hall, there is no sign of the old man. From what she imagines is the living room, she hears a groan. She should go after him, finish him off. She should cut off his balls as she promised and take them back to Toni on a plate. But she has come to save Rosie – that's all she has come to do. The police can take care of this fetid excuse for a human being.

She opens the front door. Her lungs are burning. From behind her comes an incoherent shout. She turns – and stares into the twin holes of a shotgun.

The man has the gun trained at her chest. His nose and mouth are dark with crusted blood. His mouth droops, limp and odd. One lens of his glasses is cracked and one arm hangs slack, as if it has no bones in it. He adjusts the gun; it's obviously heavy, awkward for his one functioning arm. His hair, such as it is, falls outwards in wisps from his bald head, giving him the appearance of a drug-addled clown.

'Wait,' Bridget says, laying Rosie down at the foot of the stairs, straightening up, raising her arms in surrender. 'All right.'

'U'air'.' *Upstairs?* Possibly. All vowels; he is unable to make the consonants. Yes, he is gesturing with the gun towards the stairs, his eyes creased in pain. The gun is heavy. Too heavy to use?

Bridget glances outside, to the sunlit street, the sky blue beyond the houses.

'Look,' she says, 'I'm not going to call the...' She turns and kicks, quick and high. The gun flies out of the man's hands. He grabs for it, too late, clutching at nothing but air. Bridget plants her boot into his solar plexus, sending him falling back. She lunges for the gun and turns it on him.

He is flailing on the floor. More vowels come from the slack mouth – incomprehensible, save for the palpable terror beneath. He tries to push himself up, cries out in pain.

Bridget cocks the safety, aims – and shoots. Both barrels empty into the man's chest. Blood flies, spatters against the wall. His head thuds against the bare boards. A burgundy stain swells on the front of his beige checked shirt. Only then does she feel pain flash up the back of her thigh.

She throws the gun to the floor and picks up Rosie, throws her over her shoulder again and runs.

CHAPTER 53

TONI

I don't know how long I stared out of the front window. Time mushroomed, became static. I sat and sat, useless, in my chair, phone in my lap, ears pricked: for the doorbell, for your voice calling out, *Mum! I'm back!* For sirens. Anxiety is this, my love: waiting. I had spent every minute since the accident waiting for this, for this very thing to happen, and now it had. The unnamed something bad that had shimmered at the heart of me for so long had become a solid thing. It had words to name it: you had been taken. I had been so wary of Emily that I had focused all my misgivings on her, and all the while behind the scenes you had met and befriended a stranger. And now he had you. He had you, and all I could do was wait.

Your auntie had been gone half an hour. I dialled 999. I rang off. Thirty-five minutes. I dialled 999. I rang off. Forty-one minutes: once more, my thumb hovered over the 9…

The phone rang.

CHAPTER 54

BRIDGET

Bridget reaches the van, digs in her jacket pocket for her keys. The sun is fierce. She feels the heat of it on her head, feels sweat trickle down the sides of her body, down her face and neck. A dull pain in her leg where that evil worm put a fork in her, another strip of pain up the back – a torn hamstring, most probably.

It is difficult trying to unlock the back of the van with Rosie over her shoulder. She drops the keys, has to squat to pick them up. Drops of sweat land on the black tarmac. With a shout, with all her strength, she stands up again. If she could only set Rosie down, untie her, put her in the front cab, but there is no time. She's safest in the back.

Finally, with a clunk, the key turns and the van doors swing open. There are old bed sheets on the tin floor, which she uses to protect the amps, the stage equipment. She wishes she had blankets, cushions, but the sheets will have to do. She lays Rosie down on them, taking care not to bang her head. The angle is wrong; she feels her back twinge and is overtaken by a fit of coughing. Too many roll-ups; too many sneaky late-night joints. Hands to her knees, she coughs once, twice, and straightens up. She is dying of thirst. Rosie is out cold. He must have given her chloroform or something, God knows. Bridget pulls at the sheets and tries to roll the edges, make some kind of buffer, but it is hopeless. She will have to drive slowly. Rosie will be rolling around; she will bruise. But there is no time.

She drives carefully, against all instinct, twenty miles per hour, no more. Round the corner, at the common, she swerves into the kerb and parks. She checks her watch: it is just over forty minutes since she left the flat. She calls Toni, who answers after one ring.

'Bridge?'

'I've got her. I've got her, Tones. She's OK. She's OK.'

Her sister is weeping. Bridget can't bear the sound.

'Did you call the police?'

'No, I—'

'Good. Well don't. I've got her now and she's OK. Stay there, sis. I'm coming home.'

Bridget drives as carefully as she can, hits the end of her road just as the hour is up. At the back of the flat, she parks and pulls up the handbrake. She needs to get out, get out now, but she can't. She has driven all this way, but now that she is here, she cannot send the command to her legs. Her hands are shaking. She swipes her phone screen and calls Toni.

'We're home,' she says. 'Stay there. I'll bring her to you.'

She opens the van door and swings her legs over the side, winces at the pain in the back of her thigh. The gravel blurs and redefines itself. Her head spins. It takes her a few seconds to compose herself enough to jump down. When she does, the gravel crunches under the thick soles of her boots. She winces in pain.

She limps to the back of the van and opens it up. Rosie's eyes are open, sky blue and wide with fright. She gives a muffled cry. She is lying at the edge, where Bridget laid her. Bridget climbs into the van and tears the tape from her niece's mouth.

'Emily!' Rosie cries out as if in terror and bursts into tears.

'It's not Emily, my love – it's me. It's your auntie Bridge. Oh mate, you're awake. Oh God, babe, I'm so sorry. You must have been terrified. You've had a shock, that's all. It's Auntie Bridge, lovey, oh my precious darling, my darling, darling girl.' Bridget holds her tight, checks herself against squeezing too hard.

Rosie sinks her head into Bridget's chest. They are both crying now.

'You're safe, my love. Hey, Rosie? Listen to me, yeah? You're safe. Auntie Bridget's got you. We're home.'

Rosie does not, cannot stop crying. She is gasping for air, her head nodding, her shoulders shuddering with the force of her sobs.

'It's OK; it's OK, my love. You're safe. You're safe, you're safe, you're safe.' Bridge edges one arm away from the child. 'Rosie. Honey. Do you think you can hold out your hands, my love? I want to get this tape off you. I had no time to… we had to get away. Can you do that for me, angel? Can you hold out your wrists?'

Toni mustn't see the tape. There's nothing here that she won't find out, but seeing the tape would just be one more indelible image she would have to somehow block. Along with all the others.

But Rosie won't move her head from Bridget's chest.

'Rosie? Rosie?' Shit. It is Toni, out in the car park. Her voice is getting louder, nearer. 'Rosie? Lovey?' She appears then from behind the door of the van. At the sight of her daughter, her brown eyes widen. 'Oh my God! Oh my God, Rosie, baby, my baby, oh…'

There is nothing Bridget can do now to protect her sister from even this small part of the truth. Thank God she didn't see that house, that man, smell that horrible musty lavender smell. Thank God at least for that.

With what remains of her strength, Bridget fireman-lifts her niece onto her shoulder.

'Let's get you inside,' she says. 'Let's cut you free.'

She carries Rosie into the lounge and uncurls her onto the sofa. She is whimpering. She smells of oil from the van and, Bridget realises with flashing fury, of urine.

'Come on then, Squirt,' she says softly. 'Let's get this tape off you, eh?'

Toni is beside her, sobs punctuated by sniffs. Bridget turns to her. 'Tones, go and grab the scissors will you? I don't think I can peel this stuff off with my hands.'

Toni doesn't move. Her eyes are round and red.

'Second thoughts,' Bridget says, 'you stay with Rosie. I'll go and get the scissors.'

She dashes to the kitchen and comes back to find Toni stroking Rosie's hair. Rosie is still crying but more softly now. Her teeth are chattering.

'Here.' Bridget hands the scissors to her sister. 'I'll go and run a bath, put some salt in, yeah? I'll bring a blanket.'

Toni sniffs, nods.

The water runs. The bathroom clouds. Bridget grabs Rosie's duvet, returns to the living room and arranges it over her niece. Leaving them, she goes back to the bathroom and sits on the loo seat in the steam. She can hear her sister trying to soothe Rosie but no sound yet from the girl. When the bath is ready, she tests it with her arm. Not too hot but hopefully hot enough to take away the shakes.

Rosie is still on the sofa. She is not crying, not really; the sound is more like a distressed animal, a puppy or a bird, a high, repetitive keening, beyond words and terrible to hear.

'Bath's ready,' Bridget says helplessly. 'Do you think you can walk, Rosie my love?'

Rosie nods. Toni has cut the tape and peeled it away. Rosie's wrists are red. With one hand resting on her mother's shoulder, she stands slowly, testing her legs, then bursts into tears again. This is too big, too much. They should call the police – Bridget knows it. But not now, not yet, not until she's spoken to Toni, told her about… Oh God, what a mess.

'Do you want me to carry you, love?' Bridget asks.

Rosie shakes her head, no, but says nothing. She puts one foot out, then drags the other to join it, repeating this along the hallway with slow, agonising progress until she reaches the bathroom, where she stops, one hand on the door frame. She looks smaller, as if she has lost stones in weight. Her collarbone stands sharp above her slash-neck T-shirt. The T-shirt she decided on this morning, when she thought she was heading out to her first date.

This morning – a lifetime ago.

Toni asks, 'Do you want me to come in with you, hon?'

Rosie nods. She is mute with shock, shaking violently, her teeth chattering. Bridget wonders how long it will be before she can speak, before they know exactly what happened, the extent of the damage. She was clothed. That has to mean something.

Toni follows Rosie into the bathroom. Bridget catches her sister's eye, no more than a second, before the door closes. She presses her palm to the white wood panel and closes her eyes. After a moment, she goes into the kitchen and reaches for the whisky bottle.

The sound of swilling water reaches the silent kitchen. Her sister's soothing voice trails down the hallway, her nurse's voice, the same one she uses when Rosie is sick. Bridget can't hear Rosie crying any more, guesses she must have stopped, hopes she is calmed by the heat, the salt, the caring lilt of her mother's soft words. It's not fair, she thinks only now. They've already been through enough to last any family a lifetime. She doesn't mind for herself, but Toni and Rosie have done nothing wrong. When Rosie goes to bed, Bridget and her sister will talk, then they will call the police. It is unavoidable now.

The whisky burns her throat but her hands have stopped shaking. She thinks about a cigarette but can't seem to get up from her chair. Outside the sun has begun its descent towards the back of the garages. She checks her watch: 2.48 p.m. My God, it is still daytime. The thought is inconceivable. She has had nothing since her espresso this morning. She should be hungry, but she is not – something is bothering her. Surely all that matters is that Rosie is safe? Yes, there is a man dead, in his home, waiting for someone to find him. But there is something else, something niggling away at her. Something that has to do with the fact that the sun has not yet set. The last two hours play out like a dream. Suspicion, discovery, the trace, the rescue.

It was so easy.

Was it *too* easy? And that guy. He looked like he'd never seen the sun. His house was straight from the seventies, no sign of anything more technological than a transistor radio. Something…

'She's in bed.' Toni has appeared at the kitchen door, joins her now at the kitchen table.

'Has she spoken?'

Toni shakes her head. 'She muttered something about Emily as she drifted off. I think she was worried about the audition notes. Emily was meant to be popping them over today. The mind's a funny thing, isn't it?'

'She called me Emily when I opened the van door.'

'Shock, isn't it? Poor thing.' Toni takes Bridget's glass. 'I guess we'll have to call the police now.'

'No,' Bridget says. 'I killed him, Tones.' She blinks back the maddening surge of tears that pools in the rims of her eyes.

Toni nods, once. 'How?'

'He had a gun. I kicked it out of his hands and I—'

'You shot him?'

'In the chest. After I'd kicked his head in. After I'd broken one of his arms. After I'd broken his jaw. He was defenceless and I killed him. Rosie's boots are still there. I saw them by the door. I'm going down, Tones. I'm going to prison.'

'Don't say that.' Toni reaches for the bottle. Bridget stands and grabs another glass, into which Toni empties the last of the whisky. She takes a slug. 'Death is better than he deserved.'

'Looked like he hadn't been out in years. Grey skin, you know? And he had that funny smell – neglect, dirty clothes. The house was a wreck. The front door was practically sealed. It was weird: you couldn't imagine him using a computer to send an email, let alone coming up with a fake profile. He looked like he'd arrived in a time machine, do you know what I mean? Oh God, I could have left it like that, I could have left him, but he had the gun. He was going to shoot me.'

'You won't go down, Bridge. It was self-defence. No jury in the land would send you down for killing the man who took your niece.'

'It won't look like that. Oh God.' Bridget covers her forehead with her hand. A moment later, she feels Toni's arm around her shoulders.

'Hey. You won't go to jail. Anyone would have done the same.'

'I kicked the gun out of his hands, Tones. I kicked him in the head. I picked up the gun and shot him when he was already down. He was old – did I say that? I killed him. What are we going to do?'

'We'll tell the truth. We'll go to the police before they get to us.'

'But what about the pact?' Bridget sits upright and meets her sister's eye.

Toni breaks first, looks away. 'Where was Rosie?'

'On the bed upstairs. Taped like that, like you saw, and across her mouth.'

Toni sips her whisky but says nothing.

'He hadn't taken off her clothes. He hadn't done anything to her, I don't think. And she was drugged, completely out of it. She won't remember being taken up there…'

'She was drugged?' Toni's voice rises in panic. 'You didn't say.'

'I haven't had the chance. I'm telling you now. That's why she could barely walk. Or speak.'

'I thought that was shock.'

'Well, yes. But she was out cold when I found her. I had to carry her to the van. There was no time to do anything else.'

'Do you know what he gave her?'

'No idea. Some kind of barbiturate, I would imagine. But she's safe now. She'll sleep it off. If she was going to go unconscious, she'd have done it by now.' Bridget circles her whisky in its glass, watches the light catch in the amber. 'I killed him, Tones. They'll find my prints on the gun. What are we going to do? Tones? Toni?'

But Toni is already at the kitchen door. She is heading down the hall, calling for her daughter. Bridget hears Rosie's bedroom door open, then silence, then:

'Bridge! Bridge! Oh my God, call an ambulance.'

Bridget runs to Rosie's room, digging her phone from her back pocket. Toni is leaning over her daughter, her ear to Rosie's mouth.

'She won't wake up, Bridge. I didn't know she'd been drugged, I just thought she was in shock. Bridge, she's unconscious. Call 999. Call 999 now.'

CHAPTER 55

TONI

I know I said Auntie Bridge wasn't allowed in the ambulance, and that's true, she wasn't, but the truth is, I didn't let her come with us. What I mean is, I decided before the paramedics got there that she would not come.

While we waited for the ambulance, I sat by your bedside and stroked your damp hair. We heard the wail of the sirens in the road but we stayed with you, both of us preternaturally still. And what was odd, there in the eye of the storm, you unconscious right in front of me, was that I was suffused with a strange calm. I knew you'd be all right. I don't know how to explain it any better than that: I knew it. You were breathing, the paramedics were on the way – you would be all right.

I made myself meet your auntie Bridget's eye.

'You stay here,' I said. 'I'll go with her.'

And, oh, Rosie, her face creased in confusion, as if she didn't understand what I was saying.

'Don't be daft,' she said, but her voice shrank with doubt. 'I'm coming with you.'

'Please,' I said. Having her look at me like that, well, it was… it was hard, Rosie. I felt like I was blocking her out. Which I suppose I was.

'Let me do this, sis,' was all I could think to say. 'Let me be useful, for once. Please. I speak their language; I know what to tell them. You can come for us later with the van, save us having to come back in an ambulance, OK?'

She was standing on the other side of your bed. She kicked at the bottom of the bedpost and didn't meet my eye.

'If that's what you want,' she said, eyes still on the floor.

The sirens grew loud, stopped. The ambulance light came through the front-door window. Through your half-open bedroom door I could see it flashing blue on the hall ceiling. We had a few more seconds. I tried to keep my mind straight.

'Maybe grab a change of clothes for her?' I said.

'Sure. I'll make some sandwiches or something, yeah? And a flask, in case you end up being there a long time.'

Outside, an ambulance door slammed. Bridge turned away and made for the hallway.

'Bridge?'

She stopped at the door to your room and looked back at me.

'We'll talk about what to do later, OK?' I said. 'I won't call the police is what I'm saying. I won't say anything until we see where we're up to.'

She nodded, met my eye. 'OK.'

'I'll text Emily and let her know. Only what she needs to obviously.'

'Right you are.'

She went to open the front door. Seconds later, the bustle in the hallway, your auntie reappearing, pushed aside then by the brisk-moving high-vis uniforms of the paramedics. I recognised one of them.

'Ted,' I said.

'Hiya,' he replied, his face a mix of concentration and recognition. 'Toni, isn't it?'

'Yes,' I said. 'This is my daughter, Rosie. We've had… she's taken something.'

Wordlessly, your auntie Bridge left us. There was much more I wanted to say to her, but there was no time.

Ted and the other paramedic, a woman called Sandra or Sandy, I think, put you on a stretcher. I followed them outside, stopped at our front door and called back into the house:

'Bridge?'

Bridget appeared in the hall and gave me a sad and loving smile. 'What now, woman?'

I laughed, despite everything, or maybe because of everything. My eyes stung, blurred, and then she was there, her fingertips touching mine.

'We'll be all right,' I whispered.

'Yeah,' she said. 'Go.'

I must have answered questions while we were still in the house, must have done that while they were running vital checks, but I have no memory of it. I know they put you on the stretcher in the flat and that by the time I was inside the ambulance, Ted had put an oxygen mask on your face.

The woman went to the front and started the engine while Ted shut the back doors. He asked me all the right questions: what had you taken, how long ago, had you had any alcohol. He hooked you up to a saline drip.

'So diazepam you say? Just that?'

'The truth is, I don't know,' I said. 'I know she's taken diazepam – I have that in the house for my back – but she could have taken anything before that, I don't know how many, or if she's taken other stuff.'

And there it is, Rosie: the Judas kiss. Ted's grey-blue eyes staring into mine like judgement itself while I betrayed you. While I let them think *you'd* taken an overdose. I betrayed you, to save your auntie Bridge, to save myself, but to save you too, my darling. I *didn't* know what you'd had, apart from the diazepam that I'd given you, and that was the truth. It was the bottom line. It was what was necessary, all that was necessary, to save your life. I had to be sure they would run all the tests that they would usually run in the case of unknown substance abuse – even if that meant *suicide attempt* or *overdose* being written on your medical records. The whole truth was that you had been kidnapped and that your auntie Bridget had killed a man saving you, but the only truth they needed was that you had taken some unknown combination of barbiturates. The rest was irrelevant. I had pushed your auntie away so that I could do that – tell that half-truth. I'll admit that I didn't want her to know I'd given you my diazepam, but I swear it was also because I knew she'd give herself up to save you. And that wasn't necessary. Besides, we needed her more than they needed to know the whole story.

Didn't we? Didn't we, Rosie?

You can't answer, my love. And you couldn't answer then. You were not able to contradict me and I took advantage, and there's nothing I can do, nothing I can ever do, to reverse that. All I can do is wait for you to wake up and tell you I'm sorry. And I am sorry, Rosie, my darling girl. I am so sorry.

'She'll be all right,' Ted said, smiling. 'Might be out of it for a while, but if it's less than four hours, hepatotoxicity is highly unlikely. They'll give her a reversal agent, I should think. She's breathing fine but she's unconscious, so…'

I nodded. I knew the procedure, knew your liver was at risk. If they found high serum levels, they'd give you acetylcysteine, maybe charcoal or something, I didn't know exactly which one. I hoped it wouldn't come to that, but I feared it might.

'Tough shift?' I said.

He checked his watch. 'Not yet. It will be.'

I smiled, took your hand in mine and held it. We were in the ambulance now, heading for A&E, and I was confident that you were in safe hands. I knew I'd face tough questions once the dust had settled, and I think by then I also knew that the police were inevitable now.

In A&E, the doctor gave you flumazenil. You were unconscious – it's procedure. They took your bloods, wrote *overdose* on your notes. I was interviewed by a senior nurse, no one I knew, who asked me if you'd been depressed lately, all that sort of thing. She said that when you woke up she would need to speak to you, and that I would be formally interviewed at that point. I insisted you were fine. I didn't tell her that I had given you the drugs. I did not say that, not categorically, because by then I was terrified they would take you away from me, that they'd investigate us, that they'd discover what your auntie Bridget had done, and take her away too.

We are a family, Rosie. We are a funny, fucked-up triangle family, and in that moment I didn't know who was at the base and who was at the top. All I know now is that we have tough questions ahead of us. It will be time, as they say, to face the music.

CHAPTER 56

BRIDGET

Bridget rummages through Rosie's chest of drawers: black skinny stretchy jeans, they'll do. And her Glass Animals T-shirt and her grey hoody. Shoes. She will need something to put on her feet… But try as Bridget might to block the old man from her mind, he surfaces there, blinking at her, his jaw hanging, his broken, filthy glasses. Oh God, she should never have shot him. If she'd just kicked him and legged it, if she'd been quicker, if…

Still, at least if someone goes to prison, it will be her.

Not Rosie, not Tones.

Don't think about that stuff. Thinking about it isn't going to change what's happened. Put it in a box, close the lid. Make sandwiches, a flask of coffee. Do something useful.

She limps into the living room – her leg is killing her – switches on the television. Sits down, flicks through the channels, scrolls through the films on Netflix. Switches off the television. Stands up. Looks out onto the street. No one. Not a soul. Not even a cat. She should probably clean the fork wound on her leg, change out of the bloodstained trousers.

In the bathroom, she removes her jeans, the denim bringing the sticky new scab with it as she peels it away, causing her leg to start bleeding once again. She grabs an old flannel from the airing cupboard and runs it under the tap. The wound is not deep, but there are three neat holes like a strange animal bite, which fill with red every time she lifts the cloth. She strips off and showers, holds the flannel to her leg once she is dry and finds the largest plaster she can. The wound is bleeding slower now but still comes through the plaster; she needs another two on top before it stops.

She wanders into her room and puts on fresh jeans, a clean T-shirt. She rubs her hair dry with the towel, which she returns to the bathroom. After applying some hair wax and rinsing her hands, she ambles into Toni's room, immaculately tidy, then into Rosie's, a tip of clothes, clip files, books, pens, cuddly toys, make-up, nail varnishes. On the wall, her framed poster of *Little Red and the Wolf*, posters of the Glass Animals, The xx, others – Bridget has no idea who they are. She sits then lies on Rosie's bed, pushes her face into her pillow. The smell of her is still there: her shampoo, the fuzzy smell of her when she's just woken up. To live without this smell seems impossible.

Too much. She's going to make herself cry.

Closing Rosie's bedroom door behind her, she heads for the kitchen. Her laptop is still on the table. The niggling feeling is still with her, the ease with which she was able to rescue her niece, the house, its smell, its anachronistic decor, the lack of mod cons, how mismatched this all is with the fake Facebook profile, the iPhone, the Find My Friends app…

Idly she presses the space bar and her screen saver blooms before her: Rosie on stage, in the red cape, the hood pulled over her head, the hint of those blue eyes peeping from the shadow. She looks so pretty, so young. So innocent. And despite everything that's happened, that's what she is, still. She wasn't doing anything that isn't natural, isn't a completely normal part of becoming a grown-up. When all this is behind them, Bridget hopes she will see that and be able to come to the adult world in a safe and loving way, free from shame.

She studies the photograph, drawn in by her niece's cartoonish baby blues. It was taken at that first performance, she thinks. That was when they met Emily. Bridget remembers their conversation, Emily saying she'd gone to the Central School of Speech and Drama. Bridget hadn't mentioned she'd gone to Central too – it was not her conversation to interrupt – and besides, what would she have said? Yes, I went there, but I dropped out because my little sister had fallen to pieces? No, too complicated. But she thinks about it now as she pulls the sliced bread from the bread bin, the butter, cheese and pickle from the fridge. She spreads butter on the bread, cuts cheese in thick slices, scoops glossy brown pickle from the jar.

Emily must have gone there at a different time, since Bridget cannot remember her. She should have asked her when she stopped for dinner, but that evening they were there to talk about Rosie, and besides, it didn't come up. Emily is a little older, probably. She looks it anyway. And Bridget would have remembered her. Judging by those photos she showed them, she had been beautiful, if old-fashioned, probably one of those people who are never properly young, who in middle age become what they've always been.

Emily.

That's what Rosie said when Bridget ripped the tape from her mouth. *Emily*, she muttered as she slid into oblivion, before panic overtook them once again.

Bridget leaves the sandwich stuff on the side and goes back to the kitchen table. Googles: Emily Wood.

She is on IMDb. Bridget has checked all this before, the photos of Emily's TV and theatre work. She really was so pretty then, a lot slimmer too. The blue eyes that blink huge now from behind strong lenses then were smaller, intense, penetrating. She was in *The Bill*, as she'd said, and *Casualty*. True to her claims of being a technophobe, she has no Facebook, no Instagram, no Twitter, no LinkedIn. But there is no mention of her mentoring agency, no link, nothing. Didn't Rosie have a flyer or a business card or something?

She returns to Rosie's room on the strength of nothing more than a feeling. The last time Bridget ignored a feeling, it cost her niece dear, and she's not about to do that again, no way. Rosie's rucksack isn't on the floor where it usually is. She will have taken it with her, of course, which means her purse won't be here either. Which means both are still in that house of hell, along with her Doc Marten boots.

Shit.

The old man dead in the hall. Rosie's boots and bag in his house. Bridget's DNA in his house.

The road to the police is inevitable.

But she can't – won't – think about that.

Rosie's bedside-table drawer is open an inch. Emily's card could be in there. But to search feels like a violation, even now.

This is pure paranoia: nerves jangling like a wind chime in the breeze. Post-traumatic stress, that's all it is. But that house. That house. The clean draining board, when all around was so fetid, so rank, so unsavoury. The front door to all appearances unused. That man, his nervousness, his grey pallor. The smell of him: lethargy, staleness. The lack of any technology in the house beyond an old-fashioned analogue radio. How did a guy like that get as far as Hampton Hill High Street on his own? He couldn't have taken her by force, not in broad daylight, not at that time of the morning. Persuasion then. But how? His appearance alone was off-putting enough, and as soon as he revealed himself to be Ollie Thomas, Rosie would have run a mile, wouldn't she? She would have got herself out of there, out onto the crowded street, and come home.

In Rosie's bedside-table drawer are various pieces of cheap jewellery, hair bobbles, a hairbrush, nail varnishes, a half-used packet of make-up remover pads, birthday cards, one from Bridget herself. She picks it up and reads it:

Squirt, it's not true what they say. You're not as daft as you look.
Love, your favourite auntie currently living in Twickenham.

She smiles, puts the card back. Under the other cards she finds not the business card but a flyer, folded in half.

Into the Light. Mentoring and Representation with Madame Belle.

The background is primrose, with an overlaid triangle in a paler yellow, like light cast by a spotlight. She remembers Rosie showing her the website the day after they'd met Emily. Bridget had been making the dinner, but she remembers the layout, the yellow colour.

'Cool,' she'd said, without taking too much notice, it seems to her now, thinking about it. 'You're going to be the next Emma Stone.'

With the flyer in her hand, Bridget returns to the kitchen. She should be getting to the hospital now but there is nothing she, Bridget, can do and if she's needed urgently, Toni will call her. Tones needed space. She made that very clear. Besides, for reasons Bridget cannot name, it feels important to look at this website.

Up it comes, a simple font on that same primrose yellow, the same spotlight.

Into the Light. *Mentoring and Representation with Madame Belle.*

Of course. The website's not listed under Emily Wood but Madame Belle. Beneath the header are small thumbnail photographs of ten or twelve actors, some in colour, some in black and white. She scans the faces, giving them her full attention this time instead of glancing at them from the stove. There is no one she recognises. Rosie is not on the site, which is odd. Emily must have had her headshot for weeks. Bridget looks again, clicks on the photos one by one to zoom in. There is a black-and-white shot of a boy of around twenty. He looks familiar. Enough to bug her. Something, somewhere… some chink of recognition at the edges of Bridget's… Where does she know him from? What twenty-year-olds does she know? Saph's son? He's into drama and all that stuff, isn't he? No, it's not him, too square around the jaw and this guy's hair is curly, not straight. A fan of The Promise? Nah. Too young. Who is it? Who is it who is it who is it?

Lysander.

It is Lysander. *A Midsummer Night's Dream*, end-of-first-year production, the last thing she did at Central. But Lysander is not twenty. He's Bridget's age, give or take. What was his name? He'll be in his fifties now. It can't be him. But still… my God, it's so like him, so very…

Bridget runs to her room and pulls out the large packing box she keeps in the shoe well of her wardrobe. She heaves it onto her bed and pulls off the top. Inside are photo albums, a scrapbook full of signed photos of famous actors she's worked with over the years: Colin Firth, Hugh Bonneville, Harriet Walter. Worked with in the sense that she was a stagehand. Those were the days. After she dropped out to look after Toni, she hung around the Old Vic long enough to be given something to carry. Even got the odd bit part, and it was enough, and slowly the work… didn't take off exactly but increased. She got into writing. Not as if the RSC were going to beat a path, so she found a way of creating work where none existed. There are programmes from all the theatre performances she's done: an all-female adaptation of *The Crucible* from the days when she worked with Fishnet Tight, a women-only theatre group in Wimbledon; Christmas pantos she did every year for at least a decade until the band took over… but she's getting sidetracked. Where is the damn programme for *A Midsummer Night's Dream*? If it's from college days, it will be nearer the bottom, won't it?

She tips the box onto the bed, watches the papers slide and drop to the floor. And there it is, among the loose photos and posters and flyers of her life:

CSSD presents A Midsummer Night's Dream.

She flips through. It doesn't take her long to find the headshots. Herself, Bottom, the donkey, playing opposite beautiful raven-haired, green-eyed Jacqueline Ball's Tatiana. Whatever happened to her? She went to Africa, didn't she? Ended up in charity work? And Dawn Worley, who played Hippolyta and dyed her hair pink for the role. And Lysander, there he is, Lysander… Stephen John.

'Stephen John?' she says out loud. 'What the hell is going on?'

Programme gripped tightly in her hand, she runs back into the kitchen, eyes locked on the photo. Her heart is banging. Already she knows what she's looking at, but she needs to confirm it with her own eyes until it is undeniable. At this moment it is, quite simply, surreal. Holding the programme up in front of her, she sits in front of the laptop. Emily's website reappears in a blast of primrose yellow. Bridget clicks on the young male actor's photo.

It is not only the same actor. It is the same photograph.

'Jesus.'

CHAPTER 57

Daddy died first, younger than he should have. And then, when Mummy died, I sold the farm and we came here. Our farm was in Hampshire and we moved to Ham. I liked the continuity of that. Ham, do you see? I wasn't living at the farm then, of course. I'd escaped to the bright lights, the big city, a dingy shared rental flat in Clapham North. But I moved in with him because I knew he couldn't survive alone, not without Mummy and Daddy.

I thought that now we were grown-ups, it would stop. We had left our childhood games, our plays, our theatre. Oh, the glorious plays we would enact, just for one another: the knight and his lady, the prince and his princess, the pigs and the cows and the sheep our unwitting extras! He was every bit as talented as me in the dramatic arts, but, alas, he was too particular. Strange, they called him. A bit of an oddball – something funny about that one. And of course his nerves would never have stood it. We had left such childish things behind along with our improvised costumes, our cereal-box crowns, our bed-sheet robes. I thought – hoped, rather – once we moved into the terrace that he would have left the other games behind too. The night games. The violence. But he hadn't. They didn't stop. None of it stopped until he pushed me down the stairs. Three months in a back brace is no joke. I put on weight; I was less agile, less firm of flesh. I was no use to him any more. I was no use to anyone.

The thespian world is a fickle friend indeed.

So when the house next door came up for sale, it was the perfect solution. He couldn't have managed without me nearby, no way, Jose.

He didn't clean, he didn't cook – his house was a disgrace. But that's the way he liked it. Messy child.

His rages grew worse. He would scream, wrap his hands around my neck, drag me by the hair, you name it. I bought him a tablet computer, set it up in his name, sorted out websites. Girls, very young. It was better than having to go and buy the magazines, or have them coming through the door.

That kept him going for a little while. But it wasn't enough.

He wanted live flesh. He was very specific about that. He wanted it live and young, and he wanted it drowsy and smelling of lavender. As I had been.

CHAPTER 58

BRIDGET

Bridget's breath comes in ragged bursts; her chest burns. Emily has bolstered her page with fake headshots from years ago. The woman is a fraud. She checked out, for all the rest, but she is a fraud nonetheless.

Emily, Rosie said when Bridget ripped the tape from her mouth, dazzled perhaps by the sun, not knowing who she was in that moment of panic and terror. Was it Emily that Rosie was expecting to see at the door of the van? The more Bridget thinks about it, the more this possibility becomes a probability.

She calls Toni. Toni's phone is dead.

'Fuck!'

Think. Think, Bridget. That night, the night Emily came over. She said she lived near Richmond, didn't she? That guy's house was in Ham, which is near Kingston, yes, that's the way Bridget drove, but it's near Richmond too. It lies between the two towns, doesn't it? Emily mentioned she had a brother, what was his name? Could that revolting old man be her brother?

Emily was meant to be coming over to the flat this afternoon. Didn't Toni say she'd texted her to let her know Rosie was in hospital? Which means that Emily knows where she is…

'Oh no. Oh no, no, no, no, no.'

A search for West Middlesex Hospital: the switchboard number. In panic, Bridget's eyes water, her fingers are clumsy on the keys.

Whatever happens, she has to get a message to Toni. It could be paranoia, but for now paranoia is all she has, and it is paranoia that tells her that, somehow, Emily is connected to the man lying dead in the terraced house in Ham. Is it possible she's his sister? Accomplice? If Emily shows up at the hospital, Toni has no reason not to trust her, no reason not to leave her alone with Rosie.

Bridget calls the switchboard. It rings and rings, goes to the answering machine. She tries again. Same thing. She tries again. A woman answers. Bridget gasps, gives Rosie's full name.

'It's really urgent I get a message to my sister, Rosie's mother,' she says. 'Can you tell me which ward she's in?'

She gives the details, hears the woman tapping them in. Bridget drums her fingernails on the tabletop. Come on; come on.

'She's still in A&E,' the woman says. 'She's not been moved yet, according to this. Well, she might have been moved but they've not updated the system.'

'Can you put me through? I need to get a message to her. It's urgent.'

'Hold, please.'

Music, if you can call it that, streams down the line. Bridget bites her lip against the scream she fears will escape her at any moment. The non-specific melody goes on and on, absent-minded refrains with no discernible hook, looping endlessly. Bridget swears into the mouthpiece, and, as if in response, the phone goes dead: *Fuck you.*

Her chair scrapes across the kitchen floor as she stands. It would be quicker to get there in person. Police, hospitals, schools, every single system in this country is clogged to the point of heart attack with meaningless bureaucracy, cutbacks, efficiency drives. All the technology at their fingertips, all this *communication*, and never has it been so impossible to reach another human being. She grabs the keys to the van, but on second thoughts pulls out her phone and goes to the Uber app. A cab will save time on parking. A cab will stop her driving the van through the main entrance of the hospital.

Her car is a Toyota Prius. Her driver is Rasheed. He is five minutes away.

Five minutes.

She rushes to the bathroom and pees. Four minutes. She'll grab Rosie's clothes and shove them in a holdall. On the side of the bath there are screwed-up tissues from when Rosie was crying earlier tonight. She gathers them up and pushes her foot to the pedal bin. The bin lid opens. When she sees what's inside, her stomach turns over.

'What the hell…?'

CHAPTER 59

TONI

'I came as soon as I could, dear.'

'Emily!' I burst into tears, turn immediately back to you. 'Rosie? Rosie? Look who it is. It's Emily, baby girl, she's come to see you.'

'My poor darling,' Emily says, limping over, folding my head into her bosom. 'What on earth…? How is she, my poor lamb? What on earth happened?'

'She's doing fine, Emily. Bit of boy trouble, a few too many painkillers, suspected bump on the head among other things. Shock. They're keeping her in overnight in case she has a concussion. Bloody teenagers, eh?'

Emily sits on the plastic chair by your bed and reaches for your hand. She brings it to her lips and kisses it. The sight moves me, and for a moment I can't speak.

'She's been through a lot,' I manage to say, and Emily nods and smiles and turns to you, as if to give me a private moment to compose myself.

I cannot tell her what's happened to you, baby girl. I know she's a good egg, but she's not family. I need to speak to your auntie Bridget before I say any more. I can't see us not involving the police, not now, but if there's any way we can get away without calling them, we won't. And if I tell Emily the whole truth, there's the possibility she might take it to the police. I trust her, but not with everything, not like I trust your auntie Bridge. And there's nothing to place your auntie Bridge at that house, do you see? Her fingerprints aren't on police records. The only fingerprints on their records are mine, taken when I was arrested for shoplifting, aged seventeen, nearly thirty years ago. And of course my prints are nowhere near the place, thanks to your auntie. I need your auntie Bridget more than that man's death needs solving, Rosie. He deserved everything he got. The world is better without him in it. I hope you understand, poppet. What can the police do anyway? Start sticking their noses into stuff that has nothing to do with them, that's all. The man was evil. Who knows what he would have done to you if Auntie Bridge hadn't found you?

'Can you tell me what happened?' Emily is looking at me intently now, her eyes huge behind those thick lenses. *What big eyes you have, Grandma*, I think.

'Sorry,' I say. 'I was miles away. I'm so tired. It's a long story, Emily…'

Emily's warm hand lays itself over mine.

'Call me Em,' she says, patting my hand, taking hers away.

'Em,' I say. 'Basically, she went on a date with a boy and ended up in a very bad situation. The boy turned out to be a wrong 'un, but it's all right now. A few bumps and bruises, a fright, I'm sure she'll be very careful in future.' From nowhere, I'm crying all over again.

'Oh there, there.' Emily hands me a tissue. 'And you get so anxious, don't you? I know you worry about her so. Have you… have you called the police, dear?'

'Not yet, no. We're just going to see how she is, what she says when she wakes up. She hasn't told us anything really, she was too upset, and then she took some of my pills, silly girl.'

Emily is silent for a moment. I've shocked her, I realise. She must think it's highly strange, not calling the police, but that's not my problem, not right now.

'So she hasn't spoken yet?' she asks.

I shake my head. 'I think she was in shock. I should have brought her straight here. She was all out of sorts and she wouldn't stop crying.'

'Did she come home then? What, by herself?'

I shake my head. I open my mouth to speak, but I can't. And when Emily lays her warm hand on mine again, the tears come, the way tears do when you can feel that someone cares about you.

'It's OK, dear,' she says softly. 'Don't tell me anything you're not comfortable with.'

'I should have known,' I sob. 'I should have brought her straight here, but I'm a nurse, you know, well, I used to be, and I thought I could handle it. I thought she'd be OK. She had a bath and went to bed and I gave her something to calm her down and I thought she'd be fine in the morning. But then when I checked on her she wouldn't wake up so we had to call an ambulance in the end. Maybe he'd given her Rohypnol or something, I don't know. But don't mention her going to meet a boy, will you? Not to the doctors, all right? We'd prefer to deal with this in the family. I hope you understand.'

Emily leans over and takes my hand in both of hers. It is like a warm embrace, like a hug, and I think how full of love she is, for you, yes, but for all of us too. She's grown attached to us as we have to her. I mistrusted her at first; I know I did. I was looking the other way.

'Whatever you want, dear,' she says. 'Sometimes we need to keep things in the family, don't we?' She glances over to you and returns her gaze to me.

'I'm so sorry we've been such a mess,' I say. 'With Rosie being ill and everything. She will get over it. She just needs time. We've all needed more time than any of us thought after what happened, you know, with her dad and the accident and everything…'

'Nonsense,' she says. 'Nothing to apologise for. And now, I hope you don't mind my saying so, but you look exhausted. Would you like me to fetch you some tea, something to eat?'

I shake my head. 'It's all right. My sister'll be here soon. She's going to bring a flask and some sandwiches. I'm not hungry anyway. I don't think I could face anything. And I know what the vending-machine coffee is like – it's rank. I work here, remember.'

She chuckles. 'Of course you do! Silly moo, aren't I? Brain like the proverbial sieve.' She glances back at you, baby girl, and bites her lip. Concern etches new lines on her face.

'How are you?' I ask.

'Me! Oh, I'm fine and dandy, don't you fret about me. It's you I'm worried about, dear. Listen, why don't you take yourself off a moment? Get some air – get out of this miserable place for a minute or two. There's a couch in the waiting room; you could get forty winks. I can keep an eye on her.'

I squeeze her hand. 'Thanks, Emily. Em. I could really use some air actually, I'm so stale! Not to mention needing the loo!' I pull my bag from the floor into my lap and sigh. 'If you see Bridget, tell her I'll be right back, OK?'

'Right you are, dear. Don't rush. I've brought my knitting, so to speak.' She holds up a book and chuckles.

'Emily Wood.' I lean forward and give her a kiss on the cheek. 'What would we do without you?'

CHAPTER 60

ROSIE

My head falls back. Wrong angle. Neck weird, like my head is hanging upside down. The pillow has gone. Who has taken my pillow?

'Now then, Rosie my dear,' someone, a woman, says. 'I've sent your mum out for a break, so it's just you and me.'

Emily? Emily, is that you?

'I'm just going to pop the curtain across so we can have some privacy, that's it.'

It is Emily. It so is. A whooshing sound. The something bad is a deep pain in my gut. The something bad is here. It's here and it's Emily. The feeling, the shame… is Emily. It isn't me. I'm not the something bad. I'm not the shame. It's her. That house, that kitchen, the wasp in the honey. The scones. The tea. The man from the café, standing in the doorway, the dried splashes on his glasses. Emily's face looking down at me, blinking, huge pale eyes. The chemical smell. Then nothing. Emily is the smell. Emily is the something bad. Her big eyes, then nothing. She…

'That's better.'

I want to kick, but I can't move. *Help! Someone help me! Mummy?*

'Well, I have to say, you fair gave us the slip, didn't you? As for Owen, well, I can't leave him alone for five minutes without him making a mess of everything. He really is hopeless, been that way since we were little! I suppose I should feel relieved, or happy, or free or something, but it's not as simple as that when you're tied to someone, is it? To family? I know you know what I mean.

'And so here you are. And by an absolute miracle, no one's called the police yet. I know why I haven't, dear, but I'm rather fascinated, I must say, by why your mother hasn't. Or your marvellous auntie Bridget, who I'm guessing is also responsible for shooting my poor Owen.'

Fingers on my cheek, stroking. *Help. Help me, Mummy! Auntie Bridge, help!*

'You'll be my last girl. I want you to know I've been fond of you. You're sweet in your way, and you don't have everything on a plate the way a lot of these girls do. I thought you did, you see. The theatre types usually do, or they did in my day. And you oozed privilege, up on that stage, with your nice voice and, later, your lovely manners. I must say I was taken aback when I saw your circumstances, your poor mother.

'Now this won't take long, dear, and it shouldn't hurt. I'll say goodbye then.

'Goodbye, Little Red.'

CHAPTER 61

BRIDGET

Bridget is running. Through the main entrance of the hospital, the iron taste of blood in her mouth. She reaches reception.

'Rosie,' she pants, 'Rosie Flint. Can you tell me which ward she's in? Or she might still be in A&E.'

The receptionist taps on the keyboard. She does not meet Bridget's eye, nor does she smile.

'She's in Jupiter. Level 4.' The receptionist gives a contemplative hmm. 'But it's after seven, I'm afraid. Visiting time finishes at seven.'

'This is an emergency.'

'I'm sure it is. Is it the police you need? Hey! Excuse me? Hey!'

Bridget is running. She can't stop, won't stop. Up ahead, the lift doors are opening.

'Hold the lift,' she calls. 'Hold the lift!'

She makes it and smiles at the nurse who has held the door for her.

'Visiting time is over,' the nurse says with an apologetic frown.

Bridget presses the number 4. 'I know. I'm just dropping her… her inhaler – they said to bring it.' She puts her hands behind her back. She has no inhaler, no bag, nothing in her hands. Only her keys in her jacket pocket, her cash card and phone in the back pocket of her jeans.

With a ping, the lift stops at the fourth floor. It seems to take ages for the doors to slide open.

'Sorry.' Bridget runs out of the lift first. She scans the ward names, trying not to let panic jumble the letters. A nurse pushing a trolley full of drugs passes her and frowns.

'Slow down, madam,' she calls after her. 'No running.'

'Sorry,' Bridget calls breathlessly, but she does not slow down – she does not stop running.

At the entrance to the ward, she pauses. Her senses cloud. She half walks, half runs, scanning the rooms, the beds, their occupants. Sweat pours down her face, down the back of her neck. In perhaps the fourth or fifth room, there are four beds, two empty, one with a privacy curtain around it, one containing a teenager with a grey tinge to her skin. Bridget takes a step inside.

'Who are you looking for?' the grey girl asks, something aggressive in her manner. There are bandages on her wrists.

'My niece. Rosie Flint. She's fifteen.'

'What's she in for?'

'She's—'

There's a voice coming from behind the curtain. Bridget can't hear what it's saying. But she recognises the tone, the pitch, the jaunty cadences. Emily.

She swipes at the thin fabric, pushes it back on its runners with a loud whoosh. Emily is bent over the bed. She is pressing a pillow to Rosie's face. The back of her neck is stiff with the effort – her elbows are out, her knuckles white.

'Oh my God!' the girl in the bed opposite shouts. 'Police! Help! That woman's trying to kill that girl!'

Bridget throws herself forward, grabs Emily's shoulders. Emily falls, they both fall to the floor, Emily on top, the two of them struggling like overturned crabs.

'Oh my God!' the girl shouts again. 'She was trying to suffocate her! That lady! She's fucking mental! Call the police!'

Bridget rolls Emily off her, then onto her back, sits on her belly and pins her arms to the floor.

'Murderer,' Emily hisses, her eyes huge glassy circles of pale blue. The same eyes as that man. Her brother, of course – why didn't Bridget see?

There are voices, footsteps running. Emily wrenches one arm free but it is caught by a male porter, who seems to have skidded across the floor on his knees.

'This woman is assaulting me,' Emily shouts.

'Stay calm, madam,' he says.

'She was trying to suffocate my niece,' Bridget says, breathless. 'With her pillow.'

'That's right, she was,' the girl in the bed chimes in. 'She fucking was!'

Please God someone shut that girl up.

Emily kicks, bucks, her ribcage solid, fraught between Bridget's knees.

'Get off me,' she shouts. 'Murderer! This woman is a murderer!'

The girl has begun to shriek. 'She was trying to suffocate her! That old lady there with the glasses! She was trying to kill 'er. I don't feel safe, I'm not safe, I'm not fucking safe here.'

A nurse bustles over to the girl, her hands two stop signs: calm down. Another follows, walks briskly to Rosie's bed.

'Bridge!' Toni's face looms above Bridget. 'What the hell's going on?'

'Get this assassin off me,' Emily hisses. 'Assassin! Assassin!'

There are two men now, both dressed in hospital garb, though Bridget is not sure what their uniforms mean. Each has one of Emily's arms.

Somewhere a walkie-talkie crackles. Somewhere a voice calls out: 'Police, call 999.'

'It's over, Emily,' Bridget says. 'It's over.'

Emily meets her eye. And like that, without a word, something in her appears to die. She stops thrashing. Her eyes hold Bridget's for another second before she closes them, inhales deeply through her nose. Her chest sinks, she lies perfectly still. A smile spreads across her face, as if she has entered a state of karmic peace.

Unnerved, Bridget climbs off Emily's stomach. The ward hushes; the men too become still. No one speaks. Even the shrieking girl in the bed is quiet.

Toni glances back and forth from Bridget to Emily, her eyes round, wild, her mouth open with shock and incomprehension.

'What's happening?' she says after a moment. 'What the hell is going on?'

The ward is suspended, slowed, the air thick. The porters or nurses, or whatever the two men are, have Emily locked down, but she is motionless, her face impassive, vacant, her eyes still closed as if in prayer.

'She had the pillow to her face,' Bridget says. 'Emily. She was trying to kill Rosie. She had the pillow over her face, she…'

The men hoist Emily to her feet. Slowly they walk her out of the ward, their faces stern, bewildered. Somewhere another walkie-talkie sparks into life. The nurse is talking to the grey girl, quietly, quietly. The only word Bridget catches is *police*.

Toni looks at Bridget. Their eyes lock. After a second, Toni heads over to Rosie's bed. Bridget follows, stands on the other side.

'Is she all right?' Toni asks the nurse.

'She's fine.' The nurse puts the pillow back under Rosie's head, straightens her covers before turning to Toni. 'The police will be here shortly. They'll need to talk to you both.' She looks from Toni to Bridget. 'Are you all right, madam? Are you both all right?'

'We're fine,' Bridget says over the thump of her own heart. 'Nasty shock, that's all. As long as Rosie's OK.'

'She's breathing normally,' the nurse says. 'Her heart rate is regular. Try not to worry. Stay here for now and I'll give you a shout when the police arrive.'

'Yeah. Cheers.'

The nurse walks away. Bridget stares after her a moment before returning her gaze to Toni.

'What the hell…?' Toni says.

'Emily was Ollie's accomplice,' Bridget whispers. 'Ollie, online Ollie, was Owen, Emily's brother. They were working together.'

'What? How?' Toni's brow furrows.

'We need to keep our voices down. The guy at the house, the guy I… you know. That was Emily's brother. I'm guessing it was Emily who picked Rosie up and took her there.'

'Why didn't you tell me…'

'I didn't know. Emily wasn't at the house when I— I didn't know, Tones.'

Bridget watches realisation dawn on Toni's face.

'You saved her again,' Toni says quietly, and then, after a moment, 'And now the police are coming. And Emily…'

Bridget nods. 'Yes.' She feels tired, in her bones. 'The police.'

'She called you an assassin.'

'Yes.'

An eerie calm has descended on the ward. There are no raised voices, no hints of disruption in the corridor. Wherever they have taken Emily, they must have her behind closed doors. Bridget wonders what she will do now. Will she confess to everything? And then of course they'll have to face the matter of the body. Emily knows it was her; the fingerprints on the gun will match. Arrest is inevitable now.

Slowly Bridget drags the privacy curtain back around its U-shaped runner. From the other side of her niece's hospital bed she faces Toni once again: Tones, her mad, broken little sister, the sister she has spent her life trying to save, mostly from herself. With a heavy heart, she digs in the pocket of her leather jacket and pulls out the empty packets she found in the bathroom bin. From the other pocket the ones she found under Toni's bed. She meets her sister's eye, holds it, keeps her voice low.

'We have minutes.' She throws the blister packs onto the bed. 'I found the diazepam in the bathroom bin, the rest under your bed. I only went under there to grab a sports bag. Do you want to tell me what's going on?'

Toni looks from the empty packs back to Bridget. Tears spring, overflow, run down her face, which she plunges into her hands.

'Oh God.'

'Tell me, Toni. Tell me quickly and very quietly. I can't help you unless you tell me.'

'I didn't realise she'd been drugged.' Her voice is no more than a whisper. 'You never said. I just… I just wanted to give her something to help her sleep. I gave her too many.'

'But diazepam? I thought you were going to give her a couple of paracetamol. How many?'

'Bridge, please. Too many, yes, too many, but not enough to—'

'What were you thinking? You must have known you'd knock her out even if she hadn't had anything else. And what about all these? Movicol, Imodium… Why were they under the bed?'

Toni's face crumples, reddens. 'I was trying to keep her safe.'

'You *gave* them to her? What, all at once?'

Toni nods, gives a loud sob.

'What? Was she… When?' And then it hits her. 'Before the auditions? Is that why she was sick? The diarrhoea? The constipation? Tell me. You have to tell me.'

Toni stares down at her hands folded in her lap. She looks so small. After a moment, she gives another sob. 'I just wanted… She's only fifteen. Oh God.'

'You could have burst her colon or… or seriously dehydrated her.' Bridget makes her way around the bed, grabs the spare plastic chair to sit on. She takes her sister's hands in her own.

'I would never… I just wanted to keep her safe, Bridge.' Toni's voice is a low howl. 'And she was so peaceful afterwards, all cuddled up with me on the sofa. She was my little girl… she was mine.'

'We need to keep our voices right down. We need to whisper. Look at me, Tones. Look at me.'

Toni sniffs. Her eyes are red. They are scared.

'You can't ever do that again, Tones. Yeah? You can't. I know you were trying to protect her, I know you're finding it hard letting her go, but you can't do that. They'll take her away from you. You could go to prison. I'm going to prison for sure, so there's only you now. I won't be able to look after you or Rosie for a long time, hon. And you'll lose her, Tones. They'll take her off you. Do you get that? Tell me you get that.'

Toni's mouth distorts. 'I only did it a few times. It was all right before Emily came, but then… I didn't trust her. Rosie loved her though. And then I did trust her, a bit, but I was jealous. I didn't want her coming in and taking my daughter. But I could feel Rosie breaking away from me. She will break away. She'll go off into the world and she'll never come back. It will never be the same. I can't lose her, Bridge. I can't be on my own. What if she'd got that film part? What if she'd become famous?'

'But there never *were* any auditions, hon.'

'What?' Confusion writes itself all over Toni's face.

'That's what I'm telling you. Emily and her brother were working together. Kidnapping and God knows what, God knows how many girls. I'm guessing the auditions were a way of luring them in…'

Toni wipes her face with her hand. She exhales heavily, shakily. 'I can't take it in. I can't believe it.' She bites on the knuckle of her thumb, a tiny cry escaping her. 'But why bother with the online thing? Why not just bundle her into a van?'

'I don't know. A game of trust or something. We'll find out, I'm sure. Diversion? So that Emily stayed beyond suspicion? Although I can't think how they thought the police wouldn't trace the phone. I don't know, Tones, I don't know.'

Toni nods, bites her thumbnail, tears off a thin white strip with her teeth.

'You won't tell them, will you?' she says. 'The police? About what I've done?'

'Of course I won't. But this stops here, today – do you understand? You have to promise you'll get help. Professional help. I need to know you can look after Rosie when I'm not here. You have to promise me.'

Toni meets her eye and nods, her face sorrow itself. 'I promise.'

Voices outside, in the ward. Another walkie-talkie.

'They're here. This is it.'

Toni nods, sniffs. 'What do we say?'

'Nothing. We know her, she's Rosie's agent – we thought she was nice. But apart from that, we say nothing, yeah? Just leave Ollie out of it for now.'

Bridget stands. She feels the brush of Toni's fingers across her palm as their hands slowly separate. She looks over at her niece. Rosie's legs are straight and still as a soldier's. Her tube of saline is undisturbed. It takes Bridget another second to see that her eyes are open.

CHAPTER 62

TRANSCRIPT OF INTERVIEW WITH EMILY MIRABELLE WOOD (EXTRACT)

DS Andrews: This interview is being tape-recorded and may be given in evidence if your case is brought to trial. We are in an interview room at Twickenham Police Station, Richmond Borough. The date is July 2018 and the time by my watch is 3 p.m. I am Detective Sergeant Luke Andrews. The other police officer present is Detective Constable Hope Caton. Please state your full name and date of birth.

Emily Wood: Emily Mirabelle Wood.

DS Andrews: Ms Wood, would it be all right to refer to you as Emily from this point on? For the benefit of the tape, the suspect is nodding. Also present is Stephen Richardson, solicitor. Mr Richardson, you are not here to act simply as an observer. Your role here is to advise the suspect, facilitate communication and ensure that the interview is conducted fairly. For the benefit of the tape, Mr Richardson has nodded. Emily, at the conclusion of the interview, I will give you a notice explaining what will happen to the tapes and how you or your solicitor can get access to them, all right?

Emily Wood: Yes.

DS Andrews: Emily, I need to caution you that you do not have to say anything. But it may harm your defence if you do not mention when questioned something you later rely on in court. Anything you do say may be given in evidence. Do you understand?

Emily Wood: I have been in *The Bill*, you know. [Laughs] Sorry, yes. I understand, Officer.

DS Andrews: Do you agree that there are no other persons present other than those previously mentioned?

Emily Wood: [Coughs] Yes.

DS Andrews: All right. Emily, you were apprehended apparently attempting to suffocate Miss Roisin Flint at West Middlesex University Hospital yesterday evening at approximately 7.15 p.m. Can you explain what happened?

Emily Wood: Why? [Laughs] You've just explained it yourself. That's exactly what happened.

DS Andrews: Can you tell me why this was?

Emily Wood: I'd brought the girl home for Owen, but she got away. I didn't want her blabbing, so obviously I had to shut her up, as it were.

DS Andrew: Can you tell me who Owen is?

Emily Wood: He's my brother.

DS Andrews: Can you describe your relationship with Miss Rosie Flint?

Emily Wood: I'm her theatrical agent. I offered her representation but that was a ruse. In reality, I needed a girl for Owen.

DS Andrews: So you're saying you took Rosie Flint to your property at 31 Parkview Close, Ham, Richmond Borough, which you have stated is your own home, at approximately 12.15 p.m., and that you did this for your brother, Owen? For the benefit of the tape, the suspect is nodding. Could you take us through the events as they unfolded after you brought Miss Flint into the property at number 31?

Emily Wood: That I can. [Coughs] I brought the girl into the kitchen in the usual way. We waited there for Owen, who comes by bus. He doesn't drive, you see. He came in and said hello and sat down with us at the table. We had tea together and ate the scones with butter and honey. I always bake scones when we take a girl.

DS Andrews: Emily, do you mean to say that there were other girls? That you've kidnapped others? For the purpose of the tape, the suspect is nodding. And can you tell us where they are now?'

Emily Wood: I can. In the greenhouse. Under the greenhouse, I should say. Owen loved the greenhouse. He has very green fingers. Had. But he'd let all that go lately. Which is a shame. He grew fabulous tomatoes.

DS Andrews: Emily, is the greenhouse at your property, at number 31 Parkview Close?

Emily Wood: No, dear. At my brother's. Next door. Number 29.

DS Andrews: How many girls?

Emily Wood: Rosie would have been our third.

DS Andrews: Do you have their names?

Emily Wood: Lucy Tavistock and Cosima Wright. I kept the newspaper articles. They'll be in my folder, in the unit to the left of the stove, third drawer down. The first one was years ago, 2010 or '11 sometime. Before we got the greenhouse. The last one was more recent. I started keeping tabs on her in November time. We weren't meant to be taking another but Owen was getting antsy. The Rosie Flint operation wasn't going as I had hoped. I told him we had to go slow. She wasn't biting, and the mother would barely let her out of her sight. When she got the part in the play, I changed tack. I knew exactly how I would take her, but then, when I made my move, as it were, she kept getting sick. I didn't want to take another girl, but we needed an interim. We got Cosima from a café in Putney. Tennis champ. That slowed the Rosie operation down somewhat, I can tell you. Almost had to let it drop. But we soon picked up where we left off.

DS Andrews: Emily, I'm arresting you for the abduction and murder of Lucy Tavistock and Cosima Wright. You do not have to say anything. But it may harm your defence if you do not mention when questioned something you later rely on in court. Anything you do say may be given in evidence. Do you understand?

CHAPTER 63

TONI

They interviewed us separately, there in the hospital. They took notes in their little black notepads. They were going to take us to the station, but you needed me and they could see I needed your auntie Bridge. They told us to report to Twickenham Police Station at 2 p.m. the following day so that they could take a formal statement. We agreed.

You were awake. You ate a sandwich from the vending machine, drank some water. After a stern lecture on the dangers of misusing barbiturates, they discharged you. It was a little after 10 p.m.

On the way home, in the back seat of the cab, you were OK. You were tired and pale, but you were OK. Your auntie Bridge and me were fragments of ourselves, but we put on brave faces. You told us bits and pieces. I had a million questions; I wanted a full account, second by second, but I knew you were not strong enough yet. There would be time, and at that moment it was a great comfort to me to know that, even though their drugs had caused an involuntary overdose, you had been knocked out for most of your ordeal, and nothing too unthinkable had actually happened. Still, I knew you'd been frightened, and that you'd yet to process what they'd intended to do to you.

So here we are at home. It's the next morning. The police will have interviewed Emily last night, maybe this morning. They know that some mad late-middle-aged woman tried to kill a teenage girl. But once Emily has pinned her brother's death on your auntie Bridge, they'll be here not with their notepads but with sirens and cuffs. Something tells me we won't actually have to present ourselves at the station. We'll be taken away in the back of a squad car. Your auntie Bridge will not come back.

But you know none of this yet.

Last night, when we got home, I helped you change into your PJs. Auntie Bridge brought you hot milk with honey, but to our great joy you told us you were starving, that you could murder some toast and peanut butter.

'Coming up.' Through her unimaginable turmoil, Auntie Bridge still managed to smile – all either of us wanted to do was make it right, make what were potentially our last hours together as special as they could be, and toast was as good a place as any to start.

I was alone with you in your room. You were sipping your hot milk. The moment was a lull, a kind of peace. The colour was returning to your face, a faint hint of pink beneath your freckles.

'Are you tired… love?' I asked. I could not, I realised, say *baby girl*. Not any more. I wonder now why I ever called you that. You are fifteen years old. You are not a baby.

You shook your head, drained your mug, which I slid onto your bedside table. 'I don't know.'

I wondered how much of my conversation with Bridget you'd overheard in the hospital. Did you know I gave you those pills? Would you forgive me when I told you? Would you ever trust me again? I could not wait another second. The weight of it was crushing me.

'Rosie.' I took your hand in mine. 'I need to tell you something. I need to apologise to you.'

'No, I do,' you said, tears welling. 'I lied to you, Mummy. I am so sorry.' You began to cry. I was crying too. 'I'll never lie to you again. I'm so, so sorry, Mummy.' You pushed yourself to the edge of the bed and threw your arms around me. You sobbed into my neck and I into yours.

'It's OK,' I said. 'It's all OK now. But I'm the one who should be sorry.'

'No, Mummy. If I hadn't lied, none of this would have happened.'

'Rosie. Listen to me. You have to listen.'

You sat back on the bed, wiped your cheeks with the back of your hand and gave a deep sniff.

'I made you ill. I did. Me.' There was no other way to say it. It was as bald and as shameful and as unforgivable as that.

'What do you mean?'

'Last night. I gave you my diazepam. I gave you too many, to knock you out, to make you sleep.'

'So that's why I had to go to hospital?'

I nodded, closed my eyes. 'And when you had your auditions, I gave you other stuff. You weren't nervous. I mean, you were, but not excessively. There's nothing wrong with you, my love. It was me. I put... medicine in the Rice Krispie cakes. Laxatives one time, loperamide the other – Imodium. That's what made you ill. Not nerves. Me.'

I made myself look at you. Your mouth was slack with shock. I couldn't bear the sight, but it was a sight I deserved. I should look at you, I thought. I should make myself bear it, but I couldn't. I focused on the wet tissue I was twisting in my lap.

'Last night I didn't know you'd already been doped,' I said. 'I gave you too much diazepam, I know that, but not enough to make you unconscious. I would never have done that. I just wanted to give you a good night's sleep. But I shouldn't have given it to you at all, and I'm so very sorry.' Words were not – would never be – enough. I was beyond forgiveness. But I would spend the rest of my life asking you for it. 'I was trying to protect you and, ironically, I did. I foiled Emily's plans – she was trying to lure you away from me, and if I hadn't given you that stuff, you would have gone to her and who knows where we'd be now?

'I mean, I know that's not the point, that's not the point at all, and it doesn't make it right, and I am more sorry than I know how to say. I'm going to get help, and it will never happen again, I promise. It will never happen again.'

After a moment, you took my hand, pulled it towards you like it was a gift, and I had a flash of memory – your father doing that same thing to me. In that moment, I can't explain it other than to say that I felt him with us – I felt his presence, his light or his soul or whatever you want to call it. He was there with us, my Stan, your daddy.

I met your beautiful blue eyes, the eyes he gave you, with mine.

'Me and Auntie Bridge will help you,' you said. 'That's the triangle. That's what we do. We'll be OK, Mummy. I promise.'

'I love you,' I whispered. I could not tell you that whatever the road ahead, it was just the two of us now.

'I love you more.'

'So, so wrong.' I smiled. 'I love *you* more.'

'Bloody hell, it's like a Sicilian funeral in here.' Bridget, at the door. You didn't know that in saving you, she'd killed a man, and what that meant for her, for us. She handed you your toast – an optimistic four slices – and went to sit on the other side of your bed. You grabbed her hand and shook it a moment before letting it drop onto the duvet.

'I can't eat all this,' you said, offering me the plate.

I was hungry too – who knew? I lifted a slice. It was cold. I wondered how long your auntie Bridge had been standing outside the door, not wanting to intrude. So typical of her. I loved you both more in that moment than I could possibly say.

Today, within a couple of hours, they will come. They will come and they will take your auntie away. We have hours, maybe minutes left, but to voice that will ruin what little time we have together.

Please, God, let them see it was self-defence. Please, God, don't let my sister go to prison. And for now, please, God, let the three of us have this moment of peace.

CHAPTER 64

TRANSCRIPT OF INTERVIEW WITH
EMILY MIRABELLE WOOD (EXTRACT)

Emily Wood: It's important the girl has the cup with the orange flowers whilst Owen and myself have the blue. I have the capsules for my back; I get them off the internet. I have quite a stockpile, actually, could probably wipe out a whole family if I wasn't careful. [Laughs] After that, I fetched the cloth from the cupboard under the sink. I popped a few drops – just a few, mind – of the chloroform on the cloth and placed it over the girl's mouth. She was already drowsy. She looked up at me, but she didn't see the cloth, and then she was out like a light.

DS Andrews: And can you tell me what happened after that?

Emily Wood: Yes. After that, I cleared the table and washed up while Owen taped her mouth. Then he carried her out of the back door and through the side gate.

DS Andrews: Can you explain what you mean by the side gate?

Emily Wood: Happy to. It's a gate in the fence between our back gardens. Owen fitted it so we wouldn't have to use the front doors to go into each other's houses. Nosy neighbours, what have you. It's a terrace, you see, the row. So we can't access the backs of the houses otherwise. Owen's very good at carpentry and so forth. And then, let's see, I brought her little boots and her bag through to Owen's house and popped them by the front door. And then I went upstairs to run a bath.

DC Caton: A bath, Emily? Why did you run a bath?

Emily Wood: I… Owen likes things done in a certain way. He has to have a particular lavender-scented bath soap. Our mother used it, we bathed in it as children, so we've always used it too. Only when I got upstairs, I remembered I hadn't picked any up like I was meant to. I knew he'd run out and I had it in my mind to buy some that morning. He has to have the Radox one or there'll be trouble. [Laughs] I hadn't forgotten. I'd like that on the record. Is that on the record? Oh yes, we're on tape, aren't we? So no, I hadn't forgotten. I had gone to the chemist's on the high street and they usually have it, but that morning, yesterday, I should say, they didn't have it, but I couldn't go elsewhere because I would have been late picking up the girl.

DS Andrews: Picking up Rosie Flint had been prearranged between yourself and Mr Wood?

Emily Wood: Yes. But Rosie was different. I planned to do it myself, lead her to Owen via his phone and what have you. Owen is too erratic. Having him outdoors is nerve-racking, to be frank. But she kept getting ill. The girl. Rosie. Little Red. And when the audition route failed, I knew we'd have to use our tried and trusted pincer movement. But I had to make sure that no one would be able to place me in the café at any point, do you see? All roads had to lead to number 29 and not to 31. If I hadn't forgotten the soap, we wouldn't be in this mess. Silly, really.

DS Andrews: Emily, let's go back to yesterday afternoon. You're saying that your brother, Owen, and yourself were going to *wash* Rosie in the bath? And that you needed a specific soap? For the tape, the suspect is nodding. What happened after that?'

Emily Wood: After that, well, I was very agitated because I knew Owen would be terribly cross. But I had to tell him because there was no way he wouldn't spot it if I used his Imperial Leather. So I told him. And he began to get cross.'

DS Andrews: And how did that manifest itself?

Emily Wood: Well, as it always does. He sucks air in through his mouth and blows it out. That's what he does. Over and over. And he pulls his fingers, one by one, so that they pop. And then he... lashes out, you might say.

DS Andrews: Emily? Does he become violent?

Emily Wood: How long have you got, Officer? [Laughs] Let's see, he's broken my arm, cracked three ribs, pulled clumps of my hair out. But mostly just bruises. He did push me down the stairs though. That's how I broke my back. I tell people I have a dicky hip, but it's my back. Three months in a brace, physiotherapy and what have you, but I never worked again after that. Anyway, I said to Owen, 'Now, dearest, if you don't calm down, it's all going to go to pot.' I told him I wouldn't be long, that he wasn't to worry.

DC Caton: Emily, you're saying that your brother pushed you down the stairs?

Emily Wood: I don't see what this has to do with anything. It was a long time ago.

Stephen Richardson: My client is correct – this is not relevant.

DC Caton: We're just trying to build up a picture. Emily, did he push you down the stairs?

Emily Wood: No comment.

DC Caton: Did he abuse you in other ways?

Emily Wood: No comment.

DC Caton: Emily, did he sexually abuse you?

Emily Wood: No comment.

CHAPTER 65

TONI

Your auntie Bridge and I are drinking coffee in the kitchen and going over events endlessly. It is late morning, almost midday. You are on the sofa in the living room, watching Netflix in your onesie. You are calm; you seem OK. Soon, your auntie is going to walk to Twickenham Police Station for her taped interview – that is if the police don't come and arrest her first. She's not hungry, but she wants to have one last coffee, in her special cup, with one of her favourite brown sugar cubes. She and I both know that once she leaves this house, she will not come back, possibly for a long time.

'You'll get self-defence,' I say for perhaps the twentieth time. 'Especially if you volunteer yourself. You can show them your fork wound.'

'It was a three-pronged attack, Officer.' Bridget sips her coffee. 'Death by cutlery.' She glances at me, sees that I'm not laughing. 'It'll be fine. Don't worry. I might get a suspended sentence. At least *my* record is clean.' She levels her gaze at me and raises her eyebrows.

'Not like some we could name,' I say. I am trying to join in, to save us both, but tears are coming from nowhere and all I can do is smile through them and hold her hand.

'What will you tell Rosie?'

The doorbell goes.

Your auntie Bridget jumps out of her chair and throws open the kitchen door. There's a clear view of the front door from there, as you know, and she must see the black uniforms through the glass.

'It's the police,' she says, and pulls at the hem of her T-shirt. 'This is it then.'

'Don't answer it,' I say.

'I have to.'

We are both crying. She walks towards me and takes me in her arms.

'I can't do this without you,' I say. 'I can't, Bridge.'

'You can.' Her words are muffled against my shoulder. 'You're going to be fine, sis. You can do it because you are amazing, yeah? It's in the genes.'

She lets go, and without looking at me leaves the kitchen.

'No,' I call after her, but I can't say any more. I am useless, helpless, yet again. I push my face into the cradle of my arms and weep.

The sound of the door opening. The sound of voices, serious tones. Serious, I think, but no one is reading your auntie Bridget her rights. I think I would recognise their rhythm, even if I couldn't hear the words.

A moment later, two uniformed police, a man and a woman, fill the kitchen doorway: an alarming sight, all black, white and glints of metal. No handcuffs. And thinking about it, I didn't hear a siren in the street.

'Good morning,' I manage to say. 'Can I make you both a cup of coffee?'

The woman, ridiculously young looking, with startling blue eyes and long brown hair, takes off her hat and smiles. 'That would be lovely, actually, thank you.'

'Please sit down,' I say and move over to the kettle.

I prepare coffee, listening intently.

'This is Police Constable Bell,' the woman says, 'and I'm PC Loving, but you can call me Louise.'

'Robin,' the man says.

'Call me Toni,' I say, joining in. There's a pain behind my eyes, but I ignore it. 'Everyone calls me Toni,' I rattle on in my confusion. 'My parents wanted a boy, but there you are, things don't always go to plan, do they?'

I need to get a grip, stop talking. And then you, my darling Rosie, you appear at the kitchen door and my heart tightens. This is it, my love, I almost say. There's no protecting you from the truth now.

'What's going on?' you say.

I introduce you to the police; try to ignore the shock on your face.

'I thought you were going to the station,' you say.

'We just need to have a talk, love,' I say, 'after what happened.'

'Will I have to talk?' you ask.

'We'll need to take statements from all of you,' says the female officer. Louise. 'But we're just here for a chat at the moment.'

A chat?

'You go back to your film, honey,' I say. 'We'll give you a shout if we need you, all right?'

You nod and pad back to the living room. You still look tired, I think. Droopy, that's the word.

When you've gone, the police ask how you're bearing up.

'She's doing great,' I tell them. 'She's tired, a bit fuzzy, you know? She can't remember much.'

Then they ask me and Auntie Bridge if we're all right. They tell us about victim support and counselling services. They have leaflets. My stomach is in knots. The pain behind my eyes throbs. When are they going to arrest Bridget?

I put the coffee pot on the table. Your auntie Bridge has already put out cups, milk, sugar and the biscuit tin. It is all so bloody *polite*.

'So,' PC Loving says, when we are all settled at the table. 'Last night my colleagues attempted to interview Emily Wood, but her solicitor prevented it on the grounds of exhaustion. So we had to wait till this morning to interview her, and I can tell you that she has now confessed to the abduction of your daughter and the abduction and murder of a further two girls in the west London area.'

Across the table I meet your auntie Bridge's eye. Her gaze is steady, her mouth set in a flat line.

'There's something I need to—' she says.

'If I could just finish,' the female officer says, throwing Bridge an apologetic smile. 'Ms Wood also confessed to the murder of her brother, Owen Wood, using the family shotgun stored at his property at 29 Parkview Close…'

She is still talking, but I hardly hear her. The last thing I see before my eyes fill is your auntie Bridget's face. Her eyes are round, and she clamps a hand over her mouth. On her ring finger, her silver skull looks as shocked as she does.

'Apparently he was out cold when she found him.' Here PC Loving glances at your auntie Bridge. 'Reading between the lines, he'd made her life a misery, and she took her chance.'

'So were her fingerprints on the gun?' Bridge can't take the incredulity out of her voice.

'We haven't had that information yet, Ms Casement. She says she found the gun on the floor next to him, so it seems reasonable to assume that she picked it up and, as I say, took her chance. Clearly there was a lot more to her attack on Rosie than we first thought.'

'She picked it up,' Bridget repeats, as if in a trance. 'I'm sorry I didn't – we didn't – we should have told the whole story…'

'You've both been through a great deal,' the policewoman is saying – this lovely, lovely woman, on whose cheek I want to plant a big kiss. 'We'll still need to take your statements. Ms Casement – Bridget – we'll need to record yours because you're an important witness, obviously, and we will need to question you about the assault on Mr Wood. So if you could come along to the station with us, we can do that as soon as you're ready. '

'Will there be any charges against us?' The question pops out before I have a chance to think.

'There'll be the matter of the assault on Mr Woods,' Louise says, glancing at your auntie Bridge. 'Ms Wood is alleging that Ms Casement—'

'I… I threatened him with the gun,' your auntie Bridge says.

'We'll get to that in due course,' PC Loving replies.

Your auntie Bridget hunches her shoulders. She seems smaller, far away, as if her chair has receded beyond the walls of the kitchen. Her face is impassive, a reflection, I'm sure, of my own.

'I was there,' she says. 'I hit him. I kicked him…'

'We can deal with that in your statement, Ms Casement.' It's the other officer, the man, PC Bell, was it? He is talking now. I know I should listen, but my ears are humming and I want to fly out of that kitchen and into the living room and take you in my arms and say, it's all right, it's all right! Auntie Bridge isn't going to prison! We are still a family!

But I have to keep it together.

'No one is going to press charges,' PC Bell is saying, 'and there are what you might call extenuating circumstances.' He sips his coffee.

'So my sister won't go to prison?' I ask, can't help myself.

'I doubt that very much,' says PC Loving, breaking a digestive biscuit in half. 'We have a right to protect the ones we love.'

CHAPTER 66

TRANSCRIPT OF INTERVIEW WITH EMILY MIRABELLE WOOD (EXTRACT)

Emily Wood: I knew something was amiss because he wasn't there at his back door going from foot to foot like a goose on a hot floor like he usually is, and I thought, well, that's odd. Then I thought, oh my, it's one of his rages, and my heart started with the old b-bum b-bum, you see, and I thought perhaps he was still cross about the bubble bath, so by now I've got a severe attack of the collywobbles and I'm bracing myself for a shouting fit. Or worse. It was my fault about the soap, but as I said to Owen, I didn't forget. I didn't forget the soap.

DC Caton: Emily?

Emily Wood: The chemist's didn't have any in stock and I didn't have time to go anywhere else because I had to pick up the girl from outside the café, and I had to be on the dot or I would miss her, and we'd already missed her the week before, and my scalp still hurt from where he'd pulled me across the kitchen floor by my hair.

DC Caton: Emily? Emily. Ms Wood? Would you like to take a break?'

Emily Wood: What? No, dear. Let's crack on. Procrastination is the thief and all that, *n'est-ce pas*?

DS Andrews: All right. Emily, can we focus on what happened when you returned to the property at 29 Parkview Close?

Emily Wood: Of course. So I open the door and I call out to him. 'Owen?' I call. I'm pushing on the door, my heart going ten to the dozen. 'Owen? I've got your lavender soap, dear.' And that's when I found him. He was in the hall.

CHAPTER 67

I wanted it to stop, always. And once we killed that first girl, I wanted no more to do with it. I wanted out, as they say now.

I had laid the ground long before, when I set him up with his own iPad, his websites, his porno and what have you. His young girls. I tell you, there's enough filth on there to put him away, but I guess that's not necessary, not now. And that's all I wanted, to put him away. To have the state take care of him. To be free to live what remained of my life.

When he said he needed another girl, that it was getting too strong again, I suggested we try a little technology. I suggested a long con. I believe that's the term. I told him we needed to update our methods. He believed me. He's always relied on me for everything; why wouldn't he believe his sister? I was already living half my life online by then so there was little I couldn't do. I lived for the people that I could meet, no, that I could be *on that screen. Star of the small screen, you might say. That was, after all, my career. But my acting days were over the day he pushed me down the stairs. I had to learn to walk again, one excruciating step at a time. I had to accept that mine would be a life lived in constant pain. And so technology became my escape. I suppose it was a way of continuing the art to which I had dedicated my professional life.*

I have three online boyfriends, all in their twenties.

I have seven Facebook identities, all living the most marvellous lives.

I have a neat little line in getting refunds for goods that I claim not to have received.

But these things are not relevant here.

It was technology that enabled me to avoid the shame of having to buy those filthy magazines from the local shop, and it would be technology that would lead the police to his door.

I bought Owen a phone, in his name, with his money. I set him up as Ollie Thomas and began following and friending as many local young things as I could. I went for the theatre types, the extroverts, the ones who wanted to be adored, recognised, followed. Loved. It's a numbers game for them. They collect likes as if they were trophies. They're dependent on them for their self-worth. It's an epidemic! It is so easy to infiltrate a world if you know what that world wants. And all they want is looks, youth and likes.

I contacted Rosie Flint from there. I needed a shy one, one who wouldn't cause a scene when the time came. I knew her mother was a single parent. She was perfect. Of course I knew her back to front before she'd ever met me. And Owen enjoyed his role play. It was like the old days.

I set up the agency website, the backstory, my character. And in the way of the more successful scams, much of it was true. How I had missed acting! I had missed it so much! It felt wonderful to be doing character work again. I would be outmoded, a relic, no one anyone would look at, no one anyone would give any credit to. It wasn't far from the truth. The acting profession didn't want me any more. They're all over you when you're fit and beautiful, when your limbs are strong and supple and your skin is like apricots in a basket, firm and plump and sweet. Not so great when the apricot browns and wrinkles. No one wants it then, do they? Of course not! It's left in the bowl to rot! And I walked with a limp. Three months in a brace is no joke.

I made sure to brandish my old Nokia in front of Toni, the mother. We even shared a joke about the two of us having dinosaur phones. As far as they knew, I was hopeless.

As an actor, I had a reputation for thorough preparation. I would arrive on set, lines learnt, character developed, motivations thought through. I made bold choices, added layers of meaning the director didn't even know were there. That's what got me the work. I was good, you see. I was very good. And I was always good with the young ones.

It was meant to end with her, with Rosie Flint. Owen would have his last hurrah and then enough! And due to all my work behind the scenes, the police would use the girl's phone to trace him to his house, where they would find her, the tablet, his phone. It would be over. And I would be free.

But there were so many problems. I couldn't get her away. Every time I thought I had her, she got sick. I had not banked on the nervous disposition. And then we almost had to abandon ship because Owen became too antsy and we had to take another girl just to tide him over. I didn't want to. I never wanted to. Rosie was supposed to be the last. Owen was supposed to go to prison. I was supposed to walk away. I should have dropped Rosie like a stone. When she said she'd forgotten her phone, I should have taken her home and waved goodbye and never gone back. I did not foresee that happening at all. And nor did I bank on the vigilante aunt. When I first met the mother, I thought my prayers had been answered. I should have known when I realised the aunt lived with them that she would be trouble. I didn't trust my instincts, you see – that's where I went wrong, blinded by the light at the end of my tunnel.

When I got home with the lavender soap and found him in the hallway like a broken doll, I knew it was her – the aunt. Had to be. Wasn't going to be the mother, was it? I picked up the gun and held it to his chest.

'Pow pow,' I said, though of course he was already dead. I dropped the gun and went back to my own kitchen to wait for the police. I assumed the aunt would have called them. Barnaby was there, so I held him in my arms and told him he would soon be with his brothers. There's Laurence, after Laurence Olivier, and John, after Sir John Gielgud. Barnaby isn't named after anyone. It's the name I would have given my son. If I'd had one.

But no sirens came. And I suppose I must have gone into a trance talking to Barnaby, because when Toni texted, I realised my tea had gone clap cold.

Rosie's in West Mid Hospital. She's had a nasty fright. Don't worry, she's OK but needs to rest. Would be lovely to see you. Call me when you can. T x

I smiled to myself. Rosie must still be out for the count, I thought. Owen must have given her too much chloroform; that would be just like him. And then I thought, if Rosie's out for the count and her mother is texting me, she has no idea I'm involved, and if I can't hear sirens, then the aunt hasn't yet called the police. And if the aunt found only Owen, in a house that has not a trace of me in it, then she doesn't know I'm involved either. And if Owen is dead, which he is, then Rosie is the only thing left between me and freedom.

I hadn't meant for him to die, but perhaps that was better. If he was dead, the police would never figure out he knew nothing about computers, could never have conducted such a modern operation. If he was dead, all I had to do was get to the girl and shut her up. If she talked, I would be in prison quicker than you could say Madame Belle. All I had to do was get to her, get her alone and silence her. The police would trace Owen, arrest the aunt for murder, case closed.

But of course now I've been caught red-handed trying to smother an innocent, and my role in this woeful carry-on is exposed. It is over. The game is up, as they say. My life amounts to nothing.

But there is one good thing left that I can do. One redemptive act.

CHAPTER 68

TRANSCRIPT OF INTERVIEW WITH EMILY MIRABELLE WOOD (EXTRACT)

DS Andrews: Your brother was in the hall. How would you describe him at that point?'

Emily Wood: He looked like a broken doll, like he'd fallen from a high shelf. I knew it was her – the aunt. I knew she'd knocked his block off. She's a strong woman, is the aunt. I knew the girl was gone, that the aunt had come for her. I thought the game was up, as they say.

The gun was on the floor. Our family shotgun. Silly man had obviously used it to threaten the aunt, or perhaps the aunt had taken it from the hooks on the wall and pointed it at him, who knows? Thing wasn't loaded anyway. He was moaning, and he looked like he'd taken a humdinger of a punch to the face. I picked up the gun. I went into Owen's sitting room and loaded it with the bullets that I keep in the oak dresser that used to sit in our farm kitchen.

I returned to the hallway.

'Em,' he said. And he reached out for me. Helpless – completely helpless. 'Em.'

'Goodbye, Owen,' I said.

And I pulled the trigger.

CHAPTER 69

BRIDGET

One year later

Bridget sits at the window of the upper flat, looking out onto the street where a group of boys are playing on their skateboards. They jump, pulling the boards up with their feet, spinning them, hoping to land on them but most often failing. The noise when the boards hit the road is a loud clatter. It drives Helen mad, but Bridget likes it. They are young. They are free. If they can't make a racket now, then when?

Bridget has taken the newspaper onto the tiny balcony that looks out over the street. On the little table, no bigger than a serving plate, she has already placed her pot of espresso made with the ground beans that Helen brought her from Monmouth Coffee in Covent Garden. She has planned the moment. Good coffee, good demerara. A cigarette smoked slowly on this warm but cloudy morning in late summer.

If she were young, she'd take a photo of this coffee, this silver pot, this bowl of artfully rustic sugar cubes, and put it on Instagram. But she's not young, and she doesn't need social media to tell her that life is made of pleasures as small and simple as this.

And here is another: Helen, wheeling her bike up the front path, her long hair tied back with a brightly coloured scarf, like a Land

Girl. She looks up, sees Bridget there on the balcony. The glancing expression of delight on her face when she waves is enough to make Bridget's lungs fill. Small, simple pleasures. Helen has been to Eel Pie Island for a meeting with a company who want to option a novel she wrote years ago. The woman is a walking success story; everything she touches turns to gold. Bridget teases her about it: *How come it hasn't worked for me yet, eh? You've touched me enough times and I don't see The Promise at number one.*

Helen has disappeared from view. Moments later, Bridget hears the lock on the side gate, the clank as Helen negotiates her bike and her rucksack through the narrow side return. She will be another few minutes, enough to put her bike in the shed alongside Bridget's vintage Mercian racer and Rosie's brand-new hybrid.

Getting Rosie a bike to ride to and from sixth-form college took some smooth talking, not to mention a state-of-the-art helmet and a jacket so high-vis you can see it from space, but Toni relented in the end. It would have been unthinkable a year ago.

The key rattles in the downstairs back door. With a lazy smile, Bridget gets up from her chair and fetches another cup from the kitchen. What could be better than good coffee and good demerara? Answer: good coffee and good demerara with the one you love. Small, simple pleasures.

The pleasures of freedom.

She did not go to prison. She never got near. Emily was sentenced to life imprisonment, her expression in court on hearing the sentence something like beatific calm, as if imminent incarceration represented a kind of freedom in itself. And maybe it did. Freedom from all she had left behind, a willing abandonment of personal responsibility – a surrender to the system. The details that came out in court were so upsetting that one of the jury had to be excused to be sick. Bridget heard them with mixed feelings. Revulsion, yes, of course, but sympathy too for this woman who was as much a victim as the young girls she procured for her tormentor.

And gratitude. Bridget owes Emily her own freedom, she knows: this cup of coffee, this moment on the balcony. Why Emily chose to do that will remain a mystery, but whatever the reason, this sunshine, this day, and Helen, gone from her for so long and now back, all these things are part of her life forever, and it is beyond weird to know that this is down to her niece's kidnapper.

'Hey,' Helen says, sitting on the other little chair.

'Hey.' Bridget pours her coffee, dunks a lump of sugar enough to soak half, which she knocks off with the end of a teaspoon and stirs in.

'Now that's what I call service. Thank you. Yum.'

Bridget sits back, squints against the sun as it comes out from behind the clouds. 'Half a million?'

'Of course. We can move to Florida. I've always wanted to live in a condo.'

'What actually is a condo?'

Helen giggles and sips her coffee. 'I have no idea.'

Later, Bridget does a job for a regular client over on Richmond Hill. Website update, absolute child's play, but the guy doesn't know his arse from his elbow. Easy money. She's not complaining. She gets back at six and parks on the street. She misses the car park. Sometimes it takes her a good ten minutes to find a space big enough for the van. But the set-up is perfect: her and Helen in the upstairs flat, Toni and Rosie on the ground floor.

'We can't live like this.' It was Toni who said that, after the trial. 'It's not fair on you, Bridge. You and Helen could still be together. She's not moved on, and neither have you. I'm fine now; I'll be fine as long as you don't move too far away. Come on, Bridge. What's the point in being free if you don't live your life?'

'But I can't leave you alone,' Bridget replied. 'And what about when Squirt goes to uni in a couple of years' time, what then?'

'I'm perfectly independent…'

'I know that. Don't start. It's not about that.'

'I saw this.' Toni pushed the local paper across the kitchen table. 'It's pricey, but with what we could get for this place, and if Helen were to sell her house…'

A small terrace split into two flats. Helen had shouted a resounding YES down the phone, but she wasn't back from LA in time and the property went from under their noses. They didn't get the second place either, but when the third one came up, the estate agent called them before the listing was published. Another small terrace, near the river – nearer still to the high street. Helen didn't even have to sell her house; she rented it out and still had enough to chip in a good deal more than her fair share, flash git. And now they live like this. Still a funny family, by most people's standards, but a family all the same.

Bridget presses the buzzer marked Flint.

'Hello?' comes her niece's voice.

'Open up, it's the rozzers.'

Laughter, cut off. A buzz. Bridget pushes the door and goes in.

In the kitchen, Toni is at the table and Rosie is frowning over a chopping board, green wheels of courgettes in a bowl, red strips of pepper falling from the knife. Wafts of garlic simmering in olive oil, chilli flakes possibly. And this too is a small but enormous wonder: her sister, well, sane, after everything. Six months of therapy that in the end, according to Toni, wasn't necessary, not really. The worst had happened. And Rosie has not suffered so much as indigestion for over a year. It is as if being broken for a second time has in some strange way fixed her troubled sister, her beloved Tones. Or perhaps it is the third time she has been broken: Eric, Stan, Owen. Third time un/lucky. Strange how in being plunged into the pit of someone else's sickness, there has been healing after all.

'Smells good in here,' Bridget says, sitting at the table, leaning in for Toni's kiss on her cheek.

'I've told Mum to go to the pub with you for an hour,' Rosie says, sliding the vegetables into a large frying pan. A hiss. 'I'm making veggie lasagne and it'll be ages. Can you persuade her? She's being a saddo.'

Bridget meets Toni's eye.

'Are you coming for dinner, by the way?' Rosie says. 'In, like, an hour? I'm making loads. Why don't you text Helen?'

Toni raises her eyebrows at Bridge. 'Up to you.'

'I suppose I *could* ask her.' Bridget pulls her phone from her jacket pocket. 'She'll bring nice wine, at least.'

Two texts later, dinner for four all arranged, courtesy of Rosie's new enthusiasm for vegetarianism, Bridget and Toni head out. It is still warm – warmer, in fact, than during the day now that the breeze has dropped. It is a late August evening. Rosie is seventeen. In September she will begin her last academic year before university. She doesn't do theatre any more, for no other reason than a loss of interest. She still does taekwondo, but her real passion is psychology. She wants to be a psychologist or a psychiatrist, which, Bridget pointed out to Toni, is what comes of having a fruitcake for a mother.

'Shall we go to The Fox?' Bridget says.

'Why not?'

It's only Tuesday, there's hardly anyone in. They go into the garden at the back so that Bridget can smoke.

A pint of lager each in front of them on the table, they chat about nothing in particular. Toni's job, her colleague Richard, who has found a new boyfriend and is smitten. The boyfriend used to be a male prostitute, a source of great amusement to Toni. Bridget laughs at her sister's chatter but cannot quite let go of the miracle of her, here, while Rosie is at home handling death traps such as knives and gas hobs and ovens, not to mention masked intruders smashing through the windows, armed to the teeth, dressed as ninjas.

'So this guy,' Toni can barely get her story out for giggling, 'this guy had this client who apparently liked him to blow smoke all over him while he was naked and tied to the bed. And that was it. Literally. *Tie me up, blow smoke all over me.* But the funniest bit about it, Bridge, was that when he told Richard the story, he looked at him all serious and said, "The thing was, I was trying to give up."'

They both laugh. Bridget pulls at her cigarette and blows the smoke across the table as if over an imaginary body. They both laugh again and sip their drinks. In the pause that follows, they look at one another as they often do.

'You're thinking about him, aren't you?' Toni says. 'About Eric? I can always tell.'

'Bloody hell,' Bridget says, and then, 'I can tell when you're thinking about him too.'

Toni reaches across the wooden trestle table and touches her fingers to her sister's wrist. She traces the letters, A and B, and gives a sad smile.

'I can remember you waking me up,' she says. 'I'll never forget it.'

Bridget nods, her insides flaming. She wishes Toni would stop. But at the same time, she wants her to continue. There's no one here in the pub garden, just the two of them and their depthless history, their closeness, their love.

'I bet you wish I never had,' she says.

'No, I don't. Don't say that. I don't.'

Bridget pulls on her cigarette. 'It was too hard for you. You were only fourteen.'

'And you stopped it. You stopped it happening.'

'I fucked it up, Tones.'

'Don't say that either. You didn't mean to. And the police would have done fuck-all, like they did with Mum. It was an accident.'

At no time before or since has Bridget been so glad of her strength. Until that bastard Owen, of course. Even though Uncle Eric was a weedy bloke – one of those revolting ratty little men who smoke with their thumb and forefinger pinched around their fag, like they're holding a straw in a carton of juice – she still needed

Toni's help, to hold the bedroom door open, to carry him down the stairs, to open the back door, the boot of the car.

They left him there. No one noticed he'd gone, not that day. He was always going AWOL, and besides, no one wanted him around. They drove the next night to Ham, and at two in the morning carried him to the cover of the trees. It was Toni who bought the spades from the hardware store while Bridget waited in the car, Toni who returned to the car to fetch the spades from the back seat once they'd laid the body on the rough ground of the Ham Lands. Toni who dug alongside her in the pouring rain and the dark. She was only fourteen. It was too much.

They barely made it home before seven in the morning, the two of them filthy, washing off the mud under the shower, rinsing the tub, every last trace, then sitting shivering in their threadbare bath towels, side by side on Toni's bed.

'We need to make a pact,' Toni had said. 'We will never, ever call the police. We will never tell.' She had held out her little finger, which Bridget linked with her own. 'No police.'

'No police.'

'I will never tell.'

'Thank you.'

Later that day, Bridget went into the tattoo parlour with a piece of paper on which she had drawn the letters of their names, an A and a B, like a Celtic sign: a pact, their pact, a bond of blood.

'Shall we get back?' Tones recalls her to the present. 'Dinner will be ready soon, if she hasn't burnt the house down.'

'Don't you want another half for the road?'

Toni shakes her head. 'Nah. But just this once, I'll let you push me home.'

'Bloody hell, the honour.'

Laughing, Bridget takes the handles of Toni's wheelchair. Chatting all the way, she pushes her sister through Twickenham: to their street, their family, their home.

A LETTER FROM
S.E. LYNES

Dear Reader

Thank you so much for taking the time to read *The Pact*; I am thrilled that you did and hope you enjoyed it. I very much hope you will want to read my next book too. If you'd like to be the first to hear about my new releases, you can sign up using the link below:

www.bookouture.com/se-lynes

The Pact was inspired by an old short story by Elizabeth Taylor (the writer, not the actor!) called 'The Flypaper'. The wasp in the honey trap in Emily's kitchen was my little homage to that. I wanted to use the kernel of that story and update it in order to examine whether our children are more or less safe in a post-internet world. So now that you've read *The Pact* and there's no risk of me spoiling it for you, that was why it was important for me that Emily and Owen had already kidnapped young girls without any recourse to technology. Terrible people, of course, pre-date the internet, but my job, as I see it, is not to propose answers but to ask questions and hopefully create discussion. Like most writers, I exist in a place of doubt.

I also wanted to explore how abuse is so difficult to escape, how its victims struggle to leave it behind, whether it manifests in continuing to abuse others or in losing faith in humanity in some deep way and becoming paranoid and distrustful of people in general.

Lastly, I wanted a happy ending this time. I became so attached to all three women that it would have been unbearable to leave them any other way. They had all, I felt, been through enough.

If you enjoyed *The Pact*, I would be so grateful if you could spare a couple of minutes to write a review. It only needs to be a line or two – in fact, the best reviews often are! – and I would really appreciate it. I am always happy to chat via my Twitter account and Facebook author page if you'd like to get in touch. Writing can be a lonely business, so when a reader reaches out and tells me my work has stayed with them or that they loved it, I am truly delighted. I have loved making new friends online through my first novel, *Valentina*, and my second, *Mother*, and I hope to make yet more with *The Pact*.

Best wishes
Susie

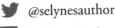 @selynesauthor
SE LynesAuthor

ACKNOWLEDGEMENTS

Firstly, thanks to my editor, Jenny Geras, who manages to be both tactful and direct at the same time. Jenny, *The Pact* is so much better because of you. The book also benefitted from my trusted writers group: Hope Caton, Robin Bell, Sam Hanson and Cat Morris – thank you particularly for saving me from the *I am Batfink, I have wings* moment.

Thank you to Kim Nash, Noelle Holten, Lauren Finger and all the amazing Bookouture team who work so hard behind the scenes and are available to help even in the evenings and at weekends #dedication. Thanks to the Bookouture authors too for their kindness and support, not to mention making me laugh a LOT.

Big love and thanks go to Louise Loving, who took me for a trip round Hounslow, showed me all the points of reference, and even included a minor car crash, which I thought was above and beyond. Thanks also for reading *The Pact* to check for any howlers. Thanks to Laura Richards, for her advice on Irish names, pronunciation, and for telling me about the folk song, *Maidrin Rua*. Thanks to Jayne Farnworth for brain storming the plot for an entire evening on Richmond Green and for your police procedural advice. Thanks to early readers and cheerleaders, Richard Kipping and Bridget McCann.

Thank you to my kids: Alistair, Maddie and Franci. Maddie, my acting girl, thanks for understanding the difference between drawing from life and writing directly from life and for advising me on teen speak. Thanks to my lovely dad, Stephen, and of course to my first reader, advisor and editor, Catherine Ball aka Mum.

To my husband, Paul, thank you for being alive, thank you for taking me to the Halls of Residence Ball in 1988 and perhaps more importantly asking if I wanted to come back to your room for some Hula-Hoops. Thank you also for waiting so patiently for a dedication. This one, finally, is for you.

Made in the USA
Middletown, DE
30 June 2023